IMPULSE

A Mageri Series Novel
Book 3

DANNIKA DARK

All Rights Reserved
Copyright © 2012 Dannika Dark

First Print Edition
ISBN 13: 978-1482017229
ISBN-10:1482017229

Formatting: Streetlight Graphics

No part of this book may be reproduced, distributed, or transmitted in any form or by any means, or stored in a database retrieval system, without the prior written permission of the author. You must not circulate this book in any format. Thank you for respecting the rights of the author.

This is a work of fiction. Any resemblance of characters to actual persons, living or dead, is purely coincidental.

Cover design by Dannika Dark. All stock purchased.

http://dannikadark.blogspot.com/
Fan page located on Facebook

Also By Dannika Dark:
THE MAGERI SERIES
Sterling
Twist
Impulse
Gravity

NOVELLAS
Closer

ACKNOWLEDGMENTS:

After an especially difficult year, this book wouldn't have been possible without the help and support of too many people to mention. First, to my readers—you guys seriously rock my world. To those who offered support, advice, editing, and direction, you have my gratitude: Teresa Gray, Carissa Cotta, Dan Marr, Kelly Rowlands, Cherrie Moore, Rachel Schneider, Anne Victory, Lea Salazar, Garee Nace, Judie Bouldry, and Michelle Madeen. I can't thank you all enough.

And a special thanks to my family, who showed me their support when I needed it the most.

The art of love is largely the art of persistence.
- *Albert Ellis*

CHAPTER 1

THE KEY TO A GOOD seduction always begins with a proper fork. Words Simon often recited whenever he cooked a meal. That man sprinkled innuendos in conversation like table salt.

I wrung my hands together beneath the table dressed with a white linen cloth. A soft glow emanated from stubby candles in red holders, and light floated across the table setting like drops of sunlight. The silverware sparkled, and the ice floating in the water-filled glasses looked like baubles.

A Breed restaurant required advanced reservations—humans went on the waiting list but never got in. Several curious eyes wandered over to my table. Unlike humans, who look away when you meet their glance, most immortals will not—they'll hold it. By their prolonged stares and low whispers it was obvious they wanted to know my situation. Honestly, so did I.

"Has anyone mentioned how stunning you are when you're nervous?"

I lifted my eyes to a tall, intimidating man in a suit jacket. Logan wore his blond hair pulled back and the smooth style drew all my attention to his riveting features. A heavy brow and severe expression greeted me, but so did an amused twitch of his lip.

"Hi, Logan." I tried to calm the butterflies in my stomach by covering it with my hand, as if he could hear their wings flapping. "Justus dropped me off about ten minutes ago."

Logan bowed his head. "I'm sorry that I kept you waiting. Family matters," he said, taking a seat.

Justus wouldn't have liked that I sat alone for so long, but a Breed establishment has a code of conduct they enforce that makes it neutral ground.

I brushed my hand over my black dress and crossed my ankles. "This is really... unexpected." The waiter breezed by with a bottle of champagne.

He watched me lick my lips and a subtle flavor of raspberries touched the tip of my tongue from the new lipstick. Not something I wore often, but when Logan said he was taking me out somewhere nice, I went into panic mode at the department store.

The black dress set off the sultry color of my dark hair, which fell loose across my shoulders. The summer was unseasonably cool and my summer glow was fading to a soft cream with a hint of honey. My green eyes were vivid, and paired against the golden amber of Logan's eyes we looked like a pair of jewels sparkling in the restaurant.

The light accentuated the blond in his hair, but when Logan spent less time in the sun, it darkened. Mine was growing unruly and while Justus offered to pay for a professional cut, I stubbornly refused. Justus was all about image—tailored suits, collectible cars, and expensive furniture. I never knew the spoils of superficial possessions in my human life and saw little reason to start now.

Logan's suit was the color of winter clouds and beneath the jacket was a casual white button-up shirt. The top two buttons were undone, revealing his warm skin tone. He looked magnificent and his athletic build gave him a formidable appearance, even with the Converse sneakers he wore. I savored a moment to drink him in; Logan Cross exuded a confident demeanor that earned admiring appraisals from a few women sitting near us.

I stroked the edge of my glass, sending drops of water splashing to the table. "If your plan is to wine me and dine me, then that's as far as it's going this evening."

He chuckled the way a man does when he knows a secret he's unwilling to disclose.

I narrowed my eyes suspiciously. "Why the elaborate show? You know I don't need all of this."

He rearranged his place settings and replied, "I'm not about to build a reputation for being a cheap date who courted you on rollerblades." There was a trace of bruised ego in his tone.

"Yes, but I'll have that mental image tucked in my memory for the rest of my life, and it's beautiful." I lowered my head, letting my hair fall in front of my face to conceal my smile. Watching a six-and-a-half-foot man flapping his arms to keep from falling murdered my chances at selecting our next date location.

"Chitahs are not meant to have wheels on their feet," he said, tapping an irritated finger on the table.

"Sorry."

He lifted my chin with the crook of his finger. "If you want to smile, don't hide it from me, even if it *is* at my expense." His thumb stroked the curve of my mouth. "You're not a submissive female, so don't behave like one."

In the short time since Logan had begun courting me, I saw compromise and fortitude that elevated him to a level of attractiveness that I hadn't appreciated when we first met. Not that we saw each other very often. There were special circumstances that I fully supported. For the first month, he was preoccupied with a new roommate.

Logan was now a caregiver for Finnegan, a Shifter we rescued from Nero. Finn looked younger than twenty-two, and perhaps he was. His naivety was almost endearing, except that he acquired it from having lived an isolated life.

Shifters had no control over their animal, and that in itself was a huge ordeal. Finn's wolf attacked Logan on the first night and mangled one of his green chairs. Truthfully, I was never fond of that chair and seeing the stuffing all over the house brought a satisfied smile to my face. Logan's condo lacked personality, so I conspired with Finn to get him to refurnish it.

Jokingly, of course.

On our first date, Justus played chaperone. There are no words to describe how awkward that evening was, but Logan seized the opportunity to prove himself to my Ghuardian. We invited him to dinner and Logan took our kitchen hostage and cooked Italian. Two more dates followed, but we spent most of our time on the phone because he was afraid of leaving Finn alone and I insisted that he take care of things at home. Logan knew how important Finn was to me and I suppose he made that his first challenge. Courtship to a male Chitah was more than roses and candy—it was proving his worth.

I unfolded the menu and gasped at the prices.

"Logan, this is too much," I scolded, two seconds from scooting my chair back and leaving.

He leaned forward on his elbows and the candlelight smoldered in the depths of his black-rimmed eyes. "This is not up for debate. Order something or I'll select the most expensive nine-course meal they offer," he said, lifting my menu from the table in irritation. I snatched it from his hands and he concealed a smile behind a closed fist.

When my bowl of soup arrived, Logan was displeased but said nothing as he admired his steak.

"I have news," he began. "It's Leo, my brother."

"Is everything okay?"

Leo was the eldest sibling and Logan respected the hell out of him. They were a family of four brothers, but the only one I'd met was Levi.

"HALO offered him a position," Logan said, taking a bite of asparagus.

"Does Justus know?"

Logan laughed lightly and licked the prongs of his fork. "Justus recommended him. They have no Chitah representation and my brother had expressed his interest. Leo's reputation precedes him. The offer came quick."

HALO operates as an independent organization whose services fall outside of the Mageri or any other governing body. Members exchange information on high-profile crimes. Justus worked long hours in his office, sometimes away from home, going over papers and tracking down the big fish. I never met the other members, but they rarely assembled because of the security risk.

"How come a Chitah never worked for them before?"

Logan furrowed his brow while he sliced into his rare steak. "Years ago there was a Chitah within the group, and he… betrayed them. The elders reprimanded him and not long after, one of the HALO members was assassinated—a Mage. They never found out who was responsible, but rumors circulated that it was one of ours," he bit out angrily. "It was a turbulent time, and they haven't offered us representation since. Justus and Leo have grown close in recent conversations and see eye to eye on many issues. Leo has integrity," he said, talking with his mouth full. "This is a good move for us, Silver. Small actions sever alliances, but it takes great efforts to mend them."

"One Chitah betrayed HALO and you were all judged for it? It doesn't seem fair. What happened?"

Logan cleared his throat and sipped the ice water—frozen cubes clinked against the glass. Something in the way he avoided eye contact made me set my spoon down.

"There's something you're not telling me," I said in a low voice. "Since when do we keep secrets?"

He sighed and tapped his finger against the candle holder. "Could we just enjoy the evening?"

I'm such an idiot, I thought. There was no need to spoil the night with my opinions on the laws. Logan heard enough of that on our phone calls.

I pointed my spoon at him. "To be continued. You know, I may fuss and snarl about all of this," I said, looking around, "but you really know how to woo a girl. Who knew Logan Cross was such a romantic?" A smile wound up his face that he tried to hide with his fist. "This has *nothing* on your secret cave. I don't think I've ever eaten in a place so—"

My hand bumped the glass of ice water.

"Oh no!" I cried, standing up to catch it, but the water poured across the table onto Logan's lap and left a damp river of ice between us. I frowned, desperately trying to sop it up and scoop the ice back into the glass when Logan caught my wrist.

"Sit down. It's only water."

Our eyes met. I had a reputation for knocking over drinks, but an old feeling I didn't care for struck me unexpectedly. Had I done something like this with my ex, a severe remark would have come my way, pointing out my stupidity and need to make a spectacle of myself. I waited for his reaction.

Logan's fingers rested on my racing pulse and his eyes flicked up to mine. Something stirred in those golden depths.

"I didn't mean to ruin everything," I said.

He lifted my hand, opened my fingers, and kissed my palm. Slowly.

"I needed cooling off," he said. "You've done nothing wrong and we both know it. Please sit," he asked, tilting his head toward my chair.

I eased back into my seat and noticed a slow burn in his gaze.

"That male will never harm you again."

After what Logan did to him, of that I had no doubt.

"That's not it," I said. "This is hard for me to get used to. It's been a long time since I've been this serious with anyone, and it seems like a few ghosts haven't left the graveyard."

It was a silly reaction and I knew the reason behind it, but old habits are hard to break. Logan somehow made them breakable.

He slid the glass to the left and his brows pushed down. "This is serious for you?"

Flustered, I picked up two ice cubes and put them in the empty glass. A few dates and I was already labeling our relationship as serious? Nice move. Time to go to the tattoo shop and ink my forehead with the word "desperate." Somewhere mid-thought, Logan rolled an ice cube over my hand and I squeaked, pulling out of reach.

He laughed darkly. "I'm glad we're on the same page."

A group of people walked by and one of the men lingered at the edge of our table. The sleeves of his blue shirt were rolled up to his elbows, displaying dark hair on his arms. He flicked his eyes between us.

"No one wants to see this," the man snarled.

Logan sat still, staring at his plate.

"I'm sorry, see what?" I asked.

His tan face mashed together when he scowled. "You should stick to your own kind... whatever that is. Relic? Maybe—" His eyes narrowed at me. "Are you a Shifter?"

Logan's chair scraped against the wood floor and he rose to his feet—towering over the man with resolute eyes.

"Quit pissing on territorial lines, Shifter. This is none of your business."

The Shifter ignored him, staring down at me. "You're a disgrace."

My heart stammered when Logan placed his hand on the man's shoulder and slowly pushed him until they faced one another.

"Say it again," Logan dared in low, threatening words. "I want you to say it again and disrespect my female."

"Your female, huh?" The Shifter bravely looked up. "Is your cock so small that you can't get your own women to—"

Logan slapped a hand across his mouth and leaned in, nose to nose—giving the man a good look at the darkness pulsing in his eyes.

"There are no laws against what we do, only opinions. Your opinion doesn't matter to me, but disrespecting this female does. Tip your head to her once more and I'll place my jacket on the back of that chair and we'll take a walk where Breed rules don't apply. Care to discuss your opinions on this matter any further?" Logan's nose wrinkled, drawing in a scent.

The man backed down in defeat. Obviously not an alpha Shifter, just a jackass.

Logan's eyes slanted, as if watching me in his peripheral. "For the record, my cock can only be measured in decibels from the screams of the female it pleasures."

I snorted and looked away as Logan turned to sit down. The man walked by me and slid his eyes down to my hips. "Keep her," he murmured. "Nothing there to grab on to anyhow."

My face heated with embarrassment.

Logan stopped and tilted his head—nostrils flaring. With alarming speed, he spun around and hit the Shifter with a solid fist. The man struck the wall and crumbled to the floor. Logan stood astride the man as two of his buddies hauled him off. I couldn't be sure if it was the Shifter's words that provoked him to violence or because he picked up my scent when I blushed. When a waiter hurried over, Logan reached in his pocket and handed him a folded bill.

And that was that.

I wasn't appalled by the sudden burst of violence—I was flattered. He could have let it go or speared him with a few words, but Logan Cross had stood up for me and let the Shifter know that he wasn't going to allow even a passing insult slide.

He took a seat and dipped his napkin in the glass of ice water, pressing it against his knuckle.

"I'm sorry that you had to listen to that," he said between clenched teeth.

When the waiter walked by, I grabbed the sleeve of his shirt. "Excuse me. Could I have my wine in a paper cup?" I flashed my eyes at Logan. "Sorry, I don't want to shatter any glasses tonight."

He wasn't laughing.

In fact, Logan leaned in and seized my left hand. His thumb stroked over my wrist, capturing the tick of my pulse, which readily quickened. My smile faded at the intensity of his stare and the inflection in his voice as it deepened. "Careful not to challenge me with a dare, Little Raven. I always make good on my promises."

When he flicked his finger on a crystal glass, a note lingered between us and I flushed. I felt it all over, from the sting on my cheeks to the warmth in my chest.

His lip twitched—restraining a smile—and I pulled my hand out of his grasp and pretended that my dress needed straightening.

Logan relished these moments. Time unrolls before an immortal's feet like a never-ending carpet, so in his eyes, he had all the time in the world to make me blush. It was a slow buildup of anticipation before we saw each other; there had been little opportunity for intimate conversation on our dates. Logan rattled my nerves and made the hairs on the back of my neck rise up with his penetrating gaze. He affected me the way sunlight does with a morning glory whenever he spoke in that manner.

In fact, Logan loved getting me flustered. I would see the glint in his eyes whenever he silenced me with his wicked tongue.

"I can't believe he had the nerve to come right up to us and say that," I said in disbelief.

Logan held a closed fist to his chin. "Breed will voice their opinions—especially when they think it concerns one of their own."

"What made him think I was a Shifter?"

"It's hard for them to tell when you don't have any distinct features. Shifters always have their noses in other people's business; they're territorial. Let's eat," he said.

After we finished our outrageously overpriced meal, I declined dessert, insisting I was full.

"I heard something interesting," I began, anticipating his reaction. "The Gathering is coming up."

Logan sat back in his chair and folded his arms. When his jaw clenched, hardening the bones in his face, I realized that dessert was going to be the can of worms I just opened. The Gathering was a long-standing tradition among Chitah. Every three years, they assembled in search of their kindred spirits. They believed that each man had one Chitah soul mate. They could live a lifetime and never find her.

Many years ago, Logan married a woman who was murdered by a Mage. While she wasn't his soul mate, he'd settled for love. He told me that most Chitah men didn't mate until they found their kindred. A man would readily leave his family for her. Logan claimed the magnetic pull could not be ignored and no force could sever that feeling—even if she chose another man. I raised the topic because I wanted reassurance. How could I get involved with a man who would drop me like a napkin if destiny walked by in a pair of stilettos? If his kindred spirit existed, then I needed to know which of us he would choose.

"Where are you going with this, Silver?"

I set my napkin on the table. It had a faint lipstick smear and I frowned. "I think you should go." He glowered at me and I leaned forward and spoke in a private voice. "Don't look at me that way. If your kindred spirit is out there, then I'd rather you meet her now instead of hiding like a coward."

"Would you be pleased if I found another?"

No, I wouldn't. I would want to snatch her by the hair and swing her around until…

"If you believe there is a woman you would pursue until the end of time, then you have to go. It wouldn't be fair to anyone you settled with, don't you think?"

"This is not a winnable argument," he said, shaking his head and pulling the collar of his jacket away from his neck. While he looked dashing in a suit, he also looked uncomfortable. "There's no reason for me to go when I've already stated my intent to court you."

"What if I said I won't see you anymore unless you go?"

His eyes skidded to mine. "Then I would go."

"Settled. I'm not trying to push you away. I'm protective of my feelings and if this is important among your kind, then be fair with me, Logan Cross. I don't want to get serious with someone who'll discard me the second he lays eyes on his soul mate. Maybe I'll have peace knowing she hasn't been born, or that this is nothing more than the power of suggestion and tradition. You'll have a few drinks and… well, I don't know what the hell goes on at those things. Karaoke?"

Logan burst out laughing and a few heads turned in our direction. "I'll go if this pleases you, Silver. But only on the condition that you accompany me and stay away from any microphones." He pushed an empty plate to the side.

"I thought it was exclusive?"

"They make exceptions if you're partnered with someone."

"Who would go with their partner? Talk about three's a—"

"Chicken?" Logan leaned back in his chair with a confident gaze and a broad smile stretched across his face.

"Throw down the gauntlet, Mr. Cross. You and I have a Gathering to attend."

CHAPTER 2

THE CAR TOOK AN UNEXPECTED turn off the highway on our drive home. Darkness spun around us when we exited the city, and I watched Logan apprehensively.

"Where are we going? You aren't taking me to your secret cave, are you? Because that's not how I roll. The dinner was expensive, but if you have some kind of expectation of payment due—"

"I would never be so crass," he said, cutting me off.

Logan had a commanding voice, but there were times when it was a seductive purr. I found each of them to be equally attractive.

Lately, cheesecake had become my new obsession and once he found out through idle table conversation, we weren't leaving the restaurant without it. The box rested on my lap and I drew in a deep breath, releasing a moan with my sigh.

"Are you going to keep staring at that box? Have a bite."

"It can wait," I mumbled.

In a quick motion, he flipped the lid open and pulled off a wedge, shoving it into his mouth.

"Hey! You're ruining it!"

"Then have a bite," he said with a mouthful, giving me a sideways glance. "It's delectable… like a certain Mage I know."

While he was still chewing on his slice, I pulled his smudgy fingers to my lips. In retrospect, I'm not sure how clever that idea really was. I took his fingertips into my mouth and sucked off the chocolate cream, my teeth scraping against his skin. Logan drew in a hard breath, and the engine roared as we picked up speed.

"Silver… *stop*," he panted. His eyes hooded with a possessive gaze.

"You were right, Logan. It's delicious." In one long stroke, I licked his thumb from base to tip.

His voice deepened. "If you keep touching me like that, I'm going to touch you back." Darkness swirled in his eyes before switching back to amber.

The car made an unsteady jerk and I freed his hand. On second thought, I'd rather make it to our destination alive than wind up tangled in the windshield because I got overzealous from a few glasses of wine.

Despite his amorous words, Logan was a gentleman. His customs were foreign, but I was learning to appreciate how Chitahs revered women. It wasn't easy for them to have a daughter and as a result, they were very protective of their sisters, respectful to their mothers, and honor bound to their wives—or mates, as they called them.

Logan's silver car eased off the road in the middle of nowhere. He opened the door, took my hand, and quietly led me to a dark meadow.

An oversized blanket smothered the grass in an open area. Wine, glasses, and a small basket lay at our feet while the universe covered our heads.

"What's this all about?"

"Sit," he requested, extending his arm.

Logan dropped to one knee, set down the box of cheesecake, and opened the wine. He filled our glasses and lit several large candles. When he removed his jacket and rolled up the sleeves of his white shirt, I noticed his muscles. They were amazingly proportioned and solid. Not big at all, but athletic. He stretched across the blanket on his left elbow, casually bending his right knee.

"Did you just see that?" I asked, pointing at a white streak that flashed across the sky.

A smile softened his eyes and a memory rushed back. When Logan protected me from Nero's guards, I had to talk him out of his primal condition. While I'd forgotten about my ramblings of meteor showers, Logan had not. Evidently, he marked his calendar for the next big show and orchestrated this entire evening. It was something I'd never experienced, and he was giving it to me on a silver platter.

I set my glass on a flat tray and placed my hand on his chest.

"Are you trying to give me the stars?"

Logan's chin lifted imperceptibly and he began to purr. That natural ability was a mystery, but it had to do with how the blood flowed through his chest and larynx. I felt it strongly around his neck and it rumbled in his chest. When that wonderful sound poured out of him, I wanted to curl against his body. He captured a lock of my hair between his fingers while keeping a steady gaze on me.

"This whole night is magnificent, Logan. Better than rollerblades." I laughed.

Lying on my back, I thought about my place in the universe as tiny specks of dust infiltrated the atmosphere in a glorious flash of light. It used to make me feel small and insignificant knowing that I would burn out like one of those stars one day. Becoming an immortal changed the way I saw the world… and myself. There was time. Time to change, time to grow—time to make a difference.

We talked for hours, drinking in the wine and each other.

"Finn will be moving soon," he said.

"Moving?"

"We're a tight family and Little Wolf needs to bond with each of us. We agreed to rotate him."

My brows arched. "Rotate him? He's not a tire."

"No, he's a young Shifter who hasn't been socialized, and nobody will hire him if they run a background check. He's not ready to go out into the world on his own."

I agreed. If something happened to Finn because we pushed him out too fast, I'd never be able to live with myself.

"His wolf may never trust us—that's a given—but Finn must learn to. I've taken an oath to look out for him, and I keep good on my word. He'll take something from each of us and become a better man," Logan said, taking a sip of wine.

I smiled and brushed a strand of hair from my face that the wind kept playing with. "What's he taking from you?"

"My furniture." He chuckled, shaking his head. "Tooth by tooth. I'm just glad that I never bought drapes."

A few more flashes of light silently skated across the inky sky above.

"Logan, why did you decide to court me? Am I just a curiosity to you because you've never dated a Mage?" When I stopped picking at a stray thread on the blanket, I glanced up and saw the disappointment on his face. "Sorry, I didn't mean to be a buzzkill. I've had too much to drink and that idiot at our table got me thinking."

Logan turned over and propped his head in his hand. "Does it matter to you that we're different?"

"I guess I'm just—"

"Looking for reasons out."

"That's not fair. Don't finish my sentences for me."

"I apologize. The way men have treated you makes my fangs ache. I'm smitten with you, Silver. Indulge me in my pursuit."

I fell into his rapturous gaze, wondering where this would lead. Too much wine provoked too many questions.

My teeth chattered.

"Let me warm you," he murmured.

Logan crawled over me, propped up on his elbows. He rested his head on my stomach and the weight of his body warmed my legs instantly. I was dizzy from the intimacy.

When a sharp sting pierced my thigh, I shouted and sat halfway up.

"I think something bit me," I complained, rubbing my leg.

"Let me take a look." Logan slid my dress up on the left side and traced his hand up my long legs. He pinched two fingers together and held them up, examining closely. "It's just an ant."

I glared at the large insect resembling a fire ant that he held between his fingers, but it was hard to tell in the dim light. "Well, tell him that I don't like being nibbled on."

He quirked a brow and flicked his fingers. "Is that so?" Logan purred.

The intensity of his stare and the proximity of his body to mine sent butterflies swarming through my stomach. Logan's energy was strong for a Chitah when his emotions ran high. Justus said I was becoming more in tune with Breed energy and it was part of my development as a Mage. Logan never had to tell me how he felt; I could feel it in his touch, taste it in his kiss, and smell it on his skin.

He leaned down and I tensed when his tongue—rough and smooth all at once—ran over the insect bite. The itching immediately numbed and I shuddered. Logan Cross may have considered his healing ability to be no big deal, but I didn't think I'd *ever* get used to that man's tongue being on me.

With a lift of his head, he drew in a deep breath and sensed my altered mood. He crawled up the length of my body and lowered himself on top of me.

"Tell me where else you've been bitten," he said playfully.

The heat of his kiss against my cold lips roared a fire to life. I circled my fingers around a soft patch of skin behind his neck, clawing lightly. The heavy taste of wine lingered on his tongue—stroking against mine—and he groaned. I felt nothing except Logan and the earth.

He broke the kiss and turned his head to the side, every breath a testament to his control.

"Logan?"

A veil of loose hair obscured his face. I cupped his chin with my hand and lifted his gaze to my attention. That's the moment I felt his heart galloping against my chest.

"Don't start something you can't finish."

"A fire?" he asked. "One that I won't be able to put out." His eyes dragged down to my lips. "Do you know what it does to me to look at your mouth when it's swollen with my kiss? Light glitters in your eyes, and the smell of your skin is a drug to me." His hand traced down my jaw. "Strong features and soft to the touch—I want to feel every inch of your body. When there's a flash of silver in your eyes, it's because I put it there. Your body is a furnace, Silver. One I'll lose control with if I play with matches."

I let go of his hair and rubbed my eyes. Logan had customs that were supposed to make him feel like more of a man, but it made me feel undesirable. When he spoke that way, I melted completely, so it was confusing when he resisted too much physical contact beyond a kiss.

"I need another glass of—"

Logan suddenly unleashed his desire like an avalanche. I was buried in it. Consumed by it as he kissed my neck.

I wiggled beneath him, trying to push him away, but all it did was create friction between our bodies.

"Keep doing that," he whispered hoarsely, settling his weight on me.

His lips grazed my neck and when his tongue flicked against my earlobe, Logan found the match that set my furnace on fire. I began to unfasten the buttons on his shirt. He stared at me with vehement desire as shifting patterns of color moved across his chest beneath my fingertips.

Logan wouldn't touch me. His mouth sucked hungrily on my neck and the blanket twisted within his clenched fists.

"Touch me, Logan. I want your hands on my body." My fingers slid inside of his shirt, craving the feel of his skin.

His hand caressed my arm and that one simple gesture was so electric that I could have set the grass on fire. There's something so wonderful about the casual movement of a man's hand across your body, moving his way down to your leg in search of bare skin.

Logan watched me intensely with magnetic eyes, observing my reaction to his touch. He tugged the dress higher until his fingers splayed across my hip, looking for the edge of my panties.

Except that I wasn't wearing any.

Stark confusion crossed his face and his fingers bit into my skin. Because the dress showed panty lines, I had gone without. Why not let him think that I did it just for him? Something about that made it sexy.

He licked his lips.

"Why, Mr. Cross… you're *blushing*."

A soft breeze chilled my skin, an owl hooted, a flash of light dashed across the sky, and Logan penetrated my soul with a kiss so deep and reverent that the light within me surged. He shifted his hips and I moaned. He knew exactly how to use his tongue and each time it stroked against mine, I gripped the blanket to resist the urge to join hands with him. It was a Mage thing, and while I'd only experienced a little of the act of binding, my body knew exactly what it wanted to do. In that single kiss, I discovered exactly what kind of lover Logan was.

Insatiable.

My sexual energy had no place to go, not without injuring him. With another Mage, this wouldn't be an issue, but I could hurt Logan with the energy that raced through my fingertips. His lips came away and he drew in a breath.

"What's wrong?" he asked. "Your scent changed."

"I can't touch you. That's what's wrong. I'm starting to feel like a live wire."

"Show me."

"No!" I protested, struggling to sit up.

"Then how do you know for sure what will happen?"

"I'm not hurting you to prove a—"

Logan pried open my fingers and placed his palm over mine. The second he did, a surge of energy knocked him on his back, several feet away in the tall grass.

"Logan!" I flipped onto my knees and crawled, wide-eyed, knocking over a glass of wine. He rolled onto his side, looking like a truck had hit him.

Or a burst of sex lightning.

"Why did you do that? Are you okay?" I brushed the hair that pulled free from his band away from his face. "Didn't your mother teach you not to stick your finger in a light socket?" I laughed, relieved to see that he was conscious.

He sighed and rubbed his face. "That's going to be a problem."

"Well, look on the bright side," I said, falling beside him in the grass. "You won't ever have to worry about buying jumper cables."

CHAPTER 3

"I DON'T UNDERSTAND WHY YOU INSISTED on coming, love," Simon grumbled as he skipped up the steps to Samil's enormous house.

I held my arms as we passed the two fierce statues of lions before the front door. "I may not hold a position within the Mageri, but as long as Nero's case remains open, then I'm going to be a part of it."

The truth was, even if they closed the case, I would still be involved.

My Creator had legal rights to me before he died, but that didn't justify the Mageri's decision to hand me over to him like property. That's why I related to Finn. Breed laws weren't established to protect the people, only to uphold outdated customs. Seven days in that basement beaten, by a man who should have mentored me, had damaged my trust in the law. I never had nightmares about Samil because he was dead and gone. It was Nero that crept into my mind in the middle of the night. He was alive and doing God knows what with innocent lives.

Simon's shoes tapped with contempt against the polished floor and he wiped the mud from his heel, leaving a brown streak on the marble.

"I don't suspect we'll find anything new," he said. "I just like to be thorough."

"If Samil had knowledge of anything that allowed him to create a stronger progeny, then maybe there's something here," I said. "A name, a diary, an instruction manual—hell, I don't know. If there is, I don't want Nero to find it."

"The Council put this house on watch from day one; ask me what I had to do in order to get us permission to enter."

"Don't be dramatic, Simon."

He spun on his right heel and lifted a brow.

"So how was Hannah in bed?" I snorted. Hannah was one of the Council members with the sharpest tongue and hairpins to match—*so* not Simon's type.

He narrowed his eyes. "You think I would bed that strumpet? For your information, I posed nude."

"For which magazine?" I bent over, unable to contain my laughter.

"Laugh it up, missy. There's a high-ranking official of the Mageri who apparently has a passion for sculpture and nude men."

"Can I see it?"

Simon smirked and reached for his zipper.

"Never mind," I muttered.

"Thanks to the guards, Nero can't touch this place with his pinky toe." Simon sniffed and crossed the room, staring at a pretentious painting encased in a gold frame. "I would have liked to kill the sod myself. You do know that?"

"Putting Adam in the challenge may have been the only legal way to kill Samil, but I don't know if I'll ever be right with it, even if Adam is. Let's not dig up bones in this cemetery."

Simon whirled around. "I do love a good bone." I glared at his T-shirt that said: *Chess players do it all Knight.*

"You are the most inappropriate man I know."

"*Moi?*" he asked, folding his arms and glaring judgmentally at me, foot tapping on the floor.

"What's that look for?"

His eyebrow rose. "You are the biggest troublemaker I know."

"So I flirt with disaster once or twice. Who doesn't?"

He snorted. "You don't just flirt with disaster, you have intercourse with it."

I was three seconds away from having a verbal confrontation when a wicked smile slanted his dimple and he sauntered across the room.

Simon pulled at the banister and headed upstairs. "There are two lessons I've learned in life: never play chess against a Sensor, and never lose your sense of humor."

Halfway up he stopped and leaned over the railing. "Oh, and never shag a woman with a tattoo."

Now that surprised me. "Why?"

"They're freaks. The lot of them."

"I thought you liked getting your freak on," I said with a laugh.

He rolled his eyes and jogged upstairs, voice trailing off. "Remind me to tell you about the time I was tied and taped to a washing machine by a woman who had the grim reaper on her back."

I searched every drawer, opened every book, and reviewed each stack of Samil's papers, but found nothing. An hour later, I called out for Simon. Silence replied. He wasn't answering his phone, either. On the third attempt, he casually strolled down the stairs with a smug grin on his face.

"Why don't you ever answer my calls?"

He tapped his front pocket. "I love the way you vibrate."

Simon mentioned that years ago he designed secret rooms as a side job, earning him enough money to freelance. While he was busy in the study looking for a magical door, I turned my attention to the basement.

The light flipped on and tiny particles of dust floated in the air as if disturbed by my presence. The stairs creaked as I made the daunting journey down memory lane. It still smelled of mold and the sole of my shoe scraped over the dark stains of degradation on the floor. I slunk down with my arms draped over my knees in the spot that was once my bed. Simon's heavy shoes clomped down the stairs and he paused halfway, soaking in the room with his eyes.

"This was where he kept me."

"Silver, come out of here."

Simon crossed the room and stuffed his hands in the pockets of his trousers. Tousled brown hair fell forward when he looked down at me with compassionate eyes.

"I wish I'd never asked you what went on down here." His voice trailed off to a whisper as he stared at the open bathroom. "At least you weren't chained."

"Chained?"

He snapped out of his haze and smashed an invisible cigarette butt with his shoe.

"Simon, what happened to you with your Creator?"

He rubbed the tattoo on the back of his neck and shook his head. "Not now, Silver. Not now."

"How long will it take me to learn how to control my light?"

He quickly responded to the change in topic. "Not sure I know what you mean."

I dropped my eyes and picked at my thumbnail. "You know, so I can be with someone who's not a Mage."

He crouched in front of me. "What gave you the idea that you could? You can't be with anyone other than a Mage in the same way."

"Justus told me when we first met that if I learned to control my power then I could be with a human," I argued.

"So now there's a human who's caught your fancy?" he said, lip twitching.

I slapped his arm. "You know what I mean."

Simon gave an impassive smile. "You can't touch them. A mortal will die and most Breed… well, that's a bit of a mood killer if you juice them up with your light. For Justus it comes easy. He shuts away his emotions; he's had years of practice. You *can* acquire enough control to level down your energy, but it would be a passionless experience," he cautioned. "The only ones immune to our touch are Vamps, and if you go trolloping around for one of them then I won't blink twice about putting a chastity belt on you."

"I think it's a little too late for that; one has to be chaste."

He turned his skull ring in circles. "Sexual energy can only be properly shared during binding with another Mage." He scratched his head as the memory of our encounter surfaced. "Intimacy is perfectly normal between us because our bodies process *that* kind of energy much differently. You can touch a Mage anywhere and the sexual energy won't release unless you join hands." He rolled the piercing in his tongue around a little. "If you want to be with someone who's not a Mage, then you're going have to give up touch, or else you'll do some serious damage."

With a hard sigh, I said, "Yeah, found that out."

Simon blinked in surprise. "Are you telling me you shagged Logan?"

"No!"

"I would be gobsmacked if you told me that you polished his knob."

"Get away from me." I laughed, shoving him. "We just kissed."

Everyone knew the custom for Chitahs during courtship was a PG experience. Most went to the next level *after* the woman accepted his claim on her. That level was more than just dating—it was a permanent commitment. Of course, we were breaking the mold because I was not a Chitah and felt it was too premature to take him as a husband.

"What Breed of women do you date?"

"I have a few regulars," he said, licking his lips. "Mage, of course. But it doesn't mean I don't have an appreciation for the lovelies. I'm an equal opportunity shagger and have never turned down a willing Sensor, Relic, or the like."

"So all this time I've been led to believe a lie? I'm never going to be able to touch another man who isn't a Mage."

"You can always have that with me." Simon raised his hands defensively when I gave him a harsh glare. "I'm just putting it out there."

"I won't forget how quickly you flew out of that bed after our drunken kiss."

His neck jerked back. "You're cross with me over that? This *whole* time?"

I was tempted to give him the finger, but instead I picked at a cuticle.

"Justus coming home was the cold shower I needed. It went too far, and I can't do that to a friend. It wasn't a rejection. You're lovely, but you don't deserve to be stuck with a cad like me."

"You got that right," I teased.

Simon stood up and showed me his back and I realized he took the comment more seriously than I meant.

"I didn't mean it like that, Simon. Don't be mad; I say stupid things sometimes—it's a sickness." I brushed the dust from my pants and stood behind him.

"Sorry to be the bearer of bad news," he said with a lengthy sigh, "but it's something you need to know. For short-term relationships it's no biggie, most aren't a stranger to interbreeding, but if it gets serious, you need to consider how much it means to you. Even with gloves, I'm afraid it's not possible."

I hugged his arm and silently wondered how Justus managed to bottle his passion. I could barely contain mine around Logan.

Simon peered down at me with an angelic face. "Still want to give it a go?"

He was incorrigible. "I could never be with a man who smokes a pipe and wears a pub cap while playing Clue, just for the effect." All smiles, I leaned in and gave him a light peck on the cheek.

"Call that a kiss? I'm a fan of the French Revolution."

I shoved him toward the steps when a dirty box beneath the staircase caught my eye. "Has anyone looked through that," I asked.

"We're out of time and I don't feel like posing for another bloody masterpiece of clay. Bring it along and I'll return it later. Of all his progeny, not one of them was willing to claim Samil's inheritance. All of this will go to the Mageri, or the fanciest junkyard in Cognito."

I stood in the doorway of Justus's hidden study. "You guys have been in here all day with that box. Do you want to tell me what's in it?"

Justus sat behind an old heavy desk, rubbing his tired face in his large hands. The skin on his brow pushed around like putty. He released a heavy sigh, dropped his arms, and leaned back until the chair creaked. "It's HALO business."

"Simon isn't part of HALO."

The sound of overpriced wine washed down his throat as he

emptied his glass and set it on the desk. His private study looked more like a temple of artifacts from his past. The only thing missing was the picture he kept of me on his desk, which he probably hid in a drawer to avoid any remarks from Simon.

"Simon has examined the contents," Justus pointed out.

"I found the box, so I think that's a crock of shit."

Simon howled with laughter from his chair and quickly cleared his throat, containing a snort. I had a right to know what was in that box and Justus knew it.

"Swearing does not become a lady." Justus suddenly snapped a finger at Simon without looking in his direction. "One word and I will tether you to the grill of my car." Simon made a gesture of zipping his lips and Justus turned his attention back to me, stretching out his tattooed arm. "No arguments. You need to get ready for the party."

Ah yes, the party. We had received invitations from Novis for a formal gathering at his home. Justus saw it as an opportunity to make connections and strengthen alliances. I had no desire to go, but Justus hadn't left me home alone since the night that Logan walked into my life.

I was pissed off already, but now I really didn't want to go. I understood the need to protect a Learner until they acquired enough skills to become independent, but that didn't make it any easier to endure being dragged to an event like a child.

"I *am* ready."

He looked over my attire. "Learner, you lack maturity."

"Maybe so, but my fashion sense is a force to be reckoned with."

"Unlike your common sense," he muttered. His eyes scraped me from head to toe as I stood in sweatpants and a black shirt that read "Fucking Classy" in cursive. It was an impulse buy when I was shopping for Sunny's housewarming gift and began as a joke. Justus rarely cursed and only purchased high-end clothing, so it was the most inappropriate shirt I could possibly wear whenever I was mad at him. Which wasn't often, but we had our moments. Because this was a cocktail party, I was certain that Justus would buckle and leave me home to avoid the embarrassment.

Unfortunately, he called my bluff.

The Aston Martin had received a detailed polish—as did Justus. When our car pulled up to the mansion, my jaw slackened.

Adam was living it up Jefferson style. I'd always met with him in public and never got to see where he lived. Aside from that, Justus didn't want me hanging out at a Council member's house.

Rumor had it that Adam was seeing someone and I was dying to meet her. There was no question that he was a catch with his debonair looks and warm heart. Adam was one of those handsome men who didn't know it, and that is an attractive quality to most women. But it was the compassion and loyalty to others that made him stand apart.

The valet parked the car, and I grinned from ear to ear as two men in expensive suits escorted me to the door. A Charmer could walk into a party wearing a garbage bag and still have every woman clawing after him. Justus didn't have to make the effort, but he did. That's just the kind of man that he was. He slipped on his most expensive watch, cufflinks, and a silk tie that made you want to grab it and pull him close. His potent aftershave was guaranteed to make lips glisten.

Between Justus and Simon, I looked like a basket case. My hair was pulled into a ponytail and the sound of my flip-flops clapping made Justus sigh more than once. Novis was waiting in the doorway to greet us.

"Think he'll adopt me?" I whispered to Simon, who ditched the usual bad-boy attire for a casual grey suit. His caramel eyes were a golden ticket into any woman's bedroom as long as he didn't open his mouth.

Novis was a striking man, although only by physical standards was he young as he was one of the ancients. His razor-cut hair was dark, complementing his piercing light blue eyes and thin-lipped smile that always had a secretive way about it. Novis appeared to be in his early twenties when he was made. In addition to being a member of the Council, he stepped up to do Good-Samaritan work, taking in those in need of refuge. He offered Adam the choice to become a Mage when the alternative was death. I admired him as a Creator.

He bowed to Justus. "Welcome, friends. Indulge in the cocktails and drinks. Please mingle and let me know if you need anything."

Justus walked by him and mumbled, "Apologies."

Novis looked me over and widened his grin. I almost returned the smile until I stumbled over the edge of a rug, knocking into a woman whose drink splashed onto the floor.

"Sorry about that; I hear there's more in the back." I thumbed in that direction and Justus bulldozed me with his eyes.

"Learner, I suggest you go to the kitchen and stay there for the remainder of the evening. There are important people here tonight; do not embarrass me." When he turned his back, it was evident he didn't want anyone to know that I was his Learner. Sure. *No problemo.*

"See ya, Simon. I'm going to kick this party up a notch." Something in another room captured his attention and he strolled off with a wave of his hand.

The champagne was delicious and full of tiny giggles. That's what I used to call the bubbles when I was a child because of how giddy it made everyone. My eyes wandered over an array of magnificent paintings that were likely originals.

I let out a burp and a head turned in my direction. It was fashioned with expensive hairpins decorated with tiny jewels. When I saw the wolfish brows and burgundy lips, I immediately recognized Hannah. She was one of the Council members and was disgusted by my shirt. I smiled politely and whirled around to escape when I caught sight of a familiar face.

Adam leaned against a doorframe, looking about as Cary Grant as any man dared to with dark brown waves of hair and a smooth shave. Standing beside him was a man wearing a trench coat. His Vampire eyes were as black as a panther on a moonless night and his features were strict.

"If this is a pissing contest, I want in." Adam chuckled.

"My, don't we look like a fancy pants tonight?" I smiled at him with my eyes. He wore a white shirt buttoned almost all the way up, tucked in a pair of black slacks. "You never told me that you live in a palace," I said, making a sweeping arm gesture and splashing my drink. Alcohol consumption was seldom and champagne went right to my head.

"I wasn't aware this was a charity function or I would have brought my checkbook," the Vampire remarked in a flat voice.

I cut my eyes at the stranger who tilted his head in a manner that implied he thought himself better than me.

"I'm Silver. Did someone forget to take your coat, or are you going to be putting on the magic act later?" I exaggerated my smile as he folded his arms.

"Silver, this is Christian." Adam dropped his eyes to my shirt and took a sip of his drink.

I slapped my hand on Adam's shoulder. "Tell me there's a karaoke machine in here because I'm ready to take my shower performance to a whole new level."

Adam didn't just laugh, he spit his drink back in the glass and set it down on a table. "You're always stirring it up, aren't you?"

"That is my modus operandi."

"Save it for later. It's too early to bring this party to a halt."

Across the room, Justus cozied up to a woman in a revealing blue dress. Her hand slipped into his pocket and she leaned in close and spoke against his cheek. I didn't see any distinct features on her so I couldn't tell what Breed she was. His amorous grin irritated me.

That was the man I met in Memphis—the one who had every woman in the bar at his disposal. He never brought women home, but there were nights that Justus came in late wearing a wrinkled shirt with smears of lipstick on the collar.

Christian looked at Adam. "The babes are always the spoiled ones, aren't they?" he said in a slow Irish accent.

"Adam is younger than me," I pointed out, exploiting the flaw in his comment. Human years didn't count and I had been a Mage for months longer.

"Looks like Simon found some competition," Adam remarked, pointing in the adjacent room.

A chessboard divided the space between Simon and a young woman. Her body was delicate and thin and covered up in a long-sleeved, pale green dress. She also wasn't sporting the generous cup size that Simon was known to revere. Her ginger hair was braided against her head, wrapped up tight with pins. Simon rubbed his chin with his aviators still on—something Justus would have also worn had he not thought it would insult the Council. When Vampires were present, people shielded their eyes from their power. Simon lifted his black knight.

"Poor bastard," Christian remarked.

Adam folded his arms. "How so?"

The woman lifted her rook and took his piece off the board. Simon's leg began jumping under the table—one of his nervous tics when the game wasn't going his way.

"She's one of Hannah's progeny." We all simultaneously glanced at Hannah, who was showing her intolerance at the rowdy behavior of some men across the room. "I think he's finally met his match," Christian chuckled. "No one beats her. Ever."

When a man walked by with a tray of food, I snagged his arm and scooped up a handful of green olives. Adam's expression shifted when I tossed one into my mouth.

"Come with me." He took my elbow and the olives scattered on the floor.

"So nice meeting you, Sister Christian," I yelled over my shoulder. Adam hurried me to the back of the house and I stumbled over my shoes as we entered a darkened room.

"What's wrong?" he asked.

"What makes you think anything's wrong?"

He lifted my hand. "Your mood ring is black."

I snatched it away. "It's just a ring."

Adam folded his arms. "The getup?" he said, nodding at my shirt.

"I always preferred acceptance to conformity."

"Woman, tell me what's wrong. I know you better than that."

"What's right?"

I turned my back and walked to the window, admiring the landscape. It looked like an English countryside with manicured shrubbery and paved walkways.

"I feel useless, that's what's wrong. Just when I'm becoming a part of something, I get pushed out of it again. I want the normal things everyone else does, Adam. But I'll never have my life back until Nero is caught. I don't have a job and Justus won't let me in on the investigation. I sit around all day and read. Justus tries to get me to work out, but I don't even feel like doing that anymore."

He sighed and groaned all at once. "So not much is new?"

I threw my head back and closed my eyes. "Do you ever wonder where we'd be right now if none of this ever happened?"

"How are things with Logan?"

I whirled around. "That reminds me… I heard through the grapevine that you have a sweetheart."

Adam massaged the back of his neck with a nervous hand and that's when I knew it wasn't a rumor. "Do me a favor and go easy on her."

Justus used the same tone when he was afraid I would embarrass him. I sagged.

"I'm really happy for you, Adam. I'm not out to sabotage your love life."

He smiled warmly, eyes still on the floor. "I care for her," he admitted. "I've waited a long time to find someone who looks at me the way she does. Maybe I am starting to believe in fate."

"Adam?"

We both turned toward the doorway. A silhouette of a lovely woman stepped into view, wearing a ruby-red dress with tiny tassels skimming across her thighs. She was familiar.

"I was looking for you *and* the wine." She leaned against the frame and smiled as he approached.

"I'll get it." He kissed her on the cheek and briskly left the room, not introducing us on purpose.

"Do I know you?"

"Kind of," she said with a melodic wave to her voice. "I'm Cheri."

Cheri was one of the prisoners released from Nero's compound and the last time I had seen her, she was nothing but a scant of a girl in dirty clothes with tangled blond hair.

Why didn't it ever occur to me? When Novis took her in,

Adam's nurturing personality would have won her over. I remembered how at ease he made me feel when we first met with his generous eyes and integrity.

"Cheri, of course. It's great to see you again. Your dress is beautiful."

"And you look…" Her gaze darted over my body.

"Just between us, I was trying to make a point with someone and lost. I may just go sit in the car for the rest of the night. So, you're dating Adam?"

"Mmm," she replied. "Quite the looker, isn't he?"

Cheri smiled when Adam appeared at her side with a glass of white wine. He stretched his arm over her head and leaned on it while she took a sip.

"They just started bringing out the chow," he said with a smirk. When he took her arm, Cheri pulled back.

"No, you go ahead. Why don't you fix me a plate and I'll meet you in there. I need to take a walk and get some fresh air." They shared a tender glance and Adam lifted her hand, gently placing a kiss on her knuckles.

"I'll be waiting," he said and turned away.

"It was nice to see you again, Cheri." We smiled at each other as I brushed by. She waved and continued sipping her wine.

"Silver," a voice barked out. "Making your Ghuardian proud I see."

Through the opening to the study on my left was Merc—one of the Council members—setting his glass of wine on the white fireplace mantel.

Each time I'd been in his presence, he made it clear that he didn't like me. There was an unspoken animosity between him and Justus; the glances they exchanged made it obvious they despised one another.

Merc stood there with his stringy light hair and beady little eyes pressed into a gladiator face. The dress shirt he wore looked painted on and the sleeves were rolled up, showing off the thick veins in his arms. This was a man voted least likely to have a political position by his fellow prison inmates.

"What's not to be proud of?" I challenged.

"Tell me, did the homeless person put up much of a struggle when you robbed them of their attire?" He laughed along with a few curious spectators.

My eyes narrowed into sharp slivers. Council member or no, this man was not about to stand there and publicly insult me.

"You might want to give your parole officer a call before they report you missing."

A man snickered and Merc invaded my space with a step of his giant black shoe. I was never told the story behind his incarceration, but he didn't know that.

"You want to cozy up to the Grim Reaper? Your call, you worthless woman," he said, lowering his voice. His fingers tugged at the ends of my hair. "Perhaps you need to be taught a lesson."

A thick body wedged between us.

"Merc, keep in mind this is a social affair and we are all invited guests. Do not throw around your position here," the man warned.

The back of his hair was short, neatly groomed, and a reddish tint with blond highlights. He was spectacularly tall and when I saw Merc's eyes flinch, I gave him a nice *fuck you* smile as he backed away and walked off.

"He really is the prick he makes himself out to be," the deep voice mumbled as he turned around.

His features were mature and rugged with a broad chest and a thick jaw covered with a closely trimmed shadow of a beard. His broad mouth and large golden eyes were Cross trademarks, but he looked Irish. Deep lines were etched high on his cheeks near his eyes—a clear mark of a man who loved to laugh.

"I'm Leo Cross."

"Logan talks about you all the time. It's a pleasure to meet you." I stumbled over my words with our unexpected introduction and reached out to shake his hand. It was a clumsy human reaction and I quickly dropped my arm. Leo held a strong presence that made me feel like I was around someone important.

"The pleasure is all mine," he said with a nod. "Come." His arm fell around my shoulders and he guided me to a private corner of the room. I folded my arms to hide the obscene writing on my shirt and we faced each other.

"I want to be frank with you, Silver. I'm much older than Logan is and I watched him come up as a boy. He was an impulsive child with a brave heart, but always getting himself tangled up with trouble. When this was still bear country, a grizzly pissed him off something fierce and Logan flipped his switch." Leo laughed and his eyes sparkled with memories. "Had I not been there, he'd still wear claw marks down his chest. Sometimes he has no sense of what is a danger to him."

Leo was the kind of man who didn't look away in conversation and I found the direction of my gaze drifting to his lapels.

"In order to ensure that our line is continued, we only mate with our own kind," he said. "I think we both know that a Mage and a Chitah mix like oil and water. You two have a number of strikes against you."

My face cooled when the blood drained from it, and I looked at a piece of lint on his sleeve, feeling just as small.

His fingers lifted my chin. "That being said, I think you two are both equally stubborn and need to come to a decision about your relationship. Logan carries a dark past that has nothing to do with you and yet—everything."

"I know about his woman and all that he lost. What makes me nervous is how sure he is about us. Look at me. If he saw me tonight he would—"

"Show you off proudly. I don't want to watch him spiral back to the man he once was. Tell him what he needs to hear before it breaks him—a decision. My brother will court you for as long as it takes, but he's doubtful where your feelings lie. That doubt is eating him alive. Any other male it wouldn't matter, but this is Logan."

Leo was afraid that his little brother would revert to the cold-hearted killer he once was.

Elegant cocktail dresses and suits swirled about the room and I realized how poorly I had played my hand.

"I appreciate your concern Leo, but it's complicated. Don't put my back against the wall and force me to rush a decision I'm not ready to make. You know how unfair that would be for both of us. There's no time limit on courtship."

Leo sighed and touched my shoulder. "You should also know that the Gathering is coming."

"I know. I told him to go."

"This is what bothers me. You don't seem to understand the risk in holding him at arm's length."

"What risk? Logan finding his soul mate? Who am I to deny him what Chitahs so fiercely believe in?"

Leo slid his hands in his pockets. "If Logan goes in his condition, he's likely to make a poor choice. Can you live with that?"

"What condition? He seems fine to me." I huffed out an irritated sigh. "And what choice? I'm not going with him so he can pick out a wife."

"He's a man who doesn't know where his female stands; *that* is a condition. You are putting him in a position where potential mates who have waited for their chance will do everything within their power to win his affection. Had he not been damaged, I wouldn't be as concerned. A long courtship gives us the opportunity to show what we have to offer. I'm afraid it's not your fault as you are a Mage and do not know the customs of how a female behaves in such situations. You continue to send mixed messages by pushing him away, and I'm only looking out for his best interest."

I knew he could scent my anger, jealousy, and confusion. His nostrils flared.

"He's been a solitary man for many years," Leo said. "After his mate's death, he was inconsolable. You brought him back to us, Silver. Men don't always make sound decisions when they're not sure if their love is reciprocated. I won't lie and tell you that it will be an easy road if you accept Logan. He's not the man he once was, and the pairing would be subject to public ridicule. You'll be on the receiving end of a lot of unkind words." Leo widened his stance and cupped his hands together. "I know you care for him. If he's going to settle, let him settle for you."

Leo tipped his head and walked away.

It felt like someone cut the rope to my anchor and kicked me out to sea. I stared blankly at a painting of a cherub angel as my chest weighted down like a bag of concrete. I didn't want to be the woman that any man settled for.

Suddenly... *chaos*.

Two armed men stormed through the front door and opened fire. My eyes widened in horror and a vase beside my head exploded from a bullet. Screams tore through the house and bodies fell from the automatic gunfire. The spray of bullets pierced the walls, shattered lamps and glass fixtures, and left a spray of blood across the floor from the crumpled bodies. Those who could flash out of the way did, but few could outrun bullets.

I dove into a hallway as a man fell at my feet with blood pouring out from a hole in his eye. Particles of debris filled the air along with the stuffing from furniture. Trays of food littered the floor with broken champagne bottles, and the air crackled with gunfire and shouts.

My back flattened against the wall. Most immortals required time or energy to heal, which is why no one immediately got up. I didn't even know if the man with a bullet in the head *could* get up.

The men stood with their backs together as they continued firing off more rounds. I flinched when gunshots erupted from all over the house. My heart was a hummingbird caught in my chest.

"Ladies and gentleman, we apologize for our late arrival, but we didn't seem to receive an invitation! Not very gracious of you." Laughter pealed out and the gunman fired off another round. "Nero sends his regards but is unable to attend due to other engagements. He wishes for us to give you his—"

I stood up, threw my arms forward, and pulled the guns from their hands using my gift. They skidded across the floor and I flashed toward the assassins before they could react. A redhead with fierce eyes rushed at them from the other direction and drove a dagger into the back of one man. He dropped like a deadweight.

Strength didn't take the other man down, the momentum of my

body slamming into his did. The young woman pulled a dagger from a holster beneath her long dress and plunged it into his chest without batting an eye.

"I've got this under control," she said coolly. One of the pins popped out of her hair, unraveling a lock of pale ginger against her green dress. I stood up, admiring her bravery. She was the kind of woman Justus would have wanted in a Learner. Fearless.

Justus ran into an adjacent room and several men scattered throughout the house. Novis was not among the bodies, thank God. Sporadic gunfire sounded as the attack came from all sides and two men dashed up a flight of stairs.

I was shaking like a tree in a typhoon.

"Help me, please!" a voice cried out.

Behind a decorative glass wall, Adam knelt beside a lady in a bloodstained dress. As a Healer, his gift allowed him to heal any Breed—although I'm not sure what his limitations were.

I stumbled over a woman who was clutching her leg.

"Hold onto my neck," I said, helping her up and taking her to the back of the house. My heart pounded, but adrenaline took over and I went on autopilot, carrying out one wounded victim after another.

Three men lined up the bodies out of sight behind the topiaries. The chaos was inside the house and victims were finding themselves trapped in the inner rooms. The only safe place to go was outside. It was a horrendous display of carnage.

I was running through the hallway to the front of the house when a spray of gunfire erupted. A man was poking his gun into each room and shooting down those who were hiding. He shot everyone in the head who charged at him.

There was no time to wait. I threw my hands forward to pull the gun, but it never came. Meaning—he wasn't a Mage. I could only pull certain metals recently touched by a Mage. He glanced at his watch and ran out of sight.

Then it grew eerily silent.

The front door crashed in and an engine roared as a vehicle skidded to a stop in the main room, pinning a body beneath a tire.

It was pandemonium. People crawled over pieces of debris and I thought I saw Merc flash into the room. Someone coughed, a few voices shouted out, and then it happened.

An explosion.

CHAPTER 4

I SHOULDN'T HAVE SURVIVED, BUT I did. The floor in the hallway looked like a war zone as pieces of a collapsed wall covered the white floor. When I coughed and looked at my palm, a slick film covered my skin and shimmered on my clothes like the wet trails that slugs leave behind.

"Ghuardian?" I coughed into my hand. "Simon?"

The cries that surfaced were horrifying, but it was the quiet moans that made my hands shake.

"Silver!" Simon called out. "Cover up your wounds!"

I stumbled through the dim hallway, stepping over chunks of mortar. "Simon, where are you?"

He caught my wrist and I looked up.

"Are you injured?" His panicked voice made my heart kick up a beat. "There was liquid fire in the truck and if it gets on any of your wounds then the injury will be permanent. I don't know how they managed to get it in an aerosol form. It's a stubborn substance, its properties not easily changed. It's airborne."

That scared the hell out of me and I looked myself over. "I think I'm okay. Where's Justus?"

My eyes widened in horror when I saw a woman with her face half gone lying in the main room.

"They won't heal. Liquid fire will seal mortal injuries." Simon grimaced and shrugged out of his jacket, tossing it over the dead woman's face. "Sodding bastards!"

In a connecting room, the woman who helped take down the two gunmen was crouched on her knees. Blood trickled from her ears and she appeared disoriented. A tall Chitah was dragging an overweight man out of what used to be the front door.

Amid the chaos, Adam stood up and took a few shaky steps before he knelt in front of a body missing a leg. In vain, he tried to heal the dead man.

I shuddered when I noticed the gashes on his face and the blood on his arms and shirt. He wiped his brow and I remembered him standing behind the glass wall. *That damn glass wall!* I sprang forward, tripping over a chunk of concrete in my flimsy shoes.

"Adam! It's too dangerous in here. The air isn't safe! You need to get outside and—"

"I can't leave them. They need help," he said in a disconnected voice, grimacing from his own pain. He lifted the man in his arms and disappeared through the rear of the house.

"Search the room," Simon yelled out. "Justus was headed this way looking for Novis before the explosion."

My tangled hair clung to my face and I tried to avoid looking at the carnage.

"Ghuardian!" I shouted in a raspy voice. "Please call out!"

I crawled over piles of broken furniture near the vehicle; it didn't appear the intent was to blow up the building as Nero could afford enough explosives to complete the job. He rigged this bomb to leave people injured. Permanently.

A foot stuck out from beneath a white sofa. I lifted one end, hoping the leg was still attached to a person. He looked to be a boy of sixteen, and while my fingers felt for a pulse, the chunk of metal embedded in his chest told me everything I needed to know.

Part of a stone archway had collapsed, along with half of the ceiling. Mage energy nipped at my skin and I crawled over the debris into the room with hope in my pocket. Sitting on a large pile, my hands worked at tossing aside chunks of rock and plaster.

A deep voice groaned beneath the rubble and as I cleared some of the debris, I found myself staring at the hilt of a sword.

Footsteps crunched behind me and my hand flew up.

"Don't come any closer," I yelled out. "I need a blanket from a safe room." I whipped my head around and saw Leo. "Get me a blanket that doesn't have any liquid fire on it!"

"Is it Justus?" Simon dropped on his knees beside me. "Good

girl. We'll do this very carefully."

Leo returned with a tightly folded blanket he handed to Simon. Something was stuffed beneath his shirt so that he looked pregnant. Leo draped the blanket over our backs, sealing us in dim light.

"Let's give it a minute for the liquid fire to settle," he said in our stuffy pocket of air.

"How is this going to work?" I asked in a worried voice.

"As best it can, love." Simon shook his head. "We'll do the best we can."

A couple of agonizing minutes passed before Simon pulled away a flat stone. I followed his cue and we carefully worked together. Others held the ends of the blanket, securing them down. There wasn't much to uncover. The hilt of the sword was flush with his belly and blood soaked his white dress shirt. Simon unbuttoned the jacket and stopped me from lifting the last bits of rubble. A bead of sweat dripped from my forehead.

"Hang in there, chap," Simon said encouragingly.

I brushed my hand across Justus's forehead, relieved he had no other serious injuries. His eyes were hooded, and I stroked his sweaty brow with my thumb.

"Hand me the sheet," Simon called out.

When the folded sheet appeared, he paused. "Carefully remove the remaining blocks from his stomach. I doubt they're coated in liquid fire, but lift them straight up."

Justus wasn't just impaled, that sword was pushed all the way to the hilt. I grimaced and fought back the sickening feeling in my stomach.

"What about his back?" I asked.

Simon tore a slit in the center of the sheet with a dagger, draping it over Justus with the handle of the sword poking through the hole.

"The blast would have thrown him down and it settled on top. What we're doing is protecting him for what's about to happen."

I pulled my hand away from Justus and looked over my shoulder. "What's about to happen, Simon?"

He stood up and snapped the blanket off in a dramatic fashion.

Crawling to his side, I cradled my Ghuardian's head with my left arm, which also kept him from moving.

"Stay still," I said against his temple, brushing my hand over the bristles of his short hair. His eyes rolled back.

When Leo stepped forward and reached for the sword, I caught his wrist.

"Silver, let him go," Simon warned. "Someone needs to pull the sword free and release him from this pain. Leo's the strongest one among us."

Novis stood in profile with his head hung low. There was a trace of guilt in his voice. "It was mounted upstairs. I've kept it for over six hundred years. Please accept my apologies."

"Can no one take away his pain?" I asked, looking between the men. A Mage kept gifts closely guarded like a fantastic hand of cards.

"Christian?" Novis yelled out.

"No," Justus grumbled. "Keep him out of this."

Simon wiped his cheek, leaving a smudge of dirt. "Distract him," he whispered to me.

How the hell do you distract someone from getting a forty-inch blade pulled from their gut?

By blurting out the most inappropriate thing, of course.

"Simon showed me what binding is. Remember that time you caught us in my bedroom?"

His eyes slanted into fiery slivers and before he could mutter a word, Leo gripped the sword and pulled. Justus peeled his lips back and his moan turned into a roaring shout.

"Ghuardian, look at me!"

His beautiful eyes—the color of summer sky—locked on mine, glazed over.

"I'm sorry I made a spectacle of myself tonight. Just one second of pain. We'll heal you as soon as it's out. Focus on my face."

He bravely locked eyes with mine and a fire flickered in them. This man possessed a control over pain that I would never understand.

Justus nodded and Leo pulled once more. I winced as the heat wafted off him.

"Someone knock him out," a voice suggested.

I snapped my head around. "Why can't you pull it?"

Leo bent over with his hands on his knees—his cheeks ruddy from the exertion. "It's wedged deep in the floor. Where's the Vampire?"

"Securing the grounds," Novis replied. "There are still men unaccounted for."

Simon palmed his forehead—something he often did when thinking. "What can we do? What can we do?"

I stood up and looked hesitantly at Novis. "Is this a regular sword? Has it been tempered with magic?"

Novis turned his head to the small cluster of men gathered behind us. "Gentlemen, you can do no more here. Go outside and help the injured."

Obediently, the small crowd dispersed with the exception of Simon. Novis stepped forward to speak with me privately and I noticed a small cut on his cheek. "Do you think you have enough control?" he whispered.

"Justus doesn't understand how it works and neither do I." After a quick glance over my shoulder, I turned my concern back to Novis. "I've never done anything like this. Moving a few knives around is one thing because small objects don't require a lot of effort, but I'm still clumsy at controlling the direction of the energy. That's a big sword. When more power is needed, I have to be emotionally charged. That's all I really know about this gift."

His eyes glittered with regret as they lowered to the scene. "Gifts are different forms of energy; if you don't learn how to use it, then it ceases to be a gift. This will require you to think of nothing else *but* control. Whatever you do that pulls a dagger, you must multiply it times a thousand, or this man shall suffer on my floor until we can locate someone more capable of pulling it free."

More capable. I didn't like the way that remark made me feel.

I once impaled my own hand moving a metal object; the metal always sought me out. This would require strict concentration to guide the sword straight up into the air.

My eyes flicked nervously to Novis and I positioned myself so that one leg was on either side of Justus. I widened my arms above the sword and took a cleansing breath.

"If I hurt you, Ghuardian, I'll accept whatever punishment you want to dish out."

That was guilt talking, because I suddenly had images in my head of polishing his entire car collection with cotton balls.

I flexed my fingers, dreading failure. My palms prickled with an electric charge as I began to slice my hands up and down in the air, feeling the energy pop even harder. Because the sword was still impaled within Justus, his power was dripping all over it. And it was *strong*.

Sweat beaded across my brow and the muscles in my arms burned. I was going on pure instinct—running my hands up and down in chopping motions with the palms facing each other. I glanced down at Justus, saw the spatters of blood on his shirt, and immediately closed my eyes. The air charged and static snapped against my palms. I looked like a robot spazzing out and hoped nobody was laughing.

"*Ffffuck*," Simon breathed. "Look at that!"

The moment he said that, I opened my eyes and gasped. You could actually see the charged energy in the air surrounding the sword like tiny blue sparks.

When the intensity reached its peak, I crouched, holding onto the enormity of that power. It swelled between my hands like an expanding ball of matter. In one sweeping motion, I stood up and lifted my arms into the air. The sword made a strange sound when it broke free from the marble and sliced upward.

Simon lunged forward as if to catch it, but the power behind the release was so strong that the handle lodged into a chunk of the ceiling that remained. We looked up at the long, red blade pointing ominously at Justus, who was covered in a blood-stained sheet. My hands tingled and sparks crackled against my skin like snaps from a rubber band. A faint bluish light radiated from them and I closed my fists.

I was a Unique, and wielding metal was only part of it. In that moment, I realized that I had the potential to do amazing things with my power once I learned to harness it.

Simon fell to his knees and covered the bloody wound with his hands, offering his healing light. Justus draped his tattooed arm across his forehead and blew out a breath as his skin color returned.

"You are a remarkable Mage," Novis complimented me. "Remarkable indeed."

"Silver," Justus summoned.

I knelt on the uneven rocks and glanced at his beautiful gold watch. The face was shattered. "Did I do that? I'll buy you a new one."

"Can you afford two large?"

I didn't even flinch. "No sweat."

He reached out and put his hand on my shoulder. "Despite your insubordination, you *are* fucking classy."

I wasn't sure if my skipped heartbeat was from the compliment or his bluntness, but I blinked and looked away. "Why would Nero do this?"

Novis answered. "He's instigating war on the Mageri. This is retaliation for the raid we conducted on his compound. It's imperative that we stop him. Men like Nero are not easy to hunt, even with the help of HALO. I fear it could only get worse. As long as Nero walks free, we're all in danger. If you come across information, you *must* give that to the Council. He has committed treason against the Mageri by this…" He turned his head with a disgusted expression. "…senseless attack. I cannot express how it upsets me that this happened under my roof. The loss would have been far greater had the people not been moved out of the house. We will have justice for the lives that were lost tonight."

CHAPTER 5

"WHY ATTACK YOUR OWN KIND if you want to start a war against the Breed?" I just didn't understand the power struggle with the older immortals. Had they become so bored with their immortality that war was a pastime?

Simon ruffled his hair and uncorked another bottle of wine. We had barely slept unless you counted the three-hour nap I took in my chair, slobbering on the table. The conversation carried through the next evening and everyone was too rattled to sleep. I cooked seven omelets for Justus to help him regain his strength, and it provided me with a distraction. The light Simon lent him to heal was draining, and my instincts to look after him kicked in.

"I don't understand who the enemy is anymore." I groaned, rubbing the exhaustion out of my face.

"Perhaps the Mageri," Simon suggested. A river of wine flowed past his lips. "Not everyone supports their laws. If he wants to gain power, then one way to do it is to dismantle them."

"That's about as effective as homegrown terrorists who anthrax the post office because they don't want to pay their taxes."

The glass tapped on the table and he dipped his finger in the wine, circling it around the rim and producing a hollow note.

"But people suddenly didn't trust their mail," he pointed out. "Sometimes the most effective way to remove a leader is to create doubt among their followers. We can only speculate and quite honestly… I'm not sure I can wake another brain cell." He sighed and dropped his head on an outstretched arm, staring at the grooves in the table. "It could have been so much worse," he muttered.

Justus walked into the room, smelling like expensive soap.

"I called Novis," he said, sitting to my left at the head of the table. "He summoned a Relic to see what can be done for Adam."

My bottom lip quivered and I pinched it between two fingers. Adam's injuries looked severe.

"Push it back, Learner. Do you think he seeks your pity?"

Relics were a type of doctor. They inherited ancient knowledge through their genes and specialized in information. Anything new they learned was retained and passed down to their children, so it was actually fortunate to be the youngest child in a Relic family. It seemed a little farfetched, but maybe a Relic could help Adam because he would have been scarred from those injuries.

I took out my frustration on a few locks of tangled hair. "I'm trying not to think about it, but you didn't see him. I didn't try hard enough to warn him about the liquid fire."

"It was already too late," Justus added in a smooth, baritone voice. "The damage was done."

Simon's leg was hopping and we listened to the heel of his shoe tapping on the stone floor.

Justus looked agitated and rubbed his bicep. "Simon, if you have something to say, then stop running a marathon underneath my table and come out with it."

"Did either of you see anyone prior to the blast? Someone that looked out of place? Maybe I'm talking rubbish."

I knew what Simon was driving at but kept my mouth shut. Merc flashing through the hall, running in the direction of the chaos. Maybe he was rushing to fight, but I never saw him after that. The risk of implicating a Council member without evidence could be damning, so I joined my Ghuardian in the head shaking.

Simon spread his arms across the table. "In proximity to where the sword was in the house, it's rather convenient that it fell on you the way it did. Novis had it mounted on the opposite side of the upstairs room."

Justus ran his hand over the spot on his belly where the sword had gone in. He was unshaven and while completely healed, he still winced every so often. Phantom pain.

"If I could remember," he muttered. "I only recall waking up."

"Maybe I'm pissed from the wine, but everyone knows the

story. It was his peace sword and had never shed a drop of blood in his lifetime… until tonight." Simon looked at me because I didn't know the story. "It hung over the Council's quarters for more years than I can remember as a reminder that peace could be found without violence. It's only my opinion, but I think Nero wanted that sword baptized in blood. Symbolic, wouldn't you say?"

I stood up from the table and rubbed my eyes. "You boys talk it out; I need to take a shower and meet up with Logan."

The doorman didn't even flinch when I let myself in at the Red Door. I was a regular. Justus enjoyed taking me to this private Breed club because most of the women didn't throw themselves at him like everywhere else, and it allowed him to be the hunter for a change. Human women could hardly contain themselves in his presence, but he got a little more space at this particular club. While the green swill they served packed a punch, I kept my nose in the familiar beverages.

The décor was relaxed with dim lights and candles on the wooden tables—yet still gave off a club vibe with plush red colors. We had a regular semiprivate table in the back where Justus could skim his eyes over the crowd and select his next conquest.

After everything that had transpired, I needed to get away from Simon and Justus for a while. I hadn't spoken to Logan and wanted to get his thoughts on everything.

Justus was meeting with someone, so I rode with Simon in his classic GTO while Justus tailed behind. Because of the enforced rules in a Breed bar about violence, he felt better leaving me there than at home alone. Justus was going to be tied up for a while on HALO business, so Simon left me the car on the condition that I fill the tank and have Logan follow me home.

For some reason that night, the Sensors were out in force and a few of them were openly exchanging. A red glow illuminated their palms during the transference, and I turned away with disinterest. It still disgusted me that one of my own memories was up for auction.

An hour passed and Logan hadn't responded to my phone calls. It wasn't like him to be late but maybe he forgot, so I decided to give him another thirty minutes.

"Looks like someone stood you up. I'll keep you company."

A man claimed the empty chair at my table without an invitation. He was tall from my vantage point. Thick shoulders gave him a hard edge—like a boxer—but it was his hair that stood out. It was short, dark, and shaved into a wide Mohawk. I lowered my eyes to the dark stubble on his chin and he snapped his gum and blew a pink bubble, watching me from behind dark sunglasses. He wore all black, and I could tell by his energy that he wasn't a Mage. Something about the way he smelled bothered me; it was a blend between stale raspberries and vinegar.

"No thanks," I said, rising from the table.

His fingers wrapped around my wrist and he gave me a thin-lipped smile.

"Sweetie, I'm not asking." I tugged my wrist but his bruising grip tightened. "My *boss* doesn't like snoopers and it seems you've been sniffing around Samil's place."

"Why don't you tell Nero to shove it up his ass, right where your head is? Let me go, because you know the rules in a Breed club." I twisted my wrist free and he leaned back in his chair with a smug grin.

"What's in the box you took from Samil's house?" he asked in a gravelly voice.

The bartender was nowhere in sight and the only other person in our section was an older Asian woman with papers scattered across her table. I turned on my heel and briskly headed to the back hallway. Simon's car was parked in the rear.

Just as I stepped out of the door, he shoved me so hard that I missed the steps and fell on my stomach.

"Going somewhere?"

I winced from the pain but quickly rose to my feet in the dark alley, ready to pull out a small dagger strapped beneath my shirt. Justus made me wear it on the odd occasion, and after the party, he wasn't leaving me alone unarmed. It was a stunner capable of paralyzing a Mage. But I could tell from his energy that this asshole was no Mage.

"I hate repeating myself," he said.

"Do I look like I have a box?"

His jaw punched out and his boots stomped down the cement steps.

"I know you don't *have* the fucking box. What I want is for you to tell me where it is."

"It's hard to take a man seriously who wears granny shades," I dared to say. "Throws off your whole scary-guy image."

That was my best effort to get him to remove his glasses. A unique eye color might reveal what Breed he was; then I would know what I was up against and how much of my ass was about to be kicked.

He threw them on the ground and stalked toward me with the conviction of a Chitah. His amber eyes were a stark contrast against his dark hair and brutal features. Logan said that it was uncommon for Chitahs to have raven locks—most of them had hair color in the shades between light brown and white. Not this guy; his brows were black and angled down, giving him an angered expression.

Through conversation, Logan taught me how to take down a Chitah.

"It's not complicated," he'd say. "You can't outrun us, so prevent us from running."

He assured me that I had a better shot than a man would, because a male Chitah would hesitate before hurting a woman.

"Sweetie, you make it too fucking easy," he growled.

I pulled out my blade.

His laugh was rough like the motor of an old pickup truck. "You think your puny little knife is going to faze me? Your mouth may be poisonous but your scent is exquisitely insecure."

I saw his moves coming a mile away. After a few dodges, I sharpened my light and prepared to lay it on him. He must have sensed the change in my plan and, quicker than I could think, he pushed me against a wall and took hold of my wrists. The knife tumbled to the ground and he leaned in close, scraping his vile fangs across the soft flesh of my neck.

I shuddered, reminded that all four of his canines could kill me in a heartbeat while anything less meant I'd be paralyzed and at his disposal.

His breath stank of sour gum, and his callused hands squeezed the skin painfully around my wrists.

"How about I torture you for a little while?" He wrinkled his nose. "Nah, then I wouldn't have the box. Tell you what, let's make this *fun*." The pitch in his voice sent a chill through my spine like a warning. "I've seen who you're tramping around with, so allow me to send him my regards."

My eyes squeezed shut in anticipation of a bite to my jugular; I'd seen what those canines could do and knew that a Chitah never gave an empty threat. Instead, he threw off a scent so pungent and thick that it coated my tongue. I wrinkled my nose in disgust and turned my head as he laughed.

Logan's scent was never that strong, nor vile. It was pure ambrosia. Chitahs also had the ability to mark a woman with a scent so undetectable that it worked as a repellent toward other Breed men. I asked Logan if he ever used it on me and he never admitted to it.

He never denied it either.

This was my first experience with another Chitah's raw power, and it was noxious and frightening all at once.

His grip loosened with an overzealous confidence that I was a meek woman who would buckle beneath his dominance. I punched him in the throat, dropped to my knees, grabbed my dagger, and with one clean swipe sliced it across his Achilles' heel.

Both of them—leaving him incapacitated.

"Good luck if you can bend over far enough to lick *that* wound. Tell Nero I'm not his bitch."

But the Chitah had already fallen to the ground, clutching his ankles and screaming in pain. I flashed across the empty parking lot and it was one of those moments you dread, like a cliché scene from a movie, when I realized that I had dropped the car keys in the alley. A text came in from Logan.

> Logan: I just found out about the bombing. Levi is joining us and we're on our way.

I asked him to pick me up at a twenty-four-hour diner at the end of the street. It took me a few seconds to flash there and I fell against the wall and caught my breath.

A silver car eased up with Logan in the driver's seat.

Overall, I behaved as if nothing out of the ordinary had happened. Nope, no lunatic shoved me around in an alleyway and sprayed me with armpit love.

Levi—Logan's younger brother—had stepped out of the passenger side to switch to the back seat when he crinkled his nose and glared at me.

"Logan, give me a minute," he said, slamming the door.

All of the Cross brothers inherited the same penetrating gaze. Although his features were rugged and quite different from Logan's, with his short hair and thick build, there was something easy about Levi. It was his generous smile and the way his bright eyes arched like golden moons. His tattoo was not dangerous, but Latin for "truth." Despite how opposite they were, Logan and Levi had a tight relationship.

His brows knitted and he lowered his voice. "Who marked you? Do you realize that if Lo catches a whiff of what you're wearing he's going to flip his switch?"

A couple crossing the street distracted Levi's attention. The man lit up a smoke while his girlfriend's heels clicked on the asphalt as she hurried toward the ice-cream shop with the pink neon sign.

"I'll explain everything in the car," I said in a tired voice.

"The hell you will. I'm not letting him *anywhere* near you," Levi cautioned, stretching out his words. "Turn around and flash your ass off; I'll cover you."

"You want me to run? That's ridiculous!"

Logan leaned over the passenger seat with a hard stare.

"I'm not playing around. Look at me, female." Startled, I stepped back. "You said you didn't want him to revert back to being a murderer? Then you better run like hell, because that man will paint blood on the moon when he finds out another male has marked you."

A chill ran down my spine. Could something so small push Logan over the edge? I didn't waste time to ponder and flashed around the corner. An old fire escape hung down from an apartment. I couldn't outrun a Chitah, but maybe he'd lose my scent. Halfway up, I heard the ladder rattle below as Logan was right on my tail.

I leapt onto the roof, fell to one knee, and jogged to the other side. The door that led inside the building was padlocked.

"*Fuck*," I hissed.

"Silver, what's come over you? Stop running from me!" Anger fueled Logan's voice.

I slowly pivoted around. Logan raked his fingers through his hair and paced toward me. As the space closed between us, the back of my legs bumped against the ledge of the building. A gust of wind blew his long hair to the right and he stopped—eyes locked on my feet.

"Don't move, Silver. Do you want to tell me why Levi pinned me to the sidewalk while you ran away?"

I swung my leg over the low wall when he stepped forward. He abruptly stopped, flicking his eyes to the perilous drop several stories below. A car horn sounded a million miles below us and a jet raced overhead.

"Stay where you are," I warned. "Don't come any closer."

Logan tilted his head to the side and his jaw hung lax as he struggled to pick up my scent. The wind cooled my cheeks as it gusted from his direction.

In a split second, it shifted.

Wild strands of black hair rippled in front of my face and tangled together. That's when his eyes widened and Logan drew in a deep breath.

The visceral look on his face caused me to lean back. Deadly canines punched out and Logan flipped his switch, becoming a slave to instinct. His malicious obsidian gaze reminded me of what it felt like to be prey in the eyes of a hunter.

I held my hands out defensively.

Silence blanketed the rooftop. The air never felt so crisp and it was the first time in a long time that I was afraid of Logan.

My legs began to shake as the excess energy within me spiraled into a vacuum. Typically, it warranted nothing more than a catnap. Leveling down was Mage 101, but it was a little difficult to concentrate on controlling my energy when a man I cared about was looking at me as if he wanted to rip me to shreds.

Maybe I wouldn't die from the fall, but as I glanced down at hard concrete below, I had second thoughts about jumping. I became disoriented, weightless, and suddenly saw the stars tumble as I fell backward. We were six stories up and I was about to become sidewalk art.

Logan surged forward with blinding speed and swung me around, placing me safely at his feet. He ran his nose up the length of my body and unfastened my blade, tasting the residual blood on the tip.

And just as suddenly as the whole thing started, the darkness in his eyes melted away. His primal mind relinquished control either because there was no imminent danger to me, or Logan was strong enough to push through it. Levi's heavy boots crunched on the rooftop when he slowly paced in our direction.

"Hey brother, everything's cool," Levi said reassuringly, holding his arms wide. His eyes darted between the bloody knife and me. A Chitah wouldn't harm a female, but I was also a Mage and Logan spent most of his life hunting down and killing my kind.

Logan rose to his feet and angrily threw his arm forward. The dagger embedded in a plank of wood that boarded up a small window by the door. Without a word, he lifted me into his arms.

"Put me down, Mr. Cross," I protested. Not that I could fight him; his grip was strong and my will was weak.

"I'm taking the female home," he announced to Levi.

His home.

CHAPTER 6

L EVI DROVE WHILE LOGAN HELD me in his lap in the backseat of the car. I napped against his shoulder, too weary to speak. Levi dropped us off at Logan's condo and went home on foot.

It was a charming neighborhood—quiet. One I could imagine myself living in if Justus would ever move out of the sticks.

Logan carried me inside and we moved through the darkened house into a bathroom where he flipped on the light. The customized tub on the left was large and well-used, judging by the packages of salts on the ledge. He set me down and paced straight ahead, disappearing behind a shower wall made of brown stones. The hot water squeaked on. I watched him with timid eyes when he knelt down before me and tucked his fingers inside of my jeans with the intent of removing them.

"Wait," I said, catching his hand.

Logan lifted his eyes to mine and pulled hard enough that the button popped off and rolled across the floor. There was nothing gentlemanly about his touch. He handled me in a familiar way—like a man who had full rights to a woman.

First my shoes, then socks, and finally he stripped away my jeans and tossed them into a wastebasket.

My heart galloped with uncertainty.

Goose bumps skimmed over my arms when he pulled off my thin shirt. When his hands reached around to unlatch my bra, I realized that Logan was about to strip me down without so much as a kiss. This wasn't romance—this was clinical. When his fingers pulled the straps of my bra, I crossed my arms and glared at his shoes.

Logan lifted my chin with the crook of his finger. "I don't expect you to understand my actions, but I will *not* have another male's scent on my female."

My heart slowed down, submitting to the power behind his words. Logan tilted his head to the side, looking at me with the same predatory eyes as the night we met.

"Another male has violated you with his scent, and I'm going to remove these dirty clothes from your body. I intend to wash you clean," he said in a voice so caged that it was as if an animal was prowling behind his words.

"Logan, I can't just get naked in front of a man unless... unless it's for the right reasons."

I was scared. Plain and simple. I could barely read the intentions of a human man, let alone a Chitah who was led by impulse, and the possessive look in his eyes made me hesitate.

He extended his long arm, cupped the back of my neck, and coaxed me forward.

"Let me make something clear. I'm drunk with your scent and when I'm near you, I find it difficult to control my instincts." His eyes slowly closed as if he were regaining control. "My body is hungry for you, Mage. Your kiss replenishes all the energy spent in restraining myself from advancing on you. It quenches my thirst and leaves me hungry for more." The black rim around his eyes swelled as if an internal battle raged. "I have no intention of taking you tonight, but my hands *will* be all over your body."

"But your eyes will not. That's my condition," I said. "This is embarrassing. Do you think that I can parade myself in front of a man so easily—one I haven't been intimate with? Then you don't know me; I don't care what kind of women you normally date."

His heated gaze soaked in every conceivable inch of my body and he stepped back, admiring the view with a lingering pause.

My jaw clenched. "What are you doing, Mr. Cross?"

I'd never been appraised like that before, and his eyes devoured me. He sensed my intent to leave and stepped in front of the door, removing his hair from the band that tied it at the nape of his neck.

"Undressing the rest of you with my eyes, Miss Silver," he

confessed with a throaty growl.

Logan licked the corner of his mouth, savoring the last crumbs of visual temptation before he reached out and flipped off the light.

"Problem solved," he murmured darkly.

I jumped when his fingers grazed across my stomach and slid down, hooking at the hem of my panties. He slowly pulled them to my ankles and I reached for his shoulders to balance myself as I stepped out of them.

Bare shoulders, but he kept his pants and shoes on. I had never felt more exposed than I did standing naked in the dark in front of Logan.

"Go wait outside; I can do this by myself," I insisted.

When he leaned in, his breath caressed my neck. "Not up for debate."

"We're going to trip and kill ourselves," I argued. "It's slippery in there and—"

"You're right," he said, mouth sliding closer to my ear. "Then we would be lying wet and almost naked together… in the dark."

My breath quickened.

"Come with me."

He tugged my elbow and with cautious steps, we entered the shower. The water quietly sprayed the floor, which was made of gritty stone, providing enough traction that my fears of falling took a backseat to what Logan was about to do.

Or not do. I wasn't sure which idea I liked better.

We moved beneath the hot water and a purr rumbled in his chest—one I'd never heard before. It was deep, sinful, and provocative. One of the most enthralling qualities about Logan was the unusual Chitah sounds he made—animalistic and led by emotions.

"Do you want to know what I find most attractive about you?" he asked, breaking the silence as he backed me up near the wall.

Logan was on bended knee and lifted my foot, placing it on his leg. My fingers searched for the wall as soft bristles circled across my ankle—soapy and wet.

"Um… my charming personality?"

He laughed softly. "Your legs."

The scrubber moved upward, swirling in heavenly motions across my knee.

"They're long and delicious. You may not be as tall as a Chitah, but no one has legs more dangerous than yours."

What was dangerous was his mouth. The more he kept talking, the less I wanted him to.

"Although, I do spend a considerable amount of time thinking about your tongue."

Likewise, I thought.

"I'll make a note of that." He chuckled.

Oh, my God. Right there in Logan's shower, I wanted to die. He wasn't a mind reader because I had said it out loud.

It had been so long since I'd been with a man that all of my confidence evaporated.

His finger trailed down my leg and I shuddered. Part of my brain fired off, wondering if that was his tongue.

Here he was, about to explore every inch of me with his bare hands, and I reacted with more innocence than I possessed.

"Reach up," he said. "There's a bar above your head. I want you to grip it."

I tentatively lifted my arms and found a solid metal bar for hanging towels. It was cold and my fingers curled tightly around it. I stared into the darkness and waited for direction.

"I'm going to put your leg over my shoulder."

My mind raced as I imagined what he looked like sitting on his knees. The wet skin of his back warmed my leg. Logan continued the slow, methodical motions along the outside of my upper thigh, but he didn't stop talking. I heard him set a bottle on the floor and cool liquid soap trickled down my skin in rivulets.

Stubble grazed the inside of my knee like worn-down sandpaper, and his heated breath caressed my skin as the water sprayed against his back. He was so close to the most intimate part of me and I knew he could smell my desire.

"Tell me one of your fantasies," he said.

I swallowed hard.

The scrubber tumbled against the wall, replaced by his firm hands rinsing the soap from my thigh. This was not a clumsy man filled with lust; Logan's hands were skilled and knew their way around a woman's body.

"When I take you, Silver, I want it to be to your liking. I don't know you intimately; do you prefer a male to be rough or gentle?"

The hot water didn't have anything on the heat of my blush as I dropped my leg to the floor. It didn't deter him as he continued to wash me.

"I don't… I don't know."

No one ever asked me; no one ever wanted to know. Logan had a way of making me nervous, and I didn't have that familiarity with him to speak so candidly about such personal things. He was well over a hundred years old. That kind of experience could make even the most seasoned woman feel like a wallflower.

"You know what you like," he said decidedly. "No better time than the present to learn more about the female I'm courting. This is something that we discuss."

By "we," he meant Chitahs. In my book, this was dirty talk, but for him it was a perfectly legitimate conversation so he could learn how to seduce a woman exactly the way she desired.

"I can't talk about this with you," I admitted in a quiet voice.

His fingers squeezed my upper thigh. Logan wasn't forceful, but he was determined when he lifted it over his shoulder.

"Tell me what you want in a lover, Little Raven," he urged. "We're not leaving this room until you confess."

His warm breath heated my inside thigh and his hands never once stopped massaging. Logan's scent reminded me of a thunderstorm—turbulent and dangerous, like an impending act of nature.

What did I have to lose?

"I want a man who knows what he wants and isn't afraid to show it." That was the truth. Most of the men I knew were indecisive or secretive. Logan's outspokenness and undeniable confidence is the reason I allowed him to court me.

A lingering kiss settled against my thigh and my fingers

tightened around the bar. He inched closer and reached around, washing my backside. I nearly lost it between the sandpapery feel of his cheek and the slippery suds.

"And?" he pressed.

His mouth slid higher.

"Someone who takes his time."

He rewarded me with another kiss on my inner thigh—only higher. A needful growl vibrated against my skin.

Desire clouded my thoughts when his cheek scraped against my soft skin, moving even closer, and his proximity was more than I could bear.

"Do you like foreplay or stamina?"

His mouth was so close that his breath touched me intimately—like scorching fire against my core. My leg reactively tried to pull him closer, but Logan was unmovable and I felt his smile spread across my leg.

"This is the most foreplay I've ever had and if you want to know the truth—I don't want you to stop."

He slid his hands upward and cool gel smoothed over my breasts. I was so startled by the unexpected contact that I stiffened. Logan placed a penetrating kiss against my inside thigh—this time his lips met with the crease of my leg and I threw my head back and it thumped against the wall. An ache throbbed between my legs and I held my breath, squeezing the metal bar.

"The most intoxicating scent on you is blushing desire." The raw timbre of his voice carried a suggestion that those words were not meant for me to hear.

Energy poured through my body like a river, forbidding me to touch him with my hands. I wanted to curl my fingers in his hair and feel the velvety stroke of his tongue as I stood languid in his arms.

Instead, he kept talking while his fingers tempted every curve and line of my body. A thumb rolled over my hard nipple and his tongue simultaneously laved my sensitive skin.

"Is this to your liking?"

Each time he spoke, his breath was ragged and heated. Did he have any idea what that was doing to me? The textures—liquid soap, firm hands, rough whiskers, and hot water. He tortured my body with his touch, yet it's what he *wasn't* doing that sent me right over the cliff.

That primal thrumming came from his throat, a purr that was deep and wild. He massaged my chest until it was slick and filmy and I leaned back. The shock of the cold stone wall against my back made me shriek out.

His laugh was delicious and dark. "I like the sounds you make and look forward to being the one who gives them to you."

Logan stood up and a stream of water spattered against my chest from the showerhead. He aimed it at me and the sudsy liquid glided down my body.

His sneakers squeaked on the tile and he took hold of my arm, wiping away the soap until a clean friction built up between us. It was more than I could have imagined as he gratified me with gentle persuasion. Logan wasn't just touching me with his hands—he was coveting me. My body wasn't simply washed with soap and water—it was revered in the gentle way that he took his time. He may not have seen me naked, but he memorized every inch of my body with his tenacious hands.

After the third round, I was about as primed as a woman could get.

"Turn around and face me," he said. "I'm going to wash your hair."

He backed me into the stream of hot water and I sighed as his fingers gingerly massaged a mango-scented liquid throughout my scalp. It didn't make any sense that Logan had so many scented toiletries and yet he never smelled like anything but a man.

"I can't believe I'm letting you do this," I mumbled with a soft laugh.

He rinsed the shampoo away and placed his heavy hands on my shoulders, making a slow descent down the curve of my back with a feathery touch.

"Logan?"

"Hmm?"

"You can't see in the dark, can you?"

"Not entirely."

I pushed away and crossed my arms. "What does that mean? You can or you can't?"

"My sight is better than average in dim light. I can't see in total darkness. Female, would it really matter after I have seen you naked with my hands? I know your body so well that I couldn't mistake you for any other woman. I have imagined you in my mind, and you're exquisite."

"Where do you intend to take this?"

Logan's hands were so sultry with every possessive stroke, and he slipped one behind my neck insistently.

"I'll go wherever you lead me. I don't have to see you to know there is a glint of silvering in your eyes and your fingers are charged with passion. You *want* to be taken." His mouth covered my ear. "And I want to be the one who takes you. Say yes and I won't stop until I'm inside of you. *Deep* inside."

His finger brushed between my legs and I gasped in surprise from the unexpected intimate contact.

"What about the courtship?" My voice trembled.

"If this is what you want—then rules be damned—it's what you're going to get." His slick finger stroked once more before withdrawing.

My heart almost slammed on the brakes. "Am I not worth sticking to your rules?"

There was amusement in his voice. "You're the reason I don't want to play by them."

"I want you to claim me in every way, Logan, but I can't touch you. I can't be with you like a normal woman. I want this, but…"

His hands cradled my neck. "But what?"

It didn't feel right. I was immensely attracted to him and swept up in the moment, but the reason he instigated this to begin with didn't set with me.

"You brought me in here because you couldn't stand me wearing another man's cologne. It wasn't about seduction or romance, or even a spontaneous move. I like being with you and feeling this way, but—"

"You're still not sure. I told you once that I would not bed a female who was doubtful, and I won't now." He sighed with frustration. "I would have been able to scent your doubt if it wasn't for all this damn *mango*."

My energy leveled down and I touched his arm. "Are you mad?"

"I'll get you a towel and show you how mad I am," he said sharply.

I snapped my jaw shut as he moved out of the room and the light burst on. The stone wall molded against my back. His arm extended through the opening, offering me a long, white towel. After covering myself up, I shut off the water and warily stepped around the shower wall.

Logan stood with his eyes respectfully closed and his arms folded.

It wasn't until I noticed the thick bulge in his wet trousers that I knew without a doubt that Logan Cross was a man of remarkable restraint.

I took my time drying off the ends of my dripping hair with a small towel, admiring his luscious, golden skin and the masculine line of his body. Broad, rounded shoulders gave his body a V shape, and the muscles on his arms and abdomen were defined and solid. A selfish part of me wanted to see those beautiful patterns rippling across his arms and torso—the ones that changed colors when he was consumed with emotion. I wanted to be the one responsible.

My crumpled clothes sat in a pile inside of the wastebasket. "What am I supposed to cover up with?"

"Me?" A wolfish smile turned up the ends of his mouth.

I finished drying my hair and noticed his glum expression. "What's wrong?"

"Aside from your unsated lust that burns my nose like gasoline? Not a thing. Do you want to know what I was going to do to you in there with those lovely legs draped over my shoulders?"

"No, please." I caught a subtle glow in my reflection and my lips were swollen from biting them.

Water trailed from his wet hair over his shoulders; nothing had changed in the baggage compartment. "Maybe you need to get back in the shower and turn on the cold water," I suggested.

"Maybe you should join me, my sweet."

He took a deep, purposeful breath and I shoved my palm against his wet chest.

"Stop doing that, Mr. Cross."

He quirked a smile. "I do love it when you call me that."

I squeezed the ends of my hair and tossed the towel in the sink. "Was it easy for you to kill all those people? Before we met."

Logan lowered his head, keeping his eyes closed. "Those were deplorable men, Silver, and I will not apologize for my actions."

"Was every single one of them a Mage?"

"Most. We've gone over this. I can't erase my past—it's not a chalkboard."

I wiped a droplet of water from my nose and crossed my arms. "I'm not holding it against you. I don't know why you chose that life, but I understand why you think it's justified. In the end, it didn't bring her back."

"No," he said, pointing a finger angrily at the floor. "Curse my life until you run out of breath, but the tragedy of who I was led me to *you*. I've never been a soft man when it comes to females, Silver, not since Katrina."

"Your wife?"

"My mate, yes. She knew me in the spirit of my youth. I chose not to leave you alone on that rooftop for a reason. I fought the instinct to track down the scent," he said, drawing in a slow breath through his nostrils. "I *know* that scent. It infuriates me that another male has marked you, and there is a familiarity to his identity. If he crosses my path—"

I cleared my throat. "I think we made the right decision tonight. It would have been for the wrong reasons and it shouldn't become something that we regret."

After a lengthy sigh, a wide smile stretched across my cheeks. I was impressed that he kept his eyes closed without the temptation to peek.

"I need something to put on," I finally said.

Logan kicked off his shoes and when he unlatched his belt, I couldn't look away. He shoved his pants to the floor and stepped out of them. It was the first time I'd seen his legs and they were more powerful-looking than I'd imagined—not like a bodybuilder, but conditioned like an athlete. He wore form-hugging briefs that were a little long in the leg and they were the sexiest damn things I'd ever seen on a man. I admired the v-cut that arrowed down his abdomen, wondering what it would be like to stroke my finger down the groove. When his thumbs hooked around his briefs, I whirled around and gaped at the tile.

"I'm not putting you on," I insisted.

"You have permission to look at me."

"How very gracious of you, Mr. Cross."

"I'm not shy about anything I have to offer you, but I need to get out of these wet clothes and put on something dry before my ass chafes."

I snorted. "I never did like peeking at my presents before it was time."

He gripped my shoulders firmly and his lips grazed my ear. "When it's time, Little Raven, I'm all yours to unwrap. And I promise that your present will be the biggest of all."

That was no lie; I'd already seen the size of the box.

I turned to give him a kiss and, although his eyes remained closed, he felt my intent and leaned down.

The kiss was deep and penetrating. It was intimate in a way that the previous ones weren't. When his tongue found mine and he slid his hands behind my neck, I nearly collapsed and flattened my hands against his chest.

"I love the way you taste," he whispered against my mouth.

My bare foot touched his when I tried to get closer. Logan teased me by brushing his mouth against mine but staving off his kiss. I nipped his bottom lip and a dangerous growl rose from his chest.

"I dare you to do that again," he whispered against the corner of my mouth. "You are always so eager to play with fire."

Provoking him was not a good idea, so I pushed away. "Let's get out of here; I've never felt so clean in my life that you could eat off me."

His eyebrows popped up. "Now that you mention it, I'm famished."

"Sorry, the restaurant is closed."

"Then let me make reservations," he offered with a suppressed grin.

Justus crossed my mind. "I need to go home."

"Hand me the phone and I'll call your Ghuardian."

"Are you going to dial blind?"

"Excellent point. Shall I open my eyes?"

It didn't seem like Justus not to check in on me. I glanced at my phone sitting on the edge of the sink and noticed it was turned off; the last thing I needed was my Ghuardian prowling the streets of Cognito in search of me. "I'll do it. He probably left a few messages and—"

My knees buckled and in a quick motion, Logan caught me.

"Easy now, I've got you." His voice was brimming with concern. When he shifted his hold, my towel hit the floor, but Logan's eyes remained closed. "Tell me what's wrong, Silver."

I blinked away the dizzy spell. "It's my energy; I'm still just a little weak and the shower relaxed me too much." My legs were shaking. "I should go before it gets too late. I need to sleep it off."

Without warning, Logan lifted me up so high that I locked my legs around his waist. Our chests moved together with each breath and I savored the way his wet hair smelled where it stuck against his shoulder. He made it easy to forget myself, and I didn't think about the fact we were skin to skin. My weary head rested in the curve of his neck and a steady vibration fluttered in his chest.

"I'm not letting you go anywhere in this condition. You'll stay here the night and sleep in my bed. I'll call Justus and let him know."

In Logan's arms, I felt protected. His body was still warm and wet from the water and I caved, allowing him to carry me when a sensible person might have pushed away. That's what my human side was telling me to do, but in the time since I'd become a Mage, there was an awakening. Everything about him was lush, like a decadent wine made from the sweetest berry. He slid his hands around my lower back.

"Can I open my eyes so I don't fall on my ass carrying you out?"

I agreed, as all he would see was the slope of my back, but when he turned in the direction of the mirror, my shriek lit up the room.

His boisterous laugh was wonderful and I felt it throughout my entire body. "Female, you are naked in my arms, and yet you will blush if I see your body?"

"It would ruin the surprise," I murmured, smiling against his shoulder.

His mouth grazed against my ear. "I'm patient," he whispered.

Instead of his bedroom, Logan walked straight through the house and into the kitchen. The cold air licked my skin, causing me to grip tighter for warmth.

"Where are we going?"

"I'm thirsty," he announced. "That was quite a chase you had me on." I felt about as silly as a toy poodle in a thoroughbred race as he bent over and opened the fridge. "Do you want milk or juice?"

"I'll have panties and a T-shirt, please."

"Sorry. We're all out."

Logan tilted his head back and took three long gulps. Meanwhile, my ass was getting frostbite from the chilly air blowing on it from inside the fridge.

"I'm really going to hate you for this in the morning," I grumbled.

"Feel free to get down and hate me for it now," he suggested with a smile in his voice. "By all means, don't let me keep you from anything."

When he let go, I held on so tight that my muscles began to quiver. "Don't even think about it."

Logan chuckled darkly and wrapped his arms around me once more. The fridge door slammed and he lingered in the center of the kitchen.

I sighed hard. "Now what?"

"I have a taste for something," he said. "I can't decide if I want to scramble some eggs or cook up that leftover—"

"If you don't get me back in that bedroom *right now*, Mr.

Cross, I'm going to scream at the top of my lungs!"

"If you insist. But please, save your screams for the bedroom. All my fine crystal is tucked away in the cabinets and I wouldn't want them to… shatter."

"You're enjoying this, aren't you?"

"Immensely," he said with a kiss to my shoulder.

"At my expense."

Logan leaned back to look me in the eyes. "Let go of your inhibitions; not everything leads to sex. There are a thousand ways to be intimate, and I want to experience all of them with you."

"Thousands? And *how* do you know that?"

He smiled, shaking his head. "I do love your fire. It makes me want to warm myself beside it."

"I haven't quite figured out if you're a gentleman or a fiend."

What kind of man pulls a woman naked into his arms and makes no advance, keeping his eyes at a respectable distance?

Logan Cross, that's who.

It was so damn hard to stay mad at him. He drove me right to the edge of a cliff in a fast car and always made it spin around at the last minute. Being with Logan was indescribable; he knew how to push my buttons without crossing any lines. Maybe that's why I didn't mind the slow seduction—I was enjoying the chase too much.

"What can I cook for you?"

"You're serious?" I moaned. "I'm not hungry. Feed me in the morning, but right now I just want to go to bed."

He carried me down the hall and stood at the entrance to his bedroom. I uncrossed my ankles and dropped to the cold floor as he turned away. The sheets were crisp and smooth as I curled up beneath them.

This was Logan, the minimalist, who didn't even hang a curtain on his window and his bed was nothing more than a mattress on the floor. The tall windows ran almost floor to ceiling and gave a picturesque view of his side of town. Luckily, there were no apartments across from us, but he faced due east and that meant the sun would be rising with us.

Logan was in the hallway talking to Justus on the phone. He

kept his voice low, but the tone was assertive and indicated he wasn't taking no for an answer. He respected Justus, but Logan was very much a man of his own who rarely held his tongue.

Moonlight shone through the open window and a mystical glow blanketed the dark room. When Logan returned, he was wearing a pair of snug black briefs that made his body look magnificent. He placed a steaming Tupperware bowl on the floor beside me and paced to the window.

"You're Ghuardian doesn't like me very much."

"What would you do if some guy called you up and announced that your little girl was going to spend the night with him?"

He arrowed his gaze at me. "I'd tear out his throat."

"So find a way to relate to him," I suggested, eying his briefs. "I see *you* found something to wear."

Logan reached down and picked up a shirt beside the bed, tossing it on my chest. It smelled like him, and I tried like hell not to take a deep breath when I slipped it over my head.

He fell beside me and slung his right arm over his face. "I apologize for arriving late tonight. Leo called us over to break the news about the bombing. I left the damn phone in the car and didn't get your messages until I was on my way."

"What did Leo tell you?"

"That you were safe, because *that* was my first concern. Leo downplayed the casualties, but I could tell by his scent that it was more serious than he made it out to be."

"It was," I said in a low voice. "Did he tell you they put liquid fire in the bomb? Everyone injured was covered in it."

"Death is a better alternative than what some of them will be faced with."

"Adam was hurt," I said ruefully. "Justus could have died. I guess we aren't so indestructible after all."

Logan rolled on his side and brushed his palm across my forehead.

"Are you sure you're all right?" he asked. "I can call a Relic if you need me to. Say the word."

"If something had happened to Justus, the Mageri would have

given me a new Ghuardian—and you know how I feel about their decisions. It would have devastated me to lose him."

He stretched over me and grabbed the plastic bowl, stirring its contents with a small fork. "Open."

"What is it?"

"Don't you trust me?"

He was always challenging me with the trust thing. I parted my lips and he held the fork to his mouth, blowing the steam before feeding me in bed. "It's pasta shells with meat sauce. Do you like it?"

His eyes watched me unblinking, waiting for a response.

"It's delicious," I said with a mouthful. "What's that zest?"

Logan lifted the fork to his mouth and licked the prongs. "My secret recipe." He gave me another bite. "I enjoy feeding you in my bed," he said decidedly.

"Not as much as I enjoy eating in it." I wiggled in the sheets and pulled them up to my neck as he shoveled in another bite.

I could get used to this kind of pampering, I thought.

"How did the intruders get in?"

"Simon learned that some of the guards were shot with metal arrows," I replied. "They're rare stunners acquired on the black market. Because stunners were made long ago, most were fashioned into blades. You can't melt down the metal or it removes the properties that paralyze a Mage. Arrows make it easier to take down a Mage from afar. Not sure why they didn't make more of them back then since they seem more practical."

"Who was the intended target?"

"We think Novis, or the Mageri as a whole. Nero may be pissed that I'm walking free and not in shackles—"

A low growl rumbled in Logan's chest at the word *shackles*.

"Nero resents the idea that we're working together and forming bonds, and he despises HALO," I said. "He thinks they're sharing too many secrets.

"Men like that think power is entitled to them. I've seen it. Very few of the ancient immortals are humbled by anyone or anything. Many are cold and indifferent."

I turned my back to Logan and he stroked my left hip. "What

troubles you?" I heard him set down the bowl.

The entire evening, that's what. My insides recoiled, thinking about how Logan could hurt me even worse than any physical abuse I had endured. I kept my heart caged—protected—and it became the compass that gave me direction. I filled it to capacity with love for those that I cared for, but I didn't know if I was willing to give it away to someone who wouldn't guard it with their life. Would he?

"Speak to me," he insisted. "What's on your mind?"

"Everything. Nothing. I'm just exhausted." I yawned. "It's been a long night and I can hardly keep my eyes open. I don't want to keep thinking about this."

"Then close your eyes and sleep."

"I'm afraid of the nightmares," I mumbled.

Logan propped himself up on his elbow and his voice became stone. "Then I'll guard you with my life in your dreams."

I awoke without any memory of dreams, but wondered if Logan had wandered into them to watch over me. In any case, I felt refreshed and stretched out my stiff legs. Morning light was cruel the way it sliced through the window like optical fire. It may have been stormy outside, but it wasn't the dark cocoon I'd grown accustomed to.

Thunder rolled. A thin film of fog covered the glass and the rain tapped against the overhang.

After a long stretch, I sat up and smiled. My red shirt had FLASH written on it with a lightning bolt. Logan was a man who was into the classics and I loved his sense of humor. His confident demeanor made his clothing choice irrelevant.

I walked to the window and drew a small heart on the foggy glass with my fingertip. Down below on the glistening street, an angry driver blasted his horn and splashed a young man standing on the curb.

A delicious aroma dragged me into the kitchen. "Smells

good in—"

I always wondered what it would feel like to be mummified—wrapped so tightly that you couldn't move and the only thing visible were your wide eyes. That was exactly how I felt in that moment.

Finn sat on one of the stools in the kitchen with his bare feet on the rungs. Dressed in a pair of sweatpants, he scraped his shaggy hair forward. His eyes were glued to a plate and his face was the color of my shirt.

Finn lived here, too. I rarely visited Logan's condo so it slipped my mind. He was here all night.

All. Night.

While nothing out of the ordinary went on in the shower—no noises or shattering glass from high-decibel screaming—the only thing that would make him turn the color of a tomato would be if he had seen us nude in the kitchen.

"Little Wolf, it would be impolite not to greet my female when she enters a room," Logan said sternly as he continued stirring something in a bowl.

"Hey, Silver," Finn grumbled forcefully.

I pivoted on my heel and hurried through the living room. Logan seized my wrist and stepped in my path.

"I've cooked breakfast. Join us. Little Wolf must learn what it means to please a woman." His hand memorized my arm, sliding up to my shoulder as if recapturing a memory. "There's no shame in what we did."

"I'm not here to teach any lessons, or especially give him one in anatomy. Now let me salvage what dignity I have left and leave."

Thunder crashed and I winced. Lightning always put me on edge and since I had become a Mage, it seemed that I was more sensitive to the intense energy in the air. Logan absently ran his fingers through my tangled hair. "Have you ever been held captive?"

He loved playing the "*have you ever*" game, only now, he was being facetious.

"Why did you parade me around like that if you knew Finn was in here?"

His voice became apologetic and he slid his hands into the

pockets of his baggy jeans. "His wolf always prowls at that hour. My hands were too full to notice he was in human form." Logan shrugged and I knew he was telling the truth.

"Fine, let's eat," I hissed, heading into the kitchen. "Finn, I'd rather not discuss it and I'm guessing that you feel the same way."

He quickly nodded in agreement and stuffed a folded pancake into his mouth.

"So what's cooking?"

Logan lifted the spatula and flipped something in the pan. "English pancakes with lemon. Also some tomatoes, sausages, and eggs."

"Well, that's different."

"How do you want your eggs?"

"Apocalyptic. I don't even want it to resemble an egg when you're done with it," I said, pointing at the hot sauce on the cabinet. "Usually I go for plain omelets but I'm having a craving for heat."

"You're not the only one," he murmured. "If my female likes it hot… then hot she will get."

Logan's words were like a full-body massage. I loved it when he stroked me with his tongue—verbally and otherwise. It didn't escape my attention either that he was using the term "my female" more often. The first time was at the restaurant on our date. I didn't object, but I silently noted it.

We sat at the kitchen island and I watched Logan squeeze lemon juice over his pancake.

"Who marked you?" he asked.

"*Now* you're curious?"

"I avoided the topic last night for a reason," he said with his mouth full. "Now that I'm calm, I want to hear all about the male who decided to mark you without consent."

Finn held a piece of sausage between his fingers and frowned. A shaggy wave of his hair crossed over his eye and he wiped it away. "What happened?"

"Nero had me followed by a Chitah. I have something he wants."

"Well he can't have you." Logan shoved a sausage into his

mouth and licked his thumb.

"He's not after me this time. I went with Simon to Samil's house and we found a box. I don't know what's in it." I pointed my fork at them. "That really pisses me off, too. It seems that my involvement with this case is at the discretion of my Ghuardian. If someone is tracking me for information, then I should at least know what I'm defending."

"You were at Samil's?" Finn wiped his greasy fingers on his sweats because Logan didn't have any napkins. His cheeks were a little plumper and his thin frame was starting to fill in. I hadn't realized how malnourished he really was when we found him until now.

"Simon was given permission to conduct another search," I replied. "Are you sure you don't know of any other houses Nero stayed at, Finn?"

"I told you everything I know," he said defensively. Finn pushed his plate forward and dropped his hands in his lap, staring at the counter.

"It's not an accusation. I'm just frustrated." I poked my eggs with the fork and Logan glared at me for not eating.

"Give him the box. It's more important than your life," Logan said.

I shook my head.

When he slammed his fork down, it bounced across the surface with a violent sound. "*Dammit*, Silver! Someone is trying to…" Logan paused.

"What? Finish what you were about to say."

"*Why* did the Chitah mark you?"

"To piss me off? To threaten me? I don't know."

Black rings circled the circumference of his eyes. "A Chitah does not threaten a female with his scent."

"He knows that you're protecting me. I can't tell you what his strategy is, but don't let him draw you out."

Logan stood up and placed the flat of his hands on the table. Every muscle in his sculpted face went rigid as his brow lowered. His blond, tangled hair concealed his eyes. "He didn't induce you to give him what he wanted by verbal intimidation. When a male wants something from a female, those are his tactics because it's not in our nature to inflict harm on a gender we revere. Even if he knew I was protecting you, it doesn't explain why the hell he put his scent all over you."

"Look, I don't know! He just said he wanted to have some fun and then he started rubbing himself against—"

Logan threw his stool across the room and stormed out as a crack of thunder sounded. Finn lifted his eyes submissively from the floor, but he wasn't shaken. Somewhere deep inside that boy was a tethered wolf.

CHAPTER 7

"Everyone have a seat because I have something to say." I watched Justus and Simon move to their usual spots while Logan claimed the chair on my right.

Logan was there to defuse the situation by explaining why he hadn't brought me home the night before. I admired the way he stood up to Justus because earning that man's respect had nothing to do with kissing ass. Justus would never respect a man who couldn't hold his own. He wasn't thrilled when he found out a Chitah was tailing me, but a smirk crossed his expression when I told him how I escaped.

"Nero hired someone to hunt me down for the contents of the box we found in Samil's basement, and I have a right to know what I'm risking my life protecting. Pencils? Old postcards?"

Justus pulled a small bowl of almonds in front of him, popping a handful into his mouth. "Samil was involved in illegal activities. Breed cannot have children with humans—it's impossible."

Flustered, I leaned forward. "You're telling me something I already know. But what are you not telling me?"

Simon leaned back and put his right shoe on the edge of the table, tying the laces together. "Genetic experimentation. The box contained records and a long list of names, which I suspect that Samil gave to his trackers—including Marco. Samil kept this little secret from Nero for obvious reasons. The blighter didn't want to give up what little control he had. I'm trying to locate all the names—they're a pain in the arse to find," he added with a wave of the hand.

"What is the list? I mean, where does it come from?"

"Haven't a clue, but everyone on that list has something in common."

"What?" I asked.

Simon's jaw tightened and he tilted his chair on the back two legs. "They were all adopted."

"How do you know that?"

"The medical records we found in the box were their birth mothers—women who went missing years ago and were never found. Do you know who your father is?" Simon arched a single brow and tapped the large skull ring on his middle finger against the wood. "Your mother was human, but we think you have Breed in you."

I caught my breath and let the silence settle in the room like a sheet slowly falling on a mattress.

"We just established that crossbreeding is impossible. I wasn't adopted. Samil may have been involved in something unscrupulous, but don't include me in your theories," I warned in a hostile tone.

"Love, you really need to get that bee out of your bonnet."

Logan removed the small bit of mint gum from his mouth and neatly tucked it inside a wrapper, keeping a watchful eye on Simon. The crinkling sound made me want to snap, and I contemplated throwing the candelabra to the ground. Instead, I watched Simon launch out of the chair and study the painting on the wall with his hands in his back pockets.

"Ever heard of the phrase: If you can't beat them, join them? Some imbeciles believe that if they tamper with the human gene pool, then they can produce more Breed. Their goal would be to decimate the human population so that they are no longer a threat. I'm trying to think of an example." He tapped his chin and turned around, leaning against the wall. "Killer bees weren't such a good idea," he mumbled.

"Simon, I get your point. What does this have to do with me?"

"Your mother was a patient. We found her records."

"You said all the women went missing," I pointed out.

"And they did. She changed her name."

I sank in the chair and felt the torturous effect of a lie shred its way through every fabric of my life.

"She told me she was in Europe but never said why," I quietly spoke. "What's in her file?"

"Not much information aside from dates and treatments administered—although it doesn't tell what was given. It's all in code. Have you ever noticed anything different about yourself? As a *human*," Simon stressed. He leaned forward with his knuckles planted on the table. Justus laced his fingers together and pressed them to his lips as if in prayer.

"I didn't exactly change into a circus monkey, nor was I the fastest girl on the track team," I said sarcastically.

Simon snorted but held it together. Logan, on the other hand, rubbed his laughter away with the palm of his hand. The sound of short whiskers rubbing against his fingers caught my attention.

"Your physical transformation when you became a Mage is unheard of. We thought there might be an explanation," Simon hinted. He was alluding to my being a Unique, but didn't speak it aloud with Logan present. "There's also the fact that it didn't happen to Samil's other progeny. Being a Mentalist, he sensed you were still alive, but I bet he had a hell of a time finding you. Took the manky bastard how many months?" he asked, looking at Justus.

"It can't be possible. I'm a Mage," I said in a doubtful voice. Logan reached over and gripped my knee.

Simon twirled a thick ring on his finger and took it off, studying the intricate design. "I don't know what they were brewing in their mad-scientist labs, but I'm only guessing they extracted the bits and goodies from a Relic or maybe one of those Shifters. It couldn't be from a Mage because we're sterile—thank bloody heaven. I'm just trying to collect as much information as possible." Simon pushed his index fingers into the corners of his eyes and rubbed.

"Well, this is stupid," I began, "but I've always been full of static. I could shock anyone without trying. Usually I had to discharge on a doorknob or something metal. One time I fried the motherboard on my computer when I turned it on. Now it seems to have regulated in my body."

Simon dragged his eyes across the table to Justus.

"Can we not stray from the fact that I called you here for a reason?" I said in a melodic, soft voice. "Aside from all the *speculation*, I want to know what else you found."

Simon pulled his fingerless gloves off and threw them in the center of the table. He flexed his hands, cracking a few knuckles, and didn't hear a damn word I said.

"The list is a neatly typed up document that arranges everyone by their age and human name. Except one person is handwritten, and by their Mage name. That person is you, love. Marco may have discovered you by accident."

"We don't believe in accidents," Logan interrupted. "Fate."

Simon rolled his eyes. "My theory is that your mum escaped before you were born and changed her name so that she couldn't be tracked. It explains why your human name wasn't on the list. It also gives a little insight as to why you were born on a plane—now that's a woman in a hurry to get somewhere. She throws a dart and ends up living in the most isolated corner of the United States."

"Hey, it's not that small of a town," I said defensively.

"Marco must have sensed there was something different about you as a human and maybe he was trying to earn brownie points by handing over what he felt was a worthy potential. Samil figured it out at some point if he jotted your name down, but I suppose some facts will remain dead and buried with the sodding idiot…" Simon grumbled. "Why go through the trouble of officially claiming you in front of the Council?"

"Samil was in Nero's debt somehow, and making it legal was a way to secure his claim so Nero couldn't steal me away. Something went wrong in the end because Samil freaked out. You can always dig him up and ask." I shut my eyes and turned away. "You think that I'm a *science experiment?*"

My cheeks heated with embarrassment and pain. I'd grown tolerant of the term "Unique" because at least it implied something special. Nothing felt special about being a Petri-dish project. "I'm a genetically created *thing* from Breed DNA?"

Justus hid his face behind a cupped hand.

Simon spoke in animated gestures. "Nero doesn't know what's in the box; maybe he thinks there's documentation that could implicate him in illegal activities. If he got his hands on the files, it would be catastrophic. The last thing we need is Nero's money joining forces with an organization on the brink of doing some serious genetic damage. I never imagined they'd figure out how to do it."

He turned his attention to Logan. "This is confidential. Even HALO will not know about this because of its delicate nature. Blab about it to Leo and we'll label you a turncoat."

They shared a private look.

Logan didn't flinch. "You have my word."

"If you betray us, Chitah, then you are not only putting her life in danger, but all of us."

Logan growled low and fierce—a sound that was predatory and dark. Simon flinched at his unblinking gaze.

"We can't do this alone," I insisted.

Justus rubbed his shoulder and his skin made a hissing sound from the friction. "Remi is the only other person I trust at this point."

I couldn't say the same because I'd only met him a couple of times. He was a Gemini and while his loyalty to Justus ran deep, it didn't feel right bringing him into my business.

After the bomb dropped, I quietly sifted through the ashes. It was one thing to go my entire life thinking that my father was a coldhearted bastard who left my mother when she was pregnant, but it was a whole other dose of nasty medicine to find out I was nothing but a genetic lab experiment.

"What makes you think that the record you found belonged to my mother? Maybe you're mistaken."

"Pictures."

"How the hell do you know what my mother looks like?"

Simon reached around and lifted a bottle of wine from a liquor table. "When we flew down with Sunny to find Marco, I did a little background check on you. The name on the file doesn't match up so she obviously took on a new identity. Lovely lady, but that birthmark on her forehead is unmistakable."

I sat back and the hard wood pinched my shoulder blade. "I'm a mutant—is that what you're telling me? That I'm a fatherless experiment scraped out of some Petri dish?" When my voice cracked, I looked away. "Feel free to get up and leave, Logan. I won't take any offense."

Logan grabbed my chair and dragged it noisily across the floor. In a swift movement, he lifted me onto his lap with my legs hanging over the other side. His rough fingers took a hold of my stubborn chin and lifted it toward his magnetic gaze. "Any questions?"

It didn't make things better, but when I buried my face against his warm neck, he soothed me with a firm stroke of his hand against my back. A vibration fluttered in his chest without a sound; it felt like something that was just for me. Logan possessed a unique calming ability through voice, sound, and even his scent.

Thoughts tumbled through my head like a jar of marbles and after they stopped rolling around, my feet hit the floor.

"Ghuardian, can I speak to you alone?"

Justus followed me into my bedroom and I closed the door to give us privacy.

"I think we should bring Novis into this," I suggested.

"Out of the question. What would make you even think to involve a Council member?"

"Since being thrown into this life, I've had to rely on my instincts because I have little else. With Adam, he earned my trust by not forcing it on me. With you, it was lack of options."

He rolled his eyes.

I stood my ground. "This is more than we can take on and I'm afraid if something happens, we won't have any protection. If you're not going to involve HALO, then we need to bring in someone with position. Novis can be trusted and might have a better grasp on how to handle this. He doesn't just sit on the Council; he's the keeper of the records. That means he's a man who knows all about confidentiality."

Justus sat in the tiny chair by the wall, or maybe it just looked tiny when he filled it. The wood creaked, and he rubbed his scalp with his thick fingers as I continued.

"I don't know Remi very well or how much advice he gives you, but we're the only people that stand in the way of what Nero wants. Four is a small number to know such a big thing. If Nero takes us out, then the experimentations will go on without anyone knowing. Tell Novis *everything*."

His features hardened, as if he were in the middle of conversation déjà vu. I wondered if he met up with Remi and received similar advice.

The next evening, Novis accepted an invitation to our home.

Novis scraped his fingers through his spiky chunks of black hair, scrunching them until whatever gel held it in place came apart. The small cut on his left cheek from the bomb was a permanent scar shaped like a backward *L*. It marred his otherwise noble features, but his reaction was indifferent when he caught me looking at it.

"How far does the oldest case date back?" Novis touched the frosty soda can.

"Twenty-eight years," Simon replied with a sniff.

"And how old are you in human years, Silver?" Novis slid his eyes across the table, watching me carefully.

"Thirty."

"Would you like to know what I think?" Novis pointed a long finger at his brow and pushed it up. "Had your mother not escaped, you would have been the *first* name on that list. Silver, I think you're patient zero."

Simon tripped over his words. "What makes you think she was the first one? This may not be the only list and I doubt that it's a completed one. The first?" he asked in disbelief.

Novis turned his attention to Justus, who was tapping his gold ring against the table. "The fact her name was handwritten on that list tells me that Samil at some point in his life was part of the experimentation. He must have acquired the list and records by theft. We know of at least two that Samil has created, and yet there is something extraordinarily different about Silver in comparison. Perhaps her splicing was the strongest from whatever genetic material they were using. Since her mother escaped before they could test her, they weren't aware that she was different from an ordinary human.

So, future experiments went on using different techniques. The Breed have unfortunately surpassed humans in the advances of science and genetic testing, achieving goals that humans haven't even dreamed of doing. Until now, I've never heard of anyone making progress in this area."

He cracked open a can of root beer and gulped down a few swallows, licking his lips. "The first eight names on the list have all been confirmed dead?"

Simon nodded. "Minus a few I couldn't locate. It's a long bloody list."

"Their deaths were not an accident. I think the children were born ordinary and they were somehow trying to bring out the Breed in the child, or hoped puberty might give it a kick start. Maybe with the first several they didn't see any change and had to dispose of them once they were adults. After that, if the infant didn't show any signs early on that the experiment worked, they simply gave them up for adoption to avoid the guilt of murdering a child or getting caught. I don't believe Samil had any special gift that made Silver what she was. He does seem to have accidentally stumbled upon a secret formula that if you kill them for a brief period, their first spark will awaken every Breed DNA within their body, something I bet the scientists never discovered. This is all hypothetical, of course, but it does explain why he did this consistently. I spoke with the two you rescued from his captivity, and Samil's preferred method was strangulation. I'm sure he discovered it by accident."

I twisted a lock of dark hair between my fingers and studied the ends. "Every Breed DNA—what do you mean by that? You can only have one egg and one sperm."

"You don't think they found a way to make a cocktail?" Novis contended. "Magic has coursed in your veins since birth and was altered when your Creator charged you with his light. You brought up the point about static, and I can tell you as a Creator that I would be very attracted to that kind of natural power in a human. True, we choose wisely with our progeny, but a Creator is addicted to the power and possibility of light." He pried the tab off his soda can and flicked it across the table. "I'm not a scientist; I can only speculate."

"Why not find a way to do all of this *naturally* instead of in a lab? Seems like so much trouble." I slid my hand out and pulled the tab to my fingertips.

Novis quirked a smile and continued. "No Breed can have children with humans. It is a genetic impossibility for the ones who are able to have offspring, and even they have limitations that often only allow them to have children within their own race. We are fundamentally different from humans. What I do know is that if you pair up Shifter sperm with a human egg, for example, the sperm will devour the egg—destroy it. We are far too strong. That's why some have been trying to alter the genetics and find ways around it. None have succeeded and it's always been common knowledge that it is an impossibility."

I sucked in a sharp breath.

"Silver, is there something you want to say?"

A memory flooded back, and words from the past crept into my mind like blood running beneath the door. Now, with perfect clarity, something that happened on the night Adam challenged Samil suddenly made sense. I needed a moment alone with Novis.

"Learner, Novis is speaking to you," Justus snapped.

"Jesus, you don't have to yell. I'm right here."

Simon chuckled and slouched as if he were melting into the chair. He was one of the most animated men I knew; whether he was talking or just thinking quietly—it seemed like Simon was always moving. His leather pants and the grain of the wooden chair didn't get along.

Novis swallowed the rest of his root beer and let out a small belch, stalling as if he wanted to say something else. "I understand why you have kept this a secret and I agree that the Council should be left out of this for now. This is dangerous information to fall in any hands—not just Nero. We'll conduct a private investigation to track down the lab and end this. Everyone involved will be questioned and scrubbed of their memory. They have no idea of the repercussions, not just in sabotaging the human gene pool in an effort to exterminate them, but they are playing genetic roulette. We cannot *conceive* of the long-term side effects, or what mutations could occur. What if nature found a way to make us susceptible to human viruses?" Novis squeezed the can until it dented, narrowing his eyes. "We're hard enough to control in limited numbers; imagine the entire world population being Breed. It would be World War Apocalypse."

"Oh, balls," Simon groaned.

"Pray tell," I said. "What could possibly have Simon Hunt's knickers in a wad?"

"I have this funny feeling I'll be going back to Europe; just when I thought I was done with that place."

"Guess they weren't done with you, my friend." Justus slapped Simon on the back.

"Laugh it up you sodding bastard, but I made a lot of enemies that left me with the taste of piss in my mouth. Perish the fucking thought that I'll be the one going. Let them put *your* Charmer rump on that plane and see how the ladies love you up for the eight-hour flight." He snorted. "I nominate Justus completely."

"I'm trying to learn from my mistakes," I began, "so I don't want to do this on a whim without telling anyone."

Probably not the best opening line. Justus placed his hands on his lap with his elbows out. He was a big guy with legs that could kick your ass all over Cognito. If the tattoo that wrapped around his arm wasn't scary enough, then it was the straight face that rarely cracked a smile unless provoked by alcohol or promiscuity.

"The objective is to shut down the labs, but we also have Nero to contend with. My question to you is: Do you think you can take down Nero, and how long will it take?"

Simon cracked his knuckles.

I sighed. "That's what I thought. If he's that untouchable, then maybe we need to focus on the one thing we don't want him to know about. We'll have to assume he's having us followed so we need to watch our step."

I threw in the "we's" and "us's" to include myself in the plan I was about to unveil.

"Just let it be known that I do *not* like this idea," I began. "If there's an alternative, then by all means, put it out there. I think you should send me home. If my mother is a part of this, then she knows something. It's a hard pill to swallow believing my mother lied to me, but then again, she rarely talked about her past. She wasn't the most loving woman, but she was protective. She never wanted me to leave that town. My mom is a difficult lady to understand. We need to question her. I can also tell you with absolute certainty that she's not about to reveal her life to a stranger if she wasn't willing to do it with me."

I circled my finger over the soda tab and it followed my movement. "Does anyone in this room know of a trustworthy Vampire?"

Simon coughed in surprise. He didn't trust Vampires and like many others, he always wore sunglasses in Breed establishments. Vamps had the ability to pull truth from a person. Apparently, Simon was a man with many secrets. But I wasn't so sure how Justus or Novis felt about them.

"She'll never confess anything willingly because she thinks that I'm dead. After we're done, we'll erase her memory."

A smile lit up Novis's face. "This one is a fine Mage you have here, Justus. I hope that you are a fair Ghuardian to this Learner."

Justus straightened his back and lifted his chin. It was an honor to receive a compliment from a Council member, yet his skeptical eyes skated over to me and my shoulders sagged.

"Does anyone have a better idea?" I looked at the quiet faces and then to Novis. "Who are the memory-eraser people?" I almost laughed at my choice of words.

"Vampires can selectively wipe your memories; we've used them before," Justus said with an ambivalent look on his face. The bristles of hair on his scalp had grown out and picked up a dark blond tint in the light. "Why is this something you feel you need to do?"

I smiled. "Because it's *my* mom. She won't recognize me, but I know what to say to get inside the house. I know the right questions to ask." I leaned forward and looked at him sternly. "It's also important that there's no funny business and she's not threatened in any way. I'm not going to sit around wondering if some Vampire is smacking her around. She might know something that's going to push us ahead on the game board."

Simon's eyes lit up; he loved game analogies.

"True that," Simon replied, his British accent shining through. I flicked the soda tab at him and laughed.

"The sooner we begin, the better," Novis decided. "I'll make travel arrangements and get Silver new identification cards. She can't use her current one for this trip."

My alternate identity was Ember Gates, which came with an ID. Our assigned names were unusual so that they would flag the systems monitored by some of our people. If you got in a sticky situation, they would bail you out. Breed had zero tolerance for confinement in a human jail or hospital.

"Guards will trail behind your car and we'll do a few switches during the ride to the airport. We have a spray that will throw off the Chitah tracking you and should Nero send a Vampire, we'll need you to remain absolutely silent. Not a single sneeze."

I looked over to Justus. "Are you coming with me?"

His mouth opened but Novis interrupted. "That's… not such a good idea." They shared a private look.

"I'm still a Learner and Justus has to escort me." *Protect me* was the phrase I was thinking, because going out of town with a man I'd never met didn't settle.

"There's no need to send in a parade of immortals," Novis said, touching the scar on his cheek absently. "You'll go with the Vampire and get whatever you can from your mother. I believe there's still work to be done here, too. Am I correct, gentlemen?"

I held Justus's gaze. I was uneasy about the idea of a total stranger accompanying me across the country, let alone a Vampire. I'd heard enough warnings about them.

"Novis is right," Justus said, clearing his throat. "My Creator living in the same city would present an unneeded distraction." Justus rose from the table and hitched up his sweatpants. "I will ensure your safety." His eyes slid over to Novis and he gave him a nearly imperceptible nod. "Keep the details of this trip private, Silver. I forbid you from sharing the details with the Chitah."

"His name is Logan, and I agree." I didn't need any distractions. Justus also seemed concerned with how involved he was getting.

Everyone pushed away from the table to stand but I remained seated. "Can I have a minute alone with Novis?"

He waved Justus and Simon out of the room.

Novis scratched his smooth chin and laced his long fingers together. The light in his eyes glittered beneath the dark brows and lashes. It was captivating to see so much age behind such youthful features.

"You can speak your mind freely."

"I've held my tongue because this could be considered slander," I said in a low voice. "Something's bothered me since you mentioned that it's impossible to crossbreed naturally with a human. Are there any exceptions to the rule that are public knowledge?"

"I can't explain how your birth was possible with absolute certainty," he admitted. "Many have attempted to crossbreed with humans for over a thousand years. Although before science came along, they tried the natural way." He grinned slyly. "It makes me wonder if they've also tried to impregnate a Shifter or even a Relic with human sperm and… I apologize. I'm listening."

I leaned in privately. "Do you remember when Adam challenged Samil in front of the Council?"

"Yes."

"Afterward, Merc said something that didn't make sense. No one batted a lash, but I guess we were too preoccupied. Do you remember what it was?"

He pinched his lip and studied the ceiling as if invisible words were written on it. "Not specifically."

"Merc asked if I was a hybrid. Doesn't that word strike you as odd? If it's common knowledge that crossbreeding is impossible, then why did he ask that question?"

Novis smoothed his middle finger across his lower lip. "Speak of this to no one until I give it more thought. You know the punishment for slander is severe."

"Novis?"

"Yes?" His voice was devoid of emotion.

"How is Adam?"

A shadow crossed his face and there was a pregnant pause before he answered. "Adam is permanently scarred. The Relic could do nothing for those that were exposed to the liquid fire."

"How bad is it? I tried to tell him to get out." I shook my head as the images came back.

"Adam saved many lives—as did you—but he was too close to the glass wall when the canisters exploded. The Relic tried the only salve he had that might have helped, but liquid fire is the Devil's formula." Sadness flickered in his stony eyes. "Adam is understandably not himself, and it will take a long time for him to accept it. He is immortal, and these scars will remain with him forever. But he must accept it and move forward. He was fortunate—some were missing whole limbs, or even worse. One gentleman that I've known many years lost half his face. Our healing light helped them recover from the mortal wounds to get them out of pain, but…" Novis couldn't even finish and he covered his eyes with his right hand, pinching at his brow.

Forever.

That word sank in like a sharp tooth. Adam had a rugged sophistication that could make any woman swoon, yet he was oblivious to it, which was probably the most attractive quality about him. It seemed wrong to dwell on the physical, but that is the impression we give the world, and Breed were especially insensitive to such things.

"How is he handling it?"

"Adam is in denial, but deep down he knows the full impact. He spoke of utilizing his gift as a service, but he'll never gain clients scarred the way he is. Maybe it's for the better. He was in an immeasurable amount of pain when the Relic tried to treat him. I've seen that kind of injury test a man and only time will tell if Adam passes. When you do see him… be kind, but don't offer him your pity."

CHAPTER 8

I leaned across Goliath—my monster-sized bed—and switched the phone to my right ear.

"Logan. I need you to stay away for a couple of days. There's a lot going on with the investigation and it'll give you time to hang out with your brothers."

"Have you forgotten I'm aware of the details?"

"Justus is firm on no visitors, so if you show up, he's going to blow a gasket. We have some important people over here." Christ, I hated lying, but at least he couldn't scent it over the phone. "It's just for a couple of days—I don't think it's too much to ask. Can you live without me?"

"Careful the words you choose," he warned.

After a brief chat, Logan gave me his word that he wouldn't show up unexpectedly. I stuffed a few things into a medium bag and put on a pair of black pants and a matching shirt. It was cool in Cognito, so I slipped into my leather jacket and carried my luggage down the hall into the main room.

"Silver, come in here," Justus said. "I want you to meet someone."

I approached the dining room and saw Justus standing in the entrance with another man. I dropped my bag and shuffled a few steps back. We never had strangers in the house and it caught me off guard.

The man was leaner than Justus, but his posture was commanding, with sharp angles and a straight back. With his hands clasped together, he widened his stance and greeted me with a smug grin. This guy looked like a young business tycoon ready to dismantle a company, yet he was also the kind of man who could easily blend into a crowd. Dark brown hair and neatly trimmed whiskers toned down the liquid black eyes that were otherwise stark against his features. This was the Vampire from the infamous bombing party—the one that had insulted me.

I glared at his leather pants and unbuttoned shirt that showed off the long silver chain around his neck. The clothes didn't look his style at all, not to mention he was dressed more inconspicuously at the party. If his intention was to piss me off, then he could have run a victory lap.

"Absolutely not," I exclaimed. "My mother will *never* let someone like him into her house. *This* is your Vampire?"

Christian tossed his arm around Justus's shoulder with a stern expression. "I've never once felt sorry for you until this very day, Justus." He laughed darkly. "Poor bastard." His voice was Irish, Scottish, or Piggish—one of those ish countries. "Does she come with instructions? Clearly, batteries were not included."

"Don't talk about me like I'm not here." My lips pressed together tightly.

"I should say the same about you; we haven't even gotten through introductions and there you are, sizing me up to see if I'm acceptable enough to meet your mum. I feel rather insulted, considering you're only a Learner and I have half a mind to walk away."

Justus cut across the room in my direction. "Christian, give us a moment."

He took my arm and led me into the hall.

"*That* is your trustworthy friend?" I whispered.

"Loyalty is hard to come by."

Simon eased in and folded his arms, looking between us.

"He's a twit," I whispered.

"*I can heaarrr youuuu,*" a deep voice sang out from the dining room.

I rolled my eyes. "Spidey hearing. Any other talents I should know about?"

Christian whistled in the other room—the kind of whistle that implied he had an answer to my question, and it was dirty.

A light flared in Justus's eyes for a brief moment before he spoke. "No arguments. Christian is the best man for the job. It was not my decision to have you leave the city outside of my protection. Remember that there are no safe places from Breed; we're everywhere. Keep your wits about you and conceal your light. Speak with your mother and then come home."

Justus walked off and murmured something to Christian in the other room.

"Why the long face, love?" Simon asked.

"Christian didn't help anyone at the party. Why did Leo ask for a Vampire when we were trying to pull the sword?"

"They're strong, and their blood can heal."

"So why didn't he heal them?"

"What the hell do I look like—a juice box?" Christian shouted from the other room.

I worked my jaw to the side, irritated by the unsolicited comments about my private conversation.

"Vamps think their blood is sacred, so they're real dicks about it." Simon brushed past me and we rejoined our guest, who was sitting in the chair nearest to the fireplace with his legs dramatically crossed.

Justus continued with the formalities. "Silver, this is Christian Poe. He's an old friend and we go back many years. Christian, this is my Learner, Silver."

The Vampire flew out of his chair theatrically and moved toward me with a one-armed bow, never taking his eyes from mine.

I could handle a man with a smart mouth because I gave as good as I got, but he was just rude. His image did not fit the bill in getting inside my mother's house. This man had a mission to mortify me—a confirmed suspicion when he stroked the chain around his neck.

Christian put both hands on Justus's shoulders and shook him, saying in a thick voice, "Don't you worry, da. I'll be sure to have her home by ten."

"Bring her home," Justus warned. "Safely. Remember what I told you."

"Ghuardian, you neglected to mention that my partner would be a halfwit."

Christian squinted as he turned around. "I'll have you know that my talents are legendary, and my reputation has spread like—"

"A rash?"

As I lifted my bag, I realized the root of my irritation was the fear of going home and facing my mother.

"So tell me all about your mum."

Just after takeoff, my plan was to kill the flight with a nap. Two minutes in, I wanted to kill more than just time.

Our trip to the airport was elaborate; Christian and I rode in separate vehicles. Guards sprayed a liquid on each car that would shield our scent from any Chitahs who worked as trackers. I looked out the tinted windows and remained quiet for the entire ride as instructed. My hair was tucked inside of a loose-knit cap and Justus had lent me his aviator sunglasses. I was beginning to understand what it felt like to be a celebrity hiding from the paparazzi.

Christian was desperate to instigate conversation, despite the fact that I was airsick.

"Could you please not talk?"

"Don't get your knickers in a knot," he replied as he crossed his leg over a knee and looked around with bored interest.

A dull ache in my stomach triggered a cold sweat and I leaned forward.

"Why don't you just puke and get it over with?"

"Is that what you say to the women you pick up?"

Christian reached out and snatched the wrist of the flight attendant. Her short brown hair bounced as she turned, but once their eyes met, her concern evaporated into a vacant smile. She was entranced.

"Yes, sir?" she asked in a monotone voice.

"Could we have a stick of gum?"

"We don't serve gum. Could I bring you a drink?"

Christian's hand traced her delicate wrist, adorned with a thin gold bracelet.

"Maybe later," he laughed darkly. "Do *you* have any gum?"

"In my purse."

"Be a dear and fetch me a piece?"

She blinked a few times and pulled slowly out of his grasp, walking up the aisle.

"No wonder," I muttered.

Christian stuck his nose right up to my cheek. "I'm sorry, what's that you said?"

I shouldered him away. "Now I'm starting to see how you pick up your dates."

"We can make them talk, but we can't force them to do something if they really don't want to. The weaker the mind, the easier it is to convince them. That fine thing with the lovely tits wanted to give me her gum. The only thing holding her back was she was afraid she might get in trouble. And if she wants to bang me in the bathroom later, then I'll be there for her. Think of me as an in-flight therapist."

"You mean a slut."

Christian clucked his tongue. "Like you wouldn't want to bed me."

The seat cushioned my back and I stretched my legs. "Sorry to burst your bubble, but that's one carnival ride I don't care to get on."

"That cougar over there wants a ticket."

I glimpsed the woman he was pointing at, who didn't look a day under ninety. "That's no cougar, that's a mountain lion."

Christian widened his black eyes. "Admit it, you find me attractive."

He used the same suggestive tone as he had with the flight attendant. Little did he know that I had a number of talents of my own, one of which included an immunity to most Breed gifts.

"From the moment I met you, Christian, I've hidden my desire. I want to marry you and be nailed together in a coffin for *all* eternity."

He flinched, confounded by my noncompliant response. "Do you not—"

"Sir, your gum."

Paper ripped and he tapped a stick of wintergreen against my nose.

"Chew. It helps with the nausea."

Fifteen minutes and another stick of gum later, my nausea abated and I could breathe again.

Christian watched me the entire time, which was unsettling. "So, you don't succumb to the Vampire magic?"

I pulled off my hat and a mess of hair fell out. "Don't get your hopes up about shagging me because clearly it's not going to happen."

Christian laughed. "Don't flatter yourself! You're *not* my type."

Which wouldn't have bothered me had it not been the way his eyes dragged over my body with disgust.

"What? Cheap, easy, and desperate?"

His crooked smile sloped down and painted a look of irritation. "No. Classy, beautiful, and refined. I *do* have taste."

My face tightened and he averted his eyes.

I reached over and snapped the shade open, sending a shower of sunlight across his lap. "Shall I have the flight attendant bring a dustpan?"

He lifted a pair of dark shades from his shirt pocket. "I could use a little sun."

I realized that everything I knew about Vampires came from the movies. "Shouldn't you be—"

"Slowly disintegrating into a pile of ash? Are you really that new?" He sighed and glanced around, but no one sat in front or behind us. "Our pupils are fully dilated, so it's irritating, like when you flip the lights on in a dark room. We have a natural tolerance to sunlight, but it takes a minute to adjust. I also enjoy silver against my skin."

I didn't acknowledge his pun.

"Worry not," he assured me. "As I said before, you aren't my type and I wouldn't want to corrupt you with sexual goodness."

"So you keep telling yourself."

"Justus was right on the money."

I snapped my head to the right. "About?"

He gave me an appraising glance before he shook his head in disdain. "You always have to have the last word."

"What else did he say?"

Christian groaned and stretched out his leather-clad legs. A woman in the aisle across from us looked like a cat who just stumbled on a canary without wings. "He warned me that by the time this trip was over, I was going to need a lobotomy."

"That *asshole*," I whispered to myself. Justus didn't allow others to belittle me, but knowing he did it behind my back really hurt.

"You shouldn't curse; it's vulgar on a woman."

"I really have no interest in what you think. The only thing I care about is getting information from my mom. Speaking of which, you're going to have to change into something less… dramatic. Nobody dresses like that where we're going. You look like Satan on a holiday."

"*You* have on a leather jacket," he said observantly.

"But I'm not wearing leather pants commando."

"You noticed." His smug grin broadened.

"As did every passenger on this plane when you walked by—not to mention the female security guard who performed the body search. So when we meet my mom, you're going to dress like a nice Southern boy because that's the only way we're going to get into that house."

"Let this be a reminder why I never visit hillbilly country."

The gum had gone stale so I wound it up in the wrapper. "Where are you from?"

"Originally? Ireland. After our mum died, I jumped ship with my brothers for America. My family was Catholic and didn't own any land; life was hard, not like today where your whole world ends when your cable stops working."

"Were you made into a Vampire there?"

"Wasn't until I came to America that I was turned. I was twenty-five when I arrived in New York. Irish had a rough go finding jobs; I changed my name to something less Irish and tried not to talk so much to hide my accent."

Imagining him not talking was like imagining the sun wasn't shining on my lap. "How old were you when you were turned?"

"Ah… that came later. By then my brothers and I had gone our separate ways. I was in my thirties."

"By choice?"

He gave me a pointed look. "Of *course* by choice. No one makes a Breed against their will."

I turned away and closed the shade, reminded of the man who made me what I was by force. We didn't speak for the remainder of the flight.

CHAPTER 9

"I FEEL LIKE A REGULAR DICKEY Dazzler in this suit," Christian said admiringly as we rounded a corner in my mother's neighborhood. One mandatory shopping trip later, he acquired a pair of ashen trousers, a white dress shirt with the sleeves rolled up casually to the elbows, and a thin black tie. He lifted a pub cap from the mannequin and when I rolled my eyes, he threw it on the register.

It was close to sunset and we needed to move because once it was dark, there was no way my mom was going to open up, even for Santa himself.

"Let me do the talking," I instructed. My finger pressed over the dirty yellow button and a bell clanged inside. I blew out a nervous breath when the locks turned and the smell of potpourri wafted through the screen door.

"Yes?"

I blinked and went into panic mode, not having seen my mother for over a year. "Hi! My name is Cassandra and this is my husband, Tom. We just bought a house in the neighborhood and we wanted to meet our neighbors."

Christian lightly stepped on my toe to stop my mouth from running a marathon. My mom looked weathered; she'd cut her hair and stopped dying it.

"You keep a lovely yard, ma'am," Christian spoke up. "Do you have a gardener that you can recommend?" I skewered him with my eyes as he broke the cardinal rule of no talking until I got us inside the house. Christian normally had a slow and assured way of speaking, but he switched his accent to American with just a hint of Southern, picking up the tempo. Clever.

My mom opened the door a little wider as she admired her yard. "I do all the gardening myself."

"You have the most beautiful yard on the block." He tucked an arm around me. "When we were house hunting, it was your pruned crepe myrtles that caught my eye. Anyone who takes such good care of their home must be good people."

Mom beamed and flattery was getting him everywhere. Sunny mentioned that my mom had turned religious, so I thought of another way in.

"We're also looking for a church," I began. "I don't know if you… uh, are a practicing—"

"What Cassie is trying to say is that you seem like a good Christian woman who could point us in the right direction. We've been so busy with the move that we haven't had time to make new friends and find a pastor. I would be more than happy to come over and help you with some of those limbs in your tree that need cuttin' down. You do a fine job on your lawn, but you don't need to be doing all this manual labor. If you won't hire anyone, then I insist on offering some time on the weekend; I have brand-new equipment in the garage just dying to be put to good use. Maybe you can help us out with a few problems; there's a nasty mess of poison ivy near the garden hose that we can't seem to pull up." He scratched his arm as if he were afflicted.

"You aren't going to get rid of that easily. It roots deep," my mom said as she swung the door wide and brushed her hands over her blue dress. "Come on in. Would you like a glass of tea or water?"

Christian shot me a victorious wink, the arrogant bastard. "Tea would be great."

The ugly brown carpet was intact, but there were a few minor changes. Photographs were missing in the hallway and she had painted the kitchen yellow.

"Now, you kids go into the living room and wait. I'll bring out the tea."

"You have a lovely home," I said.

"That was rather cliché," Christian whispered.

I gravitated to the beige recliner when he tugged my hand, reminding me that we were supposed to be happily married. We sank into the blue sofa and I sat on my hands.

"How long have you two been married?"

Christian lifted a bird figurine from the end table and I smacked his hand to put it back. "Just married last month, ma'am. We were engaged for a year and this is our first time living together."

"I want a divorce," I ground through my teeth.

"You learn more about the person you're with in the first year," she said knowingly. My brows pushed together as I considered that remark—Mom had never remarried or lived with another man.

She entered the room with a small tray and set it on the coffee table. I lifted the cold glass with etched daisies on the bottom and took a sip.

"Is this your daughter?" Christian admired a small photo of a redhead on the end table. It was my tenth-grade class picture. I hated that picture because I had a zit on my nose and embarrassing high school hair. He turned around and gave me a confused look.

"Mmm-hmm," she replied.

"She certainly didn't get her Irish hair from you, Mrs.—I'm sorry, we didn't even ask your name. How impolite!"

"Abigail Merrick."

"How many children do you have?"

"Just Zoë. She's dead now."

My jaw almost hit the floor. I was her daughter, not some goldfish that she flushed down the toilet.

"I'm so sorry; it must have been awful for you," I said consolingly.

Christian gave a short nod, removed his colored glasses, and stood up. "Abigail?" When she made eye contact, something switched off. "I'm going to ask you some questions and you're going to give me the answers."

She nodded, folding her hands across her lap. Christian carefully sat on the edge of the coffee table.

"What is your real name?"

"Sandra Meyers."

"Years ago you had a baby."

"Yes."

"Who was her father?"

"She has no father."

"What were you doing in Europe?"

"I met a man. I had no family and when I couldn't find work, he took me in. He wanted me to live with him in Germany. I thought it was exciting that he wanted to show me the world."

"How long were you in Europe?"

"A year and a half."

"Did you stay with him?"

"For a short spell. He wanted to have a baby but I didn't want children."

My stomach knotted and the desire to run out of that house was making my palms sweat.

"But he was not Zoë's father, was he?"

"I don't know. She was made in a lab. Zoë was unnatural."

"What was the name of the man you lived with, and was there anything unusual about him?"

"His name was Grady. He never touched me when we had sex. Sometimes he moved fast."

"A Mage," Christian mumbled.

Oh, how I wanted to roll up in a ball and die. "Can we not go into my mother's sex life?" I chastised.

"Tell me the details of how you became pregnant."

"Grady took me to a doctor in England, where we stayed the rest of the time. We lived together for less than a year and I wanted to go back home. It was too cold and he left me alone a lot. The doctor gave me injections and one day they took me to an office where I was locked in a small room with no windows. They put me under anesthesia several times and when I woke up, no one answered my questions. Grady stopped visiting."

Christian questioned my mom for over an hour, scrubbing the details as she revealed them. It was as if he were walking the trails of her memory and dusting a broom behind him to erase the footprints.

"Anything you want to ask her?"

The sofa squeaked when I stood up. "Ask her why she kept me."

"Why did you keep Zoë?"

"I didn't have anyone else. If Grady found me, I could give her to him and he might leave me alone."

"Did you even love me?" I shouted out in pain. She watched Christian with a vacant stare and I shoved his back to ask the question.

"Did you love Zoë?" he asked in a low voice.

She sat unresponsive for a moment. "I didn't understand her. I didn't want kids. It was a relief when she died, although I can't remember why."

"Wipe her memory, wipe it all!"

I flew out of the house into the yard, walking briskly down the sidewalk.

Halfway up the street, a black cat with multicolored eyes wove between my legs. I fell to my knees as Max slinked around my body and purred.

"Is she feeding you, panther boy?"

He meowed. How this cat knew me was unexplainable since I was a different person entirely. Did I smell the same?

"It's done," Christian announced. Max hissed at him and flew across the street behind a fence. "What's up with your pussy?"

"Guess it's your charming personality," I replied.

"That photograph wasn't you."

"I had a makeover; it came free with the Mage package."

"Justus was right. You do storm off like a child. Do not do that again; I've been instructed to keep watch over you."

I brushed the dust from my pants. "Justus has a complex about keeping me guarded like a fairy princess. No one knows we're here and I'm keeping my light concealed, so back off."

"Done and done. Thank the heavenly angels you're his problem and not mine. Let's go change and see what this town has to offer for nightlife; I'm feeling an itch in my jockeys that needs a scratch." He walked coolly toward the rental car.

"There's a cream for that," I muttered.

From across the street he shouted, "Always have to have the last word, don't you?"

CHAPTER 10

"**G**IVE ME A VODKA NEAT. And make it a double." Christian leaned against the curve of the bar on his elbows, eyeing the dance floor like a dessert cart. "Most women order sweet, delicate drinks with fruit in them."

"Well, I'm not most women and I just want to get fucked up, so why don't you go get your freak on over there in the erection section while I enjoy my drink in peace."

I wasn't offended when he gave me the finger and stalked off.

The bartender set the drink down and I knocked back a couple of hard swallows before ordering another. He lifted an eyebrow and poured me a glass of harbored resentment as I pondered the miseries of my childhood. I wasn't just an abandoned child—my mother never even loved me. I was just something to barter with if Grady found her. Maybe she'd had a reason to be afraid, but it didn't make the sting of rejection any less painful.

On the dance floor, a brunette in a nonexistent skirt backed up against Christian while he gave everyone a visual of what his bedroom play looked like. He may not have liked the South, but he didn't seem to have any complaints about the women in this town. That's when I felt the flare of another Mage.

"Watch my drink," I said to the bartender.

I walked the outer edge of the room and scoped the crowd.

"You travel with interesting company. First a Chitah and now a Vampire."

I knew the voice and turned to the man leaning against the wall. His skin was bronze and his hair neatly combed back. He kept his short beard groomed but paid no attention to the unruly brows that nearly joined in the center. Marco De Gradi was an exotic-looking man, and I could see by his style and confidence why Justus would have emulated him.

"This is a human bar, Marco. What brings you here?"

He struck a match and lit up a hand-rolled cigarette. A bright glow illuminated his face and his eyes flashed up to mine—not at all surprised to see me.

"It's my bar, smoke if you wish." His Italian accent melted off his tongue.

"Did you know that I was close to freeing the girl you gave to Nero?"

He blinked in surprise at my remark, waving a cloud of smoke from his face. I caught his attention because he'd mentioned her once before.

I folded my arms and continued. "Do you think she'll even want you after you gave her over to Nero, a sadistic monster?"

Marco flicked his cigarette and held it away from his expensive suit. "Quit playing with me and speak your mind. Why did you return?"

"I'm just here on vacation."

His fingers pinched a stray tobacco leaf from the tip of his tongue. "You're staying in my hotel; tell me your business, little liar."

"Samil hired you to track down his potentials, but what doesn't make sense is why you chose to hand over a woman that wasn't on his list. Zoë Merrick."

I caught him off guard.

Marco took a slow drag and sucked in a sharp breath. "I know who you are, *Silver*. Did you not think that I would eventually speak with Nero? You're one of his collections… courtesy of Samil."

Panic flowed through me like a mudslide.

"Don't fret; I haven't told him the good news that you're paying me another visit. Samil never mentioned you," he said with a lift in his voice. "Where *did* you come from?" His eyes shrank to horizontal slivers. Marco hadn't made the connection that I was Zoë.

"Who's the dolt?" Christian interrupted.

"Watch your tongue, Vampire."

Christian's hand flew out so fast that Marco was in a chokehold before he could remove the cigarette from his mouth. His face took on a purplish hue and his eyes bulged.

"I may not appear to be dangerous, but if you ever speak to me that way again I will tear off your head, and I have no qualms about doing it in front of an audience." Christian squeezed harder.

"Christian, leave us," I said. "This is personal business."

I didn't think he'd listen, but he released his grip, never taking his eyes from Justus's Creator. "I've got my ear on you," he said, tapping the side of his head as he walked off.

"Tell me of Rena," Marco said quietly, rubbing his neck.

I folded my arms and tapped the toe of my shoe on the floor. "Nero took her and another girl before I could free them. Do you know where else he lives?"

"He's a private man and doesn't put a return address on his Christmas cards," he said sarcastically. "Why should I help you?"

"I'm not going to bullshit you, Marco. I want Nero's ass on a totem pole. If there's any part of you that's doing this for the right reason, then you'll give us some information."

"You weren't one of the names Samil gave me. Why would he have wasted his time with you?"

"Because of *you*. I'm Zoë Merrick."

"Impossible!" he spat. Anger bled over his features and he used the palm of his hand to smooth back his hair.

"Do you want to help Rena? Absolve yourself from the crimes you've committed and help us find the captives Nero is holding. Do you know what he's doing to them? He kept them shackled like animals to a wall with a bucket for a toilet. His guards watched the property day and night. In fact, there's one guard in particular who liked to pay nightly visits."

"Stop!" he bellowed with an outstretched arm. The hand-rolled cigarette fell to the floor and his shoe crushed it, leaving a dark smudge. "Go back to Cognito where you belong."

With a sharp turn, Marco vanished into the crowd. It was disappointing that I couldn't convince him to work with us; I knew he might have information, and despite what Justus might think, it seemed worth a shot. I returned to the bar and finished my drink.

Wavy green eyes and a misshapen face stared back at me from a pool of water. I lifted my head from a gleaming toilet bowl and winced at the sharp pain in my neck.

"No one will ever kiss that face again if they knew where it's been all night."

I leaned back and coughed, waiting for the head rush to subside. Christian sat against the bathroom door of my hotel room with his right knee bent and an arm draped over it.

"Silk, you know. *Ruined*." His fingers thumbed the bloody shirt he wore. "Justus was right, you—"

"If you say that one more time I'm going to have it tattooed on your forehead," I said in a raspy voice.

"You really know how to give a man dinner and a show."

"Why is there blood on you?" I looked down. "Why the hell is there blood on *me*?" I reached for my neck. "Did you bite me?"

"You aren't my taste, but I thought we went over that. I was out back with the patio people."

I stared at him, blank-faced.

"The *smokers* outside," he continued in his thick Irish accent. "When I came back inside, you were gone. Thought you went to the toilet, so I waited by the door. Let me tell you that what goes on in the ladies room is no longer a fantasy. I thought you'd have puffy little pillows on sofa chairs where you lounged and buttered up your breasts with scented oils. My fantasies are ruined by the pungent smell of vomit and tramps spraying perfume on their fannies."

"Can you get to the point?"

His legs stretched out and crossed at the ankle. "I did another scan of the bar. I have a way of tuning out sounds one at a time as a process of elimination. It's a gift."

"Bravo." I crawled to the sink and ran a washcloth under the chilly water.

"Somewhere in the sea of voices I heard you call my name.

You get a C-plus for effort in pronunciation, but I'm afraid your speech was off because that fecking cocktail you were with spiked your drink."

"What? The last thing I remember is talking to Marco. I think. *Shit.*" My eyes flashed up. "I left my drink at the bar. Are you suggesting that I drank out of the same glass? I never do that! Whenever I leave my drink I always—" I snapped my mouth shut, remembering how upset I was. Not just about Marco, but my mom. Yeah, I probably was stupid enough to sit back down and polish it off.

"He got you all the way to the parking lot."

"Who?" My hands trembled a little bit.

"The unassuming rapist who hangs out at the bar looking for easy prey. From the state of his face, I could see that you didn't need much help. Poor bastard." Christian smirked.

"Then why are you wearing his blood?"

He watched me with dull eyes and lifted a shoulder. "I never turn down a free drink."

Scratch that off the list of things I wanted to bring up with Justus about our trip.

"Why didn't Marco knock you out with his light when you were roughing him up?"

"Justus shelters you too much. Doesn't work on Vampires, lass. Think of me like a big sponge." A crooked grin slanted up. "And the ladies like to loofah."

"If you're stronger than us and our power has no effect on you, why should we bother with the sunglasses?"

He kicked off his shoes and a white toe poked out from his black sock. "Never underestimate anyone's abilities. I've met a Mage or two in my time who could take down a Vampire with their gifts. Plus, you lot scurry around like cockroaches while we run at a human's pace. A smart Mage will stay out of reach."

"Makes sense," I grumbled, rubbing my eyes. I worked out a kink in my leg and leaned against the opposite wall. "How do you know Justus?"

"We've been knowing each other for a long time and stay in

touch; you never know when you'll need help."

"Moving dead bodies?"

"Pardon?"

"You know—the saying about how friends help you move, but real friends help you move dead bodies."

"Well," he said with a rich laugh, "I *am* the dead body."

It didn't seem possible. "Are you really dead?"

He glanced at his shirt again. "Just an inside joke; we're very much alive. Sunlight won't kill us, but you know that now. Stakes hurt like a bugger, but they work the same way a stunner does with a Mage. Years ago, they used to stake and bury Vampires as a form of punishment. If not for Gravewalkers, half of them would still be there. Gravewalkers have a knack for finding us," he said, lifting his hand slightly. "You already know we can pull truth, erase memory, and win any arm-wrestling competition. Ah, blood."

The mere mention of the word made me nauseous and I looked at the spatters on my shoe.

"A youngling craves blood and their desire is insatiable, but it gets easier as you age. Blood doesn't sustain us; the power within the blood is what we crave. It's comparable to a Mage juicing energy from another. I could go the rest of my life without having any."

"What keeps your bodies going?"

"Rejuvenation, the fountain of youth, magic—same as you. Blood helps us heal faster should we need it, but the real magic is the information that flows in your veins. A knowledge cocktail. I enjoy the taste of food, but like many Vampires, I prefer not to eat. There's a certain perk to not using the toilet all the time."

An insistent vibration interrupted us and I crawled to the sink and pulled the phone out of my purse.

> Logan: If you don't answer this message, I'm coming to get you.

"Shit." I collapsed on my back as my stomach gurgled.

"Trouble with the boyfriend?"

My fingers quickly typed out a reply.

> Silver: I'm here.
> Logan: Where is here?
> Silver: How are you? How's Finn?
> Logan: Don't change the subject. Where are you?
> Silver: I'll see you soon, I promise.
> Logan: I'm coming over.
> Silver: You gave me your word. Why don't you trust me?
> Logan: You're avoiding my calls. Let's talk.
> Silver: It's almost 11 and I'm tired. I'll call you tomorrow.
> Logan: So you ARE in TX. Who's with you?

I froze—I'd forgotten we were in another time zone. "Dammit!" I groaned, throwing my hand out and shutting my eyes. The phone skidded out of reach. "What time is our flight?"

"You have three hours. Be sure to gargle."

When I lifted my head, Christian was sending a text message. "Give me that!"

I sprang to my knees and snatched it away. "What the hell did you say?"

"Only that I had you on your back. I made sure to sign my name."

"You idiot!"

I punched his shoulder and he smirked. "In-service massage?"

> Silver: It's not what you think, Logan. I'll call you later. Miss u.

"It's your funeral. Logan is a Chitah."

Christian's eyes widened. "You're serious? You? And a *Chitah*?" He raked his fingers through his hair. "Shite, why didn't you tell me you were dating a fecking lunatic? Those bastards have a thing about hunting you for life. *Jaysus wept.*"

"Oh, grow a spine." I angrily shoved the phone in my bag.

Christian pushed himself up and stretched his arms. "I'll leave you alone to decontaminate. I've spent my entire evening in a bathroom—more hours than in my whole human life. If you don't mind, I've seen my fair share of vomit. I'll be retiring in my quarters with a 'do not disturb' sign."

Before the door opened, he showed me his profile. "How's that working out for you two in the bedroom?"

Branded by his words, I hurled his shoe at the door. "Nitey nite for you."

"Have fun electrocuting your boyfriend with your next handjob." He breezed out of the room like a summer wind. That perturbed me.

I crawled to the opening and leaned out. "Oh, and Christian?"

He paused.

"Touching is overrated. As *old* as you are and you can't get more creative than vanilla sex?"

He blinked in surprise as I gently closed the door.

Logan never returned my calls. I wondered if he entered my dreams that night to spy on me. Some Chitahs could dreamwalk with certain people. He had that ability with me, but I made him promise to stay out. No one should be allowed inside your head just because they have the key.

CHAPTER 11

Adam gripped the bars of his black motorcycle as it edged across the parking lot. It was a no-frills bike—unpolished and classic, like Adam.

It was the first time he'd been out since the bombing. Cheri wanted to meet with friends in a human bar on the seedy side of Cognito. It hadn't even been a week since he was injured, but he couldn't say no when he knew how cooped up she was in that house. Adam was especially sensitive to that need because of the fact that Nero had kept her caged for so long.

"Ugh!" Cheri protested, stumbling to her feet once he parked the bike. "I can't stand that thing! I just don't understand why it's so impossible for you to get a regular car." She clicked her tongue at the run in her pantyhose. Her polished fingernails threaded through her blond hair. "Do I look okay?"

"Like a dream," he said softly.

She looked more than okay—Cheri was stunning. From the hollow of her cheeks that made her lips look like heaven to kiss to the slope of her hips and the way they swung when she walked in heels. She'd changed since they met, but she was enamored with him from the start and he'd fallen for her harder than he should have.

"I don't know why you wouldn't let me wear the helmet," Cheri huffed.

It might have been different if his wounds were still fresh and raw; a man needed time to adjust to something like that. Novis couldn't heal him with his light, and the treatments the Relic tried were excruciating. Within days, the reflection staring back at him looked like a man who had been scarred for a lifetime. Breed were worse than humans when it came to how they viewed those with scars and deformities. This was a life-altering setback. Who would want to be treated by a Healer who was scarred? Even something as simple as giving a woman a sexy smile was an act he could no longer do without revolting her. He was damn lucky to have Cheri because most Mage women were very selective about the men they dated.

Being a Healer was the reason he was in the wrong place at the wrong time. That left a bitter taste in his mouth and he cursed his gift.

That didn't go over well with his Creator. Novis was a man with great expectations for his progeny. He provided Adam with new clothes, access to whatever education and physical training he desired. It was important for Adam to contribute to the race and prove his value.

Adam shut off the engine and Cheri placed her hands on her hips. "We're just going to have a quick drink and say hello. I'm not really in the mood to stay out all night or anything. Did you decide if you're coming in?"

Two girls sashayed by and whistled at Adam. They admired the way he looked in his torn jeans on the bike. He got that look a lot.

"Adam." Cheri snapped her fingers. "I'm going." She planted a kiss on his shield and left a smudge of lipstick. "I don't think you'd like my friends so this works out. Thanks for giving me space and time alone to have fun. Give me an hour and then we'll go home. Sound okay?"

He nodded.

Cheri sighed and adjusted the delicate gold strap of her purse on her shoulder.

He watched the door for thirty minutes. Because she had no Creator, Adam took it upon himself to keep an eye on her in public. She craved her own space and was slowly becoming her own woman again—a change he loved seeing.

Adam was still a runner and made it his morning routine to stay in shape while taking advice from Novis on how to cultivate his gifts. Adam in turn worked with Cheri and taught her how to protect her light from another Mage. He wasn't concerned about letting her go into the bar alone because humans were weak and she could take care of herself, but he decided to save her the embarrassment of the stares. He didn't give a shit what everyone else thought, but if it made her uncomfortable, then that's all that mattered.

Adam stretched out his legs, thinking about that mess with Nero. It never left his thoughts because of what they'd discovered when they saved Finn during the raid. The chain locked around the Shifter's neck was made of a metal Adam knew all too well.

Knox broke the chain with some tools he kept in his Jeep. It was confiscated by Justus, but a small piece was left behind on the floor and Adam had played with it during the drive home. Something about the sheen was familiar and when he ran his tongue over the gritty surface, he knew exactly what it was.

In the Special Forces, they'd gone on a number of dangerous assignments. The weapons were standard issue—except for the silver-tipped stakes and darts. Each job they were armed with specific weapons. Knox had a peculiar habit of rolling bullets around in his mouth—something he'd started as a nervous habit. The first time they were issued new bullets, Knox spit it out and said, "Taste this shit!"

The flavor was impossible to describe—sweet, hot, and so tart that it made your tongue curl. Regardless, they did the trick taking down their targets. One shot was all it ever took. It never killed them—no, that came later and they finally let one of the guys on the team have the honors.

He'd had a few drinks with Knox after revealing he was a Mage and the two of them concluded that every assignment targeted Breed. Adam suggested humans manufactured the metal. Someone was probably selling that shit on the black market to fill his pockets.

Fifteen more minutes elapsed; he sensed it without looking at a watch.

"Can I sit on your bike?" a voice like a lush berry asked. He looked at a woman with long legs and a nonexistent red skirt. "I saw your girl take off." She stepped a little closer. "How about we go for a ride?"

Her finger pinched a crease in his pants and he shifted uncomfortably. She wasn't his type with the heavy makeup and forward demeanor, not to mention she was a human. Now that Adam was a Mage, he figured it was more practical to stick to your own kind. A heavy cloud of perfume penetrated through his helmet and he wrinkled his nose. He preferred the natural smell of a woman.

She eased in closer with a sultry smile. "Maybe I could just climb on while you let the engine run. Would you like that?"

He'd seen it a million times since he bought that damn bike. Women didn't need to see your face. Man and machine gave off a sexual vibe.

"Pretty please?"

He looked up and catapulted off the bike. Cheri was making her way out of the bar and she wasn't alone. Some asshole had a hold of her upper arm. Friend or not, Adam wasn't about to let anyone handle her like that.

He loosened the strap to his helmet. "Take your hands off her!" he roared.

Adam crossed the parking lot in six seconds and stood beneath a beam of angry light.

"We were just saying goodbye, weren't we?" Cheri jerked her arm free and scowled.

The man's stance told him that he wasn't taking Adam seriously—not until he grabbed the guy's wrist and twisted it behind his back. Adam shoved him into the brick wall and pinned his other shoulder to keep him still. Didn't take but a minute to sense that he was also a Mage.

"What are you doing on human turf?" Adam ground through his teeth.

"The fuck are *you* doing on human turf?" the Mage countered. "Because I'm having a beer." Long hair sloppily stuck to his sweaty neck. "If you wanted to hold my hand, you should have asked."

Adam put pressure on the man's wrist until he growled out in pain and kicked him in the leg. Hard enough that Adam stepped back and lost his grip when the Mage threw his elbow out and knocked Adam's helmet. "What the fuck is up with that?"

"Leave him alone," Cheri stamped out harshly. "I mean it."

"Shut up, bitch. Nobody asked you."

Perspiration beaded on Adam's brow and he looked at Cheri. "Do you know him?"

As if it even mattered. Anger was flooding his veins like poison.

The roughneck continued poking Adam's helmet with his fingers. He was one poke away from being knocked flat on his ass.

"An old friend. *Was* an old friend," she said.

"Do you two fuck with that on?" The Mage laughed with a wheeze.

Adam's neck flew back when he was poked for the last time. In his human life, his friends called him by his last name, Razor. It was more than a name—it was a reputation. Adam could throw a sharp uppercut and no one ever saw it coming.

Knuckles hit bone and the man's jaw snapped up with a nasty split in the chin as the Mage pivoted to the ground.

A dull roar filled Adam's head and everything went fuzzy. Adam had a flashback of his sister's death and dropped to his knees, hammering into the man's face again and again. There was no reasoning. There was only anger. Rage snarled like a dragon, snapping its ugly teeth. Adam hadn't felt this way since his sister was murdered—snuffed out by a lowlife juicer.

The true reason he chose to become a Mage was that Silver bore a Creator's mark that was identical to the man who killed his sister in a dirty alley. Mortality put a cap on things like revenge, but as a Mage, he would have all the time in the world. His perception changed becoming a Healer—giving him a new direction. But maybe revenge was his only true purpose in this life.

His rage intensified into a hurricane, leaving a wake of destruction.

Suddenly, rough hands yanked him up by the armpits and threw him into the dirt. The concrete walkway scraped a hole in the elbow of his shirt. Before he could get up, a second Mage kicked him in the gut with a thick boot.

"Stay where you belong, Learner. I can always smell the green ones."

Adam swept his leg out and knocked the man onto his back.

A crowd formed and Adam hopped to his feet, gripping his side. They couldn't flash or use their Mage abilities due to the audience. No one was breaking up the fight or calling the cops—the humans were feeding off the action as they clinked their beer bottles and slurred out profanities.

He staggered back to the asshole who had put his hands on Cheri. This wasn't about right and wrong or good and evil, this was about unleashing his dragon. It lived in a dark place within him where fury slithered around like a viperous snake—hungry teeth gnashing in the darkness, hoping to pierce another with its bite. He dropped to his knees, pushed the man's shoulder back, and struck him in the jaw with four solid knuckles.

Adam's head suddenly flew back when the second Mage came up from behind and pulled off his helmet.

"Fucking hell," someone mumbled. "Look at his face."

The shame. Right under that urine-colored spotlight in front of the woman he cherished.

Adam flicked his eyes to the left and saw the girl who'd approached him on the bike cover her plum lips with her hand and turn away. The Mage behind him took one look and shook his head, leaning down to help his friend up.

Adam's knees cut into the ground and the bone felt the unforgiving press of the earth.

"You're a disgrace, and if your Creator had any sense at all, he'd put you out of your misery like a rabid dog," the Mage muttered out of earshot from the humans.

Embarrassment painted Cheri's face, and it wasn't because of his actions. She reached for Adam's arm, but he shouldered her away and stood on his own. Pain throbbed in his hand like the pulse of vengeance, and a dull ache gnawed in his gut.

Nothing like the ache when he realized how close he was to losing his lifeline—the one person that tethered him to sanity. Cheri acted as if his scars didn't matter.

They mattered. When they'd made love the night before, it was the first time she wanted the lights turned off. It seemed normal—

the way it should be—but that was never Cheri's style. He didn't bring it up, but it lingered on his mind like a false note.

Adam lifted the scuffed helmet and wrapped his arm around her small waist, pulling her protectively against him. "Why did we come here?"

They hurried across the parking lot toward his bike before anyone called the cops.

"You shouldn't have started anything," she scolded. "What got into you? He's the kind of guy who doesn't walk away from a fight; you were lucky."

"What did he want from you? These are your friends?"

"He owed me something and… well, let's just go home."

CHAPTER 12

THREE DAYS AFTER OUR RETURN to Cognito, Logan was still ignoring my calls. On the second day, I quit making the effort. Be angry, be hurt, be nonplussed, but give me the chance to explain. Was it the message Christian sent or the fact that I lied to him and went out of town?

"I'll dish it, Silver. Logan always made me nervous," Sunny confessed over the phone. "I don't like men who stare the way he does. It's deep, like he's stalking my every move."

"Logan isn't a shy man and you know Chitahs never break eye contact. He would never hurt me."

"He behaves like a predator."

"Oh, like Knox doesn't look at you like dessert?"

Sunny snorted. "That's totally different. Obviously, we're having this conversation because you like him. We've been friends for years and I know after Brandon that you'd never let any man in your life that was toxic. You barely let the maintenance man in." She inserted a thoughtful pause. "He'll come to his senses."

"Maybe I don't want him to." I curled up in the leather chair by the fireplace and tried to tuck my cold feet beneath me. "I always knew this wouldn't work out between us, but he was so damn insistent on going through the whole courting thing. I was starting to think that maybe he was different, but this proves me wrong. I just don't want it to end on this note."

Sunny sighed with a hum in her voice. "And they say women are complicated. Maybe it's good that you got him jealous; a man needs to feel the burn of jealousy to know that he isn't your only option."

"You don't give a compelling argument, Sunny. He's a grown man ignoring my calls. I guess I misjudged him."

"That's just your mean side talking," she said. "I *know* you better than that. Why don't you just go see him?"

"Why don't I write 'stalker' on my forehead while I'm at it? The old Sunny would have told me to cut my losses before I got all dickwhipped."

"On second thought, you're right. He needs to man up or get lost."

"I want that on a T-shirt."

"To wear at your wedding?" she suggested.

I laughed at the mental image and Sunny sighed dramatically.

"Silver, I've watched you go through some traumatic stuff. I never have the right words for this kind of stuff, but you deserve happiness even more than I do. What I think doesn't matter because up until now, he's treated you good. You've never looked happier. I'll support you no matter what you decide."

"Thanks for the pep talk, Sunshine. I have to go."

"Me, too. I'm helping Knox shop around for a custom suit. I can't wait to see him in something besides those tight shirts."

"Why does Knox need a suit?"

"We got the invitation, silly."

I sat up. "For what?"

"To the party, and I'm *so* there."

"What party?"

I looked over at Simon, who was leaning against the doorway with a loose grin on his face. He whispered, "I hope the suit King Kong will be wearing is not his birthday suit; that's *not* the surprise I had in mind."

"Your first year of being a Mage is a big deal," Sunny said exuberantly. "That was a fancy birthday invitation—gold embossing and everything."

Simon waggled an eyebrow and I sensed a conspiracy brewing.

"You're a dead man," I mouthed at him. He shrugged and disappeared down the hall to the study. Having a few celebratory drinks was one thing, but a party with balloons, cake, and singing made my anxiety level go up. Birthdays were never a big deal in my life, but Sunny always made the waiters sing when she took me out.

"At least there's enough time for me to find a present and buy a new outfit," she said. "Who else is coming?"

"The pope, so be sure that you dress appropriate."

"You're going to thank me for stepping in to volunteer my services; men never plan these things right. It's going to be *beautiful*. You just wait. Call me again if you need to talk."

I capitulated, making her agree not to decorate with balloons or streamers. Some battles weren't worth putting on all the armor for.

"It shouldn't be *this* hard to make a decision."

I tapped my fingers on the glass counter and watched Finn with amusement. His eyes flicked indecisively over the colorful display of candy. I tucked the movie tickets in my black pants and shrugged at the cashier.

Finn moved his finger hesitantly in circles. "I think I want the um, the uh…"

"He'll take the chocolate-covered raisins, the malt balls, and the sour candy in the big bag," I said, slapping the money on the counter. I weaved my fingers through his shaggy brown hair. "It's okay, Finn. This is your first time, so let's just pig out."

Finn had lived a sheltered life, sold by his father and passed off from one man to the next, never allowed in public because owning a Shifter was illegal. Finn was clueless when it came to the modern world, outside of what he'd learned on the computer. He could tell you all about the geography of the Middle East but didn't know how to use a gumball machine.

He was mesmerized by the smell of buttered popcorn, the dazzling display of the marquee, and the concession stand. In many ways, Finn reminded me of a toddler. I watched him experience the most basic things for the first time.

He had been badly beaten most of his life and Logan cautioned that his animal was unpredictable. We kept a close watch on him in public to make sure that he didn't lose control when overstimulated or frightened.

Nero had branded the letter N on Finn's arm as a reminder that he was nothing more than property. Finn didn't like wearing shirts that let it show, so Logan bought him mid-length sleeves. Remembering how he looked in that cell—bloody and lifeless—made my blood boil. No one deserved to be treated that way.

Despite my rift with Logan, Finn would never feel neglected as a result. He was so excited when I invited him to the movies that he hung up the phone before I could tell him the start time. Justus came along and when the car eased up to the building, I peered out the window, hoping to see Logan, but Finn was sitting alone on the stoop, playing with a yo-yo.

I looked over my shoulder. "Ghuardian, can you go in and save our seats? Find something close to the middle; I need to grab some popcorn."

Justus wore loose denims and a casual black jacket over a white v-neck. Only I knew how much that ensemble cost him. He walked with a confident swagger down the hall and a woman passing him almost dropped her popcorn to steal a lingering look at the over six-foot male with a shaved head. Justus was built tough, and even without his charm would have earned the stares. Little did she know that she was ogling an immortal.

Finn tapped his shoe nervously against the floor as he watched everyone get their drinks at the self-serve soda machines. When it was his turn, he poured every flavor available into his cup. *My God, that kid was going to be sick.* I could only laugh.

"Finn, let's sit down for a few minutes." We walked to a dimly lit area.

"What about Justus?"

I chuckled as we set our food on the table and took a seat. "He'll probably be asleep by the time we get in there; he's not really into movies. I don't have to be escorted at all times in a Breed place, but he has to come along when I'm anywhere else."

"He just left you."

"Justus doesn't have to hold my hand in public; he just needs to be in proximity. Most of the time he wanders off with some hussy, but he can still pick up on my light."

"What do you mean by that?"

I shrugged. "I'm not sure how he does it; it's just something he can do. I have to put out a lot of energy; otherwise, it blends in with the crowd. Only for emergencies," I said. "It's how he found me once."

"How long do you have to live with him?"

I shrugged. "Until the sands of time fade or he gets tired of my ass."

We both laughed.

"I'm betting on the latter," he said, grinning wide. Finn had an elfin smile that was innocent and mischievous. His bright hazel eyes soaked in the world and he grew his brown hair long enough to cover up the tips of his ears—even though the hair curled up at the ends.

"I don't know what the average is. Justus told me that some live with their Creators or Ghuardians for a year while others need a hundred. Please shoot me if we're having this conversation in fifty years."

"I've never been to a movie—thanks for asking me." Finn lifted his eyes, distracted by the neon signs. It was one of the older theaters in town and looked magnificent with red carpeting, posters trimmed in white bulbs, and theater ushers dressed in red hats.

"I think you'll like this one. It's supposed to be a good comedy."

Finn was still insecure about his ears sticking out a little. I watched him scraping his hair over them with his fingers. Someone must have picked on him growing up, but I thought it gave him character. He was also trying out a new style. Tonight it was knee-length cargo pants with a baseball hat turned backward. I made him take the hat off inside. Maybe it was old-fashioned, but I'd rather get him off to the right start. When we entered the theater, Finn held the door open for a woman and her two rambunctious children. I didn't have to ask him to do it, but his fascination with families was clear. The wistful look in his eyes watching a mother hugging her child was heartbreaking.

"Can we stay out here?" he asked. "I'm having fun."

I smirked and tossed a piece of popcorn at him. Finn stuck out his tongue and caught it with a wide smile.

"Silver, can I ask something without you getting mad?"

"It's scientifically impossible for me to be mad at you," I assured him.

He slurped the soda through the straw, watching me observantly. The flavors rolled around on his tongue and he looked uncertain. "Don't you like Logan?"

I eased back in my chair and stared at my lap. "I do, but sometimes that's not enough."

"He really likes you. Logan's a cool guy, but too serious. With you, he's different and I don't know… smiles a lot." Finn pulled his straw in and out of the cup, producing an annoying screech. "Levi dropped by a few days ago."

My ears perked up because of the manner in which he said it.

"Logan was really pissed off about something," Finn said, looking at the poster on the wall. "I guessed you two had a fight, but I didn't hear what they were talking about until I walked in the kitchen and Levi was convincing him to go to the Gathering. The next morning, Logan disappeared for a couple of days and Levi stayed over. He's funny as hell; I like that cat."

"What were they saying about the Gathering?"

He peeled open the box of chocolates. "Levi wanted to find his future pony and said that sometimes other Breeds turn up as invited guests."

"Pony?"

"It's an inside Shifter joke," he said proudly.

I laughed internally because Finn probably didn't have a clue what the punch line meant.

"I think you should go to the Gathering," he said. "Leo can get you some tickets."

"Why would I want to?"

"What better way to make up than the one place everyone goes to find love?" Finn suggested with an innocent look.

"God, you're just as bad as a chick flick." I hurled popcorn at his face and he retaliated. A few pieces clung to my hair as I ducked, sick with laughter.

A throat cleared and we guiltily looked up. Justus slid in the seat beside me and pulled a piece of popcorn from my hair.

"I heard about the attack," Finn began. "Nero, huh?"

Justus dropped his large meat hooks in my bag of popcorn and took out a fistful. "Did you hear about Silver's bravery and the lives that were saved? That was the most important part of the story."

We hadn't spoken about my pulling the sword, but I think my heart blushed when his words touched my ears. The bond between us had grown stronger, and since that night, it was as pronounced as the color on a flower.

"Leo mentioned that." Finn shook his head and his eyes darted between us. He was getting over his issues with eye contact, but when he was uncomfortable with a topic, he fell back into the old routine.

My eyes darted to Justus and I smirked. "And I always thought I was the biggest pain in my Ghuardian's side."

A close-lipped smile stretched across his face. It pushed deep lines into his cheeks and brightened his blue eyes. It was nice to see Justus that way—sometimes he was wound too tight.

"Why didn't you save our seats and wait for us?" I asked him.

Justus slipped his arm behind me. "Do you need an answer as to why I cannot sit in a room with two hundred women?"

The thought made me giggle at the virtual sex lottery we created with the vacant chairs beside him. He liked attention, but only on his terms. It irritated him when we were in normal places outside of the clubs. Otherwise, Justus had no problem parading his charm around like a beacon.

"Don't worry; I'll protect you if a love riot breaks out." I grabbed my purse and we all got up. "Let's go before Finn misses all the lame previews."

Justus walked ahead of us and our pace slowed to a stroll.

"Do you want me to give Logan a message?" Finn asked in a quiet voice.

"No, you aren't the messenger. When me and you hang out it's just me and you, okay?"

He stuck his tongue in the popcorn bag and pulled a few pieces into his mouth. "I think you should talk to Logan. He's ruined without you."

I froze in the hall near one of the posters of a futuristic man holding a laser gun.

Ruined. That was a strong word and knotted my stomach.

"Sorry."

"It's fine," I said, dragging my feet along the red carpet. "Something happened and he's too stubborn to face me and talk about it. Maybe I was in the wrong, but I don't know if I can salvage what's left of this."

"Lame. Quit making excuses; it won't kill you to talk to him. I'll call Leo for some tickets. Go or don't, but I owe you one."

"You don't owe me a damn thing, kid." I rubbed my fist over the top of his head and he laughed. I loved to hear it because it was higher than his natural voice—and genuine. "We're square."

He pulled away and gathered up his armload of goodies before they tumbled to the ground. Finn struggled with physical affection and therefore I constantly showered him with it. He liked it but just didn't know how to react. No one ever showed him love and Logan wasn't exactly affectionate with anyone other than me.

My heart stopped when I shifted the drinks around in my arms and looked up. The Chitah with the Mohawk was leaning against the wall by room number fifteen. He was dressed in black and didn't move a muscle. He also didn't bother to hide his golden eyes with sunglasses, and they bore into me like an arrow.

Maybe it was the look of fear, or shock, but Finn saw a change in my body language and he turned to face the Chitah.

"You got a problem?" Finn said in sharp, clear words. I lightly gasped at the aggressive shift in his voice.

The Chitah pointed two fingers at his eyes and then at me—a clear message that he was following me.

That single, unspoken gesture set Finn off.

The next thing I knew, popcorn showered the floor. Finn shifted so fast that I didn't have time to react.

"Finn, no!" The drinks fell from my arms and splashed on my shoes.

A ferocious red wolf with large ears stood between me and the Chitah. His lips peeled back and he snarled, showing off all his sharp teeth.

"Tell your mutt to back off," he growled. Chitahs were fearless and watching him back away from the wolf surprised me. Finn's wolf pawed the carpet and snarled, intimidating the Chitah who was walking slowly toward the exit sign.

"Look mommy, a doggy!" a little girl shouted. A flurry of panicked voices sprang up from behind and my heart began to race.

"Finn," I whispered harshly. We weren't supposed to use our gifts in public, but I was certain that no one had seen him shift.

The Chitah paced backward and his eyes darted up to mine. The moment his sharp teeth descended, Finn's wolf lunged. The Chitah tore out of the building, shoving open the exit door and disappearing into the parking lot.

I released a breath and bent over with my hands on my knees—shaking.

Justus must have felt my energy increase because two seconds later the theater door flew open. He surveyed the mess of popcorn and the wolf standing beside a pile of clothes.

Logan had warned me about Finn's animal being volatile, but I didn't think twice when I kneeled down and grabbed a fistful of his fur. He'd protected me in Nero's compound and I trusted him enough that I showed no fear.

"Don't let him shift back," Justus whispered harshly.

The wolf lifted his chin and whined before letting out a snort.

"It's okay, Finn. We'll do the movie another night."

CHAPTER 13

A STEADY TECHNO BEAT THUMPED AGAINST the seat cushions of the two-seater Maserati. My ass vibrated until I lost all feeling.

"Definite improvement, Simon," I said, turning down the music. "It's *so* you. Never thought I'd see the day you would give up the muscle car."

"I haven't sold it just yet. Side work for the Mageri was not on my agenda, so I raised my asking price. You sure you want to do this?"

"Maybe you should just drop me off."

He smiled and clicked his tongue piercing against his teeth. "I have a feeling this will be more entertaining than a monster-movie marathon. I need at least three drinks before you get us tossed out."

"Speaking of tossed out, you never mentioned why you left England to come here. What happened?" I asked.

He groaned and turned the steering wheel. "I stuck my nose where it clearly didn't belong."

"Up the skirt of a high-ranking official?"

"Officials are nothing but an official pain in the arse. There's always an ulterior motive. I prefer to stay out of politics. There are rather unsavory details that—Oh, *balls*."

"What?"

"I left the bubble gum at the flat."

Typical Simon, always changing the topic when it came to his past. I played with the zipper of my oversized black hoodie, which belonged to Justus.

The engine purred as we sped up a long road to the Gathering—a three-day social extravaganza. It was a Chitah affair, but the invitation allowed us full access. I decided to take Finn up on his offer and confront Logan myself, even if it meant ending it between us. I was a girl who needed closure.

"So what's your plan, Miss Pandora? What box will you be opening this evening? Give fair warning before sharpening your claws on his scratching post so I can record it on my phone."

"Is that it?" I almost gasped.

At the end of the road was a tremendous country club on private property. The landscape was minimal with aging trees and trimmed grass. Groups of people mingled outside of the building, which was a spectacle. A large water fountain with lights decorated the front and there were three stories of arched windows.

"Look how tall everyone is," I mumbled. The women were just as tall as the men—especially in heels.

Simon was talking to Justus on the phone. "We're here. I will." He laughed nervously. "No worries. Your Learner is taking stalker to a whole new level. I'll be sure to fill you in on…. I *heard* you, mate." He tucked the phone in his pocket with a lift of his hip. "Your Ghuardian sends his hugs and kisses."

"I bet."

Simon sniffed audibly. "You think dousing yourself in all that perfume was such a good idea? Smells like you've been embalmed with it."

"Logan knows my scent so I had to cover it up. I'll keep my hood on and you stay on the lookout."

"Nothing suspicious about that."

"Simon, just give me your support tonight. I'm going to confront him but I don't have a plan, and I just want to see for myself if…"

If Logan was interested in other women.

He tugged on one of my drawstrings. "No sulking. You don't have to explain. I get it."

I admired the glamorous surroundings. Inside, a vast sea of standing tables was woven throughout the dimly lit room. The open bar offered a variety of beverages, and I laughed when we passed an ice sculpture of a nude couple and Simon made a seductive moan.

"Don't even think about licking it," I whispered.

"Can't say a woman ever said *that* to me before," he smarted off in a thick accent.

It was a fashion free-for-all and if a dress code existed that banned tight red shorts, then the guy drinking the martini didn't get the memo.

"I feel like a turkey in a lion pit," Simon muttered, looking around warily. "I need to get pissed." He breezed off to the bar.

The men looked like chess pieces moving around a board—never staying still for very long. I withered in my corner, standing amid tall, lovely flowers. Chitah women were confident, beautiful, and graceful. The men would linger long enough to take in their scent and move on if it wasn't to their liking.

Simon handed me a frosty bottle. "Thanks," I said, leaning on my left shoulder by the window. "Do you think it's love at first sight or smell?"

He sounded like a horse when he blew out a breath. "From what they say it's a little of both. To tell you the truth, I don't feel entirely comfortable here. You do realize we're in a room with our mortal enemies."

"Never dated a Chitah?"

"Are you mad? Most of these lollies come with brothers who would like nothing more than to remove my third leg." He glanced around and mumbled to himself, "All I can enjoy tonight are the drinks."

"They sure believe in this true-love crap. Not just every three years, but let's remember they have a national gathering every five years and a global event every six."

"Sounds like the shag Olympics," Simon said with a snort.

I spit out my beer and used the sleeve of the jacket to wipe my chin. When I looked out the window, my brows arched.

"There he is," I said flatly. "The drink table on the right." My jaw slackened and I set the beer down on a table.

Beneath a trellis decorated with tiny white lights, three stunning women circled Logan Cross. They were like orbiting moons—or vultures, by the look of their carnivorous gaze. My toes curled angrily inside of my shoes.

"Careful now, you need to put a stopper in that," Simon warned. "I can feel your energy spiking. Drink your beer and look at something else, for pity's sake. If I can see it on your face, then it's oozing out of your scent glands. Or I could whisper privately about one of my sexual fantasies that involves that bartender over there," he said jokingly.

Okay, *that* caught my attention, because the bartender was sporting a handlebar mustache.

"I'll be sure to slip him your number before we leave," I promised.

Logan looked handsome in a casual dress shirt, dark slacks, and his blond hair loose. As he spoke, the women clung to his every word. Were they his type? The one in the revealing red dress dominated his attention with her long blond hair that cascaded past her bony elbows. Diamonds graced her wrist and neck—she was elegance and money. The lady in the white tailored suit with dark curls looked out of place in a sea of mostly light-haired women. The third was a tramp not a day over twenty. There was more glitter on her legs than on the grungy streets of Times Square on New Year's Eve. Her long, shapely figure captivated the men who were riveted by the way she continuously stroked her plump lips with her tongue.

"Hey, Simon?"

He flattened his shoulders against the wall and downed half of his beer.

"Do you know anything about Chitah women?" I asked, not looking away from Logan. "Do they have the same reaction as the men with the love at first sight thing? Logan said it wasn't the same."

He pulled the bottle away from his lips and it made a wet sucking noise. "No. That's why they do all that courtship business. He may find his destiny, but the poor bastard still has to prove that he's the best cat in the litter. She can choose whomever she wants. That's why they take their time courting and baby-step it; one bad play and game over."

"What happens if she denies him?"

Simon glanced at Logan. "Miserable bloke, I suppose. Theoretically, if you believe in the whole kindred spirit thing, then imagine going the rest of your life separated from the one that you know is your intended. From what they say, each of them has only one life mate—uh, only one meant to be theirs. They were born for each other."

I sniffed out a laugh. "What if the woman had two men claiming they were the one?"

"Impossible. There is only one perfect match," a deep voice to my right replied. I looked up at the reddish hair and all that brawn.

"Swank party," Simon complimented him, lifting his beer at Leo, Logan's eldest brother. "Excellent selection on the imports." The two men tipped their heads in an obligatory gesture.

I had turned to bow when he leaned in and kissed my cheek politely, as if we were family. "Thanks for the invite."

"Advantages of my position. So tell me why you are captivated by watching my brother through a window… in that charming getup?" he asked, eyeing my espionage wardrobe. "I was under the impression that you would be mending fences."

"I always sucked at manual labor. Do you mind if we just hang back for a little while? Please don't tell him I'm here, not just yet."

Leo agreed with a nod. "Enjoy the party. The blue room to the left is serving some amazing lobster," he said with the infamous Cross smile. "I'll see you two later."

Immediately, my eyes snapped back to the woman with the sea of golden hair curling her arm around Logan's waist. She was the one who touched him when he spoke, making her intention clear. Red Dress officially graduated from harlot to archenemy.

The harem gravitated to a high table with tall chairs. Glitter Girl twirled her finger around her pearl necklace as Logan laughed. God, what the hell was he talking about that had them in such a frenzy? Logan wasn't kidding when he told me once that women chased him. What really lit a fire in me was how relaxed he was with them. He was *enjoying* himself, and that bothered me the most.

Why not? They were the kind of women that every man desired, and here I was in Justus's clothes wearing cheap perfume. Expecting him not to cheat was like throwing a six-year-old in a swimming pool filled with candy and asking him not to open his mouth. I was kidding myself to think he was ever serious about me.

My fingertips crackled with energy as he leaned close to the woman in the red dress, brushed her hair back, and spoke privately in her ear.

All reason went out the window and I yanked down the zipper to my hoodie and threw the jacket at Simon. My fingers fluffed out my dark locks of wild hair and released a few buttons on my shirt. Granted, I didn't have as much to work with as the blonde, but Logan often gazed at my humble assets with hungry eyes.

Let's just hope he brought his appetite with him.

"Uh oh. I've seen that look."

"You're my date, Simon. So *be* my date."

"Use me all you want."

He proudly took my arm and we moved out the door. Simon didn't just walk—he strutted across the lawn like a male model on a runway.

Tunnel vision set in when Logan's fingers slid down her bare back as he scooted in her chair and took the seat to her right. She flipped her long hair, which would soon be twined around the grill of a certain Maserati.

Logan gradually leaned to the side until he caught sight of me, and he looked startled when I vaporized him with my gaze.

"Good evening, Mr. Cross," I greeted him warmly.

Simon cupped his hand around my shoulder, which immediately caught Logan's attention. His eyes vanished beneath his heavy brow and I bit the inside of my cheek because of how handsome he looked in a dress shirt with the sleeves rolled up.

Coursing through my veins was an unfamiliar fire that I'd never felt for a man—jealousy.

"Of all the places to run into you," I said in slow, biting words. Simon helped me into the chair across from Logan and sat on my right. "Your brother was kind enough to extend us an invitation."

"*Invitation?*" the brown-haired woman squawked. "You aren't a Chitah?" She turned her nose away as if she'd caught a whiff of my perfume. Made me wish I brought the whole damn bottle.

"Of course she's not," Glitter Girl said with a snort. "Just look at her eyes. I bet she's a Shifter, or maybe a troll!" They laughed in unison. I might have accepted the Shifter remark as a compliment, but trolls didn't exist.

"No kitty cat, I'm a Mage." I pulled a votive candle closer to me and ran my finger over the flame in a violent manner. Sparks crackled from my fingertips against the fire and caught their attention. For reasons I couldn't explain, my power was more intense whenever I was emotional. Simon discreetly pinched my side.

Mouths twisted and noses wrinkled.

"Careful who you insult with your tongue, little Mage," one of them warned, narrowing her eyes so that her lashes looked like spears. "We bite."

I caught the slightest hint of her upper fangs descending.

"Logan, wherever did you pick up this stray, dirty thing?" the bitch in red asked, tracing her fingers up his arm without taking her eyes off him.

"So, Mr. Cross, I guess you decided not to waste any time in moving on," I noted. Showing up at the Gathering was one thing, but allowing himself to be dry-humped by half the women in Cognito? *Something entirely different.*

"Logan, please assure me that you didn't chase after this insipid excuse of an immortal," Red Dress said quietly to him. She cut me a sharp glare and I flinched from the power behind her eyes. "Mage, I think it's past your bedtime."

That scrap of a woman was about to get polished off by the back of my hand.

Logan looked uneasy—stiff-shouldered—as he leaned back and tilted his head. "Why did you come here, Silver?"

I averted my eyes.

"Waiter!" Simon snapped, immersed in the game. He slipped his hand behind my neck—the one place that Logan silently claimed as his. That stirred a reaction from Logan as visible as a fissure in a dam, and he tapped his fingers against the table in a rhythm that sounded like the four horsemen riding to the apocalypse.

"I bet I can guess why he broke it off. Too much power in those fingertips, honey?" the red dress scoffed. "You could never fully satisfy him. Stick with your own kind."

My anger transformed into hurt. Simon leaned in close and whispered privately, "Don't go there. Let the trollop run her mouth all she wants, but don't give her the satisfaction of your pain."

Logan lifted his chin, taking in short breaths, stirred by the intimacy of Simon's mouth so close to my ear. The twitch in his lip made it impossible to tell if my perfume was enough to mask my emotions.

Every time she found a button to push, she would victoriously stroke Logan's arm and purr with contentment. "Someone like you could never win over a Chitah male, especially one of Logan's caliber. He comes from a respectable line of men who mate with women of class."

"Well, apparently I was good enough for Mr. Cross to date," I snapped.

"Male curiosity can be forgiven; after all, these are virile men." She squeezed his arm and constricted my heart. "It seems the only one with an infatuation here—is *you*."

The waiter poured white wine in crystal glasses and presented a platter of chocolate-dipped strawberries on the center of the table. I lifted a glass and took a long sip, struggling to ignore the verbal assault.

"Any luck tonight, Mr. Cross? Pickings look pretty slim," I said, dragging my eyes to each woman sitting at the table.

"I think I can answer that," Red Dress replied softly. Her nails caressed the groove of his jaw and brushed across his lips. I tried to remain nonchalant about it. *I really did.* But when I caught the wolfish smile on Logan's face and his arm sliding behind her back—game on.

CHAPTER 14

If Logan wanted to play dirty, then I was prepared to roll with the pig.

The intention of going to the Gathering was so that I wouldn't have to live in the shadow of destiny. It was a chance to see how real this kindred spirit thing was. Would it change anything? It wounded me to see him collect these women like pet rocks and throw them in my face for sport.

Simon tucked me against his side and kissed the top of my head reassuringly. We laced our fingers together on the table, and a soft jazz song lifted the mood of the crowd around us. If this were the Olympic games of jealousy, I was going for gold.

The one striking detail about the party was the ratio of men to women. Logan was entertaining a table with four ladies, and that riled up a few of the men standing nearby as jealousy and contempt flared in their expressive eyes.

"So tell me about the success rate, Mr. Cross. You plunk down how many millions of dollars to throw this shindig, and what—maybe a few hookups?"

"She bores me; let's leave," the blonde whispered in Logan's ear. His bright eyes latched onto mine and through his peripheral, he caught Simon's index finger suggestively stroking my palm.

"You recover from heartbreak rather quickly," he bit out. A muscle tensed in his jaw, intensifying his bone structure.

I leaned away from Simon. "Maybe staying with our own kind is for the best," I said regretfully.

A glass lifted. "I'll drink to that," Red Dress said.

"Don't you need to go get spayed or something?" I retorted.

For just a second, I caught Logan's lip twitching.

The woman in the white suit bolted out of her chair and leaned over the table, pointing her polished finger at my face. "You're nothing but a low-class Breed. You spoil this party with your presence and I don't care who the hell invited you. A Mage shouldn't stick their nose in our world, let alone be sniffing around *our* males. You have tramped around long enough and wasted this male's valuable time. He bought tickets to the freak show, but it's time you take your ridiculous carnival somewhere else."

"That's enough," Logan said in clipped words. Anger penetrated his features. "If you cannot hold your tongue then leave this table."

"Go on, I'll keep him company," the blonde cackled, gaining an advantage to her trophy as the brunette stormed off. Her hand disappeared in his lap scandalously and his eyes hooded. The look of arousal on his face shredded me apart and clouded my thoughts.

"Simon, could you pass me a strawberry?" I batted my eyelashes and tried to remain calm, but calm had already picked up the check and left the party.

This was far better than I imagined, and yet so much worse. It was a royally bad idea from inception.

With his fingerless gloves, Simon plucked out the largest berry on the platter. He ran his pierced tongue over his bottom lip—something he often did in chess when he was anticipating his opponents move. He pinched the stem and held it to my mouth so that I could eat from his hand. In Simon's defense, he didn't have a clue that he was digging his own grave with a spoon.

The smooth chocolate touched my lower lip, pulling it down in one erotic motion.

Logan's reaction was explosive and drinks flew across the table.

"You are making a spectacle of yourself!" He leapt to his feet, canines extending. Logan leaned forward and snatched the strawberry, crushing it in his tight fist. Juice streamed between his fingers and he threw the pulp into the grass.

"I'm just the expendable curiosity, so what do you care?" My chair toppled over when I attempted to scoot it back on the grassy surface. "Continue with the orgy you got here; real *classy*. I thought this was all about finding *the one*. These cheap whores don't look anything like soul mates—more like one-hour stands."

The girl in the short skirt flew out of her chair and her fangs punched out. Simon held up his hands in a threatening gesture—energy blazing at his fingertips. Woman or not, this was a different world than I was used to and he perceived her as a threat. Some of the men closed in on us and the impulse to run became strong.

Logan's eyes were two planets that I gravitated toward—bright, powerful, and mysterious.

He paced around the table like a force to be reckoned with and glared down at me with a stony face.

"Come with me," he said, touching my arm.

As we turned, a tall man with a shaved head pushed his hand against Logan's chest. "Why don't you leave some for the rest of us, Cross?"

A staring match began between the two men. I rolled my eyes and was trying to walk off when the Chitah blocked me with an outstretched arm.

Logan stepped closer and the man's nostrils flared as if picking up a scent. He suddenly took three steps back and pivoted around, rejoining his table. Something passed between them on a level I didn't understand.

Logan took my hand and we distanced ourselves from the crowd. Crisp white moonlight filtered through the branches of the tree we stood beneath, leaving pale highlights on the ground.

"Did you come here alone to hurt me?" I asked, folding my arms.

"I should ask you the same question. I came to show my support for Levi."

"Funny. I didn't see your brother at the table."

He arched a brow. "I keep polite company."

"Lending out your leg for dry-humping?"

His lip twitched and he covered it with a fist.

Logan's amusement fueled my anger. "You could have answered my calls."

"I was busy," he said, lowering his hand and tilting his head to the side.

"Doing what?"

He squinted his eyes a fraction. "Did you see inappropriate behavior outside of me sharing their company? Would you prefer if I stood alone in the corner, cursing anyone who speaks to me? It may come as a surprise to you, but my family holds an important status among my Pride. I'm trying to rebuild my reputation. Some of these people I've known for years, Silver."

The top of his white dress shirt was unbuttoned. Logan's features were riveting—so different from other men. His smoldering gaze alone was capable of holding me captive.

"I was fooling myself," I said quietly. "We're not a permanent fixture and I have no claim on you. It doesn't matter if there's any truth to kindred spirits because it's what you believe."

Logan widened his stance.

My voice cracked beneath the weight of my own words. "You demonstrated that regardless of any promise made, I'm not worth a phone conversation. If your life revolves around finding your soul mate, then who am I to deny you of that chance?" Tears were on the doorstep, so I bit them back and transformed that pain into anger. "But if women are nothing more than a conquest to you, then this is one island that you'll *never* explore. I don't belong here."

I had started to walk off when Logan backed me up against the tree and flattened his hands on the trunk. Splinters of bark showered in my hair and he leaned in close enough to kiss.

His eyes shifted—one minute radiant and piercing and the next, drunk and heavy with lust. It was like staring at something wild and unmerciful.

"Do you want him?" Logan drew in a deep breath through his nose and I shivered.

"What I have with Simon is platonic. You cut me out of your life over a text message. You're older than I am, and these are childish games we're playing."

"What do you want, Little Raven?" he breathed against my cheek. "Why can't you say it?"

His knee parted my legs and he pinned me to the tree with his entire body. I sighed from the immediate warmth. Logan was a pounding heartbeat of energy and at nearly six and a half feet—that was a lot of energy. While I couldn't see what he was doing, I knew that he licked his lips because his tongue grazed my cheek.

"*Say it,*" he beckoned, sliding his leg further between mine.

"Maybe this wasn't meant to be," I said in an unconvincing voice.

Skin rubbed against skin as he moved even closer and kissed the tender spot on my neck. "This is one argument that I won't let you win. You're wrong."

I peered around his shoulder. The red dress with the plunging neckline was moving our way like a devil's parade.

"Logan, come keep me company." Her beady eyes narrowed on mine as she analyzed our position. "It's so dull in there without you; I want to hear more of your stories. Don't let the Mage steal away the time you could be spending with a Chitah."

Her steps slowed and she got a better glimpse. Simon would have considered it a tactical maneuver the way she ran her fingers along the fabric of her neckline until it reached her breast. Was she also putting out a scent that only Logan could detect?

"Your harem awaits, Mr. Cross."

He pushed himself so hard against me that all I felt was body heat searing me through his clothes. When my fingers smoothed up his neck, a seductive vibration rumbled against my entire body from neck to hips. I should have complained about the bark chewing into my back, but all I felt was his knee moving between my legs. If I didn't know better, I'd say he was doing that on purpose.

"You outshine all those females," he said in a softened whisper.

"I don't need you to tell me that; I know what I'm worth."

He brought his head around and spoke against my lips. "I'm going to kiss you now."

"Maybe I don't want you to kiss me," I breathed against his mouth. The tension was an electrical storm as each brush of our lips set my body aflame.

Logan licked his lips and mine. "Then don't. I'll stand here and tell you everything I want to do to your body until you crave nothing but my kiss. And then I'll withhold it until your body aches for my touch."

"That's arrogant," I murmured.

His leg shifted and I sucked in a sharp breath at the pressing ache between my legs.

Logan's mouth was the next breath I drew in. His tongue insisted its way in—moving in such a provocative motion that every stroke devoured me. His strong arm slipped around my waist, but I wasn't going anywhere because he caged me to that tree with every inch of his body.

My fingernails lightly clawed the skin on the back of Logan's neck and his lips peeled back.

"Do that again and I'll lose control," he growled in a rough voice against my ear.

Logan's hands lazily slipped beneath my shirt and gripped my waist possessively. I groaned when his hips circled against mine. Energy swirled within me as I became the kerosene and he was the fire. His lips found that sensitive spot below my ear—kissing and circling his tongue until a shudder racked my body.

"Am I forgiven?" he whispered against my skin.

My impatient fingers pulled at his shirt and I heard the soft pop of buttons coming off. He tasted indescribably wonderful as I kissed his chest, keeping my focus on leveling my energy down.

Red Dress didn't exist anymore.

When Logan pulled back, the look he gave was synonymous with raw sex. Anticipation widened his pupils and soaked me in.

"I'm not like your women," I pointed out. "You won't miss that?"

"They have nothing I desire. You're an intriguing, stubborn, lovely Mage, and I would have you no other way." He straightened his back and despite the cold air, an inferno blazed between us.

"Did you want to stay here a little longer and mingle?"

"I've seen enough," he said, tenderly stroking my cheek with the back of his hand.

I smirked when I noticed his disheveled shirt and my pale brown lipstick smeared across his chest. I liked the idea of marking him—a secret I kept to myself.

"Did that woman really turn you on?"

Logan laughed and reached over his shoulder, tying his hair to the nape of his neck with a small band he had fished from his pocket.

"No, Little Raven. I picked up your scent at the table beneath all the heavy layers of emotions. I never thought you would be jealous over me and I must admit… I like it very much," he said with a sardonic smile.

"Say the word and I'll go back and turn you on some more. Would you like me to kick her bony ass by the lobster table or in front of the ice sculpture?"

I walked past him when he swung me back around and playfully spanked me. I laughed and bravely ran my hand over his firm backside.

"Careful, Mr. Cross. I hit back."

"And I deserve it," he said, levity absent in his tone. "Would you have allowed Simon to feed you that berry?"

Hand-feeding was a sign of trust among Chitahs, but I knew it was something far more intimate that wasn't done with just anyone.

"If that's what it took," I said coolly.

Before I knew it, he had snaked his arms around my waist and leaned down as if to kiss me.

"You play dirty," he said against my lips.

Logan backed away, strutting across the lawn like a man who just won the lottery. "I'll go tell that date of yours that you'll be leaving with me," he yelled out.

No matter which way I sliced it, if I accepted him in my life, then I would always be the woman he settled for. The other thought that ate away at me like a parasite was that I had my whole life for him to find his soul mate and leave me. I was already planning our failed relationship. Even more disturbing was the phrase "my whole life," because now my life was a lot longer than it used to be.

I kept a slow gait along the winding trail. My shoes were dirty at the edges and I frowned, wondering how much Justus had paid for them. A peculiar smell hovered in the breeze. Beyond the trees in a clearing, a young couple stood in the moonlight. They looked Finn's age. Her wispy dress floated like a butterfly and she covered her arms with a white shawl. They were too far out of range for me to hear their conversation, but I knew he had marked her. I didn't know the custom of the Gathering; the whole thing felt foreign as I watched how they interacted with one another. She twisted her hair back playfully and ran off. He paused for a moment before going after her at Chitah speed. Was that all there was to it?

I hoped that she gave him a good chase.

"Well, well, well," a familiar voice said.

I sharpened my light, knowing exactly who was behind me.

"Lookie what we have here," the black-haired Chitah said mockingly.

Not wanting a confrontation, I rushed forward when the Chitah grabbed my upper arm and twisted hard. "Not so fast. We have a box to discuss."

"What's in there, your IQ? Because you seem to have lost it."

His fingers squeezed bruisingly and I gasped. "Your reluctance to give up the contents has only piqued his interest that something of value is inside. I'm warning you, Mage; think carefully about how you decide. You have your hand in the fire pit and don't even know it. I could decimate you."

"Shadow me all you want, but I'm not afraid of your threats. Tell Nero that he's wasting his time. Now let go of me before I put three hundred volts into your sorry ass."

"I wouldn't suggest that in present company." His fingers opened up like a spider stretching its long legs—setting me free. I apprehensively hurried past him with my eyes on the building.

"You've made your choice," he said from behind me.

He yanked my shirt so hard that I swung around and slammed into the ground, scuffing my chin on the dirt. I felt my lip split when a sharp pain sliced through the bottom. He flattened me on my stomach and before I could increase my power, the Chitah crushed his heavy body on top of my back. My arms were pinned. I could barely breathe.

"Logan!" I wheezed. "Get off me!"

"He'll tire of you eventually," he said, shoving my face against the dirt. "I sure as hell would if my female couldn't give me a blowjob without frying my junk."

I became paralyzed with fear when his sharp teeth scraped against the back of my neck.

"By the way, my name is Tarek. It's only right that we get the introductions out of the way since I'll be claiming you."

A bold, suffocating stench leapt on me like a black panther.

It was nothing like Logan's, and I realized that each of them had their own unique imprint. Logan's was heady, like freshly brewed spices, seducing me like nothing else—a siren's call, soaking into my pores and intoxicating my senses.

Tarek's was like poison and my nose burned from how heavy it was. I charged up, ready to strike—but he was gone.

CHAPTER 15

I SPIT OUT A PEBBLE AND rubbed my nose with the back of my arm. One minute Logan was moving at an aristocrat's pace across the grounds and the next, he was sprinting.

Tarek's scent stopped Logan in his tracks and he covered his face with the crook of his elbow. His gaze lowered and locked on the blood trickling down my chin. A swirl of darkness swallowed up every bit of gold in his eyes and in less than a second, Logan flipped his switch.

His muscles went rigid, a vein protruded from his neck, and all sense of the man I knew evaporated—replaced by something primal and thirsty for bloodshed.

"Hey, Lo!" Levi yelled from behind. "Are you taking the car or is this a split?" He came up and slapped Logan on the back. His jaw slackened when he caught the scent in the air.

"Pull it back, brother. Don't you dare flip out here! Look at me," he demanded, grabbing Logan's jaw. "Focus on my eyes. There are too many elders here and if you lose control then you're going to end up regretting this for the rest of your short life. They'll make sure of that. Hell, *I'll* make sure of that."

I managed to sit up and speak calmly. "Logan, this isn't about you. He's trying to instigate something, hoping that I'll surrender to his demands. He doesn't know that I've fought worse battles against the copy machine at my old job. Calm down and let's go home."

Levi turned to face me and spoke gravely. "He *can't* ignore it. A male has officially marked you at the Gathering; I don't think you realize what that means."

By the lengthening of Logan's fangs, I had an idea.

"What you two need to remember is that I'm not a Chitah and

his cologne was not my type."

"Only kindred spirits are marked at a Gathering."

If I hadn't been sitting, my knees would've buckled.

"Well, he's not *the one* for me." I stood up and brushed the dirt from the back of my pants.

Levi stepped forward and pointed a serious finger. "You weren't just marked, honey—you were claimed. We're a walking spice rack and there are messages that you can't detect as a Mage. Maybe to you it's all the same, but to us it's a big damn deal."

"I'm a person, Levi. Regardless of your customs, I have the right to reject him because of something called free will."

My heart stammered when I noticed that Logan was gone. "Go find Simon and tell him I'm going home with Logan," I said in a rushed voice.

Levi ran his hands down the length of his pants and bent over. "You can't leave with Logan. You can only leave with the Chitah who marked you—it's our custom. Logan is tracking his scent and we need to find him before this escalates from ugly to fucking catastrophic." He cursed under his breath.

"I'm a Mage," I said in a low voice. "I'm not going *anywhere* with Tarek."

"Tarek?" He straightened his back and spoke through clenched teeth. "*Tarek* marked you?"

"Nero hired him. Don't any of your leaders care about traitors?"

"We don't get involved with Mage business unless it concerns us, but Leo will need to know," he said as he scanned the crowd. "Tarek comes from a powerful family next to ours. There's a history with him that goes way back. This is not good." Levi turned around and took off in the direction of the clubhouse.

We pushed through the door and saw a crowd of people in the center of the room. There were shouts as we shouldered our way through. Some didn't seem to care for my new perfume as they caught a whiff and arrowed their judgment at me. No, I wasn't a Chitah, and that made it all the more controversial. I paused with trepidation when I reached the center. Three men held Logan while Tarek faced him with his thick arms crossed.

"Sweetie," Tarek greeted in mock adoration with an outstretched arm. "I think it's time we get going."

Logan lunged, straining every muscle as the men struggled to contain him.

"You know the rules," a voice out of sight warned. "No violence at the Gathering."

There were disapproving grumbles in the crowd.

Simon appeared and fell quiet, watching the scene. I tensed when Levi's hand touched the back of my neck and he whispered, "If Logan challenges him here, then the punishment will be severe. Violence is forbidden when elders are present in any peaceful gathering. He could be put to death."

I gasped, and my heart fluttered like a hummingbird.

"They'll detain Logan so he won't follow after you. Tarek will drive you home because he's supposed to announce his intent to the father, or in your case, Justus."

The lack of help was infuriating.

My sharp voice cut through the room. "I am a Mage. I don't know what bearing that holds here, but no Chitah can claim me. These are not my customs and I forbid it."

An older man with a long face emerged from the crowd. I stepped forward and stood beside Logan.

"We are not asking you to consummate your relationship, Mage. If you are under *our* roof then you abide by *our* rules. The tradition of the Gathering is longstanding, and if Tarek has claimed you as his life mate, then he has full rights until we investigate further."

"My answer is no."

"Courtship hasn't begun," the older Chitah pointed out. "Therefore, he must be given one year to court you."

My knees almost buckled. "Bullshit!"

His eyes narrowed dangerously and he spoke in an authoritative voice. Meanwhile, Tarek held his position with a smug grin on his unshaven face. "This is a respectful act, one in which you will be given the choice to accept or deny him. It is not an arranged marriage, nor would we legally recognize the coupling as you are not a Chitah—that's irrelevant at this point. There are rules within our kind that are honored, so allow me to quell this little outburst by suggesting that you speak with your Council. You'll find there is little they can do in this regard. I am ordering that the three of you leave the premises; this outburst is an insult to all present."

The crowd murmured and it suddenly dawned on me why Logan hadn't spoken. *His switch was flipped.* The only thing carrying him from one breath to the next was pure instinct. Yet the voice of the elder kept him contained.

"If Logan Cross is willing to sacrifice his life for you, then he will place a challenge," the elder said. "But this is a night of peace and if you are not able to adhere to those rules, then there will be consequences. Tarek will escort you home."

"Sacrifice his *life*?" I involuntarily grabbed Logan's hand. I couldn't breathe.

It wasn't the elder who answered, but Tarek. "I've claimed you as my kindred, so courtship rules no longer apply. If Cross wants you bad enough, then he'll have to challenge me to the death. That is not custom—that is law."

His grin was poisonous—a silent explanation that if I had just given him what he wanted, then he would have never escalated it this far.

"Enough of this," the elder Chitah growled. "This is not the place to instigate a challenge. Should you choose to disobey—"

"No," I insisted, knowing that a stupid decision could end with Logan's death, especially given the state he was in. "If I have no alternative, then I agree, but only on the condition that I leave here with Logan. That is *custom*, not law."

A few unsettled murmurs silenced when the elder spoke again. He was more concerned about defusing the situation than resolving it.

"So be it. Tarek, let the dark-haired female go on her own. Young Mage, remember that you have tread into Chitah territory. You cannot avoid what is his right. I will ask that all of you leave the premises so that we may continue with our ceremonies." He waved a hand and the crowd dispersed.

Logan's grip became iron. I tucked my hand inside of his shirt and his skin was hot. "Logan? Come back."

A thin ring of gold appeared in the center of his eyes and Logan fought against his primal nature until he won.

As we moved out the door, Tarek rubbed his chin and looked me over. "Sweetie, I'm going to treat you *so* right. You'll find in time that I'm the better man and have much more to offer you than Cross does."

Logan corralled me out of Tarek's reach with his left arm. The frightening thing was how *calm* Logan's demeanor was. Fierce eyes locked onto the dark-haired Chitah and they fell into a staring match. The men who escorted us stood aside as if this were an ordinary occurrence. Tarek finally blinked.

Logan drew in a hard breath of air and held it, as if it might transform into flames and incinerate his enemy. When he spoke, his voice was as sharp as a guillotine.

"Listen to me, Tarek, and listen well. If you *ever* lay an unwanted hand on Silver, I will hunt you down to the ends of the earth and watch your blood run cold."

CHAPTER 16

"God, I love the smell of home." I unzipped my hoodie and tossed it in the chair near the door. "Justus is out with your brother for a while, so we have the place to ourselves. Do you want something to eat or—"

Logan came to a hard stop and maneuvered in front of me like a shield.

"Don't move," he said in a deep voice.

It took me a minute to comprehend why. The sofa cushions were askew; books were pulled from the shelves and littered the floor. Someone had ransacked the place. Justus always kept an immaculate house with the exception of sweeping. The floor was made of stone, so I guessed he thought that dirt just belonged there.

"Are they still in the house?" I whispered.

He spoke over his shoulder. "I didn't pick up a scent in the hall so it's hard to tell. If they are, they've been here awhile." He tensed and took a few shallow breaths. "Do as I say. There are at least two of them; the scent in the house is strong. They could be—"

Our attention snapped to the kitchen when someone cursed.

"Goddammit! Are you sure you checked the bedrooms?" a voice barked.

"Logan, the box! That's what they're looking for. It's in the private study."

"Go. I'll—"

"The hell you will!" I hissed, grabbing his arm. "You're coming with me."

He lifted a brow and looked down his nose. "Do you think I can't handle myself?"

"Maybe I don't want blood all over the furniture. I know you can handle yourself, but someone else may be in the bedroom and I'm not armed tonight."

Understanding sparked in his eyes and Logan never left my side.

We hurried down the hall to my Ghuardian's room and I tugged the candleholder on the wall. A sharp click sounded behind the full-length mirror, revealing the hidden study.

"Look for a brown box," I said, flipping on a lamp. It was one of the few rooms in the house with electricity and his vast book collection was illuminated. Everything was visible, and there was no box.

"Maybe this?" He waved a thick leather folder with a snap latch. I opened it up and found papers neatly clipped together. It looked like medical records and I nodded. Simon had been organizing.

Logan opened the door to the garage and I glanced at the desk with the medieval sword mounted on the wall behind it. Beside an expensive bottle of wine was a thick red book with HALO inscribed on the face. A strange sense of duty compelled me to tuck it beneath my arm.

We had our pick of luxury cars in the underground garage; Justus took his affection for vehicles to an obsessive level. He was a collector and his cars were nothing less than pure class. Every single one of them was treated like a lady, receiving as much affection and pampering as only a woman deserved.

Logan scanned the unholy display of exhibitionism and muttered, "Good God."

"You know, Logan, I've just accepted the fact that I'm never going to lead a normal life."

"The bike," he said, jogging to the Ducati. We pushed it down the tunnel and I pulled a switch, lowering the false ground which led to a private trail in the woods above us.

Logan rolled the bike onto the lift and threw his leg over the seat. "Get on. I'll start her up and you hang on tight."

"What if they're waiting for us?" I asked, curling my arms around his stomach.

There was no hesitation when he looked at me over his shoulder. "Then we'll fight together."

We hit topside and Logan started up the engine. The tires spun in the dirt, sending chunks of grass and rock into the air as the bike roared through uneven terrain. We skidded and nearly hit a tree, but he regained control. All I could do was hold on tight.

When the bike hit the asphalt, Logan gunned it. My teeth chattered from the cold air against my bare arms. Adrenaline poured through me like a beverage as we soared through the streets of Cognito.

The heat from Logan's apartment burned my chilled skin. I cupped my arms and shivered in the hallway.

Logan lifted my wrists and blew a heated breath against my hands. I smiled and ran the backs of my icy fingers down his torso as he hissed, scolding me with a slanted brow.

"Thanks," I said with a wicked smile.

I tiptoed through the dark living room and kissed Finn lightly on his ear. He was sound asleep, snuggled up in a blanket decorated with wolves.

While Logan called Justus, I had time for a quick shower. I put my dirty clothes back on and rejoined him, taking a seat at the kitchen island. Some of Tarek's scent had washed off, but apparently not enough, judging from Logan's twitching nose.

Because it involved a security breach, Justus stopped off at Simon's apartment and dragged him out of bed without a moment to spare. I couldn't resist a short smile when I noticed his attire. Simon wore white, body-hugging long johns and nothing else.

"What's with the underwear? I thought you went commando," I asked.

He rubbed his nose with the palm of his hand and collapsed on a stool to my left. "I'm trying new things."

"Why only one nipple ring?"

Simon glanced down and grumbled. "Hurt like a bugger; told the blighter I changed my mind." He flicked it with his pinky finger. "I'm too bleeding irritated about the whole affair to take it out."

"You faced a firing squad, and yet you weep like a baby over a needle? I'm revoking your man card."

"Let's pierce *your* nipples and see how much you warm up to the idea."

"I'll agree to that," Logan said, setting a glass of chocolate milk in front of me. He swept my hair back and lowered his voice. "I'll be happy to assist with any healing you'll need."

"Sit down, Chitah," Justus barked, losing his patience.

Logan pulled up a stool and detailed the events of the evening—minus the Gathering—because I was too shaken up to deal with all the questions. Justus reached in his back pocket and pulled out his phone to call Novis. Eavesdropping on their conversation, I was startled to discover that Justus owned other property. He paced into the living room to speak more privately and Simon took that as his cue to crash—sprawling his arms across the surface of the countertop.

"Where are we going to stay?" I withered in my seat.

Justus sauntered back into the room, twirled the phone on the granite countertop, and leaned heavily on his elbows.

"When I took you in as my Learner, I should have moved us to a safer house. This was a home of convenience, but it's not fit to offer the security needed against this disgrace of a Mage who continues to wreck lives. Such a blatant disregard for the law," Justus murmured. "I'll ensure our new home has a suitable garden where you can sprinkle his ashes." Anger bled from his face and he sat on his stool. "Novis opened the doors to his safe house during our transition. Tomorrow, I'll pick up a few things and get the new house in order."

"Simon, do me a favor." He grumbled as I lifted the leather case and slapped it on the counter. "Scan it like normal people do in spy movies, but get rid of all these papers. You can hide a flash drive up your ass a lot easier than you can a giant case."

He yawned and sat up, scraping his hands through his tousled hair. "Spoken like a true secret agent."

Logan scratched his jaw as if considering something important. "I've got a scanner and flash drive in the closet along with a computer. Care to take a look?"

Simon burst out laughing. "You barely have furniture; this I would like to see."

Logan lifted a finger, pointing to the coat closet across the hall.

Simon slid out of his seat and scratched his ass, bare feet smacking on the floor as he opened the door. "There's nothing in here, unless you count the out-of-style jackets and size-fifteen trainers."

That's when Logan stood up and leaned on the counter. "Did you ever read the story about the Lion, Witch, and the Wardrobe? One of my favorite novels."

Simon stared at the jackets, stepped into the closet, and closed the door.

"Bloody hell!" he exclaimed.

I hopped off my stool and went inside the stuffy closet, standing among the coats. "Fascinating," I muttered.

When Simon closed the door behind us, the wall slid away, revealing an enormous room. I gasped and opened the door, staring at Logan, who shrugged guiltily.

Logan had purchased the apartment next to his, knocked out all the walls, and plastered over the windows.

"Where's the front door?" I asked.

Logan paced to the far end of the room and turned off the overhead lights, leaving the smaller fixtures dimly lit. "The door is a fake. I would have purchased the whole floor, but the lady up the hall wouldn't sell. She's taken a shine to me since I made the offer."

Simon snorted while bending over to admire the surveillance monitors. "I've got one of those in my building," he said.

The images on the screens were the condo, the hall, and a few street corners. On one monitor, Finn rolled over on the sofa and stuck his foot out of the covers.

Embarrassment heated my face and I shot Logan an arctic gaze. "Do these record all the time or—"

"I review the footage each day and erase." Logan quirked a smile.

We shared a private look. He lowered his head, silently assuring me that he had erased the footage of our post-shower stroll through the living room. I hoped.

"Not bad," Simon complimented him. "You still need one on

the roof."

"That's an understatement," I said, shaking my head. "How come I've never seen the cameras?"

"Micro cameras," Simon replied knowingly. "How many inches?" he asked, running his fingers along the monitor.

"Thirty-two," Logan replied.

Simon's dimple flashed as he turned around. "Mine's bigger."

I should've been angry, but shock was in the driver's seat, taking me for a spin.

Two short, green sofas and a chair furnished the room. While we never talked about such irrelevant things, I was beginning to think that Logan's favorite color was green. Everything else was all black or metal. I'd never seen so many gadgets and weapons on the shelves. I knew Logan was a man for hire, but this was so far from how I'd imagined it.

"Who *are* you?"

"You mean who *was* I," he corrected. "This isn't my life anymore."

Logan took a seat on the sofa across from Justus and revealed the truth about his past. No one looked surprised, likely because Simon had thoroughly checked out his background prior to him getting involved with the case. No wonder Justus was adamant about us not dating, but somewhere along the lines, he'd conceded defeat.

Logan had shamed his family by the life he'd led, but they never cut him out. He worked hard to right the wrongs of his past and it was an admirable trait. The family dynamic among Chitahs fascinated me; they were so different from how humans treated one another. It gave me hope that not all things about immortals were objectionable. I once was a cynical human, and that wasn't a healthy outlook to carry now that I was part of this world.

Simon began the tedious process of copying all the data to digital form. Justus slumped into a chair and looked as if he were taking a mini nap in his hand.

Logan threaded his fingers through my hair absently. "Do you need anything?" he asked quietly. I melted a little at his soft side.

"Sleep," I said quietly.

His nose wrinkled. "You're more than welcome to put on one of my shirts," he whispered. "I can still smell him."

I stretched out my long legs. "What are you going to do for a job?"

Logan chuckled. "I've acquired enough money that my finances are in good shape. You need not worry. But I am not a man of leisure. Something will come to mind."

"Done," Simon announced. "Smart girl, grabbing this." He tossed the red book beside Justus, who flinched and opened his eyes.

"What's in the book?" I asked.

Justus rubbed his face wearily and stretched out his muscular legs. "Did you open it?"

"I may be nosey, but if that book is HALO business, then it's none of mine. I don't want to work for you when I grow up."

I rested my hand on Logan's leg without consciously thinking about it. He was extremely responsive to my touch—something I'd noticed on our first date after wiping a smudge of mustard from the corner of his mouth. For just a split second, darkness had swirled in his eyes, and he never looked at me the same after that. There was a new level of intimacy in his gaze.

Logan slid down the seat a fraction and his muscles tensed beneath my fingers.

"Is there anything you can tell me so I know that it was worth saving?" I asked.

Justus sat up and glanced at the book, turning the gold ring on his right hand in circles.

"Old tradition. Old book. It keeps record of every criminal HALO has captured since inception. A fact book, but the contents reveal punishing details. Some remain incarcerated and it's not public knowledge as to why. I would rather have the book destroyed than end up in the wrong hands. Once the investigation with Nero is over, Simon will destroy the electronic device, and the information will be written in this book," he said, patting it with his rough hand. "Modern technology makes me uneasy. I can guard this better than something that can be crushed beneath my shoe by accident or hidden inside of a cavity."

I snorted at the visual. "Or copied in ten seconds," I added, seeing his point.

He nodded in agreement. "Most of the material is stored here," he said, tapping his head. "Members of HALO could recreate this if we needed to. But people with agendas prefer their evidence written."

"What you do isn't illegal, is it?"

His eyes darted toward Logan and he stood up. "No, but not all knowledge is meant to be public. Time to go."

"Can you give me a minute alone with Logan?" I asked.

Logan switched off the computer and walked them out. I went into the kitchen and watched him as he came back in and drank the rest of my milk.

"Tarek's just blowing smoke to piss you off," I said. "Don't fall into his trap."

"He has rights to court you as a kindred spirit, Silver." Logan placed his knuckles on the kitchen island and leaned hard on them.

"They can't force me to date him or stop dating you. I'll find a way out of this, but his tactics are dirty and I don't want you to do anything stupid."

The black rims in his eyes thickened and my heart fluttered. "I'm going to challenge him," he declared.

Just then, Finn appeared at the edge of the kitchen doorway with an ugly case of scrambled hair.

"I know what that means, Logan. If you challenge him, it's to the death. Absolutely not."

His lips pressed into a hard line. "I'm afraid you have no say in this."

"All this male posturing is exhausting! Tarek's feelings aren't real. Don't destroy yourself for the sake of pride."

He rocked on his knuckles, leaning into his anger. Finn eyed him apprehensively as his eyes darted between us. "He—"

"Marked me. That's all. Why must you make this into a life or death decision?"

"Because you are the one I would—"

"Throw your life away for?" I wanted to knock some sense into him and beat all that macho out of his impulsive nature, but he held fast to his Chitah ways.

Logan growled with ferocity as his eyes raged like burning torches.

I leaned forward with my palms flat on the table. "Help me understand, because I need to know why a man who supposedly cares for me would risk leaving me alone for the rest of my life. Don't you realize what you're risking? This isn't a situation on the street where you have no alternatives. You have a *choice*, and you can walk away from this a better man. How do you think I'd feel knowing that because of *me*, you got yourself killed in some challenge of honor and bullshit? You wouldn't be the only casualty. Think of your family."

Logan was seconds away from retorting when he bit his tongue and strode out of the room. A door slammed and water pipes roared behind the wall.

"And there you have it. Don't ever date outside of your Breed, Finn. On second thought, just don't date. I can't take this, I just can't," I said, shaking my head. "If he challenges Tarek… it's over between us."

CHAPTER 17

NOVIS RESIDED IN A REMOTE area of Cognito and due to the long drive, I dozed off in the back seat of Logan's car. The tires rolled over a bump and I snapped awake when my head thumped against the window.

Tall, high-voltage fences circled the outer perimeter by the first gate. We exited the car while the guards searched inside, and I dumped myself in the backseat when it was over. By the time we hit the second gate, I was dozing off again. The doors opened and Justus stepped out of the car while Simon practiced a few new curse words and joined him. A stocky man with a fat jaw walked around the car and searched beneath it. I fell across the backseat and closed my eyes.

Several minutes elapsed and tapping sounds beneath the car roused me from my nap. The door suddenly opened and a heavy hand ran up my leg to pat me down. In less than a second, he was yanked out of the car.

"Lay another finger on my Learner and I'll cut it from your hand," Justus threatened.

Someone made a call and Novis instructed the guards to stand down. Justus switched off the classical radio station when we reached the front of the house.

"Wait in the car," he ordered.

The Aston Martin didn't have enough room for all of us, so Justus had borrowed Logan's car.

"I'm bloody well freezing," Simon complained from the front seat.

"Maybe you should have put on more than your undies," I said with a snicker.

He fiddled with the vents, trying to turn on the air. "Doesn't your boyfriend have a heater in this piece of rubbish? Had I known I'd be dragged out here and paraded like a whore while my balls were thoroughly inspected by Novis's guards, I might have put on a pair of trousers," he grumbled.

"Where did Justus go?"

"Talking with round three of the guards by the door. You'd have more luck getting inside a nun than this place."

"You're going to hell in a handbasket," I muttered, rolling over.

"Get up, Silver," I heard Justus say.

I must have dozed off again. I rubbed my sleepy eyes and peeled my face from the seat. Justus impatiently held my ankles and pulled me out of the car. I stumbled to my feet and leaned against him because let's face it—the man's a radiator and I felt like a cat snuggling up for a winter's nap. He hooked his arm around my waist and we did a zombie walk inside.

"What's wrong with her?" I heard Adam say.

"It's past her bedtime." There was a pregnant pause. "Your heroism did not go unnoticed," Justus said with admiration.

"So why don't you look me in the eye and tell me that? Save the speech for someone who cares. Feel me?"

"Novis is requesting your presence in his office," a sharp voice interrupted.

"Take her," Justus said. "She needs to rest after tonight."

"What happened?"

"A couple of vandals were inside my home and she walked in on them. She's all right," he said, patting the top of my head.

Justus passed me to Adam and my shoes slid across the floor dreamily for what seemed like miles.

"Step up."

Foreign words, of course. The tips of my shoes hit resistance and I came to a stop. "Carry me," I said, remembering a time when Adam was all I had. Time overlapped and everything became fuzzy.

"You can't carry her up *those* stairs; you're going to break both of your necks. Just put her in the study on the sofa," a woman's voice said, edged with frustration.

"Shut up," I muttered.

Light as a feather, my legs left the ground and that was as good as gold for my appointment to count some sheep.

The next morning I gave every stiff muscle in my body a vigorous stretch, the kind that makes you so relaxed that you could fall asleep again. A few strands of hair clung to my face and when I lifted my head, I stared at the stain of drool discoloring the brown fabric of a sofa.

The white glare from a small window cut my retinas like shards of glass. Beneath it was a small table and a couple of white bookshelves lined the walls. Nothing fancy; it looked like a peaceful retreat for having a cup of tea on a rainy day. My bare feet touched the chilly floor and when I stood up, my legs wobbled and I collapsed on my back. The door abruptly swung open.

"You okay?"

I threw an arm over my face to block the sun. "Adam?"

Two hands planted firmly on my hips. "For a minute there, I thought you were polishing the floor."

We fell into our old game of banter.

"Bite me."

"You're way too sour. Here," he said, pulling me up when I suddenly cried out. "Did you hurt yourself?"

"No, give me a second," I said. "My leg fell asleep and it's killing me. I'm not kidding, Adam. If you touch me I'm liable to throw up."

I expected a retaliatory comment, but it was so quiet that I could hear the dust settling on the floor. Cold horror washed over me; it was the worst thing I could have possibly said to him.

He backed away and I squinted through the beam of light. Adam filled a dark corner and turned his head to the left. The right side of his face had one scar from jaw to chin, but the five o'clock shadow was longer than usual and trying to cover it. Still, the hair didn't grow in very well and it was noticeable.

"Please, Adam. Come help me up."

"You're capable."

"What are you doing on the floor?" a bright voice inquired from the doorway. It was Cheri.

Adam pivoted around and brushed by her, leaving us alone.

"Come with me," she said. "I can lend you some clothes and show you to your room."

After a few shakes, my leg cooperated and I limped behind Cheri, following her upstairs.

"How have you been doing?" I asked.

"I'm very fortunate that Novis took me in," she replied. "It was supposed to be temporary, but it's working out splendidly."

"I'm glad to hear that."

Cheri had never learned what it was to be a Mage until recently. It was something I could relate to and on top of that, Finn suggested one of Nero's guards assaulted her when she was his prisoner. *Poor girl.*

Her perfume created a floral trail that was heavy, like a bouquet of red roses.

"This is the guest bathroom," she said, waving her right arm. "There's only one toilet on this side of the house."

We reached the fourth door at the end of the hall and she paused. It felt more like a hotel than a house.

"This is *your* room. Novis wants Justus to take the first one by the stairs. He said it was an appropriate distance between a Ghuardian and his Learner." She winked and my brows knitted at the insinuation. "You'll have your privacy up here because the rest of us are in the other wing. There're a few clothes in the closet—hope you like them."

"Thanks, Cheri. I'm not really picky. Of course, I'm sure you figured that out by now from the show I put on at Novis's party," I said with an unpleasant twinge of guilt.

"I don't really remember what you were wearing that night."

"Adam needs you," I blurted out. Her eyes slowly crawled up to mine. "What I mean to say is that I'm glad you found each other. I know it must be difficult, but I think you're going to help him get through this a lot easier. I bet he treats you like gold."

We drifted inside the bedroom and she floated to the mirror, adjusting the blond locks of hair that fell to her shoulders. "He's nice," she said in a short breath. "But…" Her lips pressed together.

"I'm going downstairs. If you get hungry, we keep leftover scraps in the kitchen before throwing them out to the birds."

The door closed with a hollow sound.

Adam was smitten with her and Cheri calling him *nice* really put me off. Nice is buying someone a cookie or visiting a lonely aunt. Nice is not how you describe a man who stands by your side and nurses you through the darkest period of your life—reminding you that it's possible to be happy again.

Still, she must have been a better woman than I gave her credit for because she stuck around even after what had happened to him. I put my doubts aside and surveyed my room.

The accommodations were modest: A twin bed, mirror, dresser, and two sitting chairs tucked on either side of a small table by the window. Apparently Novis enjoyed light colors because the walls were pale yellow and the furniture celery green.

I selected the least hideous of outfits from the closet and put on a dress. My face soured at my reflection. My long legs looked awkward in the outfit, which was a mix between country and church. It hung to my calves and she hadn't left me any shoes. I pulled off the belt attached to the turquoise monstrosity and tossed it on the bed. The last thing I needed was something to accentuate my narrow hips.

Long, black hair covered my broad shoulders and I pinched my cheeks for a little color. Let's just hope the fashion police weren't on patrol.

I headed downstairs and stepped through a waterfall of sunshine pouring in through a large row of windows. The house was a tomb and lacked the warmth of a home. Looking up at the cobwebs in the corners of the tall ceiling, I surmised there was little preparation in the move. A spike of energy suddenly pricked my skin and I jumped.

"Can I offer you a plate of food?" Novis asked politely.

I spun around on my heel and he was standing in the open doorway. "Yes, please. I thought I could hold out until lunch, but I'm starving." My stomach made an embarrassing sound and Novis suppressed a smile.

He scrunched his black hair so that it stuck out in every direction. By physical appearance, Novis was close to Finn's age, and he even sported black cargo pants and a cotton shirt that made him appear even less ancient. His casual appearance clashed with the flamboyance of his mansion; the money all but dripped from the ceiling. It wasn't flaunted in an arrogant manner, but Novis had acquired many collectibles in his lifetime and the décor was not cohesive.

"Thanks for opening your home to us, Novis. I hope it doesn't put you in a bad position with the Council."

"You're more than welcome here, Silver. The important thing is that no one was hurt when you walked in on those men. Come, there is food prepared." He placed his hand lightly on my back and I joined his side. "You don't seem impressed with the other members of the Council."

I shrugged, not wanting to say anything inappropriate. "I'm sorry about the way I behaved at your party."

He laughed lightly. "Which part? The scandalous attire that broke my dress code or the fourteen lives you saved? No need to apologize, it is I who should make amends for being the owner of that sword."

He sighed, clearly displeased as we moved through a long corridor dressed with paintings on the wall. "What you did to help Justus was admirable—a true display of your unique ability. The first time I tapped your energy, I sensed there was something different about you. There was a shadow blocking—no, guarding your light. You're the reason that Adam is my progeny, and he has proven himself a loyal Learner. I fear, however, that his progress has taken a few steps back with the recent turn of events. Only time will mend the tragedies of the past."

"I see you took Cheri in as a permanent resident. I thought she would eventually go out on her own, or be appointed a Ghuardian by the Mageri."

Novis paused and lowered his tone. "I'm not so sure how permanent that will remain."

There was an awkward silence as we entered the kitchen.

A small table filled the corner and I took a seat. It was bright and cheery with a semicircle of windows surrounding the table.

Quaint was the term I was searching for when describing the room, which seemed out of place with the rest of the house—the kind of kitchen you'd find at your grandma's house. Wooden cabinetry, white tiles, and a fresh fruit bowl by the sink.

Novis uncovered a plate on the counter and carried it to the table with a pitcher of orange juice. He seemed like a real easygoing fellow, except that he was eons old. That in itself was intimidating—to see the experience of age behind those sparkling, young eyes. On my third bite of my buttermilk biscuit, he restarted the conversation.

"I want you to know that you can confide in me. If there is information that must remain confidential from the Council for their protection, then I will honor that. I fully support the Mageri and my top priority will always be to uphold the law, but some situations are… delicate. My gift to you is my trust. Justus prefers for his affairs to be private, so I knew it wasn't his idea to call me over the other night."

A smile crept across his face as he studied me with keen eyes. "You don't have to choke on the biscuit. Swallow, and taste the juice," he said, sliding the glass toward me. "This is not an accusation."

Thank God. I hadn't chewed since he began talking and I thought I was going to need the Heimlich maneuver. Some immortals were elusive with their words—speaking in riddles—so his motive wasn't clear. I swallowed hard and chased it with a few gulps of freshly squeezed juice.

"Why are you telling me this?"

He sat back in his chair and studied me. Behind the black lashes were the palest blue eyes I'd ever seen, reminding me of Siberian Huskies.

"There are times we cannot always confide in our Ghuardian or Creator. Their duty to protect will often close an open mind. You have leverage in your home, whether you believe it or not, and a Learner is not without power to influence decisions. I'm willing to help should you ever need it. That's all I wanted to say. Now go ahead and enjoy your breakfast more slowly." He smiled and raised his brows. "I have some personal business to attend to."

Novis left the room and I nibbled on a slice of tomato, watching a bird dive at a squirrel. The wind bullied a wooden swing, knocking it against the trunk of the old oak tree outside. Novis was a curious fellow because it was obvious that he kept some things the way they were from the previous owner of this house; as if he secretly wanted to be part of that normal world that humans live in.

My mind was reeling, wondering why he wanted to reiterate his trustworthiness.

"And Silver?"

Startled, I looked up at Novis, poking his head through the open door. "Yes?"

"I'll see if I can rummage up some suitable clothes. That dress…" His voice fell to a teasing whisper. "*It's not you.*"

CHAPTER 18

1 Message Received 6:34am
Logan: I'm sorry. Msg me when you wake up
Silver: Hi. You there?
Logan: Forgive me. When can I see you?
Silver: In your dreams
Logan: Don't tempt me, I made a promise. How long will you be away?
Silver: I don't know
Logan: What do you know?
Silver: I miss you
Logan: And I miss you, Little Raven… every time I shower
Silver: You are so wrong for that
Logan: Smite me. Do you feel safe there?
Silver: It's a beautiful fortress
Logan: Perfect. I've arranged for Sunny and Knox to stay low for a while. I know how you worry.
Silver: Where are they?
Logan: Can't say
Silver: I'll call you later tonight after my shower
Logan: Now I'm jealous
Silver: Of what?
Logan: The soap

I TOSSED MY PHONE ON THE bed and hurried into the hallway. Just as I turned the corner, I ran into Adam. He quickly spun around with his back to me, ruffling his hand through his thick, brown hair.

"Are you going to hide from me forever? Because I don't think this is very conducive for our conversations," I said.

A layer of anger coated his tongue. "Do you think this is easy for me?"

When he tilted his head, I could see a fraction of a mark on his right jaw. I wanted to cry and throw my arms around him, but I remembered Novis's words about what a man needed, and it wasn't pity.

"No, I don't, Adam. I wish it had been me."

He spun around and shook me. Hard. "No, you *don't*."

Shocked by the forceful way in which he handled me, I pulled away and looked up.

Adam lowered his eyes. The scar on the left side of his face was the most prominent because it ran from his hairline down to his cheek, about an inch above his mouth. It cut straight through his eyebrow and left a mark where the hair didn't grow; he was lucky he hadn't lost his eye. The right side of his face had an angled scar running from the temple down to his chin. Not even his five o'clock shadow covered it up. Curved scars ran along the inside of his right arm and bicep—probably where he tried to block the glass as it struck him. A small cut marked the right side of his neck and made me realize how easily he could have had his jugular severed. *Where else was he scarred?*

Adam wasn't grotesque by any means, but he was marked.

I cupped his chin in my hands. "Remember what you once said to me? You never wanted to see me looking down. Take your own advice, Adam. You're a Healer, and that's something to be proud of. Many people are alive because of what you did. You're compassionate, handsome, and—"

He jerked his head away and stepped back. "Don't lie to me. Don't you *dare* mother me and tell me there's nothing wrong; I think we both know that's a line of bullshit and I don't need you to stand there and tell me I'm handsome."

Adam's boots hammered down the stairs and I wondered if the man I once knew was lost. If he was that despondent with me, then perhaps Cheri was the only one who could get him through this.

Low voices drifted from one of the sitting rooms downstairs. Grandiose paintings lined the tan walls accented with brass wall sconces. A large, thin rug with elaborate designs smothered the floor. Novis held a captive audience as he filled their glasses with amber-colored alcohol from a decanter. Justus and Simon were seated while Adam leaned against a doorframe. Cheri stood at his side, holding her arms tightly. She rubbed her cotton-candy-colored lips together, but it looked more like she was suppressing a smile when she caught sight of me.

"That's a really sassy dress," Simon began. "It's very—"

"Cheri's. She was kind enough to lend me some of her clothes," I interrupted. Simon's mouth usually ran without a filter.

Justus smoothed his hand across his arm. "Anything of value has been moved to our new home. We're working on the security."

"What's the damage?" I cringed at how easily that flew out of my mouth.

Simon widened his legs. "The whole place was trashed—including the cars. Sodding bastards destroyed the lot of them."

My eyes floated to Justus. "We should have taken one of the nicer cars but the Ducati was the only thing that we could move quietly up the ramp. I'm so sorry."

"I still have the Aston," Justus said, rubbing his chest as if pained. "It was the only car I truly enjoyed—aside from the Mercedes."

Destroying a man's car collection is as good as instigating war.

"Wipe that look off your face," he snapped.

Justus stalked toward me and I nervously bit my lip as all eyes fell on us. The tension was palpable, but no one would stand between a Ghuardian and his Learner.

"I see the guilt formulating in that head of yours," he said, smacking my forehead lightly with his palm. "They were just cars. Your life holds more value than a piece of machinery."

Kind words delivered in a harsh tone. A good woman could really soften his hard edges in ways he desperately needed. Justus was a proud and noble man, but too detached from making emotional connections with others. There was so much spirit in him and when he laughed—it was full-bodied and turned heads.

The news about his cars was a mood killer and as this was no formal meeting, I tipped my head to Novis and went outside alone.

The air was clean and crisp, and I measured my pace across the lawn until I reached the twisted tree. The only home I'd known as a Mage had become my security blanket, and now it was ripped away. Justus was the one certainty that I knew would be there for the rest of my life. After all, that was his job. But when I thought about the rift between him and Marco, it left me with doubts.

I sat on the wooden swing and gripped the ropes. Everything was up in the air—my relationship, my home, my identity, and our safety. Because of me, Sunny was in hiding.

The swing suddenly yanked back and I was thrown forward. The wind lifted the soft tendrils of my hair and dashed them over my shoulders as Adam's strong hands pushed me from behind. I screeched when the ropes jerked unsteadily.

"Woman, you are the biggest fraidy cat I know."

"Adam, please stop," I begged.

He eased up but wasn't about to stop pushing. That would mean facing me and he was wasn't ready.

"Are you still happy with Novis?"

"He's a generous Creator, and I've been fortunate," he replied.

"Do you think he'll release you from his custody? I keep wondering if Justus will ever allow me to be independent. Novis is constantly bragging about you."

"Is that so?" he mumbled.

I scraped my shoes against the dirt and skidded to a stop. Neither of us spoke and I reached behind me, scrunching my fingers through his brown hair. My hands remembered Adam the way he was as they slid down the stubble along his jaw. The scars looked years old by the way the skin had fused, and I had to remind myself this only happened just recently.

"You need to shave."

"Maybe I'll try a beard for a while."

"You didn't answer my question," I pointed out.

"I'm too new to understand what it means to be an independent Mage in this world, Silver. Don't rush; you've always been impatient."

"Happy with Cheri?"

"That's one woman I don't deserve." His voice wasn't proud as I had expected it to be, but doubtful.

"She's the lucky one," I remarked. "We're going to live a really long time, Adam." I sensed him moving away from me and I turned my head. "I just want you to remember that I'm always going to be here to kick your ass." I stood up with my knee perched on the swing, staring at his back. "Do you think a thousand years from now we'll still be friends and remember this moment? It's sad to think we may forget about all this."

Adam pivoted on his heel. "How the hell can you say something like that?"

I froze.

With a pinch of his fingers, a pack of cigarettes appeared from his shirt pocket and he angrily pulled one out, punishing it with his teeth as he plucked a black lighter from a deep pocket in his jeans. "I'm going to remember this for the rest of my life," he said, pointing to his scars. "And if you ever forget, I'll be here to remind you."

"I didn't mean it that way. I'm sorry."

"How many people do you think will take a Healer seriously with this face? I had a potential career doing something that mattered." He sucked on the butt of his smoke twice to get a lungful.

"Since when did you start smoking?"

Adam took another drag and didn't reply.

"This isn't you, Adam. Don't self-destruct."

"I've done some bad shit in my life and God knows if those people were innocent. I was a follower, doing what I was told without blinking. They were all Breed; how's that for bedtime stories? I thought I could atone by walking away, but it follows me like a shadow. So, what do you really know about me, Silver?"

"That isn't who you are—it's who you *were*. I know you, Adam. Not many people come along in your life and stick their neck out like you did for me. No, maybe I don't know who you used to be, but that doesn't matter. Don't become that man again."

Adam was reaching what Logan must have faced years ago—a

crossroad. It was a turning point, and he was driving in the wrong direction.

He stared at the house with a vacant expression, flicking the cigarette between his fingers.

"Give yourself time. No one expects you to bounce back to your old self after just a few days. I know what you're going through." I reached for the cigarette and he switched hands.

"It's not going to kill me."

My foot kicked up a plume of dirt. "Well, it'll give you bad breath."

He turned his sharp eyes to mine. "Yeah? Who am I going to kiss?"

"How about your girlfriend, for one?" I gave an exasperated sigh. "I'll always be here when you need to talk. I don't know what else to say; I can't make it better."

Adam traced his thumb across his lower lip, buried in his thoughts.

"You have a lot of love to give, and you're the most loyal man I know. Just give yourself some time and remember that nobody cares if you have marks on you. We're all marked in some way."

"I'm a husk of a man, Silver. I'm dead inside."

It was a jarring remark because deep down, I knew he was one step away from the edge.

CHAPTER 19

Logan gazed out of the bedroom window at the dense fog below, crawling up the dark street like a biblical plague. A petite young woman with a stylish black jacket quickened her step along the sidewalk. She jerked her head around when a small object fell from her arms and bounced on the gritty concrete. He couldn't tell what it was when she snatched it up, but he shook his head, disapproving of how often human women went out unescorted at unsafe hours. In her defense, she couldn't possibly know she lived in a city full of dangerous immortals. But on the other hand—humans were always dangerous. Her pointy heels clicked along the pavement until the fog swallowed her up.

His eyes hooded when he caught Silver's scent on his tongue. The sheets were thick with it, and he had no intention of washing them until it was gone.

Logan never used scented soaps and shampoos—that was all Finn. The first time they went to the drugstore, he found Finn sitting on the floor with all the body lotions, applying each one. A Chitah had no interest in perfume because their sense of smell was so acute that it picked up the soft fragrance of a female—the feminine bouquet that was unique with each flower.

Logan was enthralled by Silver's scent. Beneath the mango shampoo that lingered on his pillow was something much softer. It was her own unique brand… *all over his bed.*

His forehead tapped against the glass. Caring for Finn required patience and time, something that might cost him or gain points with her in his courtship—there was no way to tell. Now she was locked away and he couldn't get to her if she needed him.

Logan expunged any thought that she was in danger. Novis

would ensure she was safe; he was a Council member, after all.

Silver was capable, fierce, and yet her naivety compelled him to look out for her. That fiery temper was so opposite of his mate from long ago. Katrina was a demure creature with womanly charm and a vivacious laugh. The kind of woman that knew how to use her beauty, and the bounty of her body could have seduced any male. Time had added tough layers to Logan, but he was beginning to feel again. Not just a prickling sensation, but a roaring inferno.

His heavy sigh placed a thin film of condensation over the glass and Logan cocked his head. Drawn on the window was the shape of a small heart.

"I'm all packed. I think." Finn stumbled in the room and dropped his bag on the floor. "Do you mind if I take the blanket? I kind of like it."

Logan watched his reflection in the glass. He had the wolf blanket tucked underneath his left arm—neatly folded.

"It's yours," Logan said. "This isn't permanent, Little Wolf, but the only way you'll bond with us is to switch between homes. Your wolf and I have an understanding: I stay fifteen feet from him, and he doesn't piss on my chair."

Finn snorted. "Sorry about that."

"The chairs were old and it's time for a change." Logan touched the center of the heart with his finger, leaving a small dot in the middle. "Your wolf may never trust us because we're not the same, but it's imperative that *you* trust us. We're family."

"Straight up?"

"A Chitah is good on his word," he said, turning around. Logan placed a fist in front of his mouth to keep from laughing. Finn was wearing a pair of Logan's sneakers. They were so large on his feet that it looked cartoonish.

"What's going on with that?" Logan pointed.

Finn looked down and tapped one shoe against the other. "Maybe it's part of being a Shifter; I really don't know much about my own kind. It feels like… instinct." He shrugged. "For some reason, I had to take something that smelled like you, and well, these sure smell."

Logan folded his arms, pushing out his biceps. "You'll get along well with Lucian; he'll help you with your education. I think it's about time that you start impressing people with more than your wood carvings. You have the potential to do great things."

Finn's closed-lip smile was the kind that stretched wide as he kept his eyes to the ground. The fact that Finn rarely kept eye contact didn't set well with Logan. Shifters were a Breed with submissive traits around a dominant male—with the exception of alphas. Something about Finn made him wonder if it was possible he was born an alpha but years of abuse had whipped him into submission. That's part of the reason that Logan kept a close eye on him—a tethered alpha was an unpredictable and ferocious animal.

"Is Lucian my age?"

"Somewhat," Logan replied. "By appearance, yes. He's our younger brother, but in years, he's about fifty."

Finn's eyes widened and swallowed the floor.

"You'll get along," Logan reassured him. "He's smart and you'll have plenty to talk about. He also likes cartoons."

That pleased Finn because he used to watch cartoons before his father sold him. Nero's guards had never allowed it, but when they were drunk enough, Finn would sneak on the Internet and learn what he could about the outside world.

Anger prickled in the pit of Logan's stomach when he thought about the guard that Silver had seduced for her freedom—one he hunted down and found a month later working as a helper in a greasy diner. It was rewarding to fight him like a man. No use of his gifts, just fist to bone. Diego carried a solid punch, but Logan's right arm was a demon unleashed, and blood trickled from his knuckles like tears of joy. Logan would have ended his life except for the fact that he might lose his standing with Silver. She didn't understand his ways and valued life. Maybe she wouldn't have found out, but it wasn't worth the risk. Chitah women Logan understood, but he had to be delicate with this Mage.

"Logan?"

He blinked. "Sorry. Say that again?"

"Are we still going to hang out, or is this like an isolation thing?"

Logan crossed the room and ruffled the mop of brown hair on Finn's head. "Your location is changing, nothing else. Behave yourself and remember that a man should never act as a boy. Lucian has a bad habit of mouthing off when he shouldn't. He's smart, but doesn't always notice when boundaries are crossed. Don't follow his lead. When you stay with each of us, take the best parts as examples of the kind of man you want to be."

"Confident."

Logan furrowed his brow. "That wouldn't be Lucian."

"No, you. That's what I'm taking from you."

Surprise flickered in Logan's eyes. He picked up a peppery scent that told him Finn spoke the truth. What really grabbed his attention was the way Finn kept his eyes locked on Logan's—unflinching. It was so uncharacteristic of him, and yet he held his gaze just as bravely as any Chitah could. Logan wasn't accustomed to this kind of admiration from a young male who looked up to him. Lucian never aspired to emulate his older brothers, going his own way despite their guidance. He was intelligent, but there was never a sense that he looked up to Logan. Not that he really had any business doing so with the lifestyle that Logan chose.

Here he was, rendered speechless by a single word from a young Shifter wearing a pair of red sneakers twice his size.

Logan cupped his hands firmly on Finn's shoulders. "When you finish up with a good dose of the Cross brothers, if you're not ready to go out on your own, then it's your choice which of us you want to live with. My door is always open, and… I hope you'll choose me. I'd be honored."

Finn used his fingers as a comb and scraped his hair over his ears. "You bet. Not sure what kind of job I'll be able to get, but yeah, that would be cool. You're all right, Logan. When I first met you, I thought you were kind of a shithead."

"Get in the damn car," Logan said with an amused shake of his head. "I'll be down in a minute."

Finn lifted his bag and nearly tripped as he flopped out the door in those oversized shoes.

Logan lifted the T-shirt from his bed in his fist and drew in a deep breath. He thought about her wispy black hair and how it looked like a storm whenever the wind captured it. She possessed a wildness like he'd never encountered in a woman before.

Logan pulled off the shirt he was wearing and slipped his arms through the red T-shirt. When her fragrance touched his skin, his fangs elongated.

That Mage had no idea how provocative her gaze was—riveting green eyes surrounded by inky lashes. It was a sore subject because they reminded her of Samil; somehow she had acquired some of his striking features during her transformation. Her cheekbones were high and proud. Her mouth, on the other hand, was stubborn. Lips so lush and yielding that he could savor them for an eternity, and when their tongues met, every nerve in his body awakened. He remembered the feel of her in the shower, the smooth contours of her soft breasts, lean torso, and the way her stomach curved in when he stroked his knuckles against it.

Sweet nectar sifted from her pores—a scent that filled him with carnal desire.

In the shower, the smooth line of her legs had drawn him upward into forbidden territory, but he couldn't resist stroking her just once. She'd gasped, releasing a scent of desire so heady that Logan's canines punched out and he imagined taking her against the shower wall. It was an erotic impulse that frightened him; he'd never been with another Breed and didn't know if the same bedroom rules applied. He doubted it.

The thought floated away in the darkened room and Logan looked at the faded heart on the window. A small object on the windowsill caught his eye and he bent down, collecting a wood carving in the shape of a wildcat. Its angular body curved impressively, ready to strike its prey. The teeth were sharp and the eyes were—*Logan's*. Finn had carved a cheetah with all the wildness and nobility he saw in Logan.

Down on the street, Finn stood beside the car with his thumbs tucked in his front pockets. He looked up at Logan and waved.

"Uppercuts!" Novis shouted.

I swung my arm three times in a sequence of punches.

"She clocked me!" Simon complained.

"Get up!" Hysterical with laughter, I punched my arms out. "I don't even care anymore."

"Then forfeit!" Simon demanded.

The interactive video game had consumed our attention for the past hour. Novis owned every kind of game imaginable. Simon gave it a whirl, even though on numerous occasions he'd argued that video games held no intellectual challenge. His skepticism stemmed from a fear of the unknown.

"What kind of sissy punch is that?" Simon mocked as he ducked to the right.

Novis declared, "She has you beat."

Out of nowhere, Simon pummeled my character in a whirlwind of swings and knocked him out. "That was far more exciting than cards." He flexed his bicep and kissed it.

"That's really mature."

"Let me show you what else I've got," Novis said, pulling Simon's attention away.

"That was fun." I collapsed on the tan sofa, out of breath.

Cheri spread across Adam's lap like a cat—stretching and yawning. She finally stood up and tugged his hand. "Let's go to bed. I'm tired of watching them."

He tilted a beer bottle against his lips and muttered, "I'm not sleepy."

She leaned forward suggestively. "Me either."

In that uncomfortable silence, I gulped down my lukewarm soda. When Adam didn't budge, she parted through the room like a knife through butter. Cheri glanced over her shoulder and they shared a look, but I couldn't tell what was going on between them. Something personal and none of my business.

Novis eyed the doorway when she left, and I wondered if he disliked her for the simple fact that they were both in his care and knocking the headboard.

A personal chef had prepared our homemade pizza served

with beer, soda, and chips. In private, Novis was laid-back. There were moments I could almost imagine the young man he once was.

"I may need to borrow that," I teased.

"You'd probably have to borrow the telly while you're at it." Simon smirked and got ready for his first round of bowling.

The pizza crust was no longer fresh and I dusted the crumbs off my fingers, sending a shower of sprinkles on the sofa. I could feel Adam's glare. It was a peeve of his to eat on furniture and he didn't join in our party. I wondered how Cheri scored in that department, because I loved the idea of a man feeding me in bed.

An unlit cigarette dangled from Adam's mouth as he read the label on his beer bottle.

Simon rolled a strike. "In your face! Care to wager and make this interesting?"

"Ladies and gentlemen, please fasten your seatbelts. We are now reverting back to childhood," I mumbled. "How many guards do you have outside of the house, Novis?"

"I'm not exactly sure." He barked out a laugh. "It's safe, if that's where your concern lies. The perimeter is well lit, armed guards are on post, and every window in this house is secured with an alarm. No one gets inside unless we allow them access."

"I thought Justus's door would have kept Superman out," I said.

"Anyone can pick a lock," Simon muttered.

"Worry not. One of my best security advisors is helping Justus with your new home. You won't have guards, but he'll make sure that a cockroach can't get in without clearance."

"Thanks, Novis. I knew it was easy to find us down there after Logan did, but I didn't think they would—"

"What do you mean, *Logan* did?" Adam's voice cracked through the conversation like a leather whip. "I thought Justus hired him to track Nero."

I had spoken without thinking, and that's what happens when you live with a lie.

Simon finished his turn and spun around. "You didn't tell him?" He shook his head. "Did you think he'd never find out Logan took you, Silver? Badly played."

"When I want your advice, I'll ask for it."

"What do you mean, *took her*?" Adam rose from his chair and crossed the room.

Simon's eyes skipped to mine and I knew part of it was because he had trouble looking at Adam's scars. "Shall I tell him? The man has a right to know the truth so I'll give you the opportunity before I spice it up with *my* version."

My hand flew up and on cue, Novis opened the door and the two extracted themselves from the soon-to-be crime scene.

Time to come clean. "Logan was hired to deliver me to Nero, but when it came down to the actual hand-off, he backed out. Logan was never instructed—let me rephrase that—Logan had no intention of hurting me. In fact, he protected my life."

"Sounds like a fairy tale," he said mockingly. "Why don't you give me the long version." He lit up the smoke, took a deep drag, and dropped it in a soda can. "I'm going to have some words with him," Adam decided.

"No, you're not. That isn't your place, Adam. I know you care about me, but stop trying to find a reason to hate him."

"Why would you choose a man like him?" He turned his back to me and stared at the door.

I stretched my fingers across his back. "He's honorable."

"He's a criminal."

"People change. You above anyone should know that. Your opinion matters to me, but you've always been so damn judgmental. Be angry because I lied to you, but don't hold a grudge against Logan because he turned his life around for me. I don't know where things are going between us. What he's offering is a lot to consider, and I'm not taking it lightly."

"I can't believe I saved his life," he said in a disgusted voice.

Furious, I slapped him on the back. That comment sliced me raw. "How can you say something like that? You may resent the hell out of your gift or the planet, but don't you dare wish someone dead that I care about. I'd stand up for you if someone said the same thing."

"He tried to *kill* you."

"Don't be melodramatic. Logan protected me."

Adam showed me his profile with the scar running along his jaw. "Are you going to act like it's no big deal? Doesn't some small part of you wonder if he'll always be truthful? Cross is the kind of man you can buy for the right price. That says a lot about his character."

"You were bought for free, remember? I fought against caring for him but the feelings are there—I can't deny them. He's not the man he used to be and has the potential to become so much more. I'm not exactly a catch. There're a few unsavory facts about me that you'd probably be disgusted by if you found out."

"Such as?"

Hybrid. Science experiment. Mutant. Freak of nature. "Nothing."

Adam was so caught up in our conversation that he turned around. No insecurities divided us any longer. It was just him and me.

"Nothing you say will change my opinion of you." He inched in a tiny bit closer, watching me with his smoky brown eyes that held the faintest reflection of the light he inherited from Novis.

"Don't be so sure."

"So tell me," he urged in a softer voice.

I kept my lips pressed and he shook his head. "Still the same old Silver, stubborn as ever."

"Still the same old Adam, *pushy* as ever," I retaliated.

We were closer than we should have been and when I leaned back, he flinched as if I'd slapped him. His hand reactively covered the scar on his face.

I gripped his wrist firmly, trying to pull it away. "It's not *that*, Adam. It has nothing to do with your scars."

He jerked his arm away and scratched the whiskers on his jaw. Novis was right—Adam *was* different. There was no recovery period, no time to adjust and come to terms with what had happened. Adam wanted validation that he was still desirable as a man and I couldn't give it to him. A kiss wouldn't erase his damaged thoughts. Wasn't Cheri enough?

The door swung open and Simon filled the entryway. "Have you two kissed and made up? I haven't finished my game."

CHAPTER 20

SOMETHING WAS ON MY MIND the next day—and that was Adam. I tossed and turned most of the night thinking about our talk. Could that kiss have saved him? Common sense told me no, but I felt guilty that I couldn't reciprocate his feelings. What if rejecting him put him over the edge? Maybe it wouldn't have led to anything, but I was afraid of opening a door that we'd decided to keep closed.

A piece of the puzzle was missing, and a little *girl chat* was in order.

Novis had left a pair of faded jeans and a blue cotton shirt neatly folded outside my bedroom door. It was obvious that they were men's clothes and were probably his. We were about the same height and he had a slim build—although I needed a belt.

Cheri closed the bedroom door and strolled across the room, relaxing in the chair by the window. The sunlight caught her enviable waves of blond hair.

"There's something I've wanted to ask you, Cheri. Do you know why Nero left you and Ray behind that night?"

"The other girls were more cooperative and we were new. He drew more light from me than anyone else." She hugged her arms as if the temperature had dropped.

"Sorry. It's not right what we went through and I'm sure you had it ten times worse than I did. It just never made sense that he left you behind because of the lengths he went through to acquire us. Do you know what your gifts are?" I only asked because some Mage gifts were immediately known while others took years before they discovered their talents.

She shook her head gracefully. "He kept me chained the whole time. Honestly, I don't really care. Samil never gave me the choice to become a Mage," she said bitterly.

God, I knew exactly how she felt.

"What happened to Ray? I thought he was staying with you."

"No," she said nonchalantly. "He was Samil's Learner before Nero bought him; the Council evaluated Ray and he was offered independence."

Lucky bastard, I thought. "Do you two keep in touch?"

She tapped her nails on the table. "Why should I? And I have a question, if you don't mind. How did *you* manage to escape?" she asked with a dash of suspicion that made my eyebrows pop up. "Was it that Shifter boy?"

"No. I tricked one of the guards and stole the key."

"Oh? Which guard?"

"Diego."

Finn's job had been to feed Nero's potentials and clean their stalls. Despite his best efforts, they rejected his friendship. Diego worked the late shift, and Finn had heard from the other captives that he was taking Cheri out of her room on numerous occasions. After a while, she quit talking.

Here I was, grilling Adam's girlfriend because I was being overprotective—the same thing I chastised him for doing.

"I'm sorry, Cheri."

"For what?"

"Bringing up Diego."

"What do you mean?" Cheri laughed. "Ohh," she said, looking as if she'd reached an epiphany. "Don't worry, I'm not jealous or anything."

"Jealous?"

"Diego was a good fuck, but that's about it. Not much of a conversationalist, if you catch my meaning. I never could get the key from him, but he brought me snacks and sometimes a magazine. Anyhow, you do what you have to do. Isn't that right?" She winked. "The quiet ones always have the biggest cock."

Not a single word formulated in my mouth as I stared at her, dumbstruck. A minute of silence passed and I commanded my mouth to come back from the land of silent movies.

"Did you tell Adam?"

Her thin brows pushed down. "Adam doesn't need to know who I sleep with; that's *my* business."

Not slept, but sleep. It was like a Jekyll and Hyde act; she didn't seem at all like the kind of woman that Adam would fall for. He didn't know anything about who Cheri was, but I began to wonder if he'd even care.

Her eyes narrowed, watching me like a hawk.

"You shouldn't keep secrets from people you love. It's in the past and he'll understand."

"Love?" She laughed and stared at an emerald ring on her middle finger. "I don't love Adam. *God* no!"

Now her hyena laugh was really starting to piss me off.

She pressed her lips together and stared aimlessly out the window. "He's great in the sack—don't get me wrong—but a little bit on the sweet and sappy side. I mean, how many guys ask you during sex if you're okay and want to have a conversation? He talks too much in bed, describing what I feel like." She snorted and scooted her chair back. "But after his accident…" Her expression became petulant and she waved her hand, cutting off the thought. "It's been nice chatting, but I really don't need to tell you any of my personal life. You two may be buddies or something, but I don't know you."

Cheri's heels tapped on the hard floor and when she reached for the doorknob, she spun around. "And I may not love Adam, but you need to keep your distance. Claimed, honey. Take care."

My body refused to move. I sat so still that the chair was moving with the room like a musical carousel, but I was a statue.

A messenger appeared at my door a short time later and escorted me to a private office.

"You wanted to see me?" I closed the door and nervously rubbed my hands together.

Novis smiled. "No need to be anxious. Please, come sit with me."

We relaxed on the sofa by the window. On the outside ledge of the window, a group of sparrows fought for position by the birdfeeder.

"I've called you on official business. Your measuring has been recorded in our books and your skills documented," he began.

Measuring was an official ceremony where the Council documented the common and rare talents of each new Mage. They tapped into their light in addition to witnessing their abilities. Novis had conducted the ceremony and taken special interest in my ability of telekinesis with certain metal objects. The only secret that I had kept from them was that I was a Unique. Novis only tapped into my light, but hadn't drawn enough that he would know for certain how different it was.

Justus stood proudly when my name was entered in their record books and I was officially written into the history of the Mageri.

I nodded as he continued. "Your contributions to the ongoing investigation have also been acknowledged. The Mageri is aware of your act of valor and they are offering you a position. It is a rare privilege to receive a job offer by the Mageri in your first year, Silver. It's not a paid one—it's an apprenticeship."

"Like, an internship?"

"Precisely."

"Does Justus know?"

"This is Mageri business," Novis emphasized. "Until you make your decision, it is not his affair. The Mageri is above his Ghuardianship to you."

I considered the offer. "Why me and not Adam? I wasn't the only one saving lives that night."

A grim look shadowed his face and he watched a one-legged bird hop on the feeder, pecked at by the stronger ones. "It was offered to him."

"He turned it down? Why?"

"He felt it was a consolation. Adam resented the offer because he felt they were implying that it's all he's good for, and his mind was already set on being a new kind of Healer to all Breed. We had talked about it at length and I'd prefer he not share the knowledge of his gift with others, but I think it's what he was leaning toward doing. Maybe this was a blessing; some gifts should not be made public. It would have only brought him more danger. No, Adam is not ready. He's…" Novis licked his lips and looked up, searching for the right words. "…lost. You were second choice. The Mageri would have left the position open until another candidate caught their attention, but you were also on the list. I presume they see it as a—"

"Adam helped during the raid at Nero's compound," I interjected. "I don't want to steal his glory—what's rightfully his."

Novis lifted a wisp of hair from his temple and crunched it between his rolling fingers. "Nothing in life is rightfully yours until you take it."

"He outshines me, Novis. We both know that."

"Your humility intrigues me. Most would have no trouble claiming their good deeds. You spend far too much time thinking about your shortcomings rather than what you have to offer. Adam is fighting a darkness in his life; something all men face at some point."

"Adam is not a bad man, Novis."

His face softened and he lifted a finger, pointing to my foot on the floor. "See that shadow? That's the dark part of you that you don't want anyone to see. It follows you. Run from it, and it will always be on your heels. We all live with that darkness and must find a way to turn our backs on it. You cannot force a man to change direction if he is not able to see the shadow for himself. In time, Adam has the potential to be an incomparable Mage. But this is not that time."

"You would have made a great father," I blurted out. My teeth clamped down on the inside of my cheek as my mouth operated faster than my brain.

Novis lifted his eyes to the window and shared a private moment with the sunlight. "I was a father once. In my human life, we married young and had many children. That was so long ago," he said in a soft voice with melancholy eyes.

Time moved through the room at a quiet pace, stretching

along the walls and blanketing the floor. A cheery sparrow infiltrated the silence with his incessant chirping as he bounced along the window and flitted off.

"I get myself in trouble a lot."

He smiled. "I can see that you're really selling yourself short. Sometimes those who take risks and think outside the box stand out more than those who play by the rules."

"I thought the Mageri liked rules?"

He tipped his head left and right, mulling it over. "The Mageri likes loyalty, but these are valid points you bring up."

I shifted excitedly in my chair. I wanted purpose in my life and although Justus assured me good deeds were purpose enough, my spirit was listless.

"This position will be working as *my* apprentice, Silver. As tasks are required, I will summon you for assistance. It's a position you have the choice to accept, and you can leave at any time such as you could with any job, although I hope that you choose to stay. An apprenticeship with the Council can lead to greater things. This is about earning trust and gaining experience, regardless of what you may be asked to do. It's a foot in the door and a great honor to be approached without submitting an application." He crossed his legs and wove his fingers together. "When there is a need for confidentiality between us, it will be shared with no one. There are no exceptions to this rule. Do you understand this?"

"I understand."

"You need to. Don't accept this if you're going to share information on a whim and breach our trust; it's a very serious matter. This includes your Ghuardian and especially Logan. A personal relationship brings expectations of honesty, but this does not fall within those lines. There are repercussions for deception that go beyond termination of employment. You are young and impulsive and I will help you with this. I do not want to see someone with such potential throw it away."

"How much of this was your decision?"

"None. I work on the Council but I have no control over who they assign to me," he added, giving me an impish grin. "You are a very suspicious person by nature. Do learn to trust, Silver. Suspicion can be a valuable trait, but too much of it can increase paranoia and ruin relationships." Novis uncrossed his legs and patted his thigh. "I've made the offer but I cannot force your decision; do you have any questions you want to ask before you consider your answer?"

I tugged at my hair, braiding the tips. "What would I be doing?"

"Whatever is required."

"Which is what? Cooking? Gardening? Clipping your toenails?"

Novis was amused. "An apprentice has a number of duties, but you are not a maid. You would be part of investigative matters, deliver messages, and I would consult your opinion. There are a number of situations where I require a representative to speak in my place. What I ask may not always be easy—it could even be dangerous. That is why a personal apprentice is assigned a private guard so there will be no further need for Justus to escort you in public. I take the safety of all my people seriously. A position working for a Council member gives you inside knowledge that some would want to acquire. Justus is forbidden to interfere in any decisions involving official business. He may not like it, but he is loyal to the Mageri and will abide by it."

After some consideration, Logan would just have to accept it. We agreed to be honest, but if loyalty was part of the job requirements, then my obligations would be to Novis.

"Are you sure about this?"

Novis offered a broad smile and the natural light within his eyes glimmered like ripples of sunlight. "It's not a choice for me; the choice is yours."

"I'm not saying I'll be insubordinate, but Justus will even tell you that he struggles with my stubbornness. I don't like being controlled and when I start feeling that way, I react."

It was only fair to warn him that I wasn't the best team player, even if I really wanted this.

"I have no desire to control you, so put your mind at ease. My job is to mentor you. Your honesty is commendable; many would lie and say they'd do everything that was asked of them. I'm guessing you are not defiant without reason, but your heart is in the right place most of the time, even if your head is not."

He really did know how to say the right thing.

My insides were roaring like the cheering section of a football stadium.

Novis cleared his throat. "We select the most loyal and trusted humans to bring in as a Mage, and that's a control we've had for only the past two hundred years or so. This is how the Mageri contains the population, not all of it is up to the Creators. It's not uncommon for a Creator to have never met his progeny, and they are selected by the Mageri. If you've read our history books, then you're aware of the necessity that was behind a Creator building up his progeny in ancient times. We were without laws, territories, and Creators had the ability like few others to build an army of guards."

"I'm well-versed in our history, thanks to Justus. It makes sense that a Creator wouldn't want to have more progeny; what would be the point? We live in a modern society and it's too much additional responsibility." I shrugged.

"Exactly. Now a Learner is seen as a burden and they must be cared for like children. However, there are still battles raging and lives lost. We must replenish our losses with new blood. That is the way of politics these days, and it gives the Mageri a direct hand in who is selected, whereas before they had none. They groom the new ones to abide by our laws. You… you're so different because you were *not* chosen. You have a streak of rebellion and the spirit of humanity. Perhaps the Mageri feel they can smooth that out, or maybe they're willing to change with the times. Who knows?"

"I respect the fact we have laws, Novis, but I don't always agree with them. They exist only to serve the Mageri, not to protect the lives involved. When the Council forced me to return with Samil, I was terrified about what kind of world I was giving myself up to if my own people wouldn't protect me. What kind of leaders would send me home with the man who hurt me simply because he had a right to claim me? How was that protecting my rights? Justus is an obedient Mage and had to follow your orders, but he wasn't right with it. The Mageri is forward in so many ways, but backward in others."

"In our defense, we didn't know all the facts."

"You didn't ask, even after accusations were made and the resistance was obvious. I'm not saying laws are bad, Novis, only that they should be there to protect the people."

"Laws provide structure among the Breed, but yes, some are outdated. What is that old saying… Paris wasn't changed in a day?"

"Rome wasn't built," I corrected.

He chuckled. "I was never very good at remembering idioms. Many things to discuss. Many things to learn. Would you like time to consider the offer?"

"Not really," I said with a soft smile. "Novis, I accept."

"Splendid!" He clapped his hands together. "I'll contact the Mageri with your answer and send out the invitations."

"Is this a party?"

He stood up and straightened his shirt. "Formalities. We'll have a small gathering and I'll make the announcement to your Ghuardian once the Mageri is notified."

"Should I dress up?" Mischief hooked the corner of my mouth into a dangerous grin.

"You'll find that I have a sense of humor and my judgment is not as impaired as Justus's to such things. You are very young and run high on your emotions, but I do trust you will make a sound decision on this."

"Understood."

"Until then, let's keep this between us. Your first test of secrecy—this is your mission, should you choose to accept it."

I tucked my hands in the pockets of my jeans as we walked to the door. "Do you think I could leave the property for a little while? Logan wants to see me. I know we're under protection, but I'm safe with him. I'd ask Justus, but that's going to be a waste of breath. Since you have seniority…"

"Is this my first test as your employer?" He smirked and stretched out his long arms. "Of course you may. Your personal affairs are none of mine. You may be a child among your own kind, but you are a grown woman. I trust you are safe with the Chitah," he said. "You should protect yourself as much as possible, but you cannot shelter yourself from living life."

"Thanks for understanding. What do I call you now?"

Titles were common, as by custom I was still to address Justus as Ghuardian.

"Call me Novis."

CHAPTER 21

Justus had a few loose ends to tie up with the new house, so he dropped me off at Logan's for a few hours. The Ducati was still parked out front and Justus decided to pick it up later. What I really wanted was a quiet evening, but Logan had other plans.

The bike made familiar turns up the stretch of highway and I gripped his waist.

"Where are we going?"

Wherever it was, we were poorly dressed for the unexpected cool front; meteorologists were predicting an early winter. Cognito had unusual weather and I often wondered if the tremendous energy from the Breed worked as a weather magnet. Nevertheless, my blue cotton shirt was not cutting it. When the bike rolled up a private road, I slapped his shoulders as we cut through a crowd of tall Chitahs.

"Logan, why are we at the Gathering? I don't want you doing anything stupid like confronting Tarek."

The bike swerved around a branch and eased to a stop by the curb. Logan kicked off the engine and shifted around—his hair pulled tight at the nape of his neck. The color in his eyes melted like honey and sunlight, and my fingers wanted to graze along the contours of his face just as much as they wanted to slap it.

"I make good on my promises, Little Raven. You asked me to claim you in every way and that's what I intend to do. This is the last night of the Gathering and we're about to shake things up."

"When did I—"

"In the shower," he finished.

My mind went blank. "Logan! I was sexed up and barely

conscious." Ignoring me, he took my hand and all but dragged me toward the main entrance.

"Wait, stop for a minute!"

He tilted around with a twinkle in his eye.

"If you do this, what does it mean?" I tugged at my hand to reclaim it but Logan kept a firm grip. "Are you going to fight him?"

"No," he quickly answered. "Little Wolf told me what you said. I won't challenge Tarek if it means losing my position with you."

"Finn shouldn't have said anything; that's something you were supposed to figure out for yourself."

"I'll tell the elders the truth. They'll either believe me or not, but I will not keep this a secret any longer." I swam in relief knowing that Logan would expose Tarek's lies.

Logan's nostrils flared as he took in a breath of air, then his jaw slackened and eyes hooded. Something changed in his expression that made my heart beat faster. He moved closer and the heat of his body insisted that I bridge the gap between us. The heel of my shoe scraped on the concrete and I looked up at him.

"I still intend to claim you, Little Raven." He cupped the back of my neck with a gentle touch and planted his insistent lips on my mouth. A current raced through my hands for a moment and dissipated. I touched the fresh stubble on his face—soft and coarse all at the same time. My kiss wandered down and I nipped his chin with my teeth. I liked doing that because it provoked him to growl. Logan traced his fingers over the soft flesh of my neck and I gasped, trying to catch my breath. He was usually so firm with his hands and feeling them barely touch my skin made me want him so much more.

"Expose him, Logan. If that's what it takes to break his claim, then do it. But don't use me for your own personal revenge."

His eyes sought understanding as they fell over me adoringly. Very tall people were slowing their pace and dropping stares as our bodies twined and his long arms snaked around my waist. I wasn't a Chitah, and that made it controversial.

"Why are you looking at me like that?" I asked apprehensively.

A brilliant pattern erupted across his warm skin. It was striking and more pronounced than I'd ever seen it before. We were drawing a crowd in front of the entrance and they circled us with curiosity drawn on their faces.

"People are looking at us, Logan."

A breeze lifted a tendril of my hair and it floated in front of my face. He captured it and held it between his fingers, admiring the black mixed with chocolate undertones. "It's time for me to come clean about something I should have told you a long time ago."

The butterflies in my stomach were lining up on the tarmac, preparing for takeoff.

"Do you want to know the truth of why I didn't give you over to Nero when I came for you that night?"

"Because he questioned your word as a Chitah, and you're a prideful, stubborn man, Mr. Cross."

My smile waned when his voice deepened. "No. That's what I led you to believe."

Logan shifted his stance and suddenly I felt swallowed up by his height and presence.

"When I stood outside of your door in my raincoat, I had every intention of delivering you and holding to my agreement with Nero. I could smell your fear and uncertainty, which would have made it easy to force you to comply. I should have taken you immediately, but I extended the visit for a reason. Do you know why?"

Spectators circled around us, but I was oblivious. Was this public display part of his plan? I watched him with skeptical eyes as he loomed over me. His expression was unreadable and I was so rattled by his gradual admission that I tried to push him away.

"Ask me why." His grip tightened around my waist, fingers digging into my jeans. "It's time that you learn the truth about me."

"Is this part of the show?" I whispered.

"Well, well. So generous of you to have delivered my girl. I've been missing every inch of her," Tarek shouted exuberantly.

Logan's arm hooked around my waist and he forced me behind him. It was unnecessary since a physical confrontation at the Gathering was forbidden.

Tarek strutted down the sidewalk with a round, pink bubble

pressed to his lips. He snapped the gum and winked at me with his cutting eyes. The crowd parted, allowing him to enter the circle. He was dressed in jeans and a sweatshirt with a symbol on the front I didn't recognize.

"Bring the elders!" Logan demanded.

A few men hustled off and speculative glances surrounded us.

"You think the elders are going to help you?" Tarek reached in his pocket and unwrapped another piece of gum, tossing the paper on the pavement. He raked Logan over with arrogant superiority and when he saw me, he punched out his tongue seductively and blew another bubble. Logan's body stretched into hard muscle beneath his black shirt.

"Logan Cross, is this where you intend to hold your challenge?" Tarek asked, spreading out his arms dramatically. "Always had to be a showman."

"I am not challenging you," Logan replied indifferently. That caught Tarek by surprise and he studied Logan with extreme measure.

Murmurs increased behind us and three older men approached. They were seasoned with peppered hair and weathered faces. These men were old enough to have witnessed the rise of the great pyramids. It took hundreds of years for a Chitah to age five years once they reached adulthood, so I could only imagine how ancient these men were. They lined up on our right and both Tarek and Logan faced them, bowing respectively.

The bearded one spoke first. "I thought we settled this matter."

Logan submissively lowered his eyes. "Respectfully, I ask for a moment of your time."

My arms involuntarily wrapped around his waist—something I didn't notice until he placed his hand over mine. Here I was—a Mage—surrounded by men I knew to be my natural enemy.

Tarek stalked forward. "He has nothing for you—nothing but lies. I have claim on this female and he's infringing upon my rights—*my* territory. We'll be leaving."

One more step and Logan might have lunged, but an elder raised his hand. "We will allow him to speak his piece so that we may return to the ceremonies. Tarek, you are silenced."

Tarek folded his heavy arms and angrily slid his jaw back and forth.

"With all due respect," Logan began, "you've made an error in your decision. Tarek holds no claim to this female because he has already met his kindred spirit." Eyes widened among the elders as they darted between Tarek and Logan. "Years ago—while it was not done officially—Tarek privately claimed a female as his kindred spirit. Her name was Katrina, and she denied his claim and chose me."

I held my breath. Pieces of his past were fitting together in a most dramatic turn of events. His woman was pregnant and murdered by a Mage—the reason Logan went on a homicidal rampage—but I never knew the full story because the subject matter was too delicate. It broke him once, and there was no need to test those breaks again. But she was Tarek's intended?

The next part he all but roared out. "And he forced himself on her once she was mine!"

I let go of him and stepped back. His voice ripped through the night and tore open a hole, deep and wide, opening a river of pain and silence as the elders twitched their noses and picked up the scent of truth.

"As you remember, Seth, Katrina was murdered. Tarek's motive tonight is personal and I beseech you to revoke his courtship rights."

"Can I speak now?" Tarek asked, spitting out his gum. "Is the word of a male with a soiled reputation all that is needed to deny me what is rightfully mine to pursue? While Cross may be of a high-ranking family, it's no secret to anyone here what kind of work he does."

"Did," I corrected.

"Silver is *not* yours," Logan growled in a low, threatening voice. It lifted every hair on my arms and sent a chill down my spine. He was one of the most intimidating men I'd ever met, and the ferocity in his tone made one of the elders flinch.

"She will be," Tarek spoke in a soft and self-assured voice.

"Not if I challenge you."

I squeezed Logan's arm as a reminder.

"So go on then, Logan Cross. Challenge me. Or are you weak and afraid?"

"Afraid like you were with claiming Katrina?" Logan lifted his chin proudly. "You had your opportunity, but you were ashamed to let anyone know she was your intended. *Ashamed* because she did not come from wealth or status, *ashamed* because she was not good enough for you."

"That's a lie!" he bellowed.

"Go tell it to her gravestone," Logan hissed.

Tarek pointed an angry finger and stalked forward. "She was mine, and you stole her from me. You were jealous of my position and family and couldn't stand to see me have it all, so you had to steal my life mate? What nobility!"

Tarek stumbled over his lies and the moment he realized it, he backed down.

One of the elders thoughtfully stroked his chin and addressed Tarek. "You're admission is enough; there's no need to recant as we can scent the truth in your words. Your legal rights to court this Mage as a kindred spirit are severed. If that is all—"

"One more thing," Logan said, circling around to face me.

He pulled me against him and my face pressed against his firm chest. Confused, I was trying to push away when suddenly Logan's unique and robust scent filled my head and swarmed through my body like an intimate act. It was heady and intoxicating—different from any other time I'd experienced it. The power was concentrated, and the effect was immediate.

"Logan, what are you doing?"

The crowd murmured and slanted eyes placed their judgment upon us.

He lowered his head and spoke softly against my forehead. "What I should have done a long time ago." His eyes blazed when he looked up to the elders and declared, "I am claiming this female for the right to courtship. No other male will court her without a challenge, or unless she makes a decision."

"Logan, you already did this with me."

"Not officially," he said softly.

Logan spoke loud enough that everyone heard him, but soft enough that his words were mine. "I'm Logan Cross of the Cross family, and I *claim* you, Silver, in front of my elders and these witnesses. I will prove myself a worthy male and avow to honor your good name and protect you with my life. I do this, Little Raven, not because I'm possessed by you, but there is something that I've kept from you for a long time."

Still in his arms, I lifted my head to look in his eyes when his smile faded.

"What I've concealed from you has lit a fire in me and at the same time, it rips me apart. From the moment I set eyes on you, I knew you were mine. Ask me why."

I shook my head.

"*Ask me*," he insisted, tilting his head to the side.

"Why?" I whispered.

Logan dropped to his knee and in a silly moment, I thought he was going to propose. In front of an audience, he rolled up my shirt with his fingers and nuzzled his warm cheek against my stomach, spreading his large hands around my hips. Soft kisses pressed against my stomach before he lifted his eyes and drew me into his gaze.

"Because *you* are my kindred spirit, Mage. I have waited a lifetime to set eyes on you and the connection I feel is undeniable. There's more to it than chemistry because over time you've opened yourself up and allowed me to see that I'm a fortunate man. I was asleep—dreamwalking through my own life until I met you. My heart has reawakened."

"You said yourself that it can only be with a Chitah. Don't mess with my head, Logan."

My legs felt like jelly and my blood didn't bother to ask for directions on how to get to my hands. I barely heard the shocked voices around us because Logan became the center of my universe. I gripped the short mane of hair tied behind his neck and felt the resonant purr thrumming from his chest. How do you quell passion when it rages like a fire? I wanted to sink into his lap and kiss him for hours, but part of that may have been the drugging effect his scent had on me.

"Well, doesn't that just warm the cockles of my heart," Tarek chided. "Elders, that scrappy female he clings to is a Mage. Cross cannot find a life mate in her as a kindred, for she is *not* a Chitah," he said with emphasis.

"That did not seem to stop *you* from claiming her, Tarek," the bearded man pointed out.

Logan rose to his feet and faced the elders. "You know there is no denying your intended, and for whatever reason, she has been brought to me in this form. I can't explain it, nor can I disregard it. I'm humbly asking for your acknowledgement of this courtship."

"This is a most unusual turn of events," Seth muttered.

Eyes washed over us with disgust. The women looked like they wanted to drag me down a hill and beat me with dead skunks. In their eyes, I was stealing one of their own. A Mage couldn't have children and this only added insult to injury among a Breed who thrived on continuing their line with large families.

"For your sake, young Chitah, I hope that this is not trickery. Kindred spirits only exist among the Chitah race." There was a pause as the elders looked between one another. "We will allow the tradition of the kindred courtship under the condition that we speak with you privately at a later time. Otherwise, a *mating* between a Chitah and Mage will not be acknowledged by our laws, so don't get any ideas in your head."

Logan nodded. "Agreed. May I request a favor? That Tarek and his companions are detained until we're off the property. I don't trust that he won't attempt to retaliate, and I want to get this female home safely to her Ghuardian."

Several men stepped out of the crowd and surrounded Tarek, escorting him to the other side of the property as the elders turned away. The crowd dispersed and a gust of wind blew from the north, sending a few leaves tumbling down the street.

Still reeling in shock, I shoved Logan in the chest. "How could you do that to me? This isn't a game where you can toy with my emotions in order to get back at your enemy."

I couldn't contain the tears that burned my eyes and clung to my lashes. I covered my face with my trembling hands, lost to the possibility that Logan had manipulated a situation so that he could get what he wanted. Lost to…

He closed the distance between us and lowered my hands. Logan cupped my cheeks and gently wiped away my tears with his thumbs.

No words. No argument. Logan melted a kiss against my lips that burned like fire. My lashes were wet with a maelstrom of emotions, but I couldn't fight the intensity that built with every seductive stroke of his tongue. So deep and penetrating that tingles roared through my body and I gripped his arms, feeling the rope of muscle.

His hands remembered me, moving down the slope of my shoulders.

The kiss abruptly ended. Logan Cross looked down at me with a crushing gaze and held me hard—the way a man does when they never intend to let you go, whether you wanted them to or not.

"I'm still mad at you," I said in an unconvincing voice.

"Fire should never be tempered in a female because that's what fuels her passion, causing it to ignite." He lifted my chin with his hand and stroked his thumb gently across my lips. "All a male can hope for is to be consumed by it until there is nothing left of him."

CHAPTER 22

We left Novis's mansion on a sunny Thursday morning for the official move. My mood was glum. Despite its medieval embrace, our house had grown on me. I was going to miss leaping out of bed on the balls of my feet because the stone floor felt like a sheet of ice. I'd miss the crackling fire in the great room where I spent most of my time reading on the fur rug, and the amplified sounds of Justus's sticky feet treading up the stairs after his workout, or the hiss of a candle as the flame bickered with the wax.

The Aston Martin veered off the main highway, coasting up a long country road paved with dirt.

"You should move into the city," I suggested. "It would be a nice change to be near civilization and walk to the market."

"Too dangerous," he replied.

Justus seemed uncomfortable at times with modern society and I wondered if it had to do with him being an older immortal stuck in his ways.

I glared at the garage that looked more like an airplane hangar. Justus lifted the latch of the middle compartment and locked away his aviators.

"*This* is your idea of security?" I sighed inwardly at the idea of living in an open garage.

When the garage door lifted, so did my skepticism. Justus had been shopping and two glamorous cars were on display. One was a black Porsche, but I didn't recognize the model of the second vehicle. The ornament was a leaping cat of some kind, but I didn't know my cars well enough to tell. It looked a little plain, but I had a feeling the price tag was anything but.

"Hidden security cameras are installed around the perimeter and are motion sensitive. Alarms will go off with movement—anything bigger than a wolf," he said, pointing outside as the garage door closed. "I'll be inviting Novis over to get his advice—one of the settings is a silent alarm, but the security guy spoke too fast and I'm not certain what the others do." Justus coughed into his fist and worked out a kink in his shoulder. "There are traps throughout the property."

We stepped out of the car and slammed the doors.

"Maybe that's not such a good idea," I said, watching the garage door close. "What if I have to escape and I end up caught in one of your bear traps? I like to take walks, you know."

"No sneaking out, and until we get this situation contained—no walks."

He opened a panel in the wall and scanned his thumb. I didn't even see the lines because they were cleverly hidden within a large rack of tools. The wall slid to the side and I stared into a metal elevator.

"You have a thing for subterranean homes, don't you? I hope the electricity runs all the way into the house or I brought my hairdryer for nothing," I grumbled.

We stepped inside and the door closed.

"What's that?" I asked, pointing at a flat panel on the wall.

When the elevator stopped, Justus placed his thumb against it and the door opened. It seemed excessive, but I was already beginning to feel safer knowing that a couple of thugs wouldn't be able to kick in the door.

"You need to be in the system to get in, but you won't have to go through the same security measures when leaving the house. It would defeat the purpose of a quick escape."

I peered into a dark hallway lit with a caged bulb. After a few paces, we hit a dead end and I hugged my arms.

Justus bent over and stuck his face in front of a retinal scanner. "We'll get you recorded into the system later," he mumbled as a lock released behind the metal door.

It was another narrow hallway and I gripped his arm

apprehensively. "I take it there are no windows down here. You're going to make me the palest Mage in the history books."

"I can arrange for a tanning bed," he said, as if a snap of the fingers would make it so.

"No thanks," I sighed. "I'll just remain vitamin-D deficient for all eternity."

The last door had a fingerprint *and* retinal scanner.

"Hope you don't ever get pinkeye," I said, watching the door open. "Holy shit!" I gasped.

"Home sweet home." Justus looked inside the house indifferently and then back at me.

We'd officially graduated from the Stone Age. The old world vibe of our previous home had grown on me, but this one was sleek and modern. Immediately, goose bumps paraded all over my arms with victory flags waving. I could hardly contain my excitement as I stepped inside.

Beautiful wood flooring ran throughout. On the left was a dining room void of any unnatural light. The walls held flameless sconces, the table was hammered wood, and the room was warm and cozy. But the one item that stood out was the painting that had once hung in our dining room. It was an image of a beautiful maiden in a stream reaching for a man. He held the sun in his right hand and reached for her with his left, but their hands never touched. Almost everything looked unfamiliar, but there were just a few items that Justus had picked up from the old house.

The kitchen was a few steps to the right.

"Stainless steel!" I said excitedly.

Justus laughed. "Coming from a woman who doesn't like to cook."

The room lacked oven mitts and spice racks, and I had a feeling that it had never been used. Justus preferred to order out or make sandwiches, but lately I'd been making more of an effort to enjoy cooking. In the beginning, I'd refused to cook for Justus, but that's when I thought he was a prick. Now there was a certain pleasure gained when he savored something I made—even if it was something as simple as spaghetti and meatballs. Justus loved eating meat and most of the things I knew how to cook didn't involve a rack of ribs or five pounds of brisket.

Just past the kitchen was a small lounge—not much to see except some bookshelves and chairs. Straight ahead was the living room.

"This is *unbelievable*," I muttered.

It was bright and lavishly decorated with a faux fireplace that generated heat. My jaw dropped at the massive television mounted on the wall—something we never had at the old house. A charcoal-colored shag rug covered the center of the room between the matching sofas. If his previous leather sofa matched the price of a car, I could only imagine the cost of the new living room set. All it needed was wheels.

The decor had a very masculine vibe with black leather chairs and a few curvy ones that looked European.

"I can't believe we have power," I said, stroking the tall lamp.

"Is that a pun, Learner?" He barked out a laugh and scratched the back of his head.

"What is *that*?" I asked in one extended breath.

To the left was a wall of flat screen monitors with no space between them. They were bordered by curtains, neatly roped and tied.

"Watch this," he said.

A tiny remote beeped in his hand and the monitors popped on. After a few selections on the keypad, the scenic images began to change, giving the monitors the illusion of a giant window. Bright images filled the room: A sunset, mountains, snow falling, and a view of the ocean. They were moving and so crisp that it brought nature inside to us. He stopped on the fish tank and set the remote down.

"How much did all of this cost?" I couldn't process the totals in my head.

"Money is of no concern." He waved off the question, throwing his heavy weight into a swivel chair. "I'm paid well for my services and have a rather large piggy bank."

"You have one obese pig," I murmured.

Justus kicked off his shoes and stretched out his thick legs. "They're for surveillance. The security guy offered a few suggestions about screensavers and I thought you might enjoy them."

"This is not my life," I said in disbelief.

My eyes ate up every square inch of that place in awe as I wandered into a hallway with a mirror at the end. Justus dragged his feet across the floor and rubbed the back of his neck.

"Follow me. This is just a hallway with a big mirror."

I snorted and cupped my elbows and we walked to the other side of the living room. There were only two doors in the short hall.

"This is the guest bedroom. Our quarters are below," he said.

"I thought we *were* below."

When he flipped on the bathroom light and stepped into the shower, I laughed.

"Shut the door and lock it."

I turned around and did as he asked. "Now what?"

"Turn on the water," he said with his arms folded.

"If this is how you seduce women, let me start by telling you that your technique is all wrong. For one, you have way too many clothes on."

He leaned forward with a heavy sigh and tugged at the hot-water handle, tensing the muscle of his bicep. His tribal tattoo wrapped around it, climbing up to his shoulder.

Suddenly, the floor began moving. I might have lost my balance, but the descent was slow and smooth.

"It only activates when the bathroom door is closed *and* locked," he stressed. "The spare key to the bathroom is inside of the blue vase in the hall. This was a customized security feature installed by Simon years ago."

"No kidding," I murmured.

"The plumbing system is fully functional. The edges are seamless in the floor and watertight. Directly below the floor, Simon installed thin crevices to direct the water down a channel behind the walls that leads to one of our pipes. Otherwise, it would splatter on the floor below and call attention to the fact this lower level exists."

"So when we have visitors, they're going to have to take a shower with the door open? Was that Simon's idea, or yours?"

He arrowed his eyes at me and I grinned.

We stepped off the lift and it sailed into the ceiling with the help of a long metal cylinder beneath it. Justus ran his foot over a black button on the floor the size of an orange. "Just step on this when you want the lift to come down."

The room was similar to our old training facility. A thin mat covered the floor and the weapons were mounted on the walls.

"I hope there's a bathroom down here because if I have to go through a bunch of secret doors and lifts to pee, it's going to be a tight race to the finish line."

We crossed the room and I opened the only door visible. It was a hallway similar to the one upstairs with the mirror at the end and wood flooring. Beautiful round lamps with delicate etchings lined the walls between four doors. The first room was the bathroom and the library or office was across from it. I recognized some of the books, but it lacked a fireplace and a desk filled up space by the far wall.

The last door on the right contained a modern bed with a wide mattress, dark wood siding, and a low headboard. Hurricane lamps sat on a few tables and sconces lined the walls.

"That better be your room," I said, glaring at the candles.

He walked behind me and opened the opposite door. "I think you'll find these accommodations more suitable."

When the door swung open, my breath caught. It looked like someone had painted a forest on the walls with soft colors. Track lighting gave the room dimension and a visual illusion of realism. Justus had even taken the time to buy plants, although I couldn't tell if they were real or fake. It was twice the size of his room.

Then there was the bed on our right. He didn't bring Goliath—my old bed. It was too big and I hated sleeping in it. Instead, a beautiful gold-and-green blanket was draped over a smaller bed that was the perfect size. An impressive rock wall climbed up to the ceiling behind the headboard. In the corner to the right—out of place—was my red chaise. My days of sleeping on that thing were over, I quietly decided.

Justus watched with uncertainty, scratching his bristly jaw. I wanted to reach out and hug him with the gratitude I felt, but he sensed it and stepped back with a handsome smile.

"It's so beautiful. I don't even know what to say," I gushed.

His cheeks became ruddy. "The house is unchanged from the way I left it—aside from the extra security measures. This was the only room that I…" Justus rubbed his shoulder and struggled with his words.

There were so many special touches that it far exceeded his endeavors in filling my closet with expensive outfits. On top of the nightstand, the small wolf that Finn had carved sat beside a bottle of expensive peach lotion. I rarely wore that brand anymore, mostly because I'd unconsciously been letting go of who I was as a human, and some things reminded me too much of that life. Justus had no need to verbalize his feelings for me; his words filled the room.

"There's a walkway back there," he said, pointing to the other side of the room. "It goes around to a closet behind the wall of your bed. I've already laundered your clothes and they're neatly folded and hung. We share a bathroom in the hall, so keep all of your personal items put away—especially those pink razors."

His nose wrinkled and I almost burst out laughing. I always left them in the shower and on the sink to reuse. We'd had a fight once because he said it was an insult for me to keep using a disposable item when he had the money to buy more. *Of course* he could afford it, but that wasn't the point.

I won the argument when I threatened to quit shaving.

"Join me in the workout room early tomorrow; you've slackened in your training. After seeing what you can do, we'll practice on some of your skills," he said, touching his belly where the sword had gone in. "Studies will continue afterward."

My life was in a perpetual state of transition, and I was beginning to look forward to the change instead of fearing it. Nothing is ever the end of the world; it's just the beginning of a new chapter.

"You may want to dress up. Guests will be arriving this evening and Logan called." Justus turned his back to leave.

"What did he say?"

He looked over his shoulder. "You were to keep your trip confidential, Learner."

"I *did*."

"Then why did he ask who Christian was?"

The word *shit* repeated in my brain about three hundred times after the door closed.

CHAPTER 23

I SAT WIDE-EYED BESIDE SIMON, GAWKING at the giant television in front of us. He leaned over and whispered, "I'm so buying a video game system for this thing."

"I'm so never moving out," I replied.

"Finish up with your eyegasm so we can eat," Christian yelled out.

"I'm so going to kill him," I grumbled, getting up.

I took a seat on the bench of the long dining table with the hammered finish. Justus claimed the chair to my right, facing the entrance. Candles illuminated the painting behind him and demanded everyone's attention. He'd invited Novis as a courtesy for giving us a place to stay; Adam declined the invitation.

Novis dragged the chair out on the opposite end from Justus and glanced at Simon, who was sitting across from me and plunking his finger in the wine glass.

"Where did you learn your table manners?" I turned my mouth to the side.

He leaned in and stuck out his long, pierced tongue, lapping the wine from his glass like a dog. Justus slapped him on the back of the head and some of the wine dribbled on the table. Normally Justus wouldn't have cared about Simon's flippant behavior, but a Council member was present.

"Haven't had a meal in over a year; pass the potatoes," Christian said in a deep voice, sliding to my left.

"Who invited you?" I murmured.

"Your man did a knockout job, Novis." Justus raised his glass, offering his appreciation for the extra security.

"We'll get Silver set up in the system later tonight. Everything is switched on and you'll need to do periodic tests to ensure that the equipment is running efficiently," Novis said, slicing into the seasoned pork chop.

"No need to test it out," Justus replied. "Logan will be here shortly and I think we will have our first test run." The two of them laughed and Novis almost snorted.

My fork hit the plate. "What do you mean by that?"

I literally flew out of my seat and fell on the floor when a piercing alarm shrieked across the house. "What is that?"

"Logan," Justus replied, wiping the corners of his mouth with a cloth napkin. "Novis, we should get him before he wanders off into the traps."

"You'd better get him!" I yelled out. "And turn off the alarm!"

My legs were spread over the bench as I laid flat on my back. Christian peered over his shoulder. "That doesn't look very vanilla."

I speared him with my glare.

A second later, the alarm stopped screaming. "I'm going to hear that in my sleep," I groaned, pulling myself back up.

Using the tongs, I dropped some fresh salad onto my plate. Someone had made the radishes look like roses. "Does this house also come with a personal chef?"

"If you want to hire me, I'll draw up a contract," Simon replied cockily.

"You just got here thirty minutes ago."

"It's not rocket science to slice bread and use a microwave. Maybe one day I'll show Justus how to cook a proper steak." Simon laughed heartily. "I'm afraid the rest of us have to find talents to get *our* women into bed. Of course once they're there, I have other talents that keep them right where they are."

"Handcuffs hardly count," Christian said offhandedly.

"If you mean the ladies cuffing *me* to the bed so they can explore Hunt Island," he said, rubbing his chest, "...then point taken. These hands are capable of making any female climax by the mere brush of a pinky across her bare breast."

"I must have gone to the wrong island," I said with a private laugh.

The front door opened and the butterflies grew restless. I

wanted to snip off their wings because no matter how many times I saw Logan, he summoned those damn things like a spell.

Novis threw a leg over his chair with a silent grin and took a bite of his pork chop.

"Jiminy. That's some system you got there, Mage," Logan said from the hallway. I grew fond of some of the words he used that were often old-fashioned; it became one of his idiosyncrasies. Especially hearing it come out in his sultry, rich voice.

"Good thing you avoided the outer perimeter," Justus remarked, crossing the room to his chair. "A word to the wise: stay on the path."

When Logan entered the room, his fervent gaze fell on me and concealed layers of words that he would never say aloud in the company of men. *Then again, he just might.* His intoxicating stare sent a blush to my cheek.

He arrowed his gaze at Christian—the unfamiliar face in the room.

Better that I get it over with. "Logan, this is Christian Poe. Christian, that's Logan Cross."

Simon snorted. "If I introduced my penis to a vagina that magnificently, I'd never get laid."

I hurled a carrot at his head and it bounced into his cup. Novis released a short laugh and everyone settled in their seat.

Except for Logan.

When Logan was agitated with someone, he didn't narrow his eyes because he carried a gaze that could persecute and incarcerate a tough man's pride. They widened at Christian with a punishing stare and he leaned over the table, dilating his pupils into large orbs. Posturing among Breed was different from human men, and sometimes harder to pick up unless you knew better. Most people didn't look a Vampire in the eye—Simon certainly didn't—but Logan devoted his full attention to him, despite the risk.

The tension was electric when he crossed the room and stood behind me. Boyfriend or not—every Mage in that room perceived Logan as a dangerous enemy by the way they eyed him indirectly.

He brushed my hair away from the left side of my neck and bent over. "I think I'll skip dinner and go straight for dessert."

Logan stepped over the bench on my right and sat down.

In a span of ten minutes, I discussed the details of my trip to Texas. Logan only knew a fraction of the details and this was my chance to come clean with him. I left out the part where my mother denounced me as her child.

Dinner progressed to dessert and several cheesecakes slid around the table. A chocolate wedge sat on my plate and I picked at it with my fingers while Justus and Novis discussed the security system.

"So that was one night," Logan said. He cut the sharp knife into a cherry cheesecake and set the dessert on his plate while staring at Christian from across my shoulders. "What did you do with yourselves the rest of the time?"

That damn text message germinated in his mind like a virus. Logan wanted to know if the Vampire was competition, and his inability to scent Christian's emotions must have been maddening.

"I ran into Marco. We were in one of his bars without knowing it and I tried to get him to work with us."

Justus listened attentively with a frown that pressed a vertical line into his forehead. While I'd discussed the trip with him, I hadn't mentioned that part.

"My cover is blown; he knows who I am."

Justus twirled his gold ring between his fingers and stared at a candle impassively.

"I made an offer that we would help find his woman in exchange for information."

"You did what?" Justus said in a furious whisper.

"He wasn't receptive. Now that we've moved, I don't know if he could find us even if he changed his mind."

"Marco knows how to get in touch with me," Justus muttered. The disdain he harbored for his Creator colored his face scarlet.

"How long was that meeting?" Logan inquired.

"Why don't you just ask me what you really want to know?" I bit out sharply.

Simon shifted in his chair and cut in. "I'm hitting a dead end—pun intended—on my search. The higher up the list of names I go, the more tombstones I discover. I don't believe the ones I found were turned, but it's impossible to tell if they're really dead, or if it's a cover-up." His eyes floated up. "Unless the graves are empty."

"If I see you with a shovel, I'm calling the Enforcers," I said. "That's in bad taste."

"As is everything I do in life. Your point?"

Christian's hand floated over to my plate and picked up a crumb. "Let me sample your sweets," he muttered.

Logan caught his wrist and squeezed it until he dropped the piece. Christian made no move to retaliate, even though he was the stronger of the two.

"Do *not* take from *my* female's plate."

Not a breath stirred in that room as the admission was clear. Logan just announced in front of everyone present that I was more than just a girl he was courting.

"Fair enough, Chitah."

After dinner, Novis surprised us with a housewarming gift—his game system. Justus may have installed a television, but I had doubts that a satellite dish was on top of the garage. The entertainment system was perfect.

I curled up beside Logan on the sofa and talked about my stay with Novis. Despite his strained relationship with Adam, he listened with interest when I mentioned the change in his personality.

"We're less accepting than humans when it comes to physical deformities. They select a Mage based on his strength and other impressive qualities, so few exist with defects unless they acquired them as an immortal."

I needed a change in subject. "What happens when Finn shifts into his animal?"

Logan's laugh was a deep rumble. "The first time it happened, we almost killed each other, as you know."

"Cats and dogs?" I smiled warmly and watched the glint in his golden eyes.

"Something like that. We've established territories within the house whenever he's in wolf form. He shifts at will, but if he lets his temper get the best of him, then he'll shift uncontrollably."

I hadn't told Logan about Finn shifting at the theater and decided not to mention it. I didn't want one isolated incident to overshadow the fact that he was making a lot of progress.

"He told me once that when his wolf wants to come out, it feels like something scratching at the door. I've heard if they don't let the animal shift, then it tries to take over."

"Is that what it's like with you?"

Logan looked uneasy. "Sometimes I feel it coming and I can hold it back, but that's why they call it flipping a switch. Most of the time it happens and we can't stop it."

"But you can learn to control your emotions."

"Some emotions cannot be controlled," he muttered.

"Do you ever let Finn's wolf outside?"

"No," he replied, stretching his arm over the couch behind me. "Finn's wolf can't be trusted. Most Shifters have no memory outside of the first few minutes after it occurs. Wolves typically live in packs and become trained enough that they can roam free."

"Is he housebroken?"

"Remember the chair you so fondly loved?" he asked facetiously.

I threw my head back and laughed.

"The day he shits on my floor, I'm building him a doghouse."

"I'm really glad that you took him in, Logan. He deserves to have a good life and someone to call family. I liked him from the get-go and saw how much he wanted to connect with someone."

"Let's just hope his real family doesn't come calling."

Christian stood up. "I want to play."

Simon handed him the controller. I crossed my legs and absently placed my hand on Logan's thigh. He eased down in the seat, stretching out his legs. That one, subtle movement caused my hand to slide farther up his leg and his breathing grew heavier, but he said nothing.

Justus and Novis left the room in the middle of a conversation about one of the locks on the doors. Simon was rubbing his nose as if he were psyching himself up to watch a fight.

Boy, was he ever.

What happened next was so explosive it was like an accelerant on a fire. Christian managed to single-handedly strip down all civility in Logan with two simple words.

I glanced up at Logan. "Do you want to see my bedroom?"

His eyes never looked away from my hand and his lips parted as if to say something. I squeezed his leg and he let out a short groan and nodded.

The game started and Christian made a deliberate turn of his head so that he was looking at us over his shoulder. There was an odd sense of déjà vu and my brows knitted together.

"*Watch me.*"

Unexpectedly, my face flushed and I became aroused. I touched my hot cheek, unsure of what triggered such a reaction. The sensation that swam over me was erotic—a familiarity that I couldn't place and I scooted away from Logan and cupped my arms. Logan leaned forward and his nostrils flared.

Faint spotted patterns—the color of honey, cream, and desert sand—rippled across his skin. When his canines punched out, my eyes went wide.

"Logan, no!"

I locked my arms around his neck, feeling every muscle in his body flex.

"Christian, *get out*!"

Another man's name on my lips was the last thing Logan needed to hear. His switch flipped and he lunged.

With one shove, Christian sent us airborne and we hit the edge of the sofa. Logan's arm hit a small glass table and it smashed against the floor. He was about to take this five-star Justus hotel down to a one.

Logan's venom had no effect on a Vampire, but he still bared his teeth threateningly. Christian grabbed Logan's arm and twisted hard. The skin wrinkled around and Logan belted out a painful roar.

"Let go of him!" I shouted, afraid that he would break it.

Logan swung his other arm and it should have knocked Christian down, but it didn't.

It knocked me down.

The momentum caused me to lose my grip and I went spinning around like a drunken ballerina until I landed on my knees. Justus and Novis flashed in and stood warily by the door; one bite from Logan with all four fangs could kill a Mage. Novis took in the scene and stepped forward with an alarming confidence.

"Don't," I pleaded, uncertain what kind of power he might hold. Novis was a Creator, but it wasn't uncommon for a Mage to possess multiple gifts.

Justus came up from behind and hooked his hands beneath my arms to pull me out of the brawl.

"We can't leave him this way; someone's going to get hurt," I argued, pushing him away.

Justus squatted beside me with one hand on the floor and his eyes on Logan. "We have no time for you to tell him a story."

I grabbed a shard of glass from the broken table and cut my arm. A rivulet of blood trailed down to my elbow and Justus barked out, "Learner!"

I winked at him and he clenched his jaw.

Simon wasn't the only one with a flair for the dramatic. I doubled over like an actor in a play, allowing the blood to trickle down my arm.

"I'm hurt," I cried.

"Well played," Simon remarked from the sidelines.

Logan's predatory gaze lowered and one breath later, his eyes returned to normal.

"Show me your wounds," he said in an urgent voice. He dropped to his knees and turned my arm over to examine the cut. The slice was deliberate and he looked at the shard in my other hand. "I don't like trickery."

"And I don't like you smashing up my new house and spilling blood on the floor. What's this all about?"

He took hold of my other arm and lowered his voice. "Did that male put his hands on you?"

"Don't be ridiculous."

My honesty was a heavy perfume and his expression twisted when he looked at Christian. Something transpired between them and Logan rose to his feet. "Give her back her memory."

Guilt blanketed Christian's face and my jaw hung open. "What's he talking about?"

"Do as he says," Novis demanded, stepping forward with a hardened glare.

Christian walked stiffly to my side. "I was saving her the embarrassment and trouble with Justus," he mumbled. Christian fell to one knee and we locked eyes. I remembered him telling me to look deep for several frustrating minutes and then everything went away.

Everything except a memory of the hotel.

Marco had left a message for me to meet him. I went to get Christian and when he didn't answer, I slid the extra card-key through his door and opened it.

"Christian?"

Dim light filtered in through the heavy drapes, but it was too dark. I stepped cautiously inside of the room and froze, puzzled by what I saw. Christian's arms were raised and he was leaning against the wall with his bare ass to me. His hips rocked in slow, clockwise movements. It took a second to realize that someone was in front of him. A thin leg curved around his and greedy fingers locked around his neck.

"Something you need, Mage? I'm entertaining company at the moment." He didn't so much as pause in his hip swivels, but quickened them, and I heard someone beneath him moan softly.

"I have to talk to you. This is urgent."

"So is this." He punctuated his meaning with a thrust and a crooked smile as he continued to watch me over his shoulder.

In the darkness of the room, I felt my cheeks flush. "Marco left a message and wants to meet with me. It doesn't say what it's about, but I think I have a good idea. If you want to stay here then go ahead, do your thing."

"No," he said with an annoyed sigh. "Justus gave me specific instructions to watch over you." He paused and gave me a frustrated look. Slender fingers gripped his ass, leaving a shadow where the skin pinched in and he moaned. My heart quickened a beat.

"Finish what you're doing and uh… I'm going to call a cab," I said.

"Whatever you say, Mage."

My foot inched back.

"Just one thing?" He licked his lips. "I like your eyes on me," he said with smooth seduction. "I've never been watched before." He rocked faster and faster until I could hear the smacking of flesh against flesh and a woman's urgent cry.

"Watch me, Silver."

I didn't just hear the sex, but I felt the energy pour out from the human beneath him. His eyes never looked away. What held me there had nothing to do with Christian and everything to do with the energy that was dripping off them like honey. It was like something I'd never felt before, even amid the intense energy that pulsed in the clubs.

"I'm going alone," I said, forcing myself to turn away.

"Do not move," I heard him mutter.

Faster than I could track, Christian crossed the room and seized my wrist. "This isn't the time for solving mysteries, Nancy Drew. It's a setup."

I tugged my arm but he backed me into the wall. The last thing I remembered was Christian's liquid eyes.

With my memory intact, everyone got the short version because Christian was right—it *was* embarrassing. The fact that I stood there and *watched*? What the hell was wrong with me? Aside from that, I learned an important fact about myself: I wasn't completely immune to the gifts of other immortals. It was a naive assumption on my part.

"I didn't meet with Marco?"

Christian casually stood up. "Too dangerous to meet a Mage on his terms."

"What if he wanted to help us? What if—"

"Christian is right," Justus interrupted, rubbing his chin with two fingers. "It would have been a poor decision without knowing the reason you were summoned. Marco is a cunning and convincing man; I wouldn't trust him alone with you."

"Why did you erase my memory?" I snapped.

With a dramatic sigh, Christian fell into a leather chair. "To see if I could? You have a problem not doing what you're told and I don't enjoy spending my evenings guarding your door when I could be banging a stewardess. This way it saved you the embarrassment of remembering and I didn't have to worry about you wandering about."

"I thought that I was immune to your talents," I said to myself.

"It took a long time, lass. You're not immune, but it requires a lot of concentration and work on my part. It's safe to say that a passing suggestion or attempt to scrub your memory by another Vampire would not work. Unless he pinned you down and—"

Logan bent over the chair and studied him so fiercely that Christian shielded his face. "*No* such thing happened. I'm not a brute with the ladies."

I wagged my finger at him. "Don't you ever use your gifts on me without my consent, do you understand? Embarrassment I can handle."

"Amen to that," Simon remarked.

It made me realize just how conniving a Vampire could be and how vulnerable I was. Sunglasses were going on my shopping list.

Justus divided the room and stood between us, giving me his back. "I have respected you as a friend for many years, Christian. You gave me your word that you would look after her. A man doesn't have to take a woman to bed to violate their trust and you have crossed the line. If I ever find out that you've scrubbed my Learner again, I will sever our friendship. Yes, she would have defied you and tried slipping out of the hotel to meet up with Marco alone." Darkness swelled in his voice and he folded his arms. "But it gave you no right to impose your gifts on her. This is your only warning, and if you ever break my trust again, then I have a few barbed stakes that haven't been broken in. *Never* again. Are we clear?"

"Crystal."

While Justus walked Novis out, I gave Logan instructions on how to get into my bedroom. Simon stayed behind.

I put pressure on my cut until the bleeding stopped and all that remained was a raw wound. It wasn't necessary to borrow light for something so superficial when I would heal naturally—faster than a human and without scarring.

"Vampires are limey bastards and always have an agenda." Simon kicked a few shards of glass. "Go easy on Logan; I admire the hell out of him for trying to take the Vamp on with his bare hands." Simon laughed and lifted a small wastebasket to clean up the mess.

"Look at the table," I said with disgust.

"It's not as bad as all that. Pillow stuffing is everywhere and a few chairs are turned over—nothing that can't be righted. And the table was an atrocious addition to the ensemble anyhow, so I totally approve of its demolition." He kicked the leg of the fallen table and a few pieces of glass clinked on the floor. I'll have this place spotless in two shakes. Go pet your cat."

As I left the room, I gently placed my hand on Simon's shoulder. "Beneath your sexual arrogance lies a really nice guy. I hope you know that."

CHAPTER 24

LOGAN STRETCHED ACROSS MY BED with his arms folded behind his neck. I admired them, particularly where the muscle popped at the bicep. His Adam's apple undulated as if it had something to say, but he was merely swallowing. A grim expression darkened his features and he looked at me sideways.

"Did I ruin my chances with you?"

My fingers made a soft sound as I ran them along the blanket. "I'm beginning to understand your traits as a Chitah, but as a man, you have an explosive temper. Obviously you can't control it when your switch is flipped, but you need to avoid getting to the point where that happens." I smoothed my hand over his arm and he turned his head to look at me, lips slightly parted. Logan was extremely responsive whenever I touched him because I didn't initiate touch as much as his Chitah companions clearly did. "Thanks for stepping back when I needed that moment with Christian."

"You can fight your own battles," he said, rubbing his forehead. "I have more respect for your Ghuardian after tonight. That was the right thing for him to do—standing up against a friend in your defense. But if any man ever hurts you I'll put him six feet under."

I pinched his nostrils. "You're slacking, Mr. Cross. Aren't you able to smell my innocence?"

His brow quirked. "Arousal mingled with confusion and fear?"

I hadn't thought about it that way, but Logan could pick up a whole flavor of emotions and that one must have set off alarms.

"Learn to control your anger before it controls you," I said.

"I've always been in control of it, but I'm not sure that it's possible to stop myself from reacting where you're concerned."

"What you sensed back there was a misunderstanding, but it

makes me wonder. What would happen if I *was* with another man? Is that the deal breaker with us?"

His eyes closed.

"You could meet someone Logan; your kindred spirit may be out there."

"You *are* my kindred." He sat up and tilted his head to the side. "What makes you so sure?"

Logan cupped my face with his rough hand. "Because I know it in my bones. You are the only female I desire, the only water that will quench my thirst, the only sun that will warm my skin, the only lips that were made for mine."

His thumb brushed over my mouth, parting my lips, and I jerked my head back.

"The feelings can't be real, Logan. I'm a Mage, and maybe it's exciting because it's so taboo. If you thought I was your kindred spirit, then why hide it?"

His finger hooked around my belt loop. "I didn't understand it; as you said, you're a Mage. I thought I was…"

"Finish."

"Being punished. But not like that," he said quickly. "I've spent my life hunting and killing your kind. I thought no goodness could be salvaged in a Mage because you had no family, no ethics, and no sense of decency if the progeny you created were made out of necessity to strengthen your Creator and not out of love. When you discovered the box, everything made sense. Our blood must be in your veins."

"My mother was human. That's a fact. Grady was probably my father, or at least put his spark in a human's sperm." I groaned, thinking about the possibilities.

He took two sharp breaths. "Tell me what's really wrong."

"I want reassurance. Our relationship has to be a choice and I don't want to feel threatened or pressured into making a decision. Does that make sense?"

He shook his head.

"What kind of man will you become if I deny you? So enraged by jealousy that you would turn to violent measures? Would I have to look over my shoulder in fear that you might attack any man I'm seeing? Would you become like Tarek and—"

"*Never!*" Rage made every cord of muscle stand out.

"But how do you know?" I wrung my hands together as we looked at each other.

Logan softly stroked my wrist with his index finger. "The only way I could lay an unwanted finger on you is if someone cut it from my hand. I've claimed you as my kindred spirit, but I still have to win you, Silver. It's not a done deal until you accept."

"Does this mean that any man who wants to date me has to challenge you to the death? I can't live like that. These aren't my customs and I need you to trust and respect me enough to keep that temper under control. I don't want to always be looking over my shoulder to make sure my boyfriend isn't taking down the waiter for winking at me in hopes of getting a padded tip."

Logan gave me a wolfish grin.

"What?"

"I've never been called that before. It's not a term we use—boyfriend."

"What would you rather be called?"

He tilted his head to the side and a lock of hair slid in front of his nose. "Lover."

His word wasn't a suggestion—it was an invitation.

"The challenge to court must be mutual between both males. Tarek was seeing Katrina in secret when I met her. I made my intent public and sought her father's permission. When Katrina chose me, Tarek did not throw down a challenge."

"So she was allowed to date around? I'm just saying that's a heavy load to place on me so young. It feels like you're telling me that I'm your destiny and I'll never date another man again. You have no idea how messed up I am when it comes to relationships. On second thought, you might have an idea, and whenever your temper explodes like that, it reminds me of him."

Logan winced as if I had slapped him. He brushed a strand of my hair to the side and leaned in. "Tell me, then. What did he do?"

"I thought he told you while you were removing his manhood?"

Logan didn't laugh. "Females are not abused in our families. When a girl is born, her brothers will devote their lives protecting her and live in the same house until she's mated. A brother would turn on his own for striking his flesh and blood, and any male that dares hit a female will suffer heavy consequences. It's something we don't turn a blind eye to, like some of the races."

With the tip of his finger, Logan Cross lifted my chin so that our eyes met. "So tell me, female, what did he do?"

"He was jealous of everyone I talked to."

Logan's eyes filled with understanding—that my apprehension over his behavior was not unwarranted.

"Most of it was verbal abuse and honestly—I just thought that's the way things were in a normal relationship. Brandon was insecure, but it wasn't like that when we first met. Not that he was Mr. Sensitive and bought me candy, but he seemed like a good guy. I trusted him, and things went downhill when we moved in together. People change, or maybe they just don't show you who they really are until it matters." I'd spent a long time trying to forget my past. Funny how that works, because your past never forgets you. "I didn't put up with... He slapped me."

A muscle in his face twitched. "What did the police do?"

I shook my head. "For a minor infraction?"

"I would hardly call striking a female... minor." A suppressed growl sounded in his chest.

Logan was right, but law enforcement in that small town often turned a blind eye or expected you to kiss and make up. "Brandon had buttons that I tried not to push. You know how I am with my mouth."

"And this is the world you miss," he muttered. "That's not all. Tell me the rest."

I swallowed hard, because the last time I told anyone the story, it was over a pint of ice cream in Sunny's living room.

I averted my eyes and my hands played with the end of my shirt. "One night we had an argument that escalated, and I threatened to leave. I got so mad that my hand started slamming on all his buttons. I might have just shut myself up in the bedroom if he hadn't thrown Max across the room. That scared me, because he'd never done anything like that to Max and it was like a light went on in his eyes when he realized another way to get at me. He blocked the door and I just wanted him to move. So I made up a lie of infidelity. What man wants a woman who betrayed him? It's the only thing I could think of that would make him let go of me, but it didn't have the reaction I had hoped for."

Logan threw his legs onto the floor and paced around the room like a caged animal. "I don't know if I can hear this."

"Can't control your temper?"

Without slowing his pace, he backed me into the bed and flattened me out on top of the mattress. I was caged beneath his body and his hair showered down like a veil of secrecy. The blood rushed to his face as he looked at me with pensive eyes. "Finish. You have my *full* attention."

The lump in my throat expanded. "He punched me in the side and broke my rib."

After a quiet moment, Logan lifted my shirt and marked my ribs with a soulful kiss.

"I don't measure up to the Chitah women you've bragged about. I don't know why you treat me so—"

He cut me off with a soft touch of his fingers to my mouth and lifted his head. "What you lack in height, you make up for in character. Your lips are the softest I've ever known and the smell of your skin…"

The soft scratch of his jaw against my side created a ripple of light in still waters. Never before had I been seduced by compassion.

"You can't expect me to behave like a kept woman. Can I live my life and make my own decisions? I'm sure that you want reassurance that whatever choice I make is without pressure or a shred of doubt."

"Are you asking my permission to see other men?" He sat up, straddling me.

That's not what I was asking, but it pretty much boiled down to that. The freedom of choice without retaliation was crucial, and this had nothing to do with my desire to see other men.

"I don't want to feel like my life is an arranged marriage because of your claim; I want to have a choice."

He twisted around and faced the door. "Of course you have a choice in this; you're the *only* one who has a choice."

"Don't give me that," I said, hopping off the bed. "What *were* you doing at the Gathering anyhow? Just enjoying a few drinks?" He averted his eyes and I folded my arms. "Leo told me that you would be willing to settle with another mate."

"Levi asked me to join him and I obliged."

"Your outburst at the table?"

"You weren't exactly in control of your temper either, my sweet."

Point to Logan.

"I can't trust a man who isn't in full control of his rage."

"I am," he assured me.

I stepped forward purposefully. "And I'll challenge you to that. If I have to sit in front of you and make out with Simon to test that control, I will." All jokes aside, my concern was that Logan was the kind of man who would rather shed blood than tears.

Logan hooked his arm around my waist and jerked me toward him. He growled, deep and low in his chest.

"Jealous?" I asked.

His eyes settled on mine and were full of fire. "Immensely."

"I was never coddled as a child and it's been a difficult transition to be put in situations where I have to learn to trust others and accept help. Especially when people I loved broke that trust. I'm stubborn and I'll be the first to admit it, but it's with good reason. I'm sure it's a stretch from some of those needy sluts that were pawing all over you at the Gathering and probably have been for your entire life."

He pressed his lips against the base of my throat. "You're a spitfire. Those females want me for my family name, or they're sizing me up because I would produce strong boys." His lips traveled to that place below my ear that had me trembling when I felt the stroke of his tongue.

"I hope you know that I'm serious," I reminded him, breathless.

He groaned, and feeling that vibration against my neck

awakened tingles in my body.

"Good enough," I said in a raspy voice. "Now tell me what *you* want from *me*."

His eyes pulsed with amber fire as he carefully considered his answer. "All of you all over me."

My hands threaded through his hair so that I could admire his cheekbones, strong nose, and hungry mouth. "I'm serious," I said, tugging his hair.

So were his fingers that found their way up my shirt, his thumbs circling tenderly over my silky bra.

I stepped back, catching my breath before he stole it. "I want us to be able to talk to each other this way—honestly."

"You're serious about what I want from you?" Logan rose to his feet and cupped his hand around the back of my neck. "I'll tell you what I want. It's important for you to know that I come from a highly ranked family. Do you know the reason those females are throwing themselves at me? You could equate my family to princes within our territory—if I had to give the human equivalent. The top-ranking families are treated as such, which is why so many have turned a blind eye to my past deeds. The pecking order has to do with history, strength, and alliances. Money has little influence in determining social status. I love your strong will, but when you demean me in front of others, it pricks my pride. I want you to be proud to stand by my side, as I am by yours. And yes, for as long as it takes, I do not want your acceptance unless you're sure that I am your life mate. I want you to..." His words drifted off.

"What?"

He sat on the bed and clasped his fingers together.

"Logan, tell me the truth. I also want you to agree not to maul anyone behind my back for my honor. Is that a deal?"

"Deal. No lies. No going away on secret missions like you did this week without telling me," he said, skidding his eyes to mine.

"I'm sorry that you couldn't know the truth, but it wasn't my call. It was just a matter of my security and—"

"And you not trusting me. Did you think I was going to leap on a plane and lead Nero's trackers to you? Have a little faith." He tugged at my jeans, pulling me between his open legs. It was just a slight shift of our bodies, but the air between us grew heavy and hot.

"So you aren't jealous about what happened with Christian?"

"A female is a sexual creature and I've been around long enough to know about needs." The button popped free from my jeans, and his fingernail scraped along the zipper.

"What are you thinking?" I asked.

His hands wrapped around my hips and slid down my thighs—mimicking the feel of jeans sliding off. "Sometimes, Silver, I want you to let me wear the pants."

"Justus is upstairs," I warned.

His laugh sounded more like a purr. When he tried to lift my shirt, I crossed my arms.

"Why do you act so timid around me? Female, I *know* your body."

My shoulders lifted.

He traced his nose along the line of my jaw. "Remember I once said that I enjoy a slow seduction?" He smiled, drunk with my fragrance. "Lay with me."

Familiar words I once heard before. Logan's seduction had lasted longer than any I'd known, making each private moment between us burn hotter than the next. It was so gradual that it smoldered into combustible matter. But his request wasn't for pleasure. Logan wanted to talk.

He removed his shirt and with a flick of the wrist, it was on the floor. I crawled over the bed and slid up beside him, nuzzling into the crook of his arm. With each shallow breath, I privately enjoyed his natural scent.

"I love this room," I said, admiring the soft lighting and natural colors. "Justus did an amazing job."

"Not close enough," he murmured, and suddenly pulled me on top of him. Logan was smooth and hard all at once—the feel of his body beneath mine made me relax.

"Tell me what happened with your mother. There was a change in your scent when you brought her up at the table, but no one picked up on it. I did—and I want to know what happened."

As resilient as I'd been from the tragedies of my life, this was one that proved to be the hardest to overcome. My life. My beginning. From inception, I was nothing but a pawn. My cheek rested against his neck and his short stubble tickled my nose.

"Tell me what pains you."

"She doesn't love me; she never did."

Logan shifted on his side and I rolled off. I'd started to get up when he pulled me back down. We were face to face and he searched my eyes. "Don't run from me. Is this true?"

"She called me unnatural and admitted that she never wanted children. She's glad that I'm dead."

"Where is your other family?"

"There's no one else that I know of. Mom hooked up with this guy that we think was a Mage and he offered her an exciting life. Who could blame her for packing up and going to Europe? Well, he was just using her. I guess she was an easy target without family because no one would miss her. They started doing tests or experiments of some kind and he left her with the doctors. That's how I was conceived. The only reason that she kept me was out of fear that he might return, and I would be something to barter for her life or freedom. She knew something was different about him and that's what made her afraid. I don't know. I don't care."

"That explains it," Logan muttered.

"Explains what?"

He traced his finger high on my cheekbone. "Why you push people away."

"Don't psychoanalyze me!" I protested, struggling to run, but his leg pinned against mine and he held me down.

"It has nothing to do with the male who hurt you—it has nothing to do with men. You fight it so hard and you don't even know why."

He blinked softly and I began to listen.

"You grew up without the love of a parent or a sibling to protect and care for you as family should." As he said this, his cheek nuzzled against mine. "You don't know the devotion and ultimate sacrifice that family can offer to those they cherish—to know the safety it brings and how that devotion is unbreakable. It frightens you to be anchored to someone because you don't know if they'll always be there."

There it was—the hollowness of my life. It's why I doubted Justus, because the only thing that tied him to me was legal obligation. I was spent, and my weary eyes closed.

"Silver, look at me."

I refused him without words.

He gripped my face angrily. "Look. At. Me."

How could I look at anyone in the eye again now that they all knew how my life began and how nothing about my place in this world made sense? The enormity of lies that made up my life had swallowed me whole.

"I have claim on you, and because of that my brothers are *your* brothers. That's why Leo spoke with you—to keep me from making a mistake. I know his position and he's not for the pairing, but he'll support us if you should choose me."

"They're *your* brothers, not mine."

His angered words heated my cheek. "Female, open your eyes or I'm going to get some toothpicks to widen your view and we're going to look at each other all night."

I involuntarily laughed and looked up.

"They are bound to you by my claim. You will know the love of family through my brothers."

"And what about Tarek's brothers; where were they to protect Katrina?"

"They disowned him for what he did to her and it stayed a family secret. She didn't want it made public and they respected her request. I made a vow to her that I would never challenge Tarek to the death for her honor; she didn't want me to die because of her."

"Sounds familiar," I said.

"We have a hierarchy, ruled by Lords. Tarek is in a position to become Lord of his Pride when there is an open challenge. As the eldest, he retains the right, as Leo does among our Pride."

"Are the Lords your fathers?"

"No. Each Pride has a group of families that are among the most respected, powerful, and strongest. Only the eldest can claim the title in an open challenge against others. The position is not automatically handed to the son of the Lord. Should he want the title, he'll have to challenge for it like everyone else."

Logan fell on his back and continued. "I must be honest with you," he said with a nervous shift in his voice.

There was a thoughtful stretch of silence and Logan rubbed the misery out of his face.

"My father worked for HALO. He was the one who betrayed the order. My brothers and I still believe that he was in the right; he made accusations of a financial scandal among important people without enough evidence. Nothing was ever proven and as a result, my father's good name was ruined."

Logan ran his hand several times up and down his bare chest as he stared at the ceiling. No doubt the Cross family suffered for the persecution of their father.

"Justus knew him?" I asked in disbelief.

"I never met Justus when all that transpired. Our father didn't discuss his business with HALO. We respect the organization because they're independent from any law and comprised of many Breeds. The Mageri was only recently formed in the past two hundred years or so and usually have their own agenda."

"Actually, they were around longer than that," I corrected, remembering the passages from the books I studied. "But they didn't have as much control because we were too spread out. That's when they formed the Councils."

"Forgive me if I don't find your government impressive."

"So you've got a bunch of Lords a leaping?" I pinched him to lighten his mood. "Tell me more."

"We have one Overlord that rules all. It's not unlike your Mageri; you have your Councils for various territories and the Mageri is the highest authority. Except you have several making the decisions while we just have one. It's easier for us to trust one man than a group."

"What happens if you find out that your Lord is dirty but it can't be proven, or you don't trust him?"

"A Lord can only be challenged by his brothers while he's in position; it's the only way for the family to salvage their good name. Otherwise, by law we have to wait until the next challenge, which comes around every fifty years. That's why Tarek is screwed if he ever becomes Lord. He broke loyalty with his brothers and his reign would be short lived."

"Unless he killed them."

Logan slanted his eyes.

"Sorry, I'm not trying to be disrespectful," I said.

He sat up, staring at the pattern on the blanket beneath us.

"Logan, what's wrong?"

"Tarek's older brother died a few years ago. No one knows the details of the accident and the family has kept quiet about it."

The soft hush of the air-conditioning interrupted us. Logan curved his head around and regarded me with strict eyes. "What made you say that?"

"I caught a contagious disease from Simon called 'foot in mouth syndrome.' Disregard what I said because slander is not high on my priority list."

Now I knew how serious an unproven accusation was, given what happened to Logan's father.

"What is a Lord's wife called?"

Logan leaned over and tasted my neck with a languid kiss. "A *Lady*," he whispered, and his purring engine started up.

Firm lips grazed across my chin until they found my mouth. "I meant what I said," he whispered.

"About what?"

"Maybe it's time you stop wearing the pants in this relationship." His finger tugged at my zipper and his laugh was dark and devious.

CHAPTER 25

Novis sent invitations to his dinner party with a "plus one." Justus had filled my closet with exquisite dresses, but I wanted to pick out something for myself. This was a special night and while I was never comfortable wearing a dress, the occasion warranted a little fuss.

"You've been smiling all day," Logan said observantly from the driver's seat.

"Just in a good mood."

"I want to ravish you in that dress."

"That's the third time you've said that, Mr. Cross."

"Isn't that always the charm?"

The man who was courting me had purchased the dress, and he was proud of it. Yes, I had a credit card given to me by my Ghuardian, but Logan refused to let Justus pay. Maybe it was the way I ran my hands along the beautiful gowns on the rack, or the frown that followed when I flipped over the price tag, but he sensed the importance and insisted on treating.

The gown was sultry and the color of emeralds on a moonlit night. The fabric was delicate, and the dress had no sleeves and a daring neckline. Logan liked daring. In fact, he was in love with the dress the moment I walked out of the changing room covering my cleavage with my hands.

Something this elegant always seemed excessive, but sitting beside Logan, I felt beautiful.

Since the day I arrived in Cognito, I longed for purpose. This wasn't a paid position, but it was a step toward independence as a Mage. Most were centuries old and to them I was just a child. Older generations have a bad habit of holding onto prejudices and are the most resistant to change. Not all immortals were as progressive as the ones I saw in the movies.

One of the bobby pins tugged painfully at my hair, so I pulled it out and smiled at Logan. It wasn't often that I wore my hair up around him and he admired my shoulders to the point it made me nervous that he was staring so damn hard. Even during the drive, he reached up and stroked the curve of my neck beneath the hairline, causing me to shiver.

"Stunning choice, Silver," Novis complimented me when we arrived at his door. "It brings out the softness in your eyes."

Well, wasn't that the joke. I was anything but soft and we exchanged a humorous glance.

Logan bowed and I jumped when his hand snuck across my bare back. His fingers were cold and I glared at him.

"Join us in the open room for drinks." Novis stepped to the side and the warmth of his home took the chill off my arms.

Logan wore a light beige jacket and a white shirt. The man looked simply edible. I laughed when he showed up in a pair of punk-rock flat sneakers, but that was his signature style.

In the adjacent room, Justus anchored himself to a sofa with a curly blonde strapped to him like a weapon. Simon's date, on the other hand, deserved a slant of my mouth. She was tall, brunette, smothered in gold jewelry, and wore enough rouge to paint the town red—literally. Cheri sat demurely on the armrest of a white chair and Adam was nowhere in sight.

Simon's date slapped his chest with the back of her hand when she caught him gawking at me. He wasn't the only one, and Justus took on a ruddy coloring. Who could blame them? All they ever saw me wearing were jeans and sweats. I stifled a laugh when Justus introduced his companion. Her name was Honey—although I wondered if it was her stage name.

The carnivore hovering near Simon was clearly a woman who enjoyed a good cage match. Her name was Talia, and she spoke with a thick accent that sounded Transylvanian. She shredded my dress apart with her eyes the minute I set foot in the door.

Christian looked ready for a nap in a chair beside Justus. He twirled a sucker in his mouth with disinterest. He was a nondescript fellow with no distinct features—exactly the kind of person who could blend into a crowd. His facial hair was neatly groomed and shaped, and he'd combed back his brown hair for the occasion.

I drifted to a formal sitting chair and Logan took the long way around the room, keeping his eyes on Christian before taking a position behind my chair with his fingertips touching my bare shoulders.

"Does anyone know what this is about?" Justus asked quietly.

Simon cupped an elbow in his hand. "Elementary, my dear Watson. It appears that Novis has some news to share—celebratory news—which would explain the party *plus one*. The question is…" he pondered, tapping his finger against his chin, "who the fuss is over?"

"Maybe it's you. This is the first time I've seen a comb touch your hair since the Second World War," Justus remarked, polishing the face of his expensive gold watch.

Simon's date laughed wickedly and scrambled her fingers through his hair. He maneuvered to the window in an attempt to escape her. She must have been one of those trapeze artists in bed, but I could tell that Simon perceived her as intellectually inferior. Still, he was a man who liked the circus and enjoyed his cotton candy.

Novis waltzed in and reached for a glass of brandy.

"Gentleman and ladies, I have an announcement to make. No doubt you all wonder why you're here," he began as he found the end of the long table where liquor bottles glimmered in the light. Novis leaned on the edge and crossed his ankles while everyone watched him expectantly. "I've had a position open since the last individual was promoted. The Mageri contacted me earlier this week and disclosed the identity of the person they want to fill the role. As you know, Council members have little say in who they select. If a Councilman were corrupt, he would also bring in corrupt employees. The Mageri carefully reviews the candidates and makes their offer. Much to my surprise—and delight—it is someone that I know."

Everyone looked at Adam, who appeared in the entrance of the room.

Novis smirked, taking a delayed sip of his drink as he savored the anticipation.

"Bloody hell! The suspense is killing me," Simon exclaimed.

Novis finally set down the glass, wiped his finger around the rim, and stood up straight.

"I would like to officially announce and congratulate this individual who will be a fine addition as my apprentice, after having considered and accepted the offer." He pushed away from the table and cut through the center of the room. Everyone eyed one another, knowing that a position under a Council member was highly coveted.

Novis stopped in front of my chair and winked. "Silver, it will be a pleasure working with you."

There was an audible gasp in the room and my skin became feverishly hot.

"Novis," Justus cut in, leaning forward in his chair. "You might have consulted with me. I don't know that this is a wise decision. She's still a Learner."

Christian dropped his red candy in Justus's brandy glass and it clinked.

"I need not consult you in Mageri business, Justus. They are aware of her status. Most Learners are obedient and do not act impulsively—for good or bad. They would rather save their own life than risk it for others, because let's face it, that's the reason why most of them pursued immortality. She has caught their eye. The decision was not mine to make, so if you have any issues, then you'll have to go above me. Perhaps they felt I would be an adequate mentor so that her transition into our world would be smoother. With that being said, be cautious not to interfere with Mageri affairs." Novis pinched his chin with the tips of his fingers. "I expect you to give her the congratulations she is due; this is a cause for celebration, so let us eat and drink."

Tough crowd. I hugged my arms at the lack of enthusiasm, feeling suddenly underwhelmed and overdressed.

"Show your respect and commend this Mage," Logan demanded of all present. It was a command that pulled everyone out of his or her seat to reluctantly extend the courtesy.

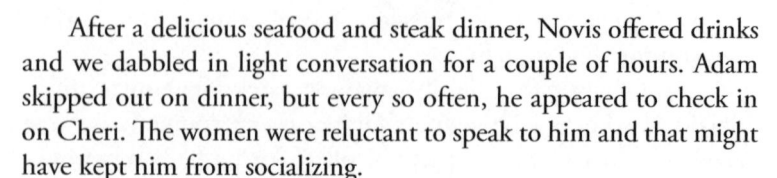

After a delicious seafood and steak dinner, Novis offered drinks and we dabbled in light conversation for a couple of hours. Adam skipped out on dinner, but every so often, he appeared to check in on Cheri. The women were reluctant to speak to him and that might have kept him from socializing.

I didn't much care for Talia—Simon's piranha—but I played nice and made an effort to remain polite.

When the men broke out the cigars, Cheri had a fit.

"Outside," she ordered, waving her hands through the cloud of smoke. "Men shouldn't ruin good upholstery with cigar smoke."

"Yes," Talia agreed. "I didn't pay a fortune for this perfume to leave here smelling like a dirty ashtray."

Simon kicked up his feet on the sofa while the men drifted out front.

I couldn't relate to their conversations about travel and the cost of gold. Talia was conceited, but Simon was too enamored by her plunging neckline and oiled-up breasts to care. Maybe I was a little jealous of how much she filled out her dress as I glanced down at my own assets. Not that they were small, but by no means were they my showcase item.

Honey appeared distraught. She rifled through her black purse for the third time.

"What are you looking for?" I asked.

"Darn. I forgot to bring my perfume. I think Justus likes it."

I sniffed out a laugh and shook my head. "You don't need any perfume, Honey. Just wear a rack of ribs around your neck and he's all yours."

Simon sprayed a mouthful of beer onto his pants. Talia rolled her eyes and made a scene about it. It was time for me to get away from this motley crew, so I excused myself to head upstairs.

Two paces up the steps, a melodic voice called out. "Silver, wait!" Cheri briskly made her way to the banister. "The guest bathroom is down here."

"I know. I just needed to stretch my legs and have a few minutes to myself." The women weren't really my crowd and listening to their cattiness was exhausting.

Her delicate pink nails curled around my forearm. "The toilet is broken," she whispered.

"Ohh." I laughed. "In that case, lead the way."

She led me to a small, pristine guest bathroom with ceramic floors. It was just a sink and a toilet and the only splash of color in the room was a painting of a magical forest.

All through dinner, Justus never spoke to me. Was he upset over the idea of me being an apprentice, or the fact that I hadn't told him? A conversation I hoped to rectify later that evening. The man was overbearing but endearing at times. I knew that he meant well, but Justus didn't have the best skills when it came to compromise. He once promised to make me a strong warrior, but I soon discovered that I didn't want to be a warrior. Just show me how to guard my light and allow me to have as much of a normal life as possible.

Normal. That word in itself described nothing about my life from conception.

At least I survived dinner.

A few of my bobby pins fell out and I carefully readjusted them, sliding the last one in. Suddenly, the lights shut off and I was engulfed in darkness as a scream rang out from the other room.

I turned the knob and when the door swung open, I ran into someone. Frozen with fear, I instinctively sharpened my light and held up my hands. Tiny sparks actually dripped from my fingertips, but all I saw before me was a shadow.

"Silver, it's me," Adam said. "I see you're all right."

My heart wandered up into my throat so I swallowed it back down. "What happened?"

"Stay in the house," he said, and walked away.

The first thing I heard when I shuffled into the sitting room was Talia.

"Oh for the love of God," she said in a thick accent. "Be a

man, Simon. Find a goddamn light."

"Bloody hell," I heard him mutter and then something hard cracked on the floor.

The lights flickered for a moment and then stayed on. Simon stood beside a broken piece of ancient pottery and a sense of normalcy returned. He glanced down and cursed under his breath. "That better not be worth my new car."

The front door burst open, hitting the wall with a thud. "Get the women downstairs," Justus barked rapidly. A flurry of men followed behind him.

Honey clutched her necklace. "Justus, what's wrong?"

Simon took Honey and Talia by the arms and hurried them across the house while yelling out, "Check if the alarm systems are disabled!"

Christian cupped my elbow and I pulled away. "Tell me you're not insinuating that I am one of *those* women that need to be tucked away in a basement? What the hell is going on?"

"Security breach," Justus announced.

Novis turned away, talking in a low voice on his cell phone.

"I thought this house was secure? Maybe it was just a power outage."

"Silver, go downstairs," Justus ordered while closing the drapes. "If the power was compromised then so was the security."

"I've got a thing about basements, if you recall. Those women aren't helpless humans. Why not let them stay up here if we have to fight?" I paced to the window on the left side of the door.

His fingers brushed over his short hair, making an abrasive, angry sound. "Mage women are not as… learned as you are."

I glanced over my shoulder. "They were never taught to defend themselves?"

"Women were never intended to be warriors," he said slowly, and I drew all kinds of conclusions from that statement. "That was never their purpose."

"Tell me you're not serious."

I never gave any deep thought to the history of some of the older women; I had assumed it was their choice to become a Mage and be equals. Now it was evident what they were choosing to become. Thousands of years ago, a Mage would have wanted strong progeny—warriors. Civilization was raw, and men fought over territories to protect their wealth. Naturally, Creators wanted brave and loyal men to serve them. Of course, that would not abate the desire to pair up with a woman to experience binding, which could only be shared with another Mage. That meant they had to make some women. Otherwise, it was a hands-off experience unless they decided to make out with a Vampire, which I'm sure was frowned upon in 1298 A.D. Given the rank of women on the Council, women's lib made it into the race eventually, but it couldn't erase the reason why these women were created in the first place.

Sex.

"That is seriously *pathetic*," I said, looking through the dark window. The guards flashed across the lawn as I caught sight of their flickering shadows. "Where's Logan?"

Novis looked up from his phone. "He's tracking."

I mentally sighed. If he had been social with a bunch of men puffing away on their cigars, then his sense of smell was likely impaired.

"Did anyone see anything unusual?" Justus inquired as he scanned the room.

"No, I was in the bathroom." The moment I said it, one of those dreadful chills swept over me.

Novis stood very close—his reflection ghostly in the glass. "What is it?" he whispered, watching my troubled face.

Shaking my head, I downplayed it. "Paranoia."

"Simon," Justus snapped. "Stay with the women. We may need to move them into the tunnels. Christian, come with me."

"Wait a bleeding minute, mate," Simon seethed. "Why don't *you* watch the women? If I have to spend another minute with that crazy hat, I'll personally see to it that—"

"Simon, *go*." My Ghuardian's voice unleashed a swell of anger and impatience. "Take Silver downstairs and lock the door behind you. Novis, where's your control room?"

"This way," he said, and they disappeared through the study.

Simon eyeballed me. There was no way he was going to get me down the stairs without a fight and we both knew it. "Stay in the house and sharpen your light," he said, pointing his finger.

When the door slammed, I began my ascent up the stairs.

"Where do you think you're off to?" Christian leaned on the banister with a sucker in his mouth. He hadn't eaten with us, but had politely sipped the wine. Upon closer examination, the level of the wine never decreased. His candy obsession was just peculiar for a grown man. Gum chewing I was used to—even smoking. But that man had a candy store in his pocket.

"Christian, go make yourself useful. A maniac could be running loose on the property—either join the men or play charades with the little girls in the basement."

His black eyes shimmered like liquid glass and he swiveled around, slamming the front door behind him for emphasis. I wondered if all Vampires were as bitchy as he was.

When I reached the first room in the hall, a picture of Adam and Cheri looked back at me from the dresser. I lifted the silver frame with the ivy etchings. Adam was handsome and smiling—all teeth. Not the kind of smile I saw on him often, but it was contagious and so genuine. I set the picture in its rightful place and returned to the hall, wondering if the reason they moved to the other wing when we stayed with them was because Cheri was a jealous control freak.

The dark hallway enveloped me like a cold blanket.

Novis had enough money to purchase the royal throne of England for his bathroom if he so wanted—bejeweled and gold-plated. Yet, he couldn't fix a broken toilet?

The bathroom door eased open. A heady fragrance of roses hit me as well as a strange feeling that I wasn't alone. Before I could react, a hand clamped around my wrist so painfully that I whimpered. From the inky darkness, a shadow emerged like honey pouring from a jar. His Vampire eyes were not charitable, his skin was smooth, and his expression was so chilling that his features were jarring. Nothing like Christian, because this guy truly looked like a monster from a movie.

"You won't remember me," he said in slow, threatening words. "Return downstairs because you don't want to know the pain I'll inflict on your bones if you choose to stay. Find Novis and tell him to come up here because it's safe."

Bastard thought he could wipe my memory. The blunt end of a handle stuck out from his hip. It was a sheathed dagger and probably a stunner.

"Would you like to go downstairs and get away from me?"

I nodded.

"Go."

What the hell killed a Vampire? Christian mentioned stakes worked the same as our daggers. I flashed to the end of the hall and lifted a wooden picture frame off the wall. Before I could smash it over my knee, he lunged. I panicked and ran into an adjacent room. Calling for help would have been as good as inviting Novis into a lion's den.

He strolled in and closed the door behind him.

"That's a pretty dress."

"I'll scream."

"Please do, it will save me the trip."

The windowpane iced the tips of my fingers.

"So," he said, tapping the knife in the palm of his hand, "why the fuck didn't you go downstairs like a good Mage?"

"I don't like doing what I'm told."

His black eyes lashed me with his disgust. I hadn't succumbed to his magic and he couldn't figure out why.

"I'll drop this knife in your chest and find out," he said, twirling it in his fingers. "Your friends are busy checking surveillance footage from what I can hear." He tapped the heavy blade against his lower teeth. "Head or chest? Head or chest," he contemplated.

"You could always stick it up your ass until you decide."

That inserted a fair amount of surprise on his face. Was it because I was a Mage or a woman? My fingers turned the latch on the window and he stalked forward.

"Going somewhere?"

The window slid up and a gust of wind blew in with the

drapery. Christian swung in the room and dropped his heavy shoes to the floor.

"Jaysus. I thought you'd never open the window," he grumbled as he approached the Vampire.

"What are you doing?" I hissed.

Christian turned to me and shrugged. "Making myself useful?"

"Why didn't you just break the window?"

"I didn't want to get billed for the glass. Novis would do it, too. Shall we continue this conversation later?"

A fight erupted between the Vampires faster than I could track, and I witnessed the raw power that made them feared. Christian threw the other Vamp against the wall and pieces of it broke away. I looked in horror at the handle of the dagger protruding from Christian's side, but he continued to fight.

The door swung open and hit the wall. Novis and Justus absorbed the scene before they darted past the Vampires to dismantle the bed.

The Vampire threw Christian across the room and demolished a table. They fell to the floor on my left, hammering each other with raging fists.

The Vampire twisted the knife and Christian grimaced.

A small piece of wood that broke apart from the table sat at my feet and I held it high. With a hard thrust, I drove it into the intruder's neck.

"Remind me never to piss you off," Christian muttered as he tossed the body off him. He pulled the knife out of his side and cleaned the blade on the Vampire's shirt. "Do me a favor, Justus, and don't ever lock that woman in a basement."

"How did he get in?" Justus wiped the sweat off his brow.

While Christian patted down the Vampire and spoke with Justus, I drifted into the hall and stood at the entrance to the bathroom. When the light flipped on, there was nothing out of the ordinary to see.

"Is this where you found him?" Novis asked.

"Yeah. And you can bet he wasn't using the facilities."

"None of the windows are broken and the alarms are still intact. I wonder how he managed to get inside," he pondered.

I gently pushed the cold, rectangle handle on the toilet. A whirlpool of water drained to the bottom and swirled the air—revitalizing the floral bouquet of rose perfume.

"Cheri."

CHAPTER 26

J USTUS HAULED THE VAMPIRE DOWN to the basement with Christian. My Ghuardian was not a man to mess around with, so I knew the interrogation wasn't going to be pretty.

Novis looked incredibly embarrassed. "Simon, please escort them home. Ladies, I apologize for the unflattering turn of events." He eased into a high chair in the lounge, watching the guests leave as Talia chewed off Simon's head in another language.

"Cheri, sit," Novis said in a hard voice.

Apprehensively, she complied, tucking in her white dress.

"I'm offering you one opportunity to clear your conscience, young Mage. Confess how the Vampire got in the house and I will be lenient with your punishment."

Adam appeared in the doorway and tossed a flashlight on a sofa. "No one else is in the house." His eyes darted between the three of us and he picked up on the tension in the room in addition to Cheri's frightened expression. "What the hell is going on, Novis?"

I cringed when Novis's face hardened with anger. Adam had crossed the line of respect by speaking in a derogatory manner to his Creator in front of others. I slipped on occasion with Justus, but maybe he was more forgiving about it because he was a Ghuardian and not my maker. Adam could hardly meet his gaze; but then, Adam hardly looked anyone in the eye anymore.

Novis turned his blue eyes back to Cheri. "I will only ask you once more."

"I don't know what you're talking about," she replied in a monotone voice.

Novis leaned back in his chair with smooth satisfaction on his face. "Now that I know you will openly lie to me, I will have no trouble removing you from my home. Effective this evening, you will be without the protection of an elder. This is your own doing and quite regretful as you could have chosen to come clean and live an honorable life."

"Novis, think of what you're doing," Adam urged. "Give her a chance to speak. Your questions are vague and she may not know what you're—"

"She knows," I interrupted. Adam's brown eyes burned me like fire and I winced.

The front door swung open and Logan filled the doorway. He took in a breath, attempting to uncover all the complicated layers of mixed emotions in the room. His jacket was gone and the white shirt was torn. In five easy strides, he crossed the room and was at my side.

"Are you hurt?"

"I found a Vampire hiding upstairs who tried to put a spell on me. He was armed with a stunner and they took him downstairs to torture him for a while."

Words I never thought I'd hear myself saying.

Logan growled inaudibly—the vibration rippled across my back when he pressed himself close.

"Cheri, what I'd really like to know is *how* did you get him inside?" Novis was blindsided by his extreme security measures being no match for one slip of a woman.

"Call Christian up here to ask her," I suggested.

Her eyes widened at the threat.

On cue, the basement door swung open. "We may need to borrow your fire pit later, Novis," Christian said in a jovial tone. "Someone help Justus get some answers from the fang while I work my magic on the damsel in distress."

Logan moved straight through the room like a match racing along sandpaper on the verge of igniting. The basement door slammed behind him and I shuddered.

Christian lifted a footstool and swung it around in front of Cheri. He took a seat and didn't seem to take notice that Adam was sharpening his light in vain as his fingers flexed.

"Let Christian question her," I said. Adam was reaching to take her hand and he glared at me. In that moment, he knew that I was the one leading the witch-hunt. "I'm not doing this to hurt you, Adam. But you need to see that she's lying to you and to everyone."

"How did the Vampire get in, Cheri?" Christian lightly held her small wrist and drew in her gaze. Within seconds, her expression went blank and the confession began.

Her entire story was a ruse. During captivity, Nero broke her will to resist. Cheri was weak in spirit, so he left her behind for a reason. After the raid, Nero got in touch and offered her a substantial amount of money to work as a spy. She helped plan the explosion by exposing the security weaknesses and left the house just in time to avoid any danger. The attack was a statement of protest against the Mageri. When Nero found out that Novis had taken us in, it pissed him off and he sent in a Vampire assassin.

Adam struggled with hearing the truth. Especially the part where she kept a guard distracted with a handjob while the Vampire slipped through the security checkpoint. *One soon-to-be-fired guard.*

The Vampire had already been hiding upstairs before anyone arrived. She warned the Vampire to remain quiet in the bathroom because Christian was invited. No one would have suspected that an assassin was in the house. So she created a diversion.

Circuit breakers? That's exactly what Cheri was. She placed her finger over a socket and reversed the electricity flow until it puffed out like a flame. That was a rare gift. She also confessed to meeting up with a couple of Nero's contacts in the previous weeks to relay information. Cheri mentioned Adam getting into a fight and jeopardizing her relationship with Nero. Adam gave a barely perceptible nod as if he understood something. Novis looked concerned, but after a few more questions, Adam was cleared of any involvement.

That bitch lied to me.

When Christian broke eye contact, she sprang to her feet and Adam caught her hand.

Cheri's lips peeled back into a snarl and she jerked her arm away. "Let go of me, you *freak*!"

Adam's neck turned a deep shade of blush. When his square jaw slackened and he angled away—I lost it.

Cheri moved gracefully in my direction and I slapped her so hard that the sting radiated up my wrist. She cupped her face in shock and flashed out the door. Novis made a call to the guards to detain her and it seemed that once again, incarceration would be in her future.

Adam's energy shifted and it scraped against my skin like an abrasive wire brush.

"Adam, wait. I didn't do this on purpose."

The same man who once held a warm tenderness in his eyes when he looked at me now held nothing but resentment. I had taken something away from him—hope that a good woman could love him for who he was.

"We're *done*," he said, cutting the air with his hand.

That short sentence demolished me. Adam left me torn in a million pieces by my own guilt. I may have had reservations about Cheri, but it was great to see him lavish his affections on another woman. From his perspective, I was out to sabotage his happiness. He stormed out of the room in one direction and I went the other.

I fled the scene and ran clumsily in my heels until I reached the tree. Gripping the rope, I hurled the swing violently at the trunk. Novis was a fair Creator, but I was appalled that he expected Adam to show up at this party and be social. Where was his empathy? Dirt covered the bottom of my dress and I cursed. It was too beautiful to be ruined.

"I hope you aren't crying; there's nothing duller than a woman who snivels all the time."

"Were you socialized as a child?"

Christian leaned against the tree, looking as relaxed as a cat in the midday sun. "You suspected her before tonight?"

"Yeah," I admitted. "Something she said rubbed me the wrong way."

He smirked. "Rub a cat the wrong way and the claws come out."

"Can I be alone?"

"Now that hurts my feelings."

The air between us stilled and an owl hooted in the distance. Christian peeled away a plastic wrapper from a butterscotch candy and tucked it inside his cheek. He wadded the wrapper into a tight ball and stuffed it in his pocket.

"Why didn't you eat dinner?"

"Not hungry," he replied.

"Are they spiked?" I learned firsthand that Sensors could spike candy with samples of emotions.

His black eyes studied me. "Remember I told you about the whole toilet experience we care to do without?"

"That's a topic I could do without."

"Suffice it to say our dinner the other night was lovely, but I won't be eating pork chops again any time soon."

I groaned in disgust.

"Novis wants us to meet with someone." Christian spoke as if he plucked it from the news headlines.

"Why do you say that?"

He tapped his finger to his ear. "I can hear them arguing, but I've only half been listening."

"So if I clap my hands really loud, that would hurt?"

"Afraid not. Amplified sounds are muted down; it's an internal self-defense mechanism. Feel free to give me a standing ovation, although most women do it after and not before."

"How did you get up to that window?" I looked up at the house and when I turned back to Christian, he was gone.

"Shadow walking, lass," he yelled from above. Christian stood on the lower branch and in the blink of an eye, he moved like liquid around the tree.

"What the hell?"

"As long as there is a shadow devoid of light, we can move through it for short distances. We are creatures of the night only because we have an advantage in the dark, but like your power, it has limitations and not everyone seems to have mastered it. I heard the Vampire blabbing on with you in the room. Good thing you were on the dark side of the house. He should have kept quiet; now my shirt is ruined."

"Don't do me any favors next time."

"Might I say that your social skills have been greatly exaggerated?"

"Not as exaggerated as your skills."

"This is a stupid idea," I complained.

"Are you questioning your new employer?" Christian mused.

I adjusted the vent in the car. "We were interrupted this evening by a killer for hire and now he wants me to be a messenger. Justus didn't look happy, either. Did you see the look on his face?" I squirmed in my seat.

"Hardly. I was too busy looking at that pet cat of yours with the big teeth."

Information had been extracted from the Vampire using torture techniques. He was to meet with his contact if the assassination against Novis was successful. The city park in Cognito was a breeding ground for sociopaths and rogues, so I wasn't thrilled when Novis asked me to deliver a message to the man paying off the Vampire.

"Considering your past with Nero, the message is better coming from you."

"No," I argued. "A guard should be doing this, not me. How did you get that Vampire to talk?"

"You can commend your boyfriend for that." His grin was toothy and he scratched at the bristles on his jaw. "That's a man with experience in the world I come from. Chitahs don't give empty threats and when he got out the kerosene, Justus had to stop him before he set the whole fecking house on fire."

I sharpened my senses when the car eased to a stop by a long row of hedges.

Christian cracked his window. "We're here," he said with disinterest.

"Do you hear anyone out there?"

"Aside from the murderer lurking in the bushes with the

machete? No."

I peered out the back window. "That's not funny," I murmured.

"What the blazes do you keep looking for?"

"You're not going to drive off and leave me here, are you?"

He tapped his fingers impatiently on the steering wheel.

"Hopefully this won't take long," I said, getting out. Christian slumped in his seat and I slammed the door.

It was my first official task working for Novis and it didn't take long for me to see the inherent dangers that came with the position. Novis had lent me a long, black coat and I flipped the hood over my face.

My heels clicked on the sidewalk and I opted against sitting on the damp, dirty park bench. Someone had spray-painted obscene graffiti on a statue of two children carrying flowers. What a shame. It could be such a beautiful park if they cleaned out all the riffraff.

It was going to be a relief when I got my assigned guard. Simon mentioned that he had trained a few of them himself, so that offered some comfort. But tonight I was on my own.

The black coat covered me from head to shoe. The only sound was a few random chirps from a listless bird who refused to bed for the night. A frosty chill tightened the air and everything glistened with a layer of midnight dew. Time slipped away as fifteen minutes elapsed.

Someone was running.

I whirled around just in time to dodge a wooden stake cutting through the air toward my heart. My hood fell back when I lifted my head and astonishment spread across Merc's face like oil paint on a canvas.

I always knew he was dirty, but working for Nero came out of left field.

Merc was a large man with a broad chest. His blond hair had that grungy look like it hadn't been washed in weeks. He looked like a misplaced rock star hooked on steroids.

"Traitor!" I spat.

His nose wrinkled. "If you are here, then Novis is still alive. Do you have a message for me?" he asked.

My fingers plucked the envelope from my deep pocket and he

reached for it with a loaded expression. Merc impatiently tore open the letter with his teeth. He scanned the message and wadded the paper into a ball, tossing it on the ground.

"Novis is a fool. Doesn't have a clue what's going on beneath his own nose. It'll make his death easier than I thought."

"How can you do this to one of your own?"

"His decisions hold too much weight, and he stands in the way of what I want. Nero is more than happy to take the credit for his death. Win-win." He punctuated the last two words, and the animosity he felt for Novis was unmistakable.

The minute Merc began his confession I knew that I wouldn't be leaving the park alive.

"The night of Samil's challenge you asked if I was a hybrid. What do you really know about me?"

His gazed lowered. "That you are an abomination."

The air chilled.

"If you're tangled with those people, then your hands are just as dirty as theirs," I said.

He lifted his hands as if to look at them in shock. "You're right!" His laugh made me want to drive my knee into his groin. "You are truly gifted at pointing out the obvious. Years ago, I had a notion to wage war against humans and joined their group. The original plan was to create a contagion that would spread among humans like a virus. After their repeated botch jobs, I could no longer fund them. It disgusts me that they continue making genetically unfit specimens like you when there's nothing to gain. They attempted to make a crossbreed that would spread Breed DNA with everyone they slept with. Can you imagine?" He laughed. "That would be my kind of slut. Then the idea was to make it transmittable by blood and they would contaminate the blood banks. The vision became clouded when their interest in the science took over the original purpose of war."

When Merc quieted, the wind raced through the trees and chilled my arms. His eyes were cold—a man without a heart or conscience.

"You know what you are, Silver? A monkey. Nothing more.

All of you should be euthanized."

"If you're so against them, then why don't you shut them all down? Or would raising hell in Europe draw suspicion?"

His brow arched. "Europe? That ended years ago. The project relocated and they monitored the children at first, but soon began dropping them off outside fire stations. It was becoming like a fucking daycare around there. Samil was packing up and probably going after that damn woman he became obsessed with."

"You knew Samil?"

"We worked together. They used him in some of their experiments because they had a theory that Creators could do some kind of special shit to DNA," he said, waving his hand. "None of us knew what they were really brewing in those labs."

"How did Samil get mixed up with Nero?"

"He was arrested for turning humans without permission from the Mageri."

"That's not a law, is it?"

His eyes narrowed. "No, it's a fucking courtesy. And when you have a Mage as old as he is suddenly making new Learners, it raises suspicion. Nero showed up out of nowhere and bailed him out. That man has an interesting way of appearing at just the right time, forcing you to be in his debt. Nero took a keen interest in the girl that Samil changed over and he paid good money for her. After that, we went our separate ways. Samil had a list of names and I *knew* what that arrogant fool was up to."

"Why are you helping Nero?"

"He's the wealthiest man I've ever met." A gleam flashed in his eye.

Merc had the ability to pull the core light and all power from a Mage—including their gifts—for a period of a day. If he found an Infuser and Nero paid him enough, I could only imagine what kind of power could be given to one man. I hoped that wasn't the reason why Nero was keeping Samil's progeny captive. Perhaps Nero knew nothing of Merc's gift.

"What did you do with Samil's light when you took it?" I asked cautiously, remembering the night of the challenge.

When Merc advanced, I backed up and he snatched the sleeve of my coat with a tight fist. "Did you really think I would let you go?"

The idea of him pulling out my core light petrified me and I struggled against him like an animal caught in a trap. My shoes flew off and Merc grabbed a chunk of my hair. He swung me around and I clawed him on the arm as he grabbed my collar with his other hand.

"Hold still, monkey," he growled, giving my head a violent shake.

Dizzy, I lost my balance and twisted out of the coat. I yelped from the sharp pain of my hair ripping out as I flew toward the ground. My forearms hit the cement and I looked back, noticing wavy strands of my black hair blowing from Merc's fist.

"I'm a hell of a lot stronger than you," he said, dropping to his knees. I flipped onto my back and Merc straddled me. He slammed my shoulders against the concrete and we fought. But it was my light he wanted, and the bones in my fingers pressed as he tried to pry my fists open with his strong hands. His body was so heavy and I struggled to breathe when he sat down on my chest, feeling the blood rush into my head.

He managed to get one palm open and Merc grabbed my chin with his left hand.

"I'll be sure to lay your body down on the hood of Justus's most prized car. What do you think?"

I scratched his face and drew blood. Merc bellowed and raised his arm to strike me with a closed fist. I could barely breathe with him sitting on my chest. Desperately, I clawed at his neck as his arm swung down.

In an instant, Merc was thrown off. I blinked at the canopy of dark tree branches above and sat up, looking down the length of my legs. Christian was sitting on Merc and plunged a stunner into his chest.

"You may be stronger than her, but I'm a hell of a lot stronger than *you*," Christian muttered.

Merc's chest became a makeshift chair as Christian pulled out his phone and sent a message.

"Is Novis coming to get him?" I asked, looking at my scraped elbows.

"Your Council is sending someone." Christian patted Merc's cheek. "Looks like you're in trouble, big boy." He pinched the wadded-up piece of paper from the ground and stuffed it into Merc's open mouth. "Never did like a litterbug."

I stood up and blew out a breath. "I'm outta here. Keep him company and try not to squash him. I've had enough drama for one evening."

CHAPTER 27

"Where do you think you're off to?" Christian yelled out.

My tattered dress dragged along the wet concrete and the chill nipped at my bare feet. With our testimonies, they had enough to arrest Merc, but I was uncertain what the Mageri would do when they got wind of the full story. It wouldn't be in their best interest to expose this kind of treachery among high-ranking officials. It would shake the confidence people had in their governing law.

"Silver, stop!"

Christian stomped across the grass, kicking up droplets of water behind his heels.

"Get back over there before he figures out how to remove that dagger!" I shouted, pointing my finger.

"Come with me. I can't let you leave alone."

"You don't have to *let* me do anything. I think I've had my fill of chauvinistic insight for one evening."

"I'm only asking you once more." His tone lowered.

"Don't threaten me, Christian. The only person who can legitimately bark orders at me is Justus. Watch Merc, because if he gets free then you're putting my employer's life in danger."

When I reached the car, I peered in the window to see if the keys were in the ignition. "Dammit!"

A loud crashing noise came from the hood and almost caused me to stumble on my ass. Christian stood on the car with his arms folded.

"That's Logan's car, and if you put a dent in it then he's going to put a dent in you."

He stared down his nose and spoke in a thick Irish accent. "You know, I don't care for your snobbery at all. You think you're better than I am and frankly, I'm sick of hearing you rabbit on. Always complaining, you can never just have a good time. Are you at least pleasant postcoital? Because at the rate you're going, you'll be lucky if that Chitah doesn't cannibalize you. Of course with that mess of hair on your head, he's likely to spit you back up."

Two headlights blinked at the end of the road and I felt the flare of a Mage.

"They're here," I said with disgust. "You're off the hook."

I lifted my eyes to the road—heavy with fog and illuminated by the umbrella of lights from old lampposts—leaving Christian behind. Little did he know how painful his comments were and little did he care. Here I was, walking barefoot in a ruined dress that Logan had paid a pretty penny for.

"You plan to walk barefoot across town?" Christian huffed as he jogged up to my side.

It was everything I could do to pretend he didn't exist. I wanted to slam my fists into a tree until they bled. This night should have been memorable in a way that didn't end in betrayal and bloodshed, because it marked a transition in my life as a Mage. It was hope that maybe Justus would see me as someone more than a student or a woman—but a Mage he could be proud of. Like everything else, it ended on a horrible note. Perhaps I was a walking catastrophe and doomed to fail at this life.

Christian hopped in front of me and began walking backward, keeping my unsteady pace.

"Are you angry?" He laughed in disbelief.

My hair tumbled out of the pins that had once held it beautifully together and he was right—it *did* look like a mess. I began ripping out the bobby pins and tossing them to the pavement. When I finished, he caught my wrist before I could flash away.

"Silver, I apologize."

"Then let go of me," I said in a hurt voice. "Novis is going to have a bodyguard assigned to me, so keep that in mind the next time you decide to grab my arm."

"It started the day you accepted his offer." He released my arm and mashed his cheek up and down with the palm of his hand. "I'm your personal guard."

"Novis wouldn't hire a Vampire to—"

"What's the matter, am I not up to snuff?" He made a sweeping arm gesture and cupped his hand over his heart. "I'm devastated."

"You can't protect a Mage, you're a *Vampire*."

"You keep saying this, but I've already come to your aid more than once. I'd say that I more than satisfy the job requirements."

"I'm going to ask him for someone else."

"You *do* that," he grumbled. "I'm not here for volunteer work."

"Could you refrain from speaking during the ride home? This was a special night for me. I don't expect you to understand; just don't speak."

He softly cursed as I returned to the car.

Halfway home, Christian pulled the car over by a newspaper stand in an empty parking lot and threw it in park.

He kept his eyes straight ahead. "I can see you're vexed by my words and for that, I'm sorry. This night was important to you. I don't want us to quarrel, not like this. I didn't mean what I said back there so put it out of your head. Novis is not going to hire someone else. Many years ago, I guarded Justus, and there is a trust between us. You have no obligation to speak to me and after tonight I'll remain in the shadows until Novis no longer requires my services. But have comfort in knowing that I will do my job and not meddle in your personal affairs. Your eyes have been hating me for the past half hour, but I can't change that."

He cracked the window and fished out a piece of peppermint from his pocket.

"We're not here to be bosom buddies, but I don't want you to doubt my ability to protect you, regardless if you make my blood boil and make me want to yank the hairs from my scalp one at a time. It is my personal belief that a good woman is a submissive one—I don't know how any man could let a headstrong woman rule his heart. You will have your privacy and I will keep my ears out of your personal life as much as I can without compromising my watch. I'm only asking if you'll accept me as your guard."

Outside the window, a small rabbit peered out from a tall cluster of weeds and hopped across the parking lot. The weight of my conscience came down on me with immeasurable force. I prepared to widen my throat for a nice dose of pride. Christian was right—this wasn't about friendship or playing nice. He was an employee and was always straightforward with me. Neither of us could back out of this situation, but we could at least come to a mutual agreement.

"I accept."

CHAPTER 28

I REDISCOVERED THE THRILL OF GOING out alone. You don't realize what a privilege it is when you can just run to the store or catch a movie without having to worry about your Ghuardian being in the mood.

And that man is *never* in the mood.

The Council had summoned me to give testimony against Merc. Novis advised that we keep the genetic breeding undisclosed, doubting that Merc would be anxious to admit his involvement. His betrayal of Novis and the Mageri was noted—punishment to be determined.

"This stuff is awful," I complained, twisting my mouth and shivering from the spicy rum. The flavor carried a thick perfume as it slid down and settled in my stomach with a burning heat. Still, it was nothing in comparison to the green swill served at the Red Door. It was a quaint little pub that Sunny picked out.

"Sorry," Sunny said apologetically. "I could have sworn you liked rum. Did Justus drop you off?"

"No. Logan lent me his car. He's out for the night playing pool with Levi and Finn. Don't tell Justus I'm here, either. He'd have a fit if he knew I was in a human bar."

She snorted. "Rebel." Sunny rested her chin on her fist and a couple of silver rings sparkled under the lamp. "Knox told me that you're in some kind of trouble, which is why we're under protection. I get it. This world freaks me out a little and I love you to bits, but I don't want to spend the rest of my life isolated in a cabin."

I turned my attention to the table next to ours where two elderly men were playing a round of cards. "I feel like shit about it too. There's a lot going on right now and I don't want to put you in any kind of danger, but being my friend does that inadvertently."

She poked a cube of ice in her glass. "I have Knox to look out for me now. We can't stay in hiding for the rest of our lives just because we're human. So, we talked about it and decided that we're coming out of the safe house. I have a life to get back to."

My eyes circled around her heart-shaped face.

"I'm not asking you, Silver. If anything happens to one of us, then it's not your fault. It's called life."

Easier said than believed.

"I'm so sorry," I mumbled.

"Will you stop saying that?" She flicked a finger in her glass and sent a spray of alcohol on my face. "If it wasn't for you I wouldn't have met Knox. My life changed for the better and I have more friends here. Life is too short to be worrying about the big *what if*."

"I never meant to put you in danger; I just didn't think that far ahead."

"Hmm," she pondered. "Are you going to tell me what's really bugging you? I know you better than that. Spill."

"Logan is getting serious. What if he turns out to be like—you know. What if it's a mistake?"

"There you go again with the *what ifs*." She lifted a straw from the table. "What if I shoved this up your nose?"

I tapped my finger on the edge of the glass. "Nero hired a Chitah to hunt me down and as it just so happens, he's an old archenemy of Logan's. He's using me as some kind of history lesson," I said, rubbing my eye. "Nero is ruining my life. I'd love to be able to get through the day without someone trying to kill me."

Sunny shook off her sweater jacket and folded it neatly on her lap. "What do you mean by using you?"

"He's playing mind games with Logan and tried to claim me as his…" I waved my hands. "…soul mate. It's a long story, but that's a big deal with Chitahs. He marked me at their Gathering and lied to his elders."

Her nose wrinkled. "Marked you? That sounds a little unsavory." Her tongue pushed out.

I laughed. "It's actually not that bad with the right guy."

"Are you saying Logan's the right guy?"

I tapped my finger on the cold glass, ignoring the twinkle that brightened her mischievous eyes. Sunny had an expressive face where not a single emotion could slip by unnoticed. When we first met, I stereotyped her. Maybe it was the dress with all the tiny cherries and the candy-red pumps, but I thought there was no way I was going to like her. We were young and she was the temp at my first office job. After a happy hour with coworkers, we'd been fast friends ever since.

"Anyhow," I continued, "this is all about a woman who came between them. Peril is a way of life for me now." I called the waitress over and ordered a beer.

"Why not get a restraining order?"

She held a small mirror in front of her face and dabbed on some peach-colored lip gloss. A man behind me wolf whistled and I snorted, giving her the look. Men were always falling at Sunny's feet like shooting stars racing to the horizon.

"Breed laws are black and white; there's no such thing as a restraining order. Logan called him out in front of their elders and thinks that he'll back down. I just don't know. I've got enough crap to worry about with Nero, among other things. My life has become so complicated. Remember when all I had to worry about was getting laid off at my job?" I sipped my beer. "Now I'm always looking over my shoulder, wondering what's next."

"Normal is boring," she said, rolling her azure eyes. "No one who ever did anything worth remembering lived a peaceful life."

"When did you get so philosophical?"

Sunny winked and pursed her lips. "I can be Confucius when I need to be. You didn't tell me what you're doing for Novis."

"Deviant, *sexual* things. He's got this outfit made of black latex—"

"Stop that!" she said with shocked eyes. I laughed at how easy she was to rile up.

"An apprenticeship means I'll be doing whatever he wants me to do, like a gofer. Although, I'm hoping the position will be a little more glamorous than that. I'll still live and train with Justus and… Oh, you have to come see the new house! It's beautiful and has electricity!" I gushed.

Her brows arched. "*That* is a step up."

We clinked glasses.

"I was very impressed. My room—I could live in there forever. It's going to be impossible to move out and leave that luxury behind."

"When will that be?"

"Don't hold your breath. You'll probably be a grandma by then."

"I'll have to check it out at your party." She smiled with her pearly whites.

"Really, do we need to do this? You know I don't like all that attention."

"It's your first birthday as a Mage so of course we're doing this. It's not every day you turn *one*. I'm so jealous that you're younger than I am. Maybe when you're a toddler, I'll buy you a tricycle." She gasped excitedly. "And when you're twelve, I can get you a training bra!"

"I need one now."

She snorted. "You have a lot more going on upstairs than you used to. What man wouldn't want a peek at those?" She reached across the table to touch. "Has Logan seen them yet?" I slapped her hand and censored my smile.

"I'll agree to the party as long as it's low-key. Lately my social functions have ended with me facing a blade, so I'm a little wary if you get my meaning."

"The only blade you'll see is the one cutting your cake, Silver. Not everything has to end in disaster, and if it does, then you need to rise up from the ashes like you always do."

I wanted to tell Sunny about my mother, but took another swallow of beer instead. Some things would have to wait.

"Don't worry about me," she said, wiping the condensation from her glass with a napkin. "We're going to be just fine."

"Just be aware of your surroundings. Don't talk to strangers, don't take candy from men in bars, and run if you see fangs. The usual."

Sunny's boisterous laugh attracted attention from the booth

adjacent to ours and she covered her mouth.

"Tell me all about Knox. You guys still doing good?"

"It's hard to explain. We just click and he gets me. I love the way we fit together physically—his body looks so hard but it's soft when he holds me. Kind of like his mouth; he sounds like a tough guy but he can melt my heart with his sweet talk. Oh, he quit smoking, so I decided to hit the gym and tone up."

"Don't be ridiculous; I'd kill for your body."

"Me too," a man to my right said. He and his friend clinked their beer bottles. I rolled my eyes and Sunny leaned in, lowering her voice.

"I had to hear the same thing from Knox. He's mad because he thinks I'm doing it for him. Then he listed everything about me he loved, in explicit detail… in front of the mirror," she said with a blush on her cheeks. "I can really see myself with him, Silver. He makes me happy and I didn't feel this with Marco. What a sleaze." Her smile turned south.

"It's hard to get an impression of Marco," I said, tearing the label from the bottle. "He's cocky as hell and I hate the way he strung you along, collecting all those humans with such indifference. He did all of that to free a woman he sold to Nero." I watched her eyes dart up to mine.

"Isn't that romantic? He used me like a dishrag and hurt all those people to atone for his sins by releasing one girl. Don't give him the benefit of the doubt, Silver. If I had never dated him, you'd still be human. Marco strung me along so he could pass you over to a man who would cut your throat." She blew out an angry breath, still blaming herself for what had happened to me. "Not the intellectual I took him for. I hope if he ever does find her that she'll see what a pig he is."

I tipped my beer in agreement and we listened to the rock music. Everything we talked about revolved around Breed. It was ironic that I spent time with those who weren't human and our conversations were about normal, everyday things.

I flared and tapped into the energy in the room, but only sensed humans. It was customary to flare around humans. Otherwise—by law—a Mage could legally kill you and claim self-defense. It wasn't easy to conceal entirely, because sometimes energy just leaked out. It was safer to play by the rules than take chances hiding.

We wasted an hour talking over a plate of nachos, making bets on when the first snow would come. Sunny remarked that surrounding cities were at least ten degrees hotter than Cognito, as if I had a problem with that. Cognito was truly a world of its own and a city that was becoming my home.

Once we said our goodbyes, I decided to kill some time before Justus checked his credit card account and discovered the frivolous charges I'd been racking up. Money was never an issue with him; it was *how* it was spent.

I loved walking the streets of Cognito with its hidden secrets. The buildings in most areas of town were old, and the city had the kind of grit that made it come alive. Streets pulsed with energy day and night. Humans mingled with us, unaware of our existence. Sometimes I wondered what they'd think if we all came out.

Most immortals preferred hanging out in places run by one of our own. The bars and restaurants were often membership only, allowing them to exclude humans. You could always tell a Breed-only establishment because walking by them was like standing beside a battery. There was a heightened charge that drew you in and felt like comfort food to my core light.

The exception was whenever I passed a group of men and sensed they weren't human. It was a dangerous city, and aside from juicers, some immortals felt like they ran the show.

But some didn't mind an open-door policy. A Mage named Victor owned the frozen-yogurt shop near the bar. He wasn't in it for the money; he just enjoyed interacting with people. I decided to swing by and plopped in a booth with a cup of strawberry frozen yogurt. A teenager was sassing up her friends at a nearby table and I listened while swirling the sprinkles and cream.

A finger plunged into the soppy cup and pulled up a scoop. Tarek stuck out his tongue to lick it up and the pink liquid ran down his hand as if it were trying to escape. I dragged my eyes upward and noticed his Mohawk made a few of the customers uncomfortable.

As if he didn't stand out enough among his own kind with the black hair I wondered why he went to the extreme with that kind of hairstyle. If it was to intimidate, then mission accomplished.

He sank his knee into the cheap vinyl seat to block my exit. "We're talking," he said, and shoved me against the window to sit. "He lies to you. Cross is keeping you around as a novelty. It's taboo for a Chitah to fuck a Mage, so naturally a lot of males want to dip their stick in a few sockets." He dipped his finger in the yogurt and swirled it. "Don't think that he'll choose you over one of our females. No matter what he tells you, we all have obligations to fulfill and that will always override a pair of open legs. You're holding onto something that you'll never have and in the end, you'd better ask yourself if it's worth it, because I can make your life miserable."

Tarek sucked the yogurt off his finger and wiped his hands on his pants. He wouldn't instigate a confrontation around humans, but if he was anything like Logan, he wasn't going to let this go. My palms began to sweat.

"Mmm, I love the smell of fear." Tarek jerked my chin to face him and put a kink in my neck. "What's the matter? Am I not your type?" he asked through clenched teeth.

"The box was destroyed."

Tarek dropped his arm on the back of the seat and I slid closer to the window.

"I'll bet you know what was inside of it."

"You're wasting your time." I wiped my clammy hands on my jeans.

He sampled the air, swirling his fingers as if catching a scent in the dramatic. "You *lie*."

A man in a long black trench coat moved like a shadow across the room. He sat down at a table with a cup of dessert and lifted his black eyes to meet mine. Christian's expression was stone as he listened to every word.

"What is Nero offering you that could be worth turning your back on your own kind?" I dared to look Tarek in the eye and blinked as if he'd scorched my retinas. The gaze of a Chitah was wholly terrifying. "I guess it shouldn't be that hard, considering you turned your back on your brothers."

Tarek yanked my hair back so hard that a splinter of pain radiated across my scalp. I winced as he kept his hold, exposing my neck right along with two of his fangs. I raised two fingers to the table, signaling Christian to stand down.

Tarek retracted his canines before someone stole a glimpse. "Give the Mage what he wants—last chance." The last two words dripped from his tongue like molasses—slow and thick.

"We're going to catch him eventually, Tarek. I'm not giving that man an ounce of anything."

He kissed my cheek. "You just introduced yourself to the biggest mistake of your worthless life."

CHAPTER 29

"THERE WILL BE NO MORE gallivanting across town if that Chitah is following you," Justus said.

He knew the word "gallivanting" irritated me, because it insinuated that I was being promiscuous. Women were his recreation, and I could always tell whenever he hooked up with one because he became grumpy for the next few days. Funny, as usually that had the opposite effect on most people.

I stared at the screens on the wall, absently flipping through images until it stopped on a snowy backdrop. "I don't *gallivant*."

"You know what I mean," he rumbled from his leather chair.

"Novis has a guard on me."

Justus leaned forward. There was a musky smell of sweat in the air as he'd just finished his workout. His neck and cheeks were red, and as he lifted his shirt to wipe the sweat from his face, the payoff of his hard work was evident. He was a fit man with solid abs.

I'd told him about Tarek while he was lifting weights, hoping that he'd finish his workout and burn off some of that "pissed off" that he carried in his pocket like spare change.

No such luck. He followed me right upstairs.

"Do you ever regret taking me in?"

Justus lifted his head and light sparked in his cobalt eyes like fireflies. A crease formed in the center of his brow, but he didn't answer.

"You helped me from the beginning for reasons I'll never understand because, let's face it, you're not the most nurturing person," I said with a short laugh. He shook his head, staring at his shoes. "Maybe it's that nobility that compels you to do the right thing. I wasn't afraid of you when we met because any man who takes such care in removing a stain from a woman's blouse can't be malicious. You have something else besides charm, and that's integrity. It's like an aura that shines around you."

The red color on his neck deepened.

"But you're not beholden to me, and I know what you've said about me to others."

"You're young," he said, rubbing his scalp. "It's my job to make you a better Mage."

"Someday I'm going to change how you feel about me, Mr. De Gradi. You just don't know it yet."

I couldn't read his expression because he was looking down, but I could have sworn I saw him smile. "You have much to prove, Learner."

"Maybe it's true that trouble follows me; look what happened to your peaceful life… *and* your cars."

I fidgeted with the mood ring on my finger. I caught him looking at it from time to time even though it was just a cheap novelty trinket.

"Enough with the cars. I am not a Ghuardian who toils over the destruction of property when your safety is my priority."

Justus sat up and smoothed a hand over his head. I could see the dark blond hinting he was overdue for a shave. There was so much that I wanted to know about him. Where did he get his tattoos, and why did he acquire them? Did he remember much about his childhood? How many women had he slept with? No, on second thought, maybe I didn't need to know it all.

My thoughts drifted to Adam. "How can a salve make scarring permanent? Why haven't they found anything to counter liquid fire?"

"Liquid fire has unique properties no one understands." He lifted a short crystal glass from the end table and swirled the last few drops. "Err on the side of caution when mentioning someone's tattoo, as the liquid fire is what seals it. In these modern times, humans ink themselves up with trivial images that hold little meaning. Marking your body should symbolize something of great importance. Unfortunately for some, it's not one received by choice. Simon's mark is a brand—one given to serve as a reminder of who he belongs to."

"But not yours. That looks pretty modern."

He twisted his right arm around and gripped his elbow. "This is three hundred years old. It's not something I got on a whim."

"But it looks so fresh, not faded. You're how old?"

My mother never shared her past, so I'd grown accustomed to not asking questions. Justus would steer the conversation in another direction, so I'd given up on personal questions months ago.

"I was made when I was roughly twenty-seven, which is a guess as several hundred years have passed since I was human. I don't think about that life anymore."

"You're only *twenty-seven*? Are you *serious*? Don't take this the wrong way, but I would have guessed you were thirty-five."

"I lived a hard life."

"How did you meet Marco?"

"During one of the Italian wars. My father was French and I fought to honor him. We advanced in the Alps; we were taken out by the enemy and Marco led their group. His attempts to make me talk were in vain." Justus laughed privately.

That explained his accent. Justus had a smooth voice and always spoke as if he were giving a presentation. It wasn't perfect grammar, but he had good enunciation. There was also a very slight, almost undetectable shift in his speech that gave a hint of an accent, but I never could place it because it wasn't pronounced and I wasn't cultured enough to identify it.

"Fast friends ever since?"

"War changes men. Once you see it from the inside, you question your own beliefs. Marco showed me a new life and we traveled. I experienced how other people lived and learned what values were important to me—what was worth fighting for."

"Where did you get the tattoos from?"

Justus leaned forward and stood on his feet, pensively rubbing his arm. "I have more pressing concerns at the moment than to discuss such things."

Justus scheduled a meeting the next evening but didn't invite me. He slipped on his black hoodie that I'd worn to the Gathering and headed out the door. Justus was hardly a man who needed to wear a jacket since he was a Thermal, so I watched him suspiciously. An hour later, I called Sunny out of boredom.

"Hey, girl! Are you coming?" she said loudly.

"Where are you?" By the noise in the background, it sounded like a bar.

"I'm at the Red Door."

"You're where?" I asked in disbelief.

She coughed and must have cupped the phone. "We're on the list now; Novis made all the arrangements so we can come here when we want." Her voice fell to a whisper. "There are some weirdos in here."

"Vampires can hear really well, so don't whisper something inappropriate. What are you doing there?"

"Knox is meeting up with some of the guys, but right now we're sitting around waiting for everyone, and he's not telling me boo," she said with enough emphasis that I knew that she was speaking directly to him. "I'm getting a little bored. Are you coming?"

My foot tapped angrily on the floor. There was no reason I had to stay home. "I'm on my way," I said.

I programmed the alarms on the way out and stood in the garage. If I was going to get in trouble for this, then it wasn't going to be while driving one of his spanking-new cars.

I knew the basics of riding a motorcycle. The Ducati seemed harmless enough. After all, I used to rock it on the five-speed with my streamers and banana seat—how different could it be?

I felt pretty badass for a few minutes. That is, until I forgot how to brake and threw myself off. I'd ridden with Adam and watched him drive, but actually doing it was more difficult than I'd assumed. It was a slow ride into the city and steering around all the traffic rattled my nerves. The bike wobbled a few times and when I arrived at the Red Door, I almost threw it on the ground.

The night air was damp and cool. I rubbed my wet nose on the cuff of my sleeve as I waved at the doorman and made my way inside. The familiar sensation of Breed energy rolled through me like turbulence; it was strange to think that I was ever scared of it.

A few eyes watched me with curiosity. I lacked distinguishable physical traits and men often assumed—or hoped—that I was a Sensor. Oh, they *loved* Sensors. Especially the new ones that offered low rates or freebie samples of their wares to gain new clientele. Sensors were all about monetary gain and immortals were dripping with wealth.

I usually kept my light concealed in a Breed club because it wasn't necessary to flare and I didn't want to attract unwanted attention. A rare few were hypersensitive to energy and could detect something different about my light. I found that out one night when I was running to the restroom and a Mage caught a hold of my waist and backed me into a wall, trying to pry my hand open.

Justus was on him in a heartbeat.

My pace quickened when I caught sight of Sunny mouthing off to someone. She stood up from the table, pointing her finger at a Vampire. *Oh, shit.*

"Sunny!"

The Vampire with short blond hair slanted his eyes at me. Harming a human may be against Breed law, but it wouldn't stop the bastard from using his gifts on her.

"My boyfriend will be back any minute," she went on. He smiled as if it didn't matter.

"You're not welcome at our table, Vamp. The club is filled with pretty girls—better snatch one up before they're all gone," I said while unzipping my jacket. He frowned and looked back at Sunny.

"Problem?" The bartender eased up and patted the Vampire on the shoulder. "Come on. These two aren't looking for that kind of fun. Off you go."

Sunny lowered her voice. "I feel like everyone is staring at me, but not in a good way."

"They are. The ones that know you're human. Otherwise, it's just a bunch of four-hundred-year-old horny men. The usual."

"You should have heard what he said to me."

I didn't need to. Most immortals had no problems telling a woman exactly what they wanted. They were too old to beat around the bush.

"Where is everyone?" I pulled out the chair with the plush red seat and sat down, smoothing my arms over the wooden table. It was one of the most beautifully decorated Breed bars in town without the loud, obnoxious music.

"Knox is in the back with Novis." She pointed. "Justus went outside a few minutes before you got here. Someone was running late."

I frowned. "Sounds very covert."

"Mmm," she agreed.

"Who else is with them?"

She shrugged and waved a hand. A pretty silver bracelet slid up her arm.

"I wonder why Knox is involved," I muttered to myself. "Is this your first time in a Breed bar?"

Sunny played with a loose curl of her hair and narrowed her violet-lined eyes. "I'm not uber impressed. A couple of the patrons look… catatonic."

I turned in the direction of her gaze and saw a Sensor making a transaction with a customer. Her hands slipped inside of his shirt, and a red glow illuminated from beneath.

"It's not so bad. Most of the men here are nice; you're going to find exceptions no matter where you go. The women, on the other hand, aren't very conversational with me, or they're busy passing out orgasms," I added, turning away from the scene.

"I bet they are with your Ghuardian." She chuckled and admired her manicured nails.

"I don't think they'd meet his standards," I mumbled.

"I'll be right back. I have to pee." Sunny glided across the room and every slink of her hips was God given. Heads turned.

I found a pen and wrote BRB on a napkin. Something didn't feel right about Justus not coming back right away because he was usually attached to Novis at the hip. I fished a hair tie from my back pocket and pulled my hair up as I headed outside. I didn't realize how warm it was in the club until the evening air stung against my cheeks. A breeze of heavy perfume drifted from the long line of humans standing by the entrance.

Justus always parked his car out front, but I didn't remember seeing it in the usual spot. I jogged over to the second lot on the right side of the building.

Halfway there, a sharp whistle cut through the air behind me. I spun on my heel and saw Christian calling me over with a crooked finger.

"Is something wrong?"

His hands slipped into the deep pockets of his coat. "You should go back inside with your friend."

"I'm looking for Justus. Sunny said he came outside but I'm worried because his car isn't parked over there," I said, pointing my finger.

"Best you go back inside," he repeated.

The gravel crunched when I turned back around.

"Tried to warn you," he muttered.

Halfway through the lot I stopped dead in my tracks. The wind changed direction and I recognized the song floating in the air. It was Mozart's Symphony No. 25 in G minor. A song I'd never heard before I met Justus, but it blared from his car in the garage on the nights he came home late.

Five steps forward and I recognized Justus sitting in the driver's seat of the Aston with his head reclined back. *Is he okay?*

Justus was gripping the back of the headrest and looked to be in pain. As he lifted his chin, the muscles in his arm bulged and his grip tightened.

I slowed my pace and got more than an eyeful. Cheap, red nails slid up his chest. He pushed her hand away and flattened his own against the ceiling of the car—grimacing. Blond hair appeared and then lowered out of sight.

That asshole was getting a blowjob.

My fingertips crackled. The fact that he left me at home so that he could get his rocks off in a vacant parking lot with some tramp really burned me the wrong way. I lifted a round pebble from the gravel below and hurled it at the car. It made a loud crack when it hit the glass and his eyes flew open. I flared with everything in me and he looked panic-stricken. Justus shoved the woman off and began to fumble with his pants.

"Unbelievable!" I shouted, turning away.

His door clicked open. "What are you doing out here when I specifically—"

"Don't you even dare!" I spun around and he quickly zipped up his jacket, sweat glistening from his brow. "Is this your important meeting? Novis and Knox are inside waiting for someone, and *this* is how you pass the time? I was always under the belief that deep down, you hated being a Charmer. Yeah, you're a flirt, but this is just seedy. Do you even know her name?"

"You should put your girlfriend on a leash." The woman slammed the car door and fastened the small buttons on her white blouse.

"You need to shut the fuck up," I said with a pointed finger.

"Silver," Justus scolded. "Behave like a lady."

Was he serious? "That's grand coming from you, Ghuardian. Why don't you behave like a gentleman? A gentleman isn't defined by extravagant Italian suits, one-of-a-kind cologne, obscenely expensive cars, or even the fact that you opened the door for a lady before she went down on you. And *that*," I said, waving my finger, "is not a lady."

Justus looked behind me as a car pulled up and stopped near the club door.

"Come with me," he said.

"Go to your meeting. I'll be inside keeping Sunny company. I'm so glad I didn't bring her out here with me; I would have been mortified. I know you're a man who makes his own decisions, but *this* is a parking lot and *that* is a whore. You're a Charmer. I get it. But where's the seduction? Do you think that this is the best you deserve?" My heart was pounding.

Justus stalked off with an angry swing in his step. This was something I expected from Simon, and I wouldn't have cared, but Justus was my Ghuardian. I'd seen him flirt countless times, but always imagined there was a selection process with his women. He bought nothing but the finest cars, clothes, furniture, watches, and yet the women he chose were so low class that I didn't even know how to process it.

The whore lit up a cigarette.

"You know he's a Charmer, right?" I asked.

A cloud of smoke blew out of her mouth and she wiped a smudge of lipstick from her chin with the back of her hand. "Honey, that's the whole appeal. Being near that Mage is like foreplay without the foreplay, see?"

"What's your Breed?" I snapped.

"Sensor," she replied with a lift of her chin. *No wonder.*

"Ah. So just a business trade."

Her eyes rolled up. "I've wanted that man since I first saw him, and I always get what I want. Justus has a reputation as a walking one-night stand; he's never with the same woman twice. Some of the dumb ones think that they actually want more than sex from him."

"And what's wrong with that?" I folded my arms.

She took another slow inhale of her cigarette. "I've heard women say he's quite good at pleasuring them, but when it comes to himself, he's a powder keg. Some Mage are like that; they have such a tight control over their energy that they never fully experience the act. I had to see for myself if I could break the man, and I like a good challenge."

"You even think about breaking that man and I'll snap your neck."

She smiled and some of her lipstick stained her front teeth. "Justus has more restraint than I gave him credit for. I offered him a trade for dinner *and* a show. Dinner was delish, but he still owes me."

Before I acted impulsively, I spun around, scraped my foot backward, and kicked gravel all over her as I stormed off. Not even my shadow could keep up with me.

"What's wrong?" Sunny asked when I returned to the table. "Justus flew by me like a hurricane and you look upset."

"Nothing," I murmured. "I need a beer."

Sunny wrapped her cardigan sweater jacket around the back

of her chair, showing off the most satiny blouse that matched her lavender polish. "I'll go get you one and put you in a better mood. Just don't run off again and leave a note on a napkin—so rude."

As she made her way to the bar, I rubbed my face in my hands. Did I really just say all of that to my Ghuardian? I felt numb. He had a right to do whatever he wanted in his free time and I certainly wasn't one to give advice on how to have a great sex life, but Justus deserved so much better.

I scooted my chair back a foot when I finally looked up.

Sitting across from me was a man with neatly combed black hair, wolfish eyebrows, and skin the color of desert sand. His cologne was as exotic as his gaze. Nothing prepared me for Marco De Gradi walking into the Red Door.

"Where is your Ghuardian?"

"What are you doing here?"

He leaned across the table and seized my wrist. "*Where* is your Ghuardian?"

"Marco?" A timid voice gasped. I glanced up at Sunny and the evening went from epic failure to catastrophic.

Before I could react, Sunny poured a bottle of beer over his head. It ran down his face and splashed on his expensive suit. Marco flew up and knocked his chair over. She ignored him and held her thumb over the rim while shaking out the fizz. His arm flew out and knocked the bottle from her hand.

"You're despicable," she hissed. "I can't believe you lied to me and used me just so you could—"

"Sunny!" I warned before she broke confidentiality.

She wasn't hurt because Marco dumped her. Sunny blamed herself for leading Marco to me, which had ultimately brought Samil into my life.

"You're just a human," he spat. "Did you honestly think I could care for someone like… you?" His eyes raked her over.

My "oh shit" alarm started blaring.

Sunny's hands balled up into fists and a couple of men tensed but stayed out of it. Many of the immortals would protect a woman, but Sunny was a human and not many men were willing to stand up and defend one.

I flared. Hard. Justus could distinguish my energy from others. He often found me in a bar without explanation, or knew when I was entering a room. It was a skill that had to be refined and an older Mage was more sensitive to energy—a skill I hadn't acquired.

Heavy boots with thick treads announced that Justus was coming. He didn't even slow down when he emerged from the hall—not until Marco turned to face him. Justus knocked over a chair and his face paled. Knox jogged in from behind and when he caught sight of Sunny's pained face, he snatched the knit cap from his head and stalked forward.

I held my breath when he stepped up to Marco, who was wiping off the beer from his sleeves.

"Who the fuck are you?" Knox asked in a gravelly voice, staring Marco dead in the eye.

Sunny's fingers traced the side of her cheek. "*That...* is Marco."

Knox threw out his arm and hit Marco like a bag of concrete. Bone cracked and Marco spun to the floor. Knox didn't throw a punch like any mere mortal man—he swung a hammer of the gods.

The bartender intervened with a look of irritation. "Get out or you go on the list."

"I have this," Novis announced with a lift of his finger.

"He leaves," the bartender demanded, pointing at Knox. "He may not be Breed, but he's instigated violence in this club. Everyone follows the rules; no exceptions."

Novis agreed. "Knox, your assistance tonight was valuable. Escort the lady home and we'll tidy up here."

Knox cupped Sunny's face and kissed her nose. "You okay? Did he touch you?"

I glanced back at Justus, who was frozen like a statue. "I'll walk them out and leave you to uh... talk to your Creator."

This was the first time that Justus had seen Marco in years. A man he once respected. I could only imagine what would happen in that back room, because that's all that Justus seemed to care about—confronting Marco.

Knox helped Sunny into the Jeep and talked with her in a low voice as he buckled her seatbelt. She was visibly shaken. After seeing them off, I headed back to the Ducati in the other parking lot. I had to cut between two buildings to get to the bike.

"Is that a number-two pencil? You're such a dumbfuck," a voice chided somewhere out of sight.

"It worked, so shut your pie hole."

I kept walking, feeling regret for losing my cool and yelling at Justus. I turned into the alley and heard a distinct snap of gum behind me.

"Well, well. How's it going, sweetie?" Tarek spit out his gum and lunged at me so unexpectedly that I didn't have time to react.

He held my arms firmly behind my back, staring down his nose at me.

"Tarek, let me go. I have people here with me and—"

A sharp fang scraped along my cheek. "Silence is golden," he murmured in slow words. "Be *silent*, female."

He pushed the tip of one long tooth into my neck—burning like acid—and I struggled like hell to get free. Chitahs had control over how many of their four canines they could extend, and God help me if all four came out.

"Let her go!"

Those three words chilled my blood with relief and fear. I peered around Tarek's arm. Justus slowly pulled the dark hood away from his face.

Tarek abruptly spun around, placing my back to Justus. My heart pounded against Tarek's chest, my breath rapid, my energy racing.

"Your punctuality is impressive, but I'm afraid I can't do that, Mage."

There was no warning for what was about to happen next. Tarek's jaw clamped down on the right side of my neck and three sharp fangs drove into my flesh.

I screamed wildly, pushing against his powerful body as his teeth pulled at my skin.

Warmth penetrated my body as if my insides were immersed in a hot bath. The venom caused my heart to hammer against my chest as if it were trying to signal a warning.

I was going to die.

The world spun like a top and the fire running throughout my veins made it feel like I'd urinated on myself. I lost the feeling in all extremities and pain roared up my spine like an unleashed demon.

Tarek flung me into the air and before I hit the ground, a strong set of arms caught me, pulling me close to his chest.

Justus held me against him until everything went dark.

CHAPTER 30

WHEN SILVER HAD CAUGHT HIM with his pants down, Justus felt the shame of it like a hot branding iron. Women were a release—like shooting up heroin. His body craved the sex but it was only afterward when the truth would catch up to him. Justus could never have a meaningful relationship with a woman, so it just made it easier to choose the ones who were cheap and easy. Never the same woman twice. His sex life had become nothing more than a revolving door. Why should it matter? He'd been alive for so many years—so long that no woman held that spark for him. Even then, Justus had hardened with time, like a fossil, and his passion had dulled.

The Sensor offered an attractive arrangement. She could pull emotions from the deepest recesses of your memory to experience all over again—for a price. Most preferred monetary gain, but she wanted sex. There was one thing from his past that he longed to experience again, if only to validate that it was real. Justus impulsively took her up on the offer when she approached him with a tenacious eagerness that was hard to resist.

Stupidly, he agreed. A Ghuardian should lead by example.

Justus bitterly yanked the hood from his jacket over his head and crushed the asphalt with hostile boots as he left Silver behind in the parking lot by the car. She often spoke without thinking, but that's what made her words slice deep.

"Do we have a room in the back?" Leo yelled out as he approached Justus from the other parking lot. "Sorry I'm late." His casual stride demonstrated that he was a man who could work well under pressure. Justus couldn't claim that control and Sunny glared at him when he stalked by her table in the club.

The private rooms were soundproof and secured for the utmost privacy. Justus closed the door behind him.

"Gentlemen," Novis said, clearing his throat, "I apologize. I've lost my voice and I'm tired. Justus has called me here to seek my council. Knox and Leo, you each have information that will carry weight in our discussion. Adam declined," he said, looking at Knox, "but he led me to believe that I can get what I need from you."

Knox pulled his knit hat over his dark eyebrows. "Just so you know, I'm done with the service. I kept the connection because the loyalty to my brothers is stronger than rank." He scratched his jaw and leaned against a glossy black table.

"Some of the jobs involved… extermination," Knox said with a guilty sigh. "We played good guy and did what we were told, but I saw some strange shit that no one ever explained. They armed us with customized weapons." He paced across the room with his thumbs tucked in his pockets. "The metal they used had a distinct flavor. Don't ask me how I know this shit. They're like those cinnamon candies with a sour fucking bite. Makes your tongue curl."

Justus took a seat beside Novis while Knox continued talking.

"It took 'em down though. Quick. They didn't die, either, so someone always had to finish them off. There were only two men on our team up for that shit. The rest of us left, except when the shit hit the fan." He shook his head violently. "In the beginning, our only job was to steal information. When the kills increased, Adam wanted out. No one told us what the hell we were doing and it wasn't until last year when my partner hacked into some files that I got an eyeful." He looked at Justus. "The chain used to tie up Silver and the Shifter is the same metal as our weapons."

Justus exchanged a glance with Leo and glared at Knox. "We're selling it to your human military?"

Knox stretched out his heavy arms and dropped them, slapping his legs. "Fuck if I know. There's a possibility that it's one of our weapons, not yours. It smells like an inside job. I doubt they'd sell this shit to you guys or it would start a fucking war.

No, they like that you're in the shadows and that's where they want to keep you." He rubbed a small circle on his belly and clenched his jaw. "If Nero has exclusive rights, then the sonofabitch that's selling it to him is living handsomely. It won't be hard to sniff around and find out who's making expensive purchases." Knox pulled the hat over his eyes and groaned. "The problem is it might be one of the guys I'm close to. I need to think this out before I start asking twenty questions."

"Understood," Novis agreed. "You could inadvertently tip off the person responsible. He won't think twice about ending your life to keep his secret; that's how humans are with money. Minimal questions—gossip, if you will—would suffice in spotting any red flags of someone with increased expenditures. Nero's smart enough that he would have opened an overseas bank account for your man."

"Has anyone studied the metal?" Leo asked in a low voice. "Uncovered its properties? How would a human engineer such a thing?"

Justus sat back in his chair. "I have a chain at my house if you want it. Call it a souvenir."

Novis shook his head. "No need. When Adam brought this to light, I went back to the compound. We've had guards on it since the raid. There was a box inside the burned building with one of the chains. I had a trusted associate study the compounds, but the intense heat from the fire diminished the effects, so the qualities are not unlike our stunners. This is something we've never seen. There's nothing to counter it, so there's nothing to study. All we can do is stop the production and distribution."

"When does this end?" Justus erupted. "When is it enough?" His knuckles whitened from his tight fists and he smoothed his hands over his knees angrily.

"You're asking when men will stop thirsting for power?" Novis laughed and cleared his raspy throat. "This is eons old. Modern technology only complicates things. Leo, tell us more about the Chitah who works for Nero and where his interests lie."

Logan's brother was not a man to ramble on. He was a lot like his father with the same admirable traits and reddish hair, Justus noticed. "Tarek belongs to a high-ranking family in an adjacent territory," Leo said. "He's been tracking Silver for information, but his involvement has become personal because he shares a history with Logan. This is where it gets muddy. Tarek tried to claim Silver."

"He *what*?" Justus felt the vein bulging in his forehead. He'd been around long enough to know about their customs of claiming a woman and how relentless they were in their pursuit.

"True," Leo confirmed. "This is a train wreck waiting to happen. Tarek is a persuasive and powerful man who *always* gets what he wants." Leo folded his arms and held everyone's attention with his riveting eyes, which were a striking contrast against his ruddy complexion. "We're known for our perseverance. Nero was smart to hire him."

"Which brings us back to the labs," Novis said. "Nero is an outlaw who must be brought to justice. However, we need to put *more* priority in the experiments. This new science poses a greater threat. I trust all of you to keep this between us, as public knowledge about such things would turn our world upside down."

Suddenly, a current surged through the room and flushed across Justus's skin like pure adrenaline. He sprang to his feet when he recognized Silver's energy.

"What's wrong?" Novis felt the flare, but didn't know her imprint.

Justus threw open the door and barreled down the hallway, shoving security against the wall as he entered the main room.

Everything spun like a dream when he spotted Marco. He nonchalantly brushed the arms of his jacket—still wearing his hair in the same style and concealing every speck of energy, even in a Breed club. This was a man whom Justus revered. He was a mentor who'd taught him how to become a man of worth. Marco had left Cognito years ago to travel abroad and never kept in contact. Even now, centuries later, Justus still felt like a Learner in his presence.

Knox almost mowed him down as he wedged himself between Marco and Sunny. There was a flurry of words, Marco hit the ground, and then everyone dispersed.

Novis snapped his fingers at his personal guard. "Bring him in the back. Most unexpected."

The guard lifted him by the back of the arms and dragged him down the hall, his feet leaving black scuff marks on the floor. Justus wanted to follow, but he was shockingly devoid of emotion. He had waited for this moment for so long—to confront his maker. Part of him needed to know why Marco chose to betray the Mageri, and the other part wanted to cut all ties. Justus lived his life by an honorable code, and Marco was the one who'd introduced him to HALO.

It was a defining moment in Justus's life, one in which he made a decision that took him by surprise.

He walked out the front door.

Justus lived his life learning to control his emotions, and this kind of rage would only lead to regretful decisions. Who was more important to him—his Creator or his Learner? It wouldn't take much to push Silver down a dark path by setting the wrong example.

He put the events from earlier out of his mind and decided to make sure his Learner got home safely before he dealt with Marco. Vampire guard or not, she was his responsibility above all else.

Tiny pebbles burst out from beneath his heavy boots as he neared an alley between the buildings. He followed the spurts of power that crackled in the air. Silver had a tendency to leak energy when she was emotional—not an unusual trait with Learners in their first years.

He rounded the corner and hit the brakes. Slowly, his fingers pulled the hood away from his face and the only thing that filled his vision was a man who was going to die.

"Let her go," Justus demanded with every ounce of control he could summon.

The man swung around with Silver caught in his arms like a fish in a net. All Justus could see was that the Chitah had bound her hands and her ponytail was swinging as she fought against him. Chitah eyes gleamed back at him violently. Justus moved forward, ready to flash, ready to fight to the death.

He gave the man with the dark Mohawk a stare that few ever lived to tell about. The anger already pumping in his blood was fast becoming toxic. Justus hesitated. He considered how fast a Chitah was and the risk of him biting Silver. If he could use a burst of light to get close enough, there would be no struggle. Just one slam of energy from his hands and good night.

Justus didn't just sharpen his light, he fashioned it into a missile.

Seconds from flashing, the energy in the air snapped like a fallen power line. The Chitah sank his teeth into Silver's neck. It felt as if someone punched the air right out of his lungs and he could only react when the Chitah tossed her at him like garbage.

Justus caught her before she hit the ground and he dropped hard on his knees, jagged concrete breaking the skin through his pants. Her body convulsed and she showed him the whites of her eyes.

"Shhh." Justus gathered her in his arms for what could be the last time. He'd never seen a Mage bitten with more than two teeth. The light of fury in his eyes almost blinded him.

It burned like ice.

CHAPTER 31

DARKNESS SWADDLED ME LIKE AN infant in the womb. Every muscle blistered with clawing pain, and yet my lungs were unable to gather the energy to scream. I was hypersensitive to everything, and a fresh slice of misery like I'd never imagined ripped across my flesh whenever something scraped against it. My chest constricted as if death had a tight grip on my light and wasn't letting go.

"You're a Chitah! What do we do?" Justus roared.

"How many punctures?"

Justus turned my neck to the left and I wanted to cry. "Three."

"That's good," Leo said. "It's four that kills… usually."

"Usually?" Justus whispered fiercely.

"Logan is on his way. Three… I don't know. That's not something I've ever seen before, but Logan may have. How strong is her light? I'm assuming she's newly made."

"It hurts," I whimpered.

"Where the hell is Christian?" Justus shouted. I'd heard him angered before, but never with such intensity.

Footsteps skidded to a stop. Knox's gravelly voice was out of breath. "I came as soon as I got the call. Anyone missing a Vamp? I found one lying underneath a cardboard box with a pencil jammed in him. Is that all it takes?"

"Only if it's deep enough. Go pull it out," Leo suggested.

"The fuck I'm pulling that thing out. What if he bites me?" Then there was a pause and his voice fell. "Is she all right?"

"Go warn Novis that he needs to leave immediately. Bring your car around and put the seats down in the back so we can transport the female."

"On it," Knox said.

"She's convulsing," Justus muttered.

Chills racked my body as my veins ran cold and my skin burned hot. The contrast between the two sensations was mind numbing. My light depleted and all I could think about was survival. I saw nothing, but I heard everything.

"So *cold*," I breathed out.

My clothes felt like electric needles wrapping around me and I showered the night with silent screams.

"Shhh."

"I feel like…" The words caught on my tongue like frozen glaciers. "I swallowed ice." Every word was exhausting and my teeth chattered. Could he even understand me?

"I'm here, Silver. Try to relax," Justus soothed.

Easier said than done. I went into convulsions.

Logan must have held his breath during the entire run because when he ended up in the parking lot of the club, his chest felt like it was going to explode.

After a few games of pool, Finn was growing bored so they went for a bite of Chinese food. The moment he got the call from Leo, the table flipped upside down and he was out the door, running. Chitah speed would beat the hell out of his second-hand car. There wasn't time to worry about the rules in public—he ran until the soles of his feet damn near set his shoes on fire.

"How many?" Logan shouted as he crossed the parking lot with Levi shadowing behind.

Justus raised three fingers. "On the neck."

Logan cursed.

Her dark, unruly hair was splayed across Justus's arms—the same locks that held the most wild and wonderful scent. Raven black with soft touches of dark chocolate. Everything about her became fascinating to him from the moment they met—especially that beautiful hair.

"I'm here, Silver. Give her to me; I know what to do." He collected her in his arms. "Get this fucking thing off her!" Logan ripped the coat away and tore at her clothes.

Justus grabbed his throat with a punishing grip. Realizing he was seconds away from being on the receiving end of a Mage power burst, he shoved Justus away.

"Put your hands on me again," he bit out. "I dare you." Ordinarily, Logan would have taken someone out for that kind of aggressive gesture, but he was her Ghuardian. "Do you want to cause her more pain?"

"Have you ever seen this before," Justus asked. "Can you even help her?"

"Once."

The victim had died. Logan knew what would bring comfort, but not how to save her as the venom ate its way through. "Who has a knife?"

The men looked between one another.

"I need to cut away her clothes," Logan said impatiently. "Now!"

Hesitantly, Justus pulled the zipper down on his cotton jacket and unsnapped a safety that held a dagger beneath his shirt.

"I want every male here to turn their eyes away or I'll use this knife to pluck them out," Logan demanded.

Logan spread Silver out on the grimy pavement and sliced away her jeans, knowing that the constricting material only made the pain worse. Then he tore her shirt up the center. The only thing against her skin that wouldn't bring insurmountable pain—was skin.

The knife clinked on the ground and Logan stripped out of his shirt and pulled her body against his. Silver's head flopped back and he cradled her delicate neck, never once laying eyes on her body after he cut away the bra. It mattered to her. If this was the last way he could honor her, then it was a request he would not ignore.

"Here's the Jeep," Leo said, waving at Knox to block the alley entrance.

Brakes screeched and Justus opened the doors. Logan stood up with Silver in his arms. Knox drove a Jeep Commander and the men pushed the seats down in the back, leaving an open space.

Levi held her legs while Logan crawled into the vehicle on his knees.

"I need someone else behind her." He sure as hell didn't *want* someone else behind her, but her body was losing heat.

They shifted around in the tight quarters and Levi crawled to the other side, bending his knees to accommodate the fit. Logan propped her head on the bend of his left arm while Levi removed his shirt and scooted in behind her. He wanted a blanket to offer her dignity, but there was nothing dignifying about holding a suffering female you couldn't help.

Logan dropped his weary forehead on Levi's shoulder as anxiety consumed him.

Justus crawled in and touched her arm and small threads of blue light filled the darkness of the vehicle.

"Your gift won't help a Chitah bite and you know it," Logan pointed out.

Undeterred, Justus continued until he slumped against the door, despondent.

Silver melted against Logan and he wrapped around her like a protective blanket.

A scream from a dying Mage echoed in his mind from the past. That man had compared three Chitah bites to molten knives against his skin and frostbite inside his bones. Logan had discovered that when he grabbed him by the arm or neck, there was no reaction except a sigh of relief. That man was given *no* reprieve—not for the heinous crime that he committed. Logan held no compassion for that Mage and now he wondered if this was his punishment. If he lost Silver, he would never be found.

"I'm so glad it's you," she whispered in his ear. "Why is it so dark?"

Her lovely eyes were lackluster as they stared vacantly up at him, rimmed with inky lashes and brows. Logan closed them with the tips of his fingers.

"Quiet, Little Bird. I'm going to take care of you now." He nuzzled against her cold cheek.

The most random thought popped in his head of her

unstoppable laugh when he'd fallen on his ass rollerblading. He regretted raising his voice with her because of pride; now he'd give anything to hear that laugh again. To see the way she threw her head back with such a sweet expression that countered her usual pensive look.

"Have the Vampire drain her," Levi whispered.

Logan growled, ready to flip his switch if another man…

"It could remove some of the venom, brother. I've never seen *anyone* with three. She could be damaged if she doesn't die from this first." Levi stretched the arm that was inked with VERITAS and scratched his short hair.

Fear sailed through Logan like a pilgrim ship venturing to new lands. The thought of having permanent damage from this, if she was lucky enough to live through it, was incomprehensible. The ridicule Silver would endure would be relentless.

"She's afraid, Logan. She would want this."

Her scent burned his nose and he glared at Christian in the front seat. "Vampire, come do it fast."

"Do it, Christian," Justus ordered harshly.

Logan brushed Silver's hair away from her lovely neck. Another man's kiss would forever mark her neck and he sickened from the thought. Christian and Leo maneuvered around one another to swap places. The moment Christian's fangs punched out, so did Logan's.

Leo spoke in an authoritative voice from the front seat. It was a natural instinct to submit to the power of the firstborn. "Logan, let him remove the venom. If you flip, we'll never be able to save her. Let's do what we can for the Mage and make her as comfortable as possible."

Instinct was a dark creature prowling inside of his mind. It was toothy with claws and always hungry. Giving himself over to instinct was feeding it power and when the beast had its fill, it became strong enough to take over. That was the way of the Chitah—an age-old defense mechanism. Instinct knew nothing about fear, logic, or rationale. It acted and reacted, making the man operate on nothing but impulse. A Chitah could sense what was going on around him—as if a passenger in his own body—but could not control himself.

Logan took a clean breath through his nose as the Vampire pierced her neck with two fangs, drinking her life.

The beast snarled.

Logan flicked his eyes up to Leo. "It was Tarek, wasn't it?" He wanted to hear it for himself, even though Tarek's scent was all over her.

The engine hummed, picking up speed.

"Careful, Logan. You know the laws against attacking one of our own. If you go up against him, he'll bury you. Either with a shovel or public opinion."

"Not if he gets buried first."

Silver's complexion became chalky. Draining blood couldn't kill her, but he wouldn't risk it in her condition. He gripped Christian by the jaw and pried him away. "Enough, Vampire," he said in disgust.

Tears leaked from her eyes and stained her cheeks with red trails of blood. Logan wiped them away and took in her scent. Even beneath the vile fragrance of venom and misery he could still taste the sweet perfume of his female.

"Don't leave me," she whispered.

Logan began purring and he felt her body relax to the power behind it. He placed a petal-soft kiss on her lips and glared at Leo. "I will tear his life apart."

"Don't," Leo warned. "You know what it would bring to our family and the punishment. You have no claim on her that would be honored."

"And what would you have me do?" Logan held on when tremors rolled through her again. Her body temperature was dropping fast.

"Concentrate on keeping her alive, that's what you can do," Leo replied. "I'll speak to the elders and see if there's a way to seek punishment."

Levi pushed himself closer against Silver's back. Possession blossomed into another emotion that Logan hadn't known in so long that rendered him incapable of selfish motives. That word was devotion.

"Call Adam," Logan said.

"If I am not able to help her, then neither is he," Justus replied.

Logan snapped. He scooted away from Silver, crawled over to Justus, and grabbed a fistful of shirt. "I'm not going to ask again. He has a gift and you're going to dial his number."

Justus threw his hands against Logan's chest with the power of a centuries-old Mage. He wielded energy the way a samurai warrior did a sword. Light flashed in his eyes and the shock threw Logan against the door of the Jeep, sending a snap of pain through every nerve ending.

"Your kind did this!" Justus shouted. "What kind of man would savagely hurt a woman this way?"

Logan's fangs punched out and he sprang up on his knees. "Ask yourself the same question, Mage. How much love has your own kind showed her? *How much?*" he roared. "A Chitah may have done this, but it's *because* of a Mage—one that hunts her and destroys lives for his own self-righteous beliefs."

"This isn't the time!" Leo cut in angrily. "Logan, watch your temper. Justus, I'll forgive you for that remark once, but insult my Breed again and I'm going to reconsider my position. Let's all take a breath before we say something we regret."

The vehicle hit a huge dip in the road and everyone went airborne for a split second. Logan raised his head toward Knox. "Do that again and I'll tie you to the undercarriage."

Logan directed a malevolent glare at Justus, who was bathed in aroma of residual lust when his duty should have been taking care of his Learner. Scattered lights from outside the vehicle streaked across the interior like falling stars.

Logan pressed his lips to Silver's ear, his words so low that not even the Vampire could hear his promise.

"On my word, Tarek will die by my hand. I will avenge you."

CHAPTER 32

"Don't move," Logan whispered firmly. Warmth enveloped me like a cocoon. I could feel his arms, smell his skin, hear the deep rolling purr thrumming in his chest—Logan surrounded me with body, breath, and heat. But I couldn't see him. A stabbing pain sliced through my neck when I turned it.

"Be still. Go back to sleep."

If it weren't for the fact that the bed was shaking, I might be able to sleep.

"I tried, but it won't work." Adam said from outside our cocoon. "My gift has limitations. I can try again. Did you call anyone else?"

Simon lowered his voice. "The first four hours were rough but it looks like she'll pull through. It's under control; not even a Relic could help at this point. Go home."

I wept and a bristly cheek nuzzled against mine. My throat felt as if I had swallowed glass and the nausea only exacerbated the discomfort. Distraction came in the form of random thoughts that flitted through my head like gnats. Why did this have to happen? Would Novis now find me incompetent? And what if the Mageri discovered how I was conceived? Did Justus still hate me?

"Get out," Logan said sharply. "You're upsetting her." The door clicked shut.

"Silver, I can sense your discomfort. I'm going to turn you over real slow… Easy… That's it."

I mentally sighed with the change in position. When he rolled away, I understood that it wasn't the bed that was shaking—it was me. An unrecognizable sound poured from my throat and I once again felt the sticky warmth of his chest.

"I'm not leaving you," he said in a low voice. "The cold is the hardest part; it'll be over soon."

His voice was gentle and rich with emotion. It relaxed my body as if he were summoning an unexplained power through his vocal chords that worked on my mind like a narcotic.

"I know what you're thinking." A finger tapped my nose. "Get off the pity wagon."

Could he hear the snort in my mind? Probably not. But it made me feel better.

As he stroked my hair, all I could think about was how I wanted him to talk to me. My fingers slipped around his side and I nuzzled into his neck.

"Do you recall the night I spent with you in the hotel room?" he asked. "That was the night I confessed you were my other half."

I shook my head, not remembering him saying anything along those lines.

"You didn't hear it because you weren't meant to. I never planned to reveal this to you, Silver," he said, drifting off. I felt the firm press of his arms around my back. "Relax, female."

The door clicked open and Justus gave an order that made Logan tense.

"Let me take over."

Simon tried to smooth over the request. "He's a Thermal and she's not improving. If her core temperature falls too low then it will compromise her light. He's her Ghuardian, let him do his job and ease her pain. Go stretch your legs, mate. You look like something the cat—"

Logan growled. "Do what you must but I won't leave this room."

There was a moment of separation and it felt like someone threw me in a mountain of snow. The bed depressed and Simon's voice went up a pitch. "You're the one who said that it must be skin on skin. Would you rather her be in pain?"

"Do *not* look at her body," Logan said in a low, threatening voice. "Don't even touch her."

"Don't tell me how to handle my Learner, Chitah."

The sheets were sandpaper fashioned from a billion needles. Justus smelled like a workout and his large hand braced around my back as his heavy arm rested on top of mine.

"Put away your fangs or you will be forcibly removed. By law, I am responsible for this Learner and if you want to challenge me, then I will rope your ass to a tree without blinking and summon every Creator who ever lost a Learner to you. Retract them. Now."

Delicious heat melted across my body and I pressed my forehead against his sticky chest and sighed. It was the first relief I'd felt from this nightmare and the tremors began to subside. "Thank you," I whispered.

There's something indescribably wonderful about waking up in the arms of a man. I didn't need my eyes to know the chest I was rubbing my face against belonged to Logan. His scent filled my nose like a thunderstorm—masculine, powerful, dark.

"Feeling better?"

"A little," I said in a hoarse voice.

I licked my dry lips and felt something with a hard edge tap against them.

"Drink."

It wasn't easy to wrap my mouth around the straw; the water sloppily shot up and dribbled down my chin, but it eased the burn in my throat and I nodded.

"Don't move," he said. I'd never heard Logan sound so drained as if he were battling exhaustion. "Your body processed a lot of venom. The first few hours you vomited blood and we had to double up on the sheets when it came out in your tears."

Blind or not, I slammed my eyes shut. Of *all* people to see me in that condition. Everyone talks about how the perfect guy will hold your hair back when you're throwing up, but how could any man want me after seeing that?

"The venom settled in your blood and ate away at your light. When power escapes from your body, you get cold, right? Multiply that times a thousand and that's what our venom does. Adam tried to help but his power is limited. You fought through it well," he said with admiration, threading his fingers through my hair. "I've never met a female with so much courage in the face of death."

I smiled in my mind because it wasn't the first time that I'd faced death. I was becoming quite a pro at it. "You thought I was going to die?"

"I did this to a Mage once. He suffered and died. I don't want to talk about this right now."

"Logan?"

His fingers snagged in the tangles of my hair. "I'm here."

"You're naked." And I felt it all the way down to my feet.

His chest rocked with laughter. "I am."

"Didn't take advantage, did you?" I said with a half smile. We were locked so tightly together that our bodies felt as one.

"Nudity is not enough to turn me on; your pain is not an aphrodisiac. I never looked at you. I… kept my word," he whispered in my ear.

I wanted to laugh at how silly that sounded given the circumstance—because I hardly cared. But it was endearing and I wouldn't mock him. "Logan?"

"Hmm?"

"Are the lights out?"

"Don't think about it. The venom still courses through your veins."

"Maybe the gods are trying to tell me something," I muttered.

"What do you mean?"

"I'm not even a year in to being a Mage and I've been murdered, tortured, kidnapped, almost burned alive, survived a bomb, was bitten by a Chitah… what am I missing?"

"Me?"

"Oh yeah… *you.*"

Soft lips melted against mine and moved to my cheek. The bristles from his jaw should have bothered me, but they didn't. I loved the intimate feel of his face against mine.

"Breed life is no walk in the park," he said. "Former humans have more mishaps in their first few years. They're too green to know how to live in this world and appreciate the dangers. Someday we should compare stories. I bet I could trump you as I was foolish in my youth."

"I heard about the bear."

The pillow rustled. "Did you now? Hmm. Yes, I was quite young. *Leopold* enjoys telling that story far more than I like hearing it."

"Why have I been naked this whole time?"

"Our venom moves through the skin and attacks the nerve endings. The only comfort that seems to dull it is heat and skin. Anything else is painful, as you know. Enough talk; we need to keep you warm." Logan threw his leg over mine and shifted closer.

"I'm a little too tired right now to be mortified that Justus saw me naked. Thanks for giving me that memorable experience that we can bring up at all of our future reunions. I'm sure by now he's already drawing up the papers to make me independent."

"That wasn't my idea," he muttered.

"I thought you would have gone into thermonuclear meltdown." I said, stretching a little.

He nipped my earlobe lightly. "I see your fiery tongue is warming up. I had to swallow my pride."

A short laugh escaped and I rolled to my back. "I didn't realize you had such a tremendously *huge*... throat."

It was awkward not being able to read his face.

"Tell me about you and Tarek," I said.

Logan took his time tucking a thin blanket up to my chin, and the feel of it didn't bother me. "Katrina was my mate, but she was *his* kindred spirit. Tarek never declared it in front of our elders. That's why he could claim you at the Gathering without rebuke. I only found out because Katrina confided in me when I began courting her openly. We met on a street corner when her hat blew off and I chased it," he said wistfully. "Their courtship was secret and he didn't prove himself a worthy mate. In the end, she wanted a male who wasn't ashamed of her."

"Why did you chase her if she wasn't your kindred?"

"I was young and Leo warned me of the consequences, but I loved her. Tarek became obsessed when she rejected him. Even after we were mated he still tried to court her. Despite how he did it secretly, it was still his right, but it was insulting to Katrina."

"Even though you were married?"

"The law allows fair competition only among kindred spirits. They respect the bond enough to give the male a chance to prove his worth, even if his intended is mated with another. Tarek threatened me instead of making an open challenge. If I had died, then he would have faced punishment. Only making his claim public could have acquitted him from the crime, but I'd be willing to bet he would have suffered the consequences rather than claim that female," Logan said with contempt.

"Why didn't he make it public?"

"He was embarrassed by her status, but it didn't stop him from wanting her. She came from a low-ranking family and it would have caused a stir. He was also courting another female from a powerful territory at the time. Her brother was a Lord, and I presume it would have been an ideal match between families. That arrogant prick thought he could have his cake and eat it too." Logan paused and grief filled his voice. "The young she carried… it was his. He forced himself on her."

I touched his shoulder. "I'm so sorry."

"She chose not to make the accusation public—afraid that Tarek might try and take her child away. The scandal never got out. His brothers threatened to expose his secret to the woman he was dating, so Tarek ended it before she found out. They were right to save that female the shame."

Katrina must have been frightened of Tarek to not seek justice. But then again, would the risk of losing her child be worth it? I couldn't imagine facing such a sacrifice.

"Could you have loved his baby?"

"I kissed her belly and told her I would love that child as my own. It wasn't a lie." Logan quieted and swallowed hard. "One month before I would have held him in my arms, she was murdered by a Mage I was in debt to. Tarek paid him off to kill me, but the Mage decided he would have a little fun of his own. I've wanted to kill Tarek for a hundred years."

"What happened to the Mage?"

"What do you think?"

The door creaked and Simon interrupted. "There's an awful lot of chattering in here."

"Hey, Simon."

"Bloody hell," he sighed. "Put a fright in me like that again and... Are you hungry?"

"Not right now. Maybe in a little bit."

The door clicked shut.

"Why did you tell me before that the baby was yours?"

"Chitahs respect the family above all else. It was the right thing to do—you can't punish a child for how they're conceived."

"My lips are dry," I said quietly.

Butterflies unexpectedly awoke from their slumber when gentle lips touched mine and his tongue slipped across my bottom lip. "Then let me wet them," he whispered. "When your body is cold, I will give you warmth." The blanket moved away and he slid against me—skin to skin—pushing his thick leg between mine.

"Mr. Cross?"

"Hmm?" *How could one sound from his mouth be so sexy?*

"I feel well enough to bathe and I want to do it alone. Can you run me some bubbles?"

"Whatever you desire, my raven."

CHAPTER 33

L OGAN WRAPPED MY BODY UP in a clean sheet and carried me to the bathroom. I couldn't argue about it since my legs were weak. He placed everything I needed within reach and I soaked for a long time in the hot water, immersed in my thoughts. Would this be enough for Tarek to back down? Something told me this wasn't the end of it.

The water was getting cold, so I pulled the plug and waited for the tub to empty before drying off. It was as if my muscles had atrophy and I called Logan in to help. It was frustrating to feel like an invalid, but he made those feelings go away with his patience and encouragement for me to do things on my own. I slipped into one of my oversized shirts and a robe that belonged to Justus. It was long in the arms but carried his smell and made me feel safe.

Still blind, I clung to anything with familiarity. For the longest time I held the little wolf that Finn had carved, admiring it all over again with the details in each groove.

Logan made me walk around the room to strengthen my muscles, and I stumbled persistently in order to regain my independence.

Living out the rest of my days locked away in my bedroom like a recluse held no appeal. Logan bundled my feet in a pair of socks, and we made a slow journey to the training room. I tripped over the mat and laughed when he snatched the back of my robe and snapped me back like a rubber band. Finding the floor switch for the lift was a challenge, but Logan had me count the steps from the wall.

"How are you feeling?"

"Better, Ghuardian. I'm a little hungry."

"Watch the rug and don't let her fall," Justus barked as we entered the dining room.

I took my seat on the bench, feeling the indentations on the wooden table with my fingertips—something I'd never noticed before. My nostrils were flaring, trying to decipher all the different smells that blended together.

"What happened to Christian?" I asked with concern.

"He's outside."

"Invite him in."

"He's not a puppy, Silver. He's your guard, and his place—"

"Invite him in. Maybe this is how *you* treat guards, but we're going to be civilized people. There are enough alarms here to warn us if a dog takes a crap on the property, so let him inside." It was the least I could do for a man who might have died trying to protect my life.

A few minutes later, a second set of footsteps followed Justus into the room and a chair scraped against the floor on the other side of the table.

Logan lightly touched my hand with two fingers and let go. I guessed he was checking my body temperature, but it was reassuring to know he wasn't going to abandon me.

No one said a word. I wasn't an idiot and knew they were having visual conversations about my condition. It made me squirm in my chair as I pricked my fingers on the prongs of the fork.

"How long was I sick?"

"Two days," Justus murmured.

I leaned against Logan's shoulder. "Tell me you didn't sleep with me like that for two days."

He spread the flat of his hand across my collarbone, stroking my throat with the pad of his thumb.

When I was sick as a kid, my own mother never took care of me as well as Logan did. She'd set a bottle of murky liquid and a couple of pills on my nightstand and let me ride it out by myself. I grew up thinking that's how it was supposed to be. If I threw up, I had to clean it. "You won't always have someone there to take care of you," she'd say. "Learn to fend for yourself."

I ran my fingers across the bridge of his knuckles.

"It's two in the morning, but we're going to have a bloody

good meal," Simon announced. "I cooked up the kitchen. Tomato soup, hamburgers and chips, chicken and mash, plenty of fresh veggies, and bacon sandwiches on the table." Simon was upbeat and had been busy cooking a potpourri of food. "What'll you have?"

"Whatever drugs you're taking." I snorted. "Um, cooked carrots if you have any and—" Before I could finish, I heard what I assumed were carrots hitting my plate. "The soup smells pretty good." I reached out, feeling for the plate and silverware.

"Let me feed you," Logan insisted.

"No, I can do it myself."

That was pride talking. I stabbed a carrot and missed the target, poking the hot veggie against my cheek. Logan's hand wrapped around mine.

Christian shifted in his seat. "Chitah, if she can't figure out how to put a carrot in her mouth then I'll shine your shoes with my tongue."

"I'm not sure if I want to win this challenge anymore." I tapped the carrot playfully against my nose several times and Simon howled like a hyena.

Wet steam dampened my face as I leaned over the hearty aroma of my soup. "Did anyone find Tarek?"

"I'm not sure we can seek retribution by law," Logan said in a low voice. "They're put in place to protect our rights, not that of a Mage. I'll speak to Leo; he may have some pull."

"Your weak laws mean nothing to me," Justus said, clearing the air.

I reached out to find Logan's hand under the table and he pulled it away. In fact, he got up out of his chair in a violent motion.

"I want a peaceful dinner," I demanded of everyone. "Don't instigate an argument with Logan for something he has no control over. Our laws don't protect their rights, either."

Ignoring the sighs and silverware hitting the table, I tested the temperature of the soup with my finger and found it agreeable. The first spoonful wet the tip of my nose and someone quietly chuckled.

After a few successful rounds, I managed to get the soup thing worked out… mostly hanging my head over the bowl like a dog.

"Give her a napkin," Simon groaned. "She looks like she made love to a tomato."

I turned my head privately to Justus. "I'm sorry, Ghuardian."

"Why should you apologize?"

"I think we both know."

"I should have hidden the keys to my bike."

"Did you find where I parked it?"

"There's a tracker on it," he said. "I'll pick it up later."

"Maybe you need to put a tracker on me," I said with a somber smile.

A piece of silverware tapped on the table from his direction. "Maybe that's not such a bad idea."

"It's a royally bad idea. You microchip your pet, not your Learner."

"Hmmm."

Super. Now I really opened up a can of worms. If he planned to microchip my bra collection, then I was going braless.

"I had no idea Marco was going to show up like that. What happened?"

Justus replied stoically. "Novis released him when he refused to answer questions."

"Why did he come all this way?"

The gentle breeze from a vent nipped at my cheeks and I shivered.

"To work out a deal, I presume." I heard the soft hush of fabric as he shrugged. "There was something else I had to take care of that was of greater importance." And the weight of his words told me that the something else was me. "Some battles aren't worth the fight. The more time that passes, the less it matters what he wants. I once respected him, but now I am without a Creator." A fork hit the plate and I jumped. "Marco is not welcome in my house… or in my life. A Creator should—"

"I know," I said, reaching out blindly with my hand in search for his. All I found was a plate. "It's a rare gift they have, and with it comes responsibility. It seems to be just wasted on the wrong people," I said, thinking of Samil.

"You have my word that I will never dishonor you the way Marco has me."

By his tone, Justus was through talking about it.

Simon rambled on about what color to paint his van. He was on the fence about selling the GTO now that he had acquired a Maserati. His apartment manager required him to pay rent for each space he occupied and it rubbed him the wrong way. Simon could afford it, but that man was all about the principle of things. They intentionally kept the topic steered away from Tarek when it was the only important thing on my mind.

If being a blind woman was my new life, then I had no choice but to face the obstacles that lie ahead. Maybe if I kept a positive outlook it would help Adam return from the land of pain and sorrow. But it didn't feel right not grieving for my own loss, and it started to consume me. I reached out my hand.

"What do you want?" Simon asked.

"Just looking for the chicken."

I heard the sharp slap of skin and jumped in my seat—my ears alert.

"Let her get it," Christian bit out. "Silver, it's at two o'clock, and careful to not tip over your—"

Ah, but it was too late. My glass went over, sending water across the table. There was a flurry of movement while Simon cleaned the mess and a few chairs scooted back. Anger roiled in me, and I was too pissed off to tolerate this coddling anymore.

"Everyone, just stop it. *Stop.*"

"Get her another drink," Justus ordered.

"Fuck the drink!" I shrieked. "You have all managed to skirt around the topic of whether or not I'm going to be blind. If you won't even answer that, then quit fussing over me like I'm an invalid!" I bowed my head to my plate.

"Look, you're upset," Logan soothed.

"*Of course* I'm upset. Why wouldn't I be upset? This isn't about Nero anymore; this is about you and Tarek. I'm caught in the center of a feud that's been brewing for a hundred years and has nothing to do with me. Yet I'm the one sitting in the dark." I kicked my chair back and stood up to leave.

Logan took hold of my arm.

"Let go of me."

"You're going to hurt yourself. Sit down."

I yanked my arm out of his grasp and fell over the table. Soup splashed on my left arm as my right hand landed in a bowl of vegetables. I swallowed the embarrassment and stayed very still.

"If I can't leave this room on my own, then everyone else needs to leave. I want to be alone," I said, stretching out the last words.

There was the unmistakable sound of Justus moving his mouth angrily as he stood up. I needed to absorb the gravity of the situation. I also needed to cry it out in private, because facing an eternity of being a blind woman deserved at least a moment of silence.

"Logan, go home and rest," I said, still sensing him at the door. "Speak to your brother and see if anything can be done. I'm not mad at you."

I sat down, wiped the soup from my arm, and buried my face in my hands. It didn't matter if they could hear my sobs, but it needed to be unleashed before it turned into anger and bitterness.

Could I endure centuries of darkness? The hate virus invigorated me with power, but I couldn't allow it. Anger would only put me on a path that went in circles and never had a change in direction.

"Aye. You want to be antisocial, is that what it is?"

"I thought you left."

Christian's shoes tapped on the floor and he took the seat across from me. "If you don't want anyone feeling sorry for you, then you aren't allowed to feel sorry for yourself, either."

"I'm allowed at least one good cry for losing my sight." I sniffed and wiped my nose on the sleeve of the robe. "Do you sleep outside every night?"

"I don't require sleep."

"There's plenty of security outside," I said with a sigh. "You don't need to stand guard when I'm home."

"An assigned guard never leaves."

"What happened at the club?" I asked.

"I found out what a pencil sharpener feels like."

"You can always take another job."

He sniffed. "You're a stubborn woman."

"So I've been told." I relied on the subtle sounds of breath, body movement, and the tone in his voice to give me insight behind his words.

He sighed. "It's what I enjoy doing, Silver. Everyone has a calling, and it gives me a sense of worth to know that I am protecting a life. We don't have to be bosom buddies."

"Maybe my life isn't worth all that trouble. I'm just a Learner. All I do is wreak havoc," I said, waving my right arm.

"Havoc wreakers write the pages of history, lass. You're in good company." Christian's voice lowered. "I had a sister who was blind."

It took a moment to absorb the seriousness of his admission. Christian was more than just an obnoxious man—he was an obnoxious man with a past. "When you were human?"

"She was younger than me by six years or so. We had to leave her behind with my da, so I don't know what became of her. But she was a bright one, always doing things on her own. You see, you don't know what life is going to deal you, but you have to learn how to deal with life. Fuck rolling with the punches—learn to punch back. Your vision will probably come back in time, but if it doesn't, then I won't tolerate your pity party for one."

"I won't tolerate you keeping the squirrels company, so let's strike a deal."

CHAPTER 34

Despite his opinion on the matter, Justus couldn't say no to me in my condition. We hooked Christian up with the guest bedroom temporarily.

It was the least I could do for a man willing to risk his life for someone he didn't know very well. Sure, Christian was abrasive—that was a common trait among most Vampires. Apparently, a sharp tongue came with a sharp tooth. I still wanted to rectify the situation between us until I could speak with Novis about other arrangements.

Sigh. And then there was *that*. Given my new affliction, there was no chance that Novis would keep me on as an apprentice.

There are no issues in life, only challenges.

The next day, I tied a scarf around my eyes and did everything I would normally do. I found my toothbrush and brushed my face... and a few teeth. It took several minutes and the cap to the toothpaste fell into the toilet, but I did it. Every mundane activity took time as my brain learned to memorize my surroundings by touch alone. What I was beginning to appreciate more was how perceptive I was in other regards. Timing out how to cook a pastry in the toaster required my ears to listen to the sizzling and my nose to tell me when it was ready.

"Ghuardian?" I knocked on his door in rapid staccato but he didn't answer. I stuck my face through the crack. "You in there?"

It wasn't like him to ignore me, so he must have gone upstairs. I was beginning to regain my sense of time—something a Mage had the ability to do. It was just after eight in the evening and he normally would have called me up for dinner.

Once upstairs, I paced to the hallway by the kitchen. "Hello?"

"Surprise!" a sea of voices shouted from the dining room.

I stumbled backward and fell into someone's arms. Logan's voice whispered in my ear, "It's your birthday and they insisted on carrying on with this. Tell me to make them leave."

"It's okay," I said, clutching my heart and leaning into him. "You smell really good. What are you wearing?"

"You," he said, and lightly nipped my earlobe.

A set of delicate arms laced around my shoulders. "Oh, Silver." Sunny was sobbing against my neck and I patted her back consolingly. "Don't be mad at me," she begged. "This is horrible timing and I wanted to cancel but everything was ordered to deliver and I asked Simon what to do about it. *He* said that you needed this and it would snap you out of your gloom," she said accusingly. "At least, that's how he put it."

"Leave it to a woman to throw you under the bus," Simon muttered.

"I didn't know what to do. I'll clean all this and we'll go home." Her voice broke and I smelled her perfume—a favorite she wore on special occasions.

"Sunshine, I swear to God if you cry at my birthday party, I'm going to make you take me to a strip club next year."

"Then I'll cry a *river* for you, girl."

We laughed until everything felt normal again. There was no point wallowing in self-pity—it's not something I'd ever done in my human life when things got tough. There was a time when I had no place to live, no job, and medical bills I paid out of pocket because of what my ex did to me. Life goes on. It was my first year as a Mage and it was only fitting that it be memorable.

My nerves vibrated like a string on a guitar when I heard the sound of bodies moving. Were they gawking at the scarf on my head or the horribly mismatched clothes I was probably wearing?

"We missed you, dollface," a gravelly voice said.

I grabbed his tremendous arms and patted them. "Knox, so good to… feel you?" I smiled. "Sorry, Sunshine. Swear to God I'm not feeling up your man."

I tugged at the tight cap he wore on his head that covered up his dark hair. It was intrusive to be so physical, but my hands instinctively sought to do what my eyes could not. "Nice suit, Knox." His silky dress shirt was tight in all the wrong places; I was so impressed that Sunny managed to get him in a suit at all—even if he won the war over wearing the hat.

"Get over here and say hello to your friend, Razor."

My heart stalled when Knox called Adam by his human surname. I hadn't known Adam was here and after our last conversation, I was uncertain he'd want to even be a part of this.

Adam once told me all he needed in life was a piece of land, purpose, and a good woman. After meeting the women at Novis's party, I had doubts that it would be possible with our kind.

Knox quietly cursed at him and I knew he wasn't going to let go of the resentment he harbored.

All of Logan's brothers except Lucian were present. Finn talked excitedly about lighting the candles and someone shushed him. He'd never experienced a birthday and I made a mental note to talk to Logan about it.

"I should have brought a piñata," Finn blurted out. He didn't mean any harm by the fact I was blindfolded and I heard one of the Cross brothers growl at him.

I laughed contagiously. "Bring it. I'm in the mood to stomp some serious piñata ass." I might have actually enjoyed swinging a baseball bat, given my mood.

They'd rearranged the room. The dining table was shoved against the left wall and the chairs and loveseat were pushed together on the opposite side. It was cozy to have everyone in the same room and allowed me to listen to the conversations. My ears flooded with sound: drinks pouring, someone tapping their foot, crunching from the vegetable tray, laughter, and disparaging sighs.

Tension flared when I bumped into Logan, who was leaning against the wall. Despite a room full of people, all I felt was his body against mine. A fire sparked in me that wasn't there before, derived from the knowledge that we'd spent days tangled up naked in a bed. His formidable presence and protective nature drew me to him even more than the sexual tension.

Logan very slowly moved away, creating a maddening friction between our bodies. I took a seat in the chair and blew out a shaky breath.

"I probably look like something the cat dragged in," I said to Sunny. "What if I had walked up here in my underwear?"

"Now *that* would have been a surprise," Simon remarked from across the room.

Her laugh was bright and she hugged me again. "Is that how you parade around the house in front of Justus?"

"Only when I want to punish him."

Logan was great. He gave me space and every so often, I felt his presence. It was hard not to; there was something about his energy when he circled around me that stimulated my light and made the little hairs on the back of my neck stand up.

"Honey, you want to sit by the most handsome man here?"

"Levi, how could I say no to a guy who manwiched me?"

He snorted and eased me onto his leg. "That was as close as I'll ever get to mating with a female, Silver. But I must say—you give good back."

I missed all the subtle facial expressions, but I caught so much more in the tone and pitch of everyone's voice. I wrapped my arms around Levi's neck and rested on his shoulder.

"I don't really remember any of it, but thanks."

I wasn't usually so public with affection, but not seeing the watchful eyes made it easier.

"I'll always have your back," he murmured.

"You need to quit while you're ahead."

When I stood up, my legs were a little wobbly and I gripped the table. Levi clutched my hips. "You should sit down," he said in a concerned voice.

"I'm fine."

Simon and Finn argued about how the universe was created while Leo bragged that his plan was to have seven children—which would be enough to scare off any woman.

A rough hand took hold of my fingers. *Adam's hand.* No words passed between us, but we came to a silent resolution. It wasn't my fault that his woman was a conniving tramp, yet now I understood him better. Our hands did the talking that our lips could not.

The room grew silent all of a sudden and Sunny began to sing.

Oh God, I was never into the whole birthday-song thing and listening to a group of men who couldn't carry a tune was more than I could stand. I backed up like a spooked mare and Logan encased me in his arms from behind.

"Red still suits you, Little Raven," he said softly, grazing his finger along the hollow of my cheek.

"What am I supposed to do now?"

"Blow out the candles," Finn suggested.

"And set my hair on fire?"

Simon howled with laughter. "There's only one candle on the cake, love." He wheezed a few times and that's when I was ready to shove his face into it. "I can't help it. He's dating a one-year-old." Simon elapsed into a fit of laughter and someone smacked him.

"I doubt it's enough to torch and cinder that wild beast of yours," Logan murmured, tugging the ends of my hair.

"Help me do this, Logan. I don't want to feel up the cake looking for the candle."

"I'll hold your hair while you blow," he said.

Levi barked out a laugh. "All right, Logan. Save the sweet talk for later."

I placed my fingertips on the edge of the table and blindly blew out a breath. There were claps, which led me to believe that I hit my mark or they were filthy liars.

"Give me the knife," Sunny insisted. "Let me cut it properly before you men hack it to pieces."

"Presents!" Simon demanded.

"I don't really—" I shook my head. This was becoming too much.

Someone shoved a light box into my hands. No paper or ribbon. The lid fell to the floor and beneath the rustling tissue was thin, delicate fabric. I lifted it with my right hand and someone whistled. My cheeks flamed up and I let go, hearing a few deep chuckles.

"Thanks, Sunshine," I grumbled.

"Anytime," she said with a smile in her voice. "Every girl needs something to feel sexy."

"Thought you could use these," Justus said in a raspy voice, handing me a small bundle wrapped in tissue paper. *What did Mr. Moneybags get me?* I wondered.

When I tore away the paper, my hands ran across an unexpected gift.

"Well, what is it?" Levi asked.

"The perfect thing for my cold feet—slipper socks." Probably worth more than I deserved. I may have been blind, but I knew that Justus was firecracker red.

Our house always ran cold and I took advantage of the fact that he was a Thermal. Many a cold night, I cozied up beside him on the sofa with the ulterior motive of warming my feet. The man was a portable space heater; what girl could resist?

Simon whispered in my ear, "We'll play this later. Promise I won't cheat."

I felt the box and laughed. "Why don't you and Knox give it a test run?"

"What game is that?" Levi asked.

I turned my mouth down. "Twister."

"I'm in," he said with a hard clap of his hands. "Knox?"

"Sorry, but there's only one spot Knox is putting his hands tonight, and it's not on red or green." Sunny was full of spirit and I gave her a mental thumbs-up.

"There's another one this way." Logan took my hand and led me out of the room.

"From who?"

"Adam," he said in a low voice.

When my feet brushed across woolen fur, I knitted my brows. "I don't remember that," I murmured.

Logan released my hand and I knelt down. Thick fibers ran between my fingers and I knew what it was—my old flokati rug. "Where did you get this?"

"I took it the night we went to your apartment." Adam's words were thick with memories as he drifted out of the room.

"It's perfect," I said graciously. The rug was the only piece left of my human life and it was my safe place when things weren't going well.

"Mine's next." Logan brushed his hand over my head and I raised a suspicious brow.

Sunny gasped and someone shushed her.

"Hold out your hand," he said. "Palm down." I lifted my left arm and did as he asked.

"I hope you don't intend to slip something on my finger because—"

Silk moved beneath the palm of my hand and a vibration rose to a crescendo, except that it wasn't coming from Logan.

My fingers pinched together and told my brain it was a soft ear, wet nose, and the hard bristles of whiskers.

"A cat?" I hesitated.

"He's yours, Silver. Not a replacement… but *yours*."

"Max? You brought me my cat?" I was overwhelmed. Who does things like this? "But Justus—"

"Approves," Justus interrupted loudly. "I don't care for animals but if he's yours, then I'll make an exception. Just keep him out of my room."

Max still smelled like my baby and I held him in my arms. Many significant events had transpired in that short period and Max had become a casualty. It was like hurricane victims having to leave their pets behind.

"Logan, I can't believe you did this. How did you find him?"

"I own his scent. When you introduced me to him that time we flew down, I put it to memory. He was still in your mother's neighborhood and it took some time to track him down. That little terror went into a crawlspace beneath a house and I had to go in there after him… with the spiders."

"Don't be such a pussy," Levi said.

Simon laughed. "That's the best joke I've heard all night. I'm going in for the cake before you manky bastards take all the good bits."

"When did you do this?"

"The night you returned from Texas," he admitted.

So *that* was the reason Logan never returned my calls; he was in Texas, hunting down my cat and arranging to transport him to Cognito.

Crap. The blindfold didn't hide the fact I was about to lose my cool in front of a room full of people. A swell of admiration for Logan filled my heart, along with regret for my behavior when I confronted him at the Gathering. He *couldn't* tell me the truth or it would have ruined the surprise. My face stung with the heat that preludes tears. Max scrambled from my arms and I leaned forward and grabbed the collar of Logan's shirt, pulling him against me.

When I nuzzled against his unshaven cheek, Max wasn't the only one who was purring. The voices around us trailed away.

He smelled my hair with a slow breath. He kissed the curve of my jaw. And then a long, passionate kiss grew between us—the kind that can shatter you into a million pieces. His lips were soft and tasted of the Bordeaux he'd been drinking. I loved the way his rough fingers stroked the nape of my neck. Every man has a place on a woman's body that he calls home, and for Logan, that was it.

"Tell me, lovely, did we do good?"

"Mr. Cross, you did so good that I could strip you out of your clothes on this carpet."

His laugh was low and dubious as he stroked his tongue along the soft patch of skin below my ear.

"Empty threats don't impress me." The flat of his hand moved across my collarbone and then down my chest until he gripped my waist. "I crave you, Little Raven. Say the word and I'll remove everyone from this house and lay you out on this rug as mine for the taking."

"Don't wake her," Logan said in a low voice. "I'll stop in tomorrow morning before the meeting with Leo. Justus, I brought cat food so *you* need to keep Max fed. You're on litter patrol as well."

Justus muttered something unintelligible as they left the room.

The party had ground to a halt when the smell of arousal bloomed in the air and Logan's brothers took that as their cue to head out. By the time the last person left, I'd fallen asleep on the sofa. Max curled up beside me, paws stretched like prickly branches around my neck.

Half asleep, I gasped and sat up, completely disoriented. Beads of sweat rolled down my brow and I shuddered. *Where was I?* Stumbling to my feet, my hands searched for a switch when my hip knocked into a shelf and I fell to the wood floor.

"What are you, a duster now? Get up." Christian's foot nudged my side.

"I don't want to get up. It's my birthday, and I'll—"

"Jaysus. Start singing that and you'll get a thick ear."

Over the past hour, something murky and cold had rolled through my body. It reminded me of when I didn't level down and the power depleted.

"Christian, I don't feel good."

His voice grew closer as he knelt down "What's wrong?"

"Sick."

"Why didn't you say anything earlier?"

He lifted me up and went downstairs. His boot kicked against a door, making a shockingly loud sound.

"Justus, rise and shine." He kept moving and put me in the sheets of my bed.

"What did I tell you about coming in here?" Justus scolded.

"Silver needs a specialist; she's not well."

"Logan said it would take time to wear off."

"I hear her breathing and heartbeat, and it's all off. She's not getting better, she's worse than she was six hours ago. Do you know a good Relic? Then you better get one."

CHAPTER 35

"Why didn't anyone call a Relic as soon as this happened?"

The woman's voice was stern and authoritative. She came highly recommended by Remi, a close friend to Justus. He personally drove her to the house but was uncomfortable with staying and offered to pick her up when she was finished.

Relics are mortals with a unique gift. They're born with ancient knowledge inherited in their genes, passed down by their ancestors. In order to retain the knowledge and continue their line, Relics only marry another Relic. They date back as far as any Breed, perhaps further, which makes their knowledge invaluable. Most become healers of some kind, or scientists, but they were also consultants. I couldn't imagine being a young child and simply knowing things I couldn't explain.

This woman sounded like she wanted to inflict pain among the men and heal later. She had a feminine voice with a sharp edge that reiterated her confidence. I liked her immediately.

"We had it under control," Justus replied defensively. "The Vampire drained the venom and I gave her some of my light. She's been kept warm and had an appetite at the party."

"Do you often throw a celebratory party for a girl who just lost her sight and almost died?" she asked in agitation. "And yet, she's still *blind*. Next time call a professional. I want everyone out of here while I examine her."

When the door closed, I could hear the soft hush of her legs rubbing together when she approached the bed. She was wearing a skirt. It's funny how much we rely on vision when our other senses will make up for our shortcomings.

"Silver, my name is Page La Croix. I'm one of Remi's personal advisors, but I'm also a healer. Have you ever met him?"

I nodded.

"I'm only doing this as a favor because Remi is a dear friend of mine and as it turns out, your Ghuardian is a close friend of *his*. Personally, I'm of the opinion that Creators should only be women, because only a man would think that having a party for an injured Mage is okay."

"He didn't mean any harm."

"They never do," she muttered privately. "I'm going to check your vitals and perform a physical examination. If you feel any discomfort, I want you to speak up right away."

Page pressed firmly all around my abdomen, checked inside my mouth and ears, squeezed my ankles, and even looked at my fingernails. The only sore place on my body was where Tarek had bitten me. She examined it closely. It was swollen and hot, yet the only thing Page noticed were three puncture holes and no discoloration.

"It'll scar," she said. "I hope you know that. Mage light won't work, nor will the healing saliva from a Chitah." Something I'd already guessed, as I was sure that Logan would have tried if he knew it was possible.

Legs from a chair tapped on the wood floor beside the bed. Page asked questions while I listened to the scribbling of a pen. "Tell me exactly how you feel."

"This morning I was all right. It started just before the party and I don't know—my body just feels lethargic. By the end of the party I could barely move and I fell asleep on the couch." I touched my eyes. "Maybe it's just being in the dark."

"And now?"

"There's a cold ache deep in my bones. Also, my light feels like it's leaking out of my body. My neck still hurts and the tips of my fingers are burning."

"No doubt from the energy leak. Silver, I'm going to be frank with you. Chitah bites don't happen very often unless it's with the intent to kill. One or two punctures—yes, we've seen that administered as a warning. Because their venom is deadly to a Mage, most never tangle with a Chitah. Other species don't have the same reaction to the venom; it takes a specific hold with your kind. If they use all four of their canines, it kills. But three is just so *rare*. Three contains enough to kill a weak Mage, but you seem to be a tough cookie," she said with a smile in her voice.

"What's wrong with me?"

"The venom hasn't left your body and it's wreaking all kinds of havoc. If we do nothing, you'll eventually weaken to a state of mortality. Do you understand what that means?"

I shook my head.

"Your light will go out. Your fingers are burning from the continual energy leakage. A Mage has natural light in their eyes—I've seen it sparkle, flicker, pulse—you name it. It explains the blindness. The venom is attacking your light everywhere, and you're noticing it in the places where it's the strongest."

I touched the tips of my fingers. "Could I die?"

"Yes. I'm not going to lie to you. A patient should always know the truth about what's happening to their body because they may have important decisions to make and they need to prepare. Your Ghuardian should have called a Relic as soon as this happened, but most men are stubborn and think they can fix things themselves. I'm going to try to heal you, okay?"

"Okay."

"My methods may be unorthodox, but it will always be your choice to deny the suggested treatment. Anytime you're not on board with the plan, just chime in. Vampire, you can come in now. I also wish to speak with her Ghuardian." Page never lifted her voice above a soft hum because she knew Christian could hear every syllable.

"What can we do?" Justus sounded like a general looking for an order.

"I'm sorry; I didn't get your name?" Page said.

"De Gradi. Anything you need, I am at your service."

Her bag snapped open and metal items clicked against the bedside table. I was acutely aware of everything happening and my nervous heart pounded against my chest.

"Her condition is deteriorating; you boys had the right idea, just not the right method. Once we draw the venom out of her bones and into her blood, *then* we drain her. If we don't expel every drop, it will redistribute and this will start all over again. Don't look at me that way, Vampire. I need you for other reasons. I can't have your blood tainted with the venom, so you won't be drinking from her."

"Already did."

"When?" she asked. "Because unless it was within the past twelve hours, you know that it won't make a difference."

"I can't give her my blood, it's—"

"Suck up your egotistical pride about the glory of your pure blood. I'm quite aware of how revered a Vampire's blood is. If it helps, I'll throw down some rose petals at your feet during the ceremony. This is the only way. Are you a friend, or—"

"I'm her guard."

"Ah," she said victoriously. "Then you are duty bound to protect her life."

"What if she turns?"

"Vampire, she won't turn. She's a Mage. Once a Mage, always a Mage. Isn't that right, Mr. De Gradi?"

Liquid poured, followed by the sound of stirring. Page sniffed lightly and slipped her cool fingers behind my neck.

"Silver, I need you to sit up and drink this… all the way down. I won't lie: It's going to taste noxious and disgusting, but I've got a breath mint if you want it," she offered. "Here."

The glass was cold and I dipped my nose in. "Oh, that's rank. Please tell me the glass isn't full."

"Drink it, Learner," Justus scolded. "Or else I will plug your nose and—"

"Stifle it," Page snapped. "I won't have you making my patient uncomfortable, so if you don't curb that tone, then I'm going to ask you to leave. If she wants to take two hours before she decides to drink this, then it's her choice to do so. I'm here to help and give her the best care that I can. Are we done?"

I'd never heard anyone order Justus around like that. When

he didn't argue back, that was my signal to drink before a world war broke out. I held my breath and gulped down whatever muck and madness it held. Like expected, it was rancid, but the glass was emptied to the last putrid drop.

"Good girl, Silver." She held my wrist and smoothed a hand over it. "I'm going to wrap a tight band around your arm. I need to find your vein, so you'll feel a stick. Don't worry, I always get it the first time."

I nodded and she prepped me—thumping and slapping the inside of my forearm. I flinched a few times and a needle slid in. Actually, it felt more like a nail.

"Mr. De Gradi, I need you to bring a couple of large containers. I'm not sure how long this will take, but I'll test her after a few hours. Get the biggest ones you can find so we don't have to keep making trips. I'm sure you don't want to recolor your flooring by accident."

"A few hours?" I exclaimed. "If you take all my blood, won't I die?"

"That's what the Vampire is here for."

A sensation swept through my body—like flames charring my bones. I grimaced and threw my head back.

"It's starting to work; give me that container pot until the Mage returns. It'll do," she said.

If I ever saw Tarek again, I was going to personally defang him.

"We don't have time, Vampire. Quit staring and get in the bed with her," Page said.

"Do you mind not calling me Vampire all the time? It's beginning to rub me the wrong way."

Page's heel tapped against the floor.

"*Christian*, this is going to take a while. No, no, no. We can't do it that way. She won't get enough. I don't want her falling unconscious because the intake needs to be continual due to the blood loss. Get in the damn bed. I've got a scalpel."

"Don't threaten me, lass," he murmured in a dark voice.

"I was simply pointing out the obvious." Page was the kind of woman I admired; she really knew how to shape these men up.

The mattress depressed.

"Absolutely not," Justus barked. Hollow containers tumbled on the floor. "Get *out* of that bed, Christian."

Page assertively lowered her voice. "You're either going to be supportive to your Learner or I'm going to tape your mouth shut. If you want this Mage healed, then you need to let go of those protective reins and let me do my job. Exactly what do you think is about to happen here? This is not a bordello, Mr. De Gradi. I don't have time for this." She sighed wearily.

"Why not do a transfusion?" he asked in a tone that challenged her.

"Time is of the essence and I don't have the right equipment for that. We can't take any chances in delaying this. I'm not certain that doing a full transfusion with the Vampire's blood would work because it'll mix too quickly with hers. The venom is working like soldiers, and if you throw his blood in there then they'll attack the enemy, or work even faster to put out her light. Think of the ingestion as a sneak attack—soldiers infiltrating behind enemy lines. I need the slow absorption that's unique to a Vampire."

Page punctured Christian's neck and the first few draws of blood were awkward. I was afraid of throwing up, but it didn't taste like blood at all. It was dark and sweet, like black liquorish and spicy red wine, except it went down like hard liquor and burned my stomach. It comforted me, and like a babe at the breast I sleepily pulled to him. My lips numbed from the sucking, and when his wound began to heal, he cut it again. Somehow, that magically tasty beverage had a way of working itself out of my stomach. I didn't understand the science behind it—whether it was going straight to my veins or speeding up my body in producing more blood—all I knew is that the need for more would take hold again.

Sometimes I would stop and rest, but as my blood was draining out of a tube at a controlled level, I went back to the vein when my body grew weak. Justus left the room, disgusted by the whole affair. Couldn't say I blamed him. I thought I'd be spending my first birthday binging on alcohol, not O positive.

"Page?"

"Yes?"

I wiped my mouth on the towel draped across the pillows. "Justus—you think he's a prick, don't you?"

Her sigh was barely perceptible. "I'm a Relic and a professional healer. He's overstepping his bounds when he interferes. I don't like people telling me how to do my job when they don't know a single thing about it. He's an imperious jackass, and you have my sympathies."

"Yeah, he's like that."

"I'm going to make some notes and do a little research, Silver. If you need anything, just yell." When Page left the room, I made a small inquisitive sound. The kind you make when you've figured something out.

"You noticed that too, huh?" Christian asked with an amused voice.

"Hard not to. I've lived with Justus long enough that it caught my attention right away. It's weird that he didn't seem to notice."

"Perhaps he was too distracted by his old guard tucked beside his precious Learner."

"I could curl up with a teddy bear and he'd tear it a new stuffing."

A shiver skated across my skin.

"Here, you need to start again," he urged.

"Why don't you just put a straw in there, Mr. Juicebox?"

"I don't exactly like spending my evenings as a cocktail, so let's get this over with, yeah?"

"Where's my cat?"

"Clawing out Justus's eyes, I hope."

"He would do that, too." I chuckled.

Christian coaxed my head to the wound and I drank.

"You know, you aren't so bad when your mouth is full."

"Do you say that to all the women?"

"A filthy mouth doesn't become a lady. You should learn to hold that tongue of yours."

"All you old immortals have a thing about how ladies should act. I can always have another Vampire delivered; I'm sure there's a takeout service."

He pulled my head back down, "Shut up and feed before I have to cut my throat again."

After a minute, he groaned and I pulled away. "Is this hurting you? Maybe we should do it somewhere else."

"Where would you suggest, lass? Because I have a lovely vein in my groin area that you could suck on." He gave a satisfied laugh.

"So it's okay for you to have a dirty mouth, but not a woman?" I flew on my back, staring into the dark void. "Maybe it's working; my fingers aren't burning anymore."

"She said there's a good chance you'll regain your sight, so do exactly as you're told."

My mind raced. What if we never caught Nero? This could go on for infinity until he got what he wanted, so why didn't I just give him the damn box? Would he leave me alone? Then there was Tarek. If he'd meant to kill me then he would have, but he wanted me to suffer. Even worse, he wanted Logan to watch. I closed my eyes. *So very tired.*

Except Christian was shaking me. "Wake up! Fall asleep on me and I'll shave your head. The blood loss is making you tired."

He tugged on my neck and I pressed my lips shut. I was cognizant of the consequences of refusing to drink, but my state of mind was akin to a fever and I wasn't thinking rationally. Christian was too strong for me to resist and he shoved my face against his wet neck. What was the point? I would always question if Logan had settled for me; Tarek would forever play his games; Nero would stop at nothing, and I could be permanently blind.

Christian hooked his finger in my mouth and I bit down on it. He rolled his heavy body over mine and forced my jaws open. Blood trickled in my throat and I choked.

"Just swallow it."

My body submitted and I commenced drinking. His warm breath was rapid against my shoulder and I heard a low groan. I snapped out of my blood frenzy to see what was wrong.

"Is that hurting you?"

"*Jaysus wept*, you really think this is hurting me? This sounds like a conversation between two teens in the back of a Chevrolet.

Don't ask daft questions if you don't know about Vampires."

I wiped the back of my hand over my mouth. "How do you manage to follow me when I'm out?"

He rolled off and the bed lightly bounced as he settled to my left. "I've got a motorcycle, but I can stay behind a good distance and track where you're going with my eyes and ears. No need for the headlamp. On foot, I shadow walk." He shifted to his side. "Can I just say that you riding that Ducati the other night *seriously* hurt my feelings? It was enough to make a grown man weep. You should learn how to properly ride."

"My options were limited and I wasn't about to take the princess car out. Justus would kill me three times over."

"I failed you as a guard," he bit out.

"Do you think that I blame you for what happened? You were attacked."

"And that's why I failed. I've been doing this job for years and I get taken out by a fucking pencil."

I belched and turned my head to my side. "I think I'm going to be sick," I muttered.

"Definitely not the effect I usually have on women."

The thought of what'd I'd been doing—drinking blood—coiled in my stomach. "No one's perfect."

"This is not just a job; it's an obligation and an honor to protect a life. I'm not leaving you unless Zeus himself throws a lightning bolt into my arse, sending me across three counties, or I'm discharged. You hear?"

I not only understood him, but I was about to throw up on him.

He gripped my shoulders and slung me over his lap. I vomited something thick and acidic—listening to it splatter on the floor. God, the *floor*. I wanted to curl up and die because my room probably looked like a slaughterhouse.

"All better? I think we'll leave that for Justus to tidy up," he said with a dark laugh.

When the wave of nausea subsided, I sighed and fell on my back. "Justus is going to be so disgusted by this that we'll probably move to a cave."

"The man is all business, but he has a playful side."

"Playful? That's hardly a word I would associate with Justus. I doubt he'll see the humor," I said in a raspy voice.

"Inside joke. I've known the man a long time. Friends that old always have stories."

That I understood. There were plenty of inside jokes with Sunny. Still, I didn't see the humor in cleaning vomit.

Christian pushed my frown up with the pad of his thumb. "Justus was ill once from a concoction he was forced to drink. As his guard…," he said with a sigh, "I had to keep him alive."

"What was it?"

"Liquid fire. While it works its way out of your system, you're extremely vulnerable. He was forced to throw it up and… Jaysus, I had to jam my finger down that wanker's throat," he grumbled.

"Who made him drink it? Is that something you can just slip in someone's glass?" Wasn't that a scary thought.

"Impossible. The moment it touches your tongue it's like…" I heard his mouth smacking around, doing a mental recall. "Well, Justus could probably compare the flavor more than I could since I don't eat much. It's vile to be sure. As for who? Old enemies. He's quite settled from when I knew him—less reckless, more stoic. Seems to work for him."

Justus had progressively become the man he is; I always had the impression he was born arrogant. Probably came from a rich family with harems.

"Drink," Christian coaxed.

"You need to shave your neck because I feel like I'm making out with a wild boar."

He laughed. "Poor bastard."

"Who are you calling a bastard?"

"The boar you made out with."

"Is a five o'clock shadow on your *neck* a fashion statement?"

"Why mess with centuries of perfection? The ladies do like."

CHAPTER 36

"No, that's all she'll need. I retested her blood and she's clear of the venom. Let her sleep it off."

"And her vision?" Justus asked. In my hazy state of consciousness, I heard the concern behind his clipped words.

Page spoke softly. "I'll be honest—I don't know. She went too long without treatment and the damage may be irreversible." There was a snap of a bag and rustling of fabric as her voice moved farther across the room. "Don't let her out of that bed, do you understand? Keep her still and watch her for the next twenty-four hours. That was more Vampire blood than I've ever seen another Breed ingest, so she'll need plenty of rest. No Mage healing, you're likely to do more damage than good. I'm being very specific, Mr. De Gradi. Silver must remain still and calm; don't agitate her."

There was a pause before she continued. "I don't appreciate you turning away as if you have better ideas. Question my knowledge all you want, but don't defy my orders. I'm here as a favor to Remi and if you have any respect for him then you'll heed my advice. She's *my* patient, do you understand me?" Her tone punctuated each word showing that Page was all business. I mentally snickered at the image I had of her: unsophisticated, dressed in discount clothes with her hair pulled up in a tight bun and holding a long, punishing ruler.

"Before you leave, can you remove him from that bed?"

Her laugh was soft and amused. "Is she your lover or your child? Because I see a woman in there who is capable of making her own decisions. Here's my card. Call me immediately if her condition worsens and do me a favor—no more parties. I think she'll feel better after a day, but no excitement. I'll check back in after I see a few more clients. Goodbye, Mr. De Gradi."

I curled up against my warm pillow, wishing the voices would drown out.

"Logan is on his way," Justus warned.

"Is he now?" my pillow said. "Then maybe he can be the one to untangle her arms from my body. Worry not, Justus. I have no interest in your Learner."

The door slammed shut.

"Wake up," Christian said with a hard shake.

"Stop it," I groaned, nudging my face against him.

"It's been a lovely evening, Silver, but I need to find my list of '*things I wish I'd never done*' and add this to it."

He snapped the towel from beneath my head and smudged it over my mouth, muttering curses when he crossed the room.

During the last couple of drinking sessions, I felt remarkably strange—as if new feelings were flooding in me that weren't my own. While a Mage could taste emotions from the light that came from another, I knew little about the complexity of Vampire blood. Perhaps it contained trace amounts of those feelings in addition to the information that transferred. I didn't understand how a Vampire could read that language, but I knew that his blood was lifeless until he rolled on top of me. Only then did it swim with flavor.

"Why the hell are you so turned on?" I accused. But it was too late—Christian was gone.

My hands ran along the walls and I counted my steps to the bathroom. I never cared for mouthwash, but after ingesting the entire contents of Christian, a gargle was in order. I shuffled back to the bed and curled up in freshly changed sheets. Someone had cleaned the floor and the dirty towels were gone. It only took three sighs before I fell into a deep and blissful sleep.

I was thankful Vampires carried no personal scent. Otherwise, it would have been a fiasco. Logan slipped into my room while I slept and covered me protectively. I loved the way he held me fiercely; every woman should know what it's like to be held by a man who would lay down his life for her. Logan Cross had proven it more than once.

His nose traced up my arm, my collarbone, and circled across my neck. Logan drew in a deep, soulful breath until his motor kicked in. Something stirred within me—a longing for his touch. I arched my back and he brushed his hands over my face.

"How's my sumptuous Mage?" he asked, each word dripping from his tongue like sweet honey. "Why did you hide your sickness?"

"I didn't want to ruin the party," I said, kissing his pliant mouth, tasting the mint that clung to his breath.

"Forgiven," he whispered against my lips. Our breathing grew heavy as I drew him in.

"Kiss me," I beckoned. Desire stirred in me like tiny firecrackers going off.

My fingers tugged on his zipper while I slid my other hand between his stomach and his jeans. His breath hitched and it felt wonderful when his muscles locked tight as I curled my fingers.

"What are you doing?" he whispered in a dark and desperate voice. Logan's excitement overwhelmed me and it was an incendiary awakening of touch and taste. I slowly pulled the zipper down and his lips grazed over mine. "We're not doing this," he said firmly.

Except we were. By the weight of his chest, the swell pressing between my legs, and the way he continually breathed in my scent—I knew Logan wanted me.

Logan's scent changed and his body language was telling me "more" by the way he submitted. I bit his lower lip and the reaction was instantaneous. He snatched my wrists, pinned them against the pillow, and clamped his teeth on my shoulder. Not hard, but not soft. Something a mother cat would do to scold their overzealous kitten. It was raw and animalistic.

I trembled, uncertain of how Chitah men were in the bedroom.

He wiped a few stray hairs from my left cheek. "Did I hurt you?"

"It's not that."

His gentle fingers brushed over the bite on my neck. The punctures would leave scars for the rest of my life, and now I was forever marked by two men I hated, but not the one that I cared for.

"I'm going to kill him," Logan said darkly. "And it'll be painful so that I can savor his remorse."

"Shhh," I whispered.

My hand popped the button on his jeans free. Some of his willpower came off with that button.

Logan sat up, straddling me. "You're ill."

The moment I placed my hands on his upper thigh, a sound came out of him that reminded me of the night I'd spent with him in a cave. It was primal and barely contained. It fueled me even more to claw at the fabric with my nails and slowly push my hands upward.

Logan captured my wrists.

"What if I said it was doctor's orders?"

"Then I would know you were lying." He took a deep breath and pressed his lips in the palm of my hand.

I closed my fingers into a fist. "Now I have your kiss."

"And what do you plan on doing with it?" He chuckled, softly stroking the wrist of my left hand.

Without answering, I slid my hand between my legs and opened my fingers, releasing the kiss. Logan inhaled sharply.

There was no weakening this man. He was a Chitah and always had the upper hand when it came to seduction. The cocksure tone in his voice returned. "How did you know it was me lying on top of you, hmm?" He stroked his finger across my jaw, in control once more.

"Because I know your smell."

He eased himself on top of me. "Don't say things like that. You don't know the effect they have on me."

But I did. His sentences sometimes trailed into a growl, but now they ended with a breath. His skin was so warm.

"Touch me," I begged in a whisper against his cheek.

"Silver, stop. I can't do this. You need to heal."

"Doc said I'm healed. Don't I *feel* all better now?" I nibbled his shoulder, rubbing my hands down his sides and his entire body reacted with a jerk. This was too much restraint for a man who had pursued me as hard as he had. "*Why* don't you want me?"

Logan hovered. Every word was a caress in all the places that I craved him. Between each of his sentences, he placed a languid kiss against my neck. "I want to seduce you, Little Raven. *Slowly*. Like a delicacy. I want to savor your arousal. Taste you. Touch you with these hands that have memorized every line and curve of your body."

"Then *touch* me."

"You don't know what you're asking. Don't put me in a position where I have to deny you."

My body sagged. "I've been asleep for years, Logan. I want this. Right now. With you. If you don't…"

He lifted my chin up with his finger. "Erase your doubts. Tell me."

"I'm blind. Maybe I'll never regain my sight. If you don't want me now, then I'll know it's because you're not okay with this. I need to know that this doesn't matter."

"My doubt has nothing to do with your ability to see."

"Then what is it?"

"Would you find a male who imposed on you in this weakened state admirable? When I said that I would take you as you are, I meant it. Blind does not mean weak; it means that we'll experience each other through touch." Logan's hand cupped my breast and I moaned. "And taste." His tongue circled on my shoulder before planting a kiss. "And sound." A quaking purr rumbled in his chest that soothed me like a lullaby. "And smell."

"I like your smell." My legs opened to him.

"A female should be courted properly and I regret going about this the wrong way. I carried a foolish notion that because you're a Mage, some rules did not apply. But you're owed the same honors that a female Chitah would get."

"Celibacy?"

He kissed my nose. "We are virile males, Little Raven. Refraining from sex is how we show a female our strength, respect, and control."

"You're also a man who likes to break rules, Mr. Cross. And I'm okay with that."

His fingers were on my hips, clawing. "You know I love when you call me that."

"Then claim me."

The heat between us rose by ten degrees. "There's no going back and undoing what's been done," he warned.

"I'm already undone, Logan. I want to feel like I'm more than just a challenge in your eyes—but a light."

His hand flattened over my chest. "Female, you are the most relevant thing about me."

I closed my eyes and murmured, "I wish I could see your face."

Logan stretched across me and a switch clicked. "Sight is overrated. Now that we're both in the dark, what shall I do with you?" His long fingers trailed up my inner thigh and paused so close to my panties that I felt the heat from his hand and moaned. "Someday, Little Raven, my eyes will feast on your body."

His expert hand massaged me so slowly that whatever doubt I had about his intentions melted away. His thumb grazed over my sex and I lifted my hips for more.

A delicious purr sounded against my ear. "You are a luscious female."

"Turn on the lights if you want."

"No." His mouth covered mine and his tongue was hot and velvety. As he deepened the kiss, he released his hold and the weight of his body settled on me.

"Ah," Logan whispered. "I seem to remember you saying something about enjoying foreplay." He sat up.

Well this is an odd way to go about it, I thought.

Logan held my bent knees, slightly prying apart my legs. "Where should I begin?" he contemplated.

When his left hand moved away, I held my breath in anticipation.

A feathery touch brushed over my panties, stroking me so insistently that I made one of those wonderful, pleading moans that every man loves to hear.

"So sensitive," he murmured, kissing my knee and licking my inner thigh.

My heart raced, my body trembled, and I knew with everything in me that I wanted Logan.

Without warning, he hopped off the bed and pulled off his

jeans. If I didn't know better, I would have sworn he was taking his time to draw out the suspense. Maybe he was reading my scent like a book and had discovered the art of cliffhangers.

His fingers leisurely slid down my leg.

"Sit up."

I never knew what to expect with Logan Cross. Nerves fluttered in my stomach and I sat on the edge of the mattress with my legs hanging off the side.

"Raise your arms," he said.

My loose shirt lifted away from my body and fell to a heap on the floor. His fingers gathered the ends of my hair, feeling the length of it as they moved down—the backs of his hands caressing my breasts.

"Don't be nervous—I won't hurt you," he reassured me, having picked up my tangled scent of arousal and tension.

"What are Chitah women like in bed?" I couldn't help but blurt out the question.

"Submissive."

"Those women at that party didn't seem very submissive."

He chuckled, lightly rubbing my shoulders. "In the bedroom, most of them will submit to a male as a show of respect. We certainly don't expect them to; it's just in their nature."

"Can I take this off?" I asked, touching the buttons on his shirt.

He stepped closer and I hooked my fingers around an opening and ripped it apart. The tiny buttons dismantled, tapping across the floor.

"Sorry," I said. "That wasn't very submissive of me."

Logan sucked in a sharp breath and his fingers dug into the skin on my shoulders. "Tell me what you want me to do to you, Little Raven," he murmured.

That took me off guard. Sex was always a recreational activity—like exercising. Which happened to be two things I didn't do very often, but when I did, there wasn't much of a warm-up.

I shrugged so that he could feel my uncertainty. "Kiss me?"

He knelt on the hardwood floor, sliding his hands up my thighs and nuzzling his cheek against my stomach until I thought that I would expire. "Where?"

That single, suggestive word charged the air with infinitesimal sparks. An awareness grew between us like a tug of war—a push and pull of energy in its most basic form.

Logan stood up and took my hand, pulling me to my feet. The distance between us made my heart race like an anxious hummingbird.

"I can scent your nervousness."

My voice was breathier than I intended it to be. "I can't help it, Mr. Cross. You have that effect on me."

"Mmm," he purred. "Step closer."

I inched forward.

"Closer."

My stubborn feet moved nearer on the cool, wood floor.

"*Closer*," he whispered insistently until our bodies touched. "Good."

The feel of his chest against mine was overwhelming. He used my body as a map to find direction and lifted my chin with the crook of his finger to kiss me. "Each time you get nervous, I want you to remember that you have me completely… in your thrall."

"Thank you for Max."

"Your heart was running free on the streets of Texas, so I wanted to bring it home."

"Where did you keep him? Finn didn't mention it."

"Levi. He's pretty keen on the fella. Chitahs aren't really big on keeping pets, but now he's been talking about getting himself one."

My fingers were doing a little exploring of their own between our small talk, admiring the lines of muscle in his broad shoulders. Logan was built for speed—svelte and tall, but his body was toned and capable. "Your hair seems longer," I noted, touching the ends of it. My fingers trailed down to the V cut along his abdomen, sliding down the grooves.

Logan dropped to his knees and hooked his fingers on the edges of my panties, slowly… *slowly* pulling them down. Some random thought struck me about how I really wanted him to tear them off with his teeth.

God yes, this *was* going to happen. He rolled his tongue below my navel, circling dangerously. "What about Justus and Christian?" I asked.

He lowered his voice. "They don't exist." His hand wedged between my legs. "Just you and me; we're the last two left on earth."

A throbbing ache took hold as he scorched me with his touch and tempted me with his words. I'd never felt so sensitive, where even the softest gust of air or brush of a finger was multiplied times a hundred.

"I'm on bended knee, Silver. Tell me you want me."

It wasn't about sex; he wanted me to accept his claim. Logan Cross was indirectly asking me to stop running and choose. I thought about what he once told me: *"Make the men in your life run for it; if they tire of the chase, then they're not worth your affections."* I wasn't ready for a life-changing decision. I just wanted this night.

"Take me to the bed," I whispered. My legs were not going to hold me up any longer.

He lifted me and I held onto his neck. "I'll take you… anywhere you ask me to," he murmured.

My heart pounded when the sheets cooled my back. Logan measured the distance from my thigh to my breast with his tongue. The darkness brought such an unexpected intensity of heightened awareness. Even the exaggerated sound of the sheets rustling beneath his knees was erotic.

"Oh, Miss Silver. You do have the loveliest bosom."

A laugh almost erupted from me until his mouth latched onto my nipple. When he swirled his tongue, I moaned in a soft breath. I'd waited for that moment for so long—the one place I wanted to feel his lips, and they were so generous and attentive.

"I'm a man of patience," he said, kissing around the curve of my breast, "but I've waited an excruciatingly long time to taste you."

"What would you have done if I made you wait years?"

"I would have learned how to give you an orgasm from a kiss."

My heart quickened. His bedroom words were even better than his bedroom eyes. I luxuriated beneath his expert touch and melted into a pool of desire. Nothing else existed, just the feel and smell of a man who handled me like a goddess.

Seconds? Minutes? It seemed like hours that he marveled over every inch of skin with his tongue until I was writhing beneath him. His arms caged me, hair sliding across my chest, and the rhythm of his wet tongue and whiskers left me breathless.

There was a tug as he pulled the mood ring off my finger.

"I thought it didn't bother you?" I asked softly.

"It's yours, but when I take you I want nothing on you—especially a token that another male has given you." The ring tapped on the bedside table to my left.

I cupped my hand around his neck and stroked my thumb against the bristles on his jaw. "Logan, I want to touch you while I still can. It requires concentration to keep my light reined in, but this is something that I need to learn how to control."

"Tell me what you want me to do."

"Lie down on your back," I said.

He growled, pleased with my take-charge command. We switched places and I sat beside him.

"When you can no longer touch me, then it's *my* turn," he said.

"Fair enough." If I lost concentration and my energy leaked, a shock would rip through him and embarrass me for the rest of my life. "Do you trust me?"

"Implicitly."

"Grip the headboard."

It creaked as he stretched his long arms behind his head. Logan's anxious breath filled the silent room when I ran my fingers up his leg, as if I had all the time in the world. Every place I touched, the texture of his skin changed. From the soft bristle of hairs to a smooth spot on his inner thigh, and then his stomach was warm and taut with grooves of defined muscles. I scored my nails across his hip and the headboard made a loud complaint.

"Do you want me to touch you?" I asked.

His hips lifted in response. Logan was a caged animal and it was exciting to feel the dangerous power of the man beneath me.

My fingers wrapped around his shaft—so smooth and rigid. With long strokes, I slid my palm to the head and then back to the base. His entire body responded—tensing as his heels dug into the mattress. I grew apprehensive when I felt the length of him; he was more man than I'd given him credit for. I leaned forward and circled my tongue in a spot on his chest. A deep rumble gathered in Logan's throat like a roar waiting to be unleashed.

"Stop," he groaned in a hoarse voice. His fingers curled in my hair.

"Why?"

I could hear his teeth scraping against his lip as he moved his hands away. "Our females…"

"Don't tell me you've never had a woman pleasure you," I almost said in disbelief. Silence replied. "So I'll be your first?"

The headboard made a terrible creak as if it might snap into pieces and temptation took over. I leaned over and licked his stomach, so near to him that he roared out and tensed all at once. "Silver, please. I'll lose control." His voice was a harsh warning and frightened me as I decided that we'd have plenty of time to explore dangerous ground.

His skin smelled masculine, sticky with heat beneath my fingertips. I ran my tongue over a spot on his lower belly and his body tensed as I kissed my way up to his Adam's apple. I licked it. Strange thing—I'd never done anything like that before. His thick purr tickled against my lips.

"You smell so good," I said in a soft breath, running my nose around his neck and through his hair. "Why do you smell so good?" I took a long, deep inhale.

When I slid farther up and nuzzled his cheek, Logan let go of the headboard and held on to my hips. "I've never been with a Mage before, Silver."

"I've only been with human men, so this will be new for both of us," I said, nibbling his ear. I hoped that Logan wouldn't compare my novice ways to the experienced immortal women he'd slept with. That thought alone almost sent me running out of the room. I was overwhelmed with how gentle, firm, and insistent Logan was in seeing to my needs. Truthfully, I felt inferior with a man who had at least a hundred years practice on me. No pressure.

He groaned beneath his words. "I'm afraid I might hurt you."

"Why?"

There was a pause and I kissed my way up to his chin, feeling the bristles against my lips. "Tell me."

"Sometimes during sex, when it gets intense, we flip our switch."

"Seriously?" I frowned. Then I remembered how fiercely he'd fought to protect me while in that condition. Deep down, Logan was in there, he was just at the mercy of his instincts. "I trust you."

"But *I* don't trust me."

"Doesn't matter," I said against his lips, kissing the corner of his mouth. "I've seen the dark side of you, Logan, and we get along just fine. I guess when you think about it, we could both end up killing each other in the bedroom."

He flipped me over and I felt like a clock about to unwind as he laid himself on top of me.

"Mmm," he purred. "My turn."

When I tried to open my legs, he closed them with his own—but I felt his arousal like a solid fact against my thigh.

Logan placed a kiss on my swollen lips, tasting them like nectar. There was a raw intensity behind every stroke of his tongue against mine, and suddenly our desire erupted into something wild. I pulled his hair; his fingers bit into my waist; flames erupted from the press of our skin, rubbing so hard that the energy snapped in my fingertips, so I pulled it back.

This is how Justus was with his women? Containing my energy forced me to become detached from the full experience; it was like eating without tasting.

The curve of his strong back against the palms of my hands made it feel like Logan was mine. I took hold of his glorious backside as memories of our hotel stay resurfaced, along with that brief moment of temptation when I saw him naked for the first time.

"I can't touch you anymore. I'm sorry," I said through shallow breaths, letting go.

"Put your hands over your head. I can feel your energy rising." Logan kissed the delicate spot on my neck that I loved the most.

"What's it feel like?"

"Like every hair on my body is standing up."

I grinned. "That's not the only thing standing up."

He rolled off me, stroking my thigh.

"Sorry," I said. "I thought it would last longer, but I lost control."

"Control is the one thing that I forbid you to have tonight. No holding back—there's no hiding who we are in here, Silver. I'll take you as a woman, as a Mage, and as my female."

His words rushed through my head like a storm. *His* female. I fought against the way the idea overlapped in my mind like layers of devotion.

His fingers on my inner thigh smoothed away my nerves. Not seeing what was coming was the most erotic experience and his hot mouth on my breast was so unexpected that I squirmed beneath him. He did things with his mouth that sent light shooting through my fingertips. I gripped my pillow tighter.

"You have a very greedy tongue, Mr. Cross."

Without warning, he slipped a finger inside me and I nearly threw him off the bed from the desire that licked over my body like a flame.

"Spread them," he demanded in a dark whisper against my ear. I complied. "I want my mouth there," he growled, stroking me once more. "When I get that privilege, I'm going to take my time. Do you understand me?"

I shook my head. *Hell no, I didn't understand.* When his fingers found a rhythm, a moan escaped that sounded more like a plea.

"You're a seven-course meal, and tonight is only the first course."

Now I knew. Each time we were together, there would be something new for us to share. His version of a slow seduction wouldn't be abstaining from sex, but feeding me experiences slowly. Nothing was predictable about this man.

"Please… I want you." My voice cracked, legs clamping together and trapping his hand.

Logan climbed over me, tracing his eager lips across my neck. "Say it again."

My pillow was about to become nothing but stuffing. "I

want you."

"No," he said. "Not like that. I've waited since the night we met—when you stubbornly challenged me—to say those words. Whisper it in my ear. *Slowly*."

The San Andreas Fault had nothing on the power dividing within me. Logan's ear brushed against my mouth. It was so intimate speaking to him that way—so close that he could hear my shaky breath. "Take me," I said impatiently. "Because if you don't touch me, then I'm going to have to touch you." When he rocked his hips against mine and I felt a thickness press between my legs, I gave in. "I want you, Logan. *Only* you."

A heady, intoxicating scent filled my nose. Pheromones, aphrodisiac, ambrosia—clashing into the most powerful mix I'd ever experienced. It was dominating and sinful, with a power so primal it triggered all kinds of responses in me.

I arched my back and just as soon as I felt the blunt head slide upward, he thrust himself to the hilt.

"*My* female," he growled in my ear.

My knees clamped against his hips and my entire body locked up. This was more than I'd imagined. Logan filled me to capacity and my body yielded to him in ways that I didn't understand. My legs were shaking.

Did that spectacular pattern erupt across skin? I didn't want him to contain his animal the way I did with my light. I wanted to learn everything about Logan Cross.

He dropped his left arm over my wrists to keep them still while the right caressed my body. Logan drove himself into me—over and over again. His persistent hips slammed against mine until it felt like we were conjoined. There was a thunder in our hearts and he kissed me so salaciously that he was everywhere. My mouth. My core. Hands on my body. Scent in my nose. Words resonating in my mind. My past. My present.

I struggled beneath him, yearning to touch as he kept my hands pinned. He growled and nipped my shoulder with his teeth. "Let's do this a different way."

Logan lifted me by the waist and turned on his back, grabbing my hips to straddle him. I tentatively climbed astride.

"Hands on the headboard, and hold on tight," he said.

Did he know what he was doing to me?

Logan guided himself inside and I held the damn headboard, ready to snap it in two. He caressed my hips, waiting patiently for me to move. I felt brave and scooted my knees up.

Logan knew me better than I knew myself.

"Tell me what you want," he said. I tensed, causing his fingers to grip tighter. "*Tell me.*"

Most of my sexual liaisons were brief interludes, with the exception of the failed relationship. My ex never wanted me on top because, in his eyes, it was empowering. Sex was never about me, but his own gratification followed by a critique on why I couldn't please him. It made me self-conscious about taking control.

This was exactly the position I wanted to be in, yet *telling* Logan what I needed was harder than I thought it would be.

"Uh…" I took a deep breath. *Get it together.* I could already feel myself blushing, even with this delicious man inside of me. I just couldn't say it out loud. Why was it so difficult?

Logan wasn't having any of it. He hooked his arms over my shoulders to keep me in place. "Neither of us will be going anywhere until you tell me what you want."

"You're making me nervous."

He pushed himself up and spoke against my cheek. "And you're making me angry. You think whatever you say will frighten me off? Your scent only tells me so much; what I really want to know is what's on your mind. So *tell me* what you want." He slid his arm around my back and stroked the curve.

"I want you to…"

"To what?" Logan fell back down against the pillow, waiting patiently for an answer.

Even in the dark, I rolled my eyes. I knew exactly what my body needed to send me over the edge, but asking for it wasn't a dialogue I was used to having. Why couldn't I just be like other women and take what I wanted, say what I wanted, do what I wanted? I had no problem doing that with every other aspect of my life. *Damn my inhibitions.*

Instead of asking, I leaned forward until my nipple brushed across his parted lips. His wet tongue circled around.

"This is what you want, isn't it," he murmured. "Then say it." His mouth came away and he waited. *Damn him.*

"Suck on me," I said in a small breath.

Logan did more than obey; he devoured me, taking pleasure in using his mouth to light up every nerve. His hand cupped my breast while his other stroked my body.

That unflinching gesture spiraled within my belly like a wound-up coil. I dropped down hard, repeating the motion again and again until each thrust caused him to moan. I don't know how many minutes went by before we were fast approaching the edge.

"Perfect," he breathed against my sensitive skin. I was on the brink as I picked up speed—reckless and focused only on my own pleasure, my own release.

I couldn't stop. My body became a locomotive and the bed thumped against the wall. He pinched my nipples hard with his thumb and index finger, twisting them until I cried out. My legs trembled and I grew dizzy as a flush of heat went through me in waves.

"Come for me, Little Raven."

Five simple words unraveled me. My body tightened as his hands spread over my hips and thrust me against him in his own needful rhythm. I grabbed a handful of his hair, pulled it back, and firmly bit his neck as I came.

Logan roared out during his release and smothered me in his scent. One he managed to keep contained the entire time and thank God for that. It only heightened my arousal, causing me to climax even harder. I cried out, unable to stop riding the wave as I moaned his name once again.

I transformed into jelly against his sticky chest. A cool sheen of sweat never felt so sweet. He tenderly stroked my damp hair away from my shoulder as our chests filled with heavy breaths.

When I sat up, an aftershock slammed into me and he immediately responded—rocking me into continual pleasure with his hands on my hips as tiny bursts of light filled my head. I suddenly became keenly aware of the meaning behind "parting is such sweet sorrow".

"That's it. Give me *everything*," he murmured. "I'm not leaving this bed until my female is sated."

His words were all the stimulation I needed. I collapsed on his chest and pressed my soft lips to his throat, feeling the wonderful tickling vibration of his purr mingled with his racing pulse. He stroked my back and shoulders with a gentle touch.

When I started to pull away, my heart stopped. Something was *very* unfinished. I still felt him thick inside of me. "I thought you… weren't you satisfied?"

He moaned. "Intently."

"Then how come—"

Logan cleared his throat with a dark laugh. "Chitahs are known for our stamina."

"Oh." I smiled impishly. "Do you want to finish?"

Logan rocked with laughter. "Silver, you're spent. Come lay beside me."

He hissed when I rose and settled down on the mattress. Once his arms wrapped around me, I wondered why we'd waited so long.

"Is that how it normally goes for you?"

Logan slid my hips closer and the air stirred between us. "No. This was different. Twice I almost flipped my switch and that's never happened before. I've never felt that out of control."

"Not even with your mate or all the women henceforth?"

He snorted and pinched my arm. "Most of the females I've chosen were submissive in the bedroom with a few aggressive tactics."

"Sounds like war."

"More like routine. Some things come natural and most of the act is anticipated. But with you… I don't know what to expect."

Logan's leg wove around mine. "Most females stay on their backs and that's what I'm used to. I only let you get on top so that I wouldn't get hit by your sex lightning."

I burst out laughing. "That's one way to put it."

His soft kiss against my ear stirred another flurry of butterflies.

"But I must say, Silver, I'm a converted man. We're doing that again," he decided.

"If Justus heard us, I'm going to die," I mumbled against his chest.

"Nothing he hasn't heard before. I'm sure," he replied coldly. "They're upstairs and I requested privacy."

"You *didn't*."

He snorted. "I *thought* you needed rest. Had I known your intentions were otherwise, I would have asked them to drive into the city for the evening. Justus was working in his study when I came down."

"Oh. Well in that case, he'll be up there until the next eclipse. He's a workaholic. Whether it's HALO or those damn weights, he's always busy with something."

"Does he still make you work out?"

I shrugged. "Sometimes. Not as much as before, but we still have our sessions."

"Well," he said, grabbing the back of my thigh, "be sure to tell him that the training paid off."

I kissed his chest lightly. "I'll do that. Right before dinner I'll commend him for getting me in shape for sex."

We laughed quietly and soaked in the cool air that drifted over the bed. I enjoyed lying in his arms and realized how much I'd yearned for it—not just to be held by a man like it mattered, but by him. I would have never imagined that my contempt for Logan would grow to something more. As a Mage, I no longer had to worry about things like unsafe sex or pregnancy, but there was still that matter of my heart.

"Are you hungry?" I asked. "I can fix us a plate and we can eat in bed."

"Absolutely not," he snapped.

"Something wrong with my cooking?"

"You fix very delicious meals, but I draw a line. A Chitah male is never served by a female; it's the other way around."

"So I can never cook?" I almost liked that idea, but then again…

He sighed. "It's as it should be."

"Compromise with me, Mr. Cross. I'm not a Chitah. You like my enchiladas, right? Just imagine how empty your life will be if you could never enjoy them again."

I sensed his smile in the darkness. "For you I will bend, but it won't be easy. I respect that these are not your ways, but you have no idea how upset I was at the dinner party you gave."

"What?" My brows knitted at the random comment.

"The one you had months ago when we first met; I helped you prepare and cook the food. When you walked in and served those males, I was coming out of my skin."

I circled a finger around his navel and a few quiet minutes passed.

"I miss Finn," I said quietly. "How's he getting along with Lucian?"

Logan's weight shifted and he patted the small of my back. "Little Wolf is making progress. I was quite impressed the night he left me," he trailed off.

"Why?"

"Nothing. Schooling is what he needs; the rest will come with time."

"It meant a lot to me that you took him in. Humans don't take in strangers so easily. Maybe a sofa for a couple of nights, but then he'd be out on his own. If someone like Finn ended up on the streets, I don't even want to imagine what kind of life he'd have."

"There are many qualities about humans that confound me," he grumbled. "I don't know much about them, but you're beginning to make me think that they're not all bad."

"Glad to oblige. It's only been a year, but it feels like that part of me is still around sometimes. You really impress me, Logan Cross. Immensely."

He turned on that deep motor in his chest that was barely audible and I felt it with the flat of my hand. He had no control over the sounds his body made, so knowing my touch or compliment could incite that response made it sexy as hell.

"When we first met, why did you get mad when I wandered off in the cave?" I asked.

"Has that bothered you this long?"

I shrugged. Sometimes little things settled in my mind, took residency, and paid rent. Perhaps I was searching for ways to disprove his claim that I was his kindred spirit.

He combed my hair back. "You almost fell to your death and it frightened me. My feelings were conflicted at the time. My apologies if I was cross with you."

"You're always cross, Mr. Cross," I teased.

"Mmm," he moaned, sliding farther down. His lips were impossibly softer against my mouth and I didn't respond, letting him kiss each corner until he had his fill.

"I love our pillow talk," I admitted. "Whenever we're in bed this way, your guard is down."

"I thought you were the only one with a guard."

I squeezed his arm. "Even now you still intimidate me. Everything about the way you speak and carry yourself—maybe it's because I know how dangerous you really are."

"Never to you," he quickly replied. "How's your neck feeling?"

I touched the marks of Tarek's bite on the right side of my neck, having almost forgotten.

"Not so bad."

"Worry not," he assured me. "Tarek's blood will run cold if it's the last thing on earth I see to."

Logan overwhelmed me with his protectiveness; I wanted to roll myself up in it and bask in that devotion. The emotion was one that I struggled to embrace, but Logan made it easy because he allowed me to stand on my own two feet. I gained a sense of what relationships were like among his kind, and I recognized from the very beginning the allowances he made in order to respect my needs. Allowances even the human men in my life never gave.

"What's it like? Being human," he asked.

Curiosity played on his words like a bow on a violin. I was intrigued that he wanted to know more about my old life.

"It's hard to explain," I began, shifting to my side and slipping into the crook of his arm. "It's like you're living life with an expiration date. You live in denial that you'll ever get old. I once carried scars as reminders of events in my life."

"Scars?"

"I had a small mark on my forehead where I hit it on the corner of a table when I was little. The only thing I remember about it was crying and my mom yelling at me. It's hard to remember the details because I was only two or three. She said I was running from her because I didn't want to put on a dress."

Logan laughed heartily. "That's my girl."

"I was reborn in this new body with only one mark—Samil's. Until now," I said regretfully. "Now I'll be reminded of Tarek."

A low growl sounded from Logan.

"If their lives are so fragile, then why do they seem so alive?"

I sighed. "The uncertainty of your life gives you a greater appreciation for it. You don't know from one day to the next if you'll be healthy or even alive. Most immortals seem blasé about life because of its permanence. They don't know the feeling of a phone call in the middle of the night that could mean someone you know is dead. One small mishap can become life altering. Then there's cancer and other things that you can't prevent. I didn't have to deal with losing anyone. Maybe that's why it's hard for me to get close with people. How Adam survived the death of his entire family, I'll never comprehend."

"I'd like to discuss this with you more in detail sometime," he stated. "Too morose of a subject when I have you naked in my arms."

"Have you given any thought to looking up your sister?"

By the way his shoulders stiffened, I knew Logan wasn't ready to discuss this. Sadie was the human infant his family had given up and it was a sensitive topic. Chitahs shared a human gene and were either born human or Chitah. Human babies were always given up. No exceptions.

Logan's heart beat just a little bit faster beneath the palm of my hand.

"I would never want to put her life in danger. Look at what Tarek did to you," he said angrily. "Why would I risk that with my flesh and blood?"

"Sometimes the risk is worth the consequence. I'm not going to drop this subject, Logan. I know how you feel about your sister. Your traditions serve to segregate your own family because these children are not immortal. Even if you choose not to raise them, they should at least know who they are and where they come from."

"Would it have given you peace of mind growing up to know what you were?"

A question I'd never considered. "I don't know, but how do you think I like finding out what I am at this stage in my life? Don't you want to know what kind of woman she grew up to be? What if she's alone and needs someone to help her? She won't live forever, you know."

He couldn't conceal his conflicted feelings. Logan's legs wrestled with the sheets and finally kicked them off. I rolled on my back, bending my knees and staring into the darkness.

"Yes," he admitted, sitting up and scrubbing his fingers through his hair. "I want to know she's being taken care of. We protect our females—our sisters—and it kills me to wonder if someone is looking out for her the way we would… the way I would. But our world has no place for a human."

"Need I remind you of Sunny and Knox?"

I cringed when I heard the sternness in his response. "Need I remind you we had to put them in hiding?"

Touché.

"Not anymore, and by their choice. They understand the risk. You don't have to bring her into our world, Logan. I'm not trying to force you to do anything that would put her life in danger. Stand in line behind her at the coffee shop and have a conversation. Check up on her and make sure she's not struggling with paying rent. You could send the money anonymously." My eyes stung from the realization that my own family was comprised of a mother who didn't love me, and a cat. "You'll regret it," I said, throwing my arm over my face.

Logan moved my arm away and kissed the corners of my eyes. "Let's continue this another time. I want to sleep beside you without tears."

Since the moment he walked into my life, Logan offered nothing but comfort. Even in captivity, he fed and kept me warm beside the fire. I healed using the power he offered, and he protected me like a shield against the men that Nero had sent. Logan treated me with such reverence but as an equal. It didn't seem like too much to ask to honor his request.

"Why did you bite me?" he suddenly asked in a rough voice.

"Sorry. I don't know what came over me. Did I break the skin?"

"No," he said absently. "Sometimes you behave in a way that's very…"

"What?"

"Our females bite to incite the male to climax," he said matter-of-factly. "It's a primal barometer to let us know when they're ready."

"You see what you want to see," I muttered, stroking the hard knuckles on his hand. "Do you think you can tolerate not being touched? It's not a novelty, Logan. It's something I'll never be able to control if I want to give myself completely to you."

Logan kissed my neck, making his way up to the edge of my jaw. "You touch me more than you know." He eased back and his voice became humored. "Plus, we can try ropes."

Skin smacked when I slapped his chest. "Behave, Mr. Cross."

He caressed the rounded curves of my chest with his skilled hand. "Did you want this only because of your blindness—to test me?"

"I want to know that I can ask for this and it's mine to take. No bargaining. No explanations. No negotiations."

"Little Raven, I'm yours for the taking," he said against my lips.

His mouth melted against mine, moving with slow indulgence. It was languid and relishing. I could kiss that man for hours and never tire.

Logan nuzzled his cheek against mine. "There's no need for you to be shy about asking for what you want in bed." I squirmed, trying to escape, and he hooked his arm around my body to keep me still. "I don't like that you shut down on me. Whatever it was like with the men in your past doesn't matter," he said, stroking the flat of my belly. "If you have needs, then I want to know what they are. If you want my mouth on your body, then you only need ask and I will taste every speck of you."

I smiled warmly at his words.

"Do I still make you nervous?" he asked, rolling me over to face him again.

Butterflies roared, taking pattern in flight. My admission was a heavy perfume in the air, and he stroked my cheek with the pad of his thumb. Logan only made me anxious when he was soft with me. My ambivalence with him was shifting day by day.

"I like that," he murmured. "You're so unlike other females and I never know what you're going to do from one minute to the next. Even your fire-breathing makes my animal growl with delight."

"Are you saying you like my sass?"

"Mmm," he said, squeezing my backside. "I also like your ass."

I laughed and tilted my head up, opening my eyes. I blinked once. Then twice. Shit! I could *see* him. The color was a hazy blue, but his light eyes rimmed in black stared past me. I shot up so quickly Logan's expression hardened.

"What's wrong?" he said, rising up. I could *see* his nostrils flaring, picking up the panic in my scent. His long hair was a tangled mess and his knee rose, blocking the view that I wanted to see the most.

"Are the lights out?" I asked.

"Yes."

"Logan, I… I can see you."

He reached for the nightstand in a panic, nearly knocking over the lamp as he switched it on.

A blaze of light ignited in my head and a blood-curdling scream poured from my lungs.

CHAPTER 37

SEARING PAIN ROARED THROUGH MY skull, reaching corners I didn't know existed. I shielded my face, unable to stop screaming from the unbearable agony that pulsed in my watering eyes. Logan threw a blanket over my body just moments before the door crashed in and there was a struggle.

Christian's voice fell to an octave that would have made a shadow hide. "Do not *move,* Chitah."

Imagining Logan pinned naked to the floor with his fangs bared might have been funny if not for the fact that flaming spears were driving into my skull. I rolled to my stomach, moaning against the pillow.

"Call the bloody Relic!" Christian shouted. "I have this under control." Justus's heavy boots stormed down the hall.

"I'm only going to ask you once to get off me, Vampire. If you don't let me check on my female, you have my word that I will personally end your life."

A Chitah's threats were never empty.

"Let him up," I yelled. "Logan, don't threaten him."

Christian's voice vibrated in my ears as loud as a scream, and yet I knew he was speaking under his breath to Logan's face. "I don't care if you're her Siamese twin; you will *not* touch her until the doctor gets here. That is on *my* order as her guard. Now put your goddamn trousers on."

Tears streamed down my face, soaking into the sheets. The pain was crippling.

"Where do you hurt?" Christian asked.

"My eyes," I cried.

"Right now? When did it start?"

"I don't know."

"Turn off the lights," Christian shouted. "All the way into the hall. I want a complete blackout!"

"She's on her way," Justus confirmed. "What happened?"

"Keep the lights off," Christian stressed as he sat down on the bed. "Look at me, girl. Move your head away from your arm. Keep your eyes closed and tell me if you feel any pain."

I rolled to my back and coolness touched my face as I sensed the absence of light.

His thumb pressed against my eyelid. "Does that hurt?"

"No. There's a dull ache, but they don't hurt anymore."

"Open your eyes."

Hell no.

"Do it, Silver," Justus urged from across the room.

My lids pried apart by sheer force—lashes opening like a flower yawning at sunrise. I touched the corners and rubbed away the tears with my fingertips. Slowly the room came into focus. There was so much detail that I could even make out the painted trees along the walls, and the strands of hair on Logan's head that were lighter than the rest.

Christian cursed under his breath.

"I can see," I whispered.

"Silver?" Logan called out from the corner of the room.

"Give me a minute."

The room was a blue haze—almost grainy. Christian's heavy brows sat over his wide eyes. My new sight brought such vivid detail. His angled jaw was square and his nose straight, with a shadow of hair across his jaw and chin. On one cheek was a single, thin line where his smile usually ended up. More like a hard smirk than a smile. Christian's eyes didn't seem as hollow as I had imagined them before, but inviting, as if he were drinking in the world through their liquid depths.

"You can see me, can't you?"

"Tell us what's happening," Logan said sharply.

Christian leaned in. "You realize that it's pitch-black in this room?"

My breath caught and I sat up, holding the blanket against me. When I shook my head, a black mane of hair spilled across my shoulders. "Did you change me?"

His mouth turned to the side. "There's more involved in creating a youngling, but I've never given over that much blood to anyone. We'll wait for the Relic. Feck me, *your eyes*," he marveled, pushing up my lid. "They're fully dilated."

I should have been petrified, but my body swelled with relief. My eyesight was back and even if I had to avoid lights for the rest of my life, then I'd be okay with that.

"Is this how it feels for you? I can see *everything*. I can even see the mud on Justus's shoes!" I laughed, and Justus reached down, blindly rubbing at the edges of his soles.

"We have more tolerance to light than you apparently do."

Logan utilized his nose to read the scents in the air. The sound of the bed stirring made him tense up. He was handsome, standing several inches taller than Justus with disheveled post-sex hair in his face. I admired his svelte body in the pair of loose denims that hung unevenly from his hips and covered most of his feet at the ends. Even in the darkness, Logan's eyes were magnificently intense—it was difficult to look directly at them.

Christian snapped his head to the right and jumped to his feet. "Stay back, Chitah."

"I know you're doing your job, but he's not a threat and you know it. I want him beside me," I ordered.

The man I'd just made love to strode across the room barefoot until his legs bumped against the bed. The look on his face was stone and his lips pressed into a thin line. Without sight, he still knew where Christian stood. I took Logan's hand and held it.

"Logan stays until the Relic gets here."

He angled toward the Vampire and lifted his chin. "Leave this room."

Christian glared at me. "You were not to get excited or upset, and apparently being around that one," he said, jerking his thumb, "is doing just that. Keep your eyes closed until she gets here. I'll get your night clothes."

Logan placed his hand on Christian's shoulder. "Put a finger on her delicates and I will put a pain in you that will give your ancestors nightmares."

Justus said nothing. Had I shamed him by having sex in my own bedroom? Was he the least bit happy that I could see, or afraid of what I'd become? If I did change into a Vampire, would he cut me loose? All those thoughts blinked out when Logan smiled at me.

My God, I could see again.

"What were you doing when this happened?" Page asked, setting her black bag down on a chair. Much to my surprise, she didn't look anything like I had imagined, but her question distracted me, as did my audience.

My chest heated up like a sunburn. The men stood like statues in a park, waiting for my answer.

"Please, Silver. It's important that I know exactly what transpired when your vision returned."

Logan cleared his throat and lifted a proud chin. "I was pleasuring my female."

My palm smacked against my forehead. "Is it possible to die of embarrassment?" I whispered to the Relic.

"Was it during sex or after you climaxed?" she asked in a clinical voice.

Yes, it *was* possible to die of embarrassment. Justus buried his face in his hand and Christian glared at Logan with disdain.

"I think I can guess," she said quietly.

How could a woman ask me such a personal question in a room full of men?

Page's cool fingers pushed on my abdomen. "I think the blood did the trick." Her mouth crumpled over to one side of her face. "I need your eyes, Vampire. Come assist me."

Christian waltzed over with his hands tucked in his pockets and disgust painted all over his features. "It's Christian. Continue to call me Vampire and I will address you the same, Relic."

Page shrugged. "Whatever floats your boat."

She blindly reached for her bag and Christian tossed it on the bed in front of her. Even in the dark, Page cut him an intentional glare. It was obvious that she fought against the same bullshit I'd been complaining about for the past year with immortal men.

"Silver, how do you feel otherwise?"

"Fabulous. I feel like myself again. There's nothing out of the ordinary—well, that's not true. For a few minutes, small sounds were amplified, but that seems to have gone away."

"I'm going to cut you," she announced.

Christian snatched her right hand, which held the scalpel. "The hell you will."

"Let go of my hand," she bit out through clenched teeth.

Justus stepped forward and narrowed his eyes in the dark. "Guard, take your hands off her," he said in a stony voice.

The threat in his tone was chilling and Christian complied, stepping away and shaking his head angrily.

"I need to assess if anything has changed in her healing abilities, and that requires testing her blood," Page said. "My advice is to assist me in doing my job, or leave the room and I'll work blind if I have to."

"Christian," I urged, but he shook his head.

She fished a scalpel from her bag and I cut the tip of my finger under her direction. It was a small incision—just enough to get a few drops of blood.

"Sorry, I'd normally do this with a needle, but I'm not that talented in the dark."

Christian snorted. "Why does that not surprise me," he murmured.

"I'll do a full CBC and a few other Breed-specific tests later, but this sample will allow me to see what's going on."

I took the glass slide from her hand, carefully holding the edges. "Let me help you," I insisted.

"Place a drop of blood on it—not too much. I have some equipment with me in the hall."

She kept her gloved hand out, palm up, and I placed the slide at the base of her fingers after collecting a sample. Her thumb pushed on the edge to keep it secure as she turned around. "By the way, keep an eye on your cut and tell me if it heals unusually fast."

A few moments passed and the blood continued to trickle. "It's not healing," Christian observed. "Patch her up, doc. I think you got what you need."

"I concur. Silver, I'll be back in a few minutes after I study the sample and we'll finish up."

Page left and Logan stormed across the room like a straight-line wind. His eyes narrowed when he found my arm and lifted it, using his nose to scent out the wound. Christian quirked a brow when Logan sucked on the tip of my finger, rolling his tongue around the nick.

"It's just a cut, Logan. No big deal."

Chitahs could release a chemical in their saliva that was a healing agent for superficial wounds, and yet his tongue on my skin still made my belly coil up.

Logan's hardened expression lightened when he sat on my left side with one arm draped over my right shoulder as if shielding me.

"Anyone up for a game of charades?" I joked.

Justus held the wall up with his shoulder and a few minutes later, Page swung the door open and felt her way inside.

"There's a cat in the hall," she blurted out in a shaken voice. "I almost tripped over it. At least, I hope it was a cat."

Justus rolled his eyes right up to the ceiling and I laughed.

"That's just Max," I said, remembering that he was part of my life again. "He's big, but he's harmless. Kind of like the man you're about to feel up."

On cue, Page's hand made contact with Justus's chest. He froze like a man who had walked up on a rattlesnake and she snapped back her arm as if she'd just stuck it in a lion's cage.

She pivoted on her heel and faced my direction. "The good news is your vision is back."

"Tell me something I don't know," I said, unsatisfied with the obvious diagnosis.

"Your blood is clear of any traces of venom as well as Vampire blood."

Page dropped her hands to her hips and for the first time, I noticed her. She was so much younger than I had imagined—possibly my age. Her face was captivating and brimming with intelligence. She kept her dark hair in a short, choppy style above her shoulders that framed her heart-shaped face. Delicate eyebrows arched over her long-lashed eyes. Not at all dressed in the frumpy clothes I'd imagined, but a very classy v-neck blouse and dark slacks, which looked even more impressive with her straight posture and slender physique. She looked like a pretty woman who tried very hard not to be. I was unable to make out the details of the exact color of her eyes, but they looked brown.

Page leaned against the wall to the right of Justus.

"I'll be the first to admit I've never done this on a Mage, or any other Breed for that matter," she said, with suppressed excitement. Knowledge was desirable to a Relic. "I do know with absolute certainty that you can't turn; I just didn't expect the side effects. Your absorption ability is unique, Silver." Her finger twirled in a slow circle as she spoke, staring upward. "It looks like the blood circulation in your eyes increased too rapidly and triggered a... Vampiric reaction with *his* blood. It should subside and I don't expect it to return; just a short-lived side effect."

"Does this mean I'm not going to be blind?"

Her brows arched. "Yes, it does. The effects you're experiencing will rapidly wear off. While this has never been attempted to my knowledge, the reaction isn't logical. It's common to feel the Vampire's emotions when the blood enters your body, but not to take on their traits. That's unheard of and has me a little mystified," she said in a soft voice. Her teeth clicked together as she lowered her eyes in thought.

"What am I supposed to do, just sit around in the dark?"

She shrugged, making an intentional physical response, knowing I could see her.

"I'm afraid if you expose your eyes to light you're only going to intensify the pain, and I don't want to risk injuring your eyes any further. What I recommend is that you stay down here or have all the lights in the house shut off since I don't know how long this will last. When you can no longer see, then it's safe to turn everything on. But start with candles, because your retinas will be sensitive. Call me right away so that I can detail what you are experiencing, anything out of the norm, that sort of thing. Move around the house all you want—you need exercise to keep the blood circulating." She stretched out her arm, looking as if she hadn't slept in days. "Cover them with a scarf or something, just in case someone flips on the lights by accident." Page glared at Justus.

"Do you need to take more of my blood?"

"I didn't see anything out of the ordinary in your blood smear; everything looks as expected. I'll stop in tomorrow for a full sample so I can get a better look at it in the lab with the proper equipment. You need to get some rest. And this time I mean it."

Her voice was stern and I squirmed like a scolded child.

It looked as if her mind was spinning from the details of my spectacular recovery. She tapped her chin with her index finger and knitted her brows. "Do you have any questions?"

Locked up in the dark? No, that about covered it. "Thanks, doc."

Her smile widened and the corners of her mouth turned up a little. It was a mischievous grin and played on her features. "You can call me Page, or Relic. I never did like the doctor tag and we're usually referred to as healers or advisors."

"Since I don't believe in calling people by their Breed name—thanks, Page."

"You're welcome." Her voice raised a pitch and she turned to leave.

"I'll escort you out," Justus offered.

"No need. I'm quite capable."

"It's dark outside," he said through clenched teeth.

"It's dark in here, too; I don't seem to recall you escorting me across the room or helping me with my things. I'll bill you directly for my services. Goodnight, Mr. De Gradi."

And just like that, Page La Croix was gone.

Logan kissed my forehead and excused himself from the room.

Justus followed him and Christian stayed behind, plucking off the tiny leaves of my plant.

"Stop doing that," I complained, taking a seat in the plush chair across the room. I kicked my feet up on the ottoman and sighed heavily. This would definitely be a birthday to go down in the annals.

"Try not to let your apathy affect your enthusiasm," Christian replied in a surly voice. "I never saw anyone less excited to have their sight back."

"You know, I'm inclined to think that letting you in the house wasn't the best plan. The idea of you barging in whenever I'm with someone in private isn't very appealing."

"And remind me how often that occurs?" Christian pushed away from the wall and paced across the room until he found a chair. "Don't think that I enjoy the idea of having to hear every squeal, moan, and slap of skin. Some things *cannot* be tuned out."

"For the cost of an ice cream cone, you can buy yourself some earplugs. You promised you'd keep your ears tuned out of my personal affairs."

"Conversations are far easier to block than… fucking. That's not so easy to tune out. There's a weak point in my brain that somehow cannot get past the sound of sucking and—"

"I get it."

A knock sounded at the door.

"Come in," I said wearily.

The door swung open and Logan drew in a scent through his nose, turning his head to the left and stalking in my direction. He knew exactly where I was and sat on the ottoman, pulling my feet into his lap. Logan's fingers worked magic as he rubbed the soles and I sank into the cushions of my chair.

"Now *this* I could get used to." I sighed. "It's a good thing it wasn't Christian's feet you ended up rubbing. How can you find me so easily in the dark?"

The coloring in his face deepened and he tilted his head to one side. Logan pulled a band from his pocket and tied his hair back—one strand fell free and slipped in front of his left eye. His jaw clenched.

"Oh, now this I've got to hear. What has the great Chitah all flustered?" I asked.

"Your scent is sweet on my tongue. Like…" He paused and looked upward as if trying to make an association. "Lemon cake."

"I smell like cake?"

"Mmhmm," he growled. "Edible, sweet cake, with a sharp tang on my palate."

"So you're saying I'm tart?" I laughed and his eyes narrowed in the dark. "I guess that means if I ever got lost in a bakery that you, Mr. Cross, would be at a loss."

"Now this I can't hear," Christian complained as he swung the door closed behind him.

Logan reached around and grabbed the plate behind him. "May I feed you?"

My toes curled in his palm and a provocative grin spread across his face. It was cubed cheese and strawberries. Not an ideal combination, but my stomach was begging.

"What happened with Leo?" I asked, nibbling the cheese from his fingertips. It was mild cheddar and tasted divine.

His lip twitched and he blew the strand of hair from his face. "The elders refuse to honor my claim under our laws. I should be entitled the full rights to challenge Tarek to the death for your honor."

"Because I'm a Mage."

He held out another piece and I polished it off. I sat back and watched him turning another piece of cheese between his fingers.

"Will it always be this way?" I asked. "Like that night at the restaurant with the Shifter—I can't change public opinion, but will the laws ever change?"

"I had this same discussion with Finn. He's developed an interest in law."

"Good for him. We're both victims of our own laws. Maybe he'll change them someday."

Logan leaned forward with an outstretched arm and I ate the cheese. This one tasted bitter and I grimaced, deciding no more.

"Tarek's family is too prominent. The elders' stance is that you're still alive, and…" Logan sighed with frustration. "They won't pursue action. By laws of the Mageri—"

"Yes," I said dismissively. "I've studied our books enough to know that nothing will be done. It just doesn't seem right. There's no higher order that holds everyone accountable. Not unless we're talking about the outlaw Breeds who want war and to invent purple ponies breathing apocalyptic fire."

"What?" Logan laughed, scratching his head.

"Nothing. I'm rambling." I sulked and stared at my hands.

"Eat," he demanded, twirling a strawberry between his fingers. "I can sense your hunger and it upsets me."

"Tarek walking free should upset you more."

"It should," he agreed. "But he'll serve his punishment. Are you going to eat from my hand, Little Raven?"

That quirked a smile on my face. "No."

Logan set the plate behind him and the energy in the room shifted. The only thing between us was a thin T-shirt and a pair of jeans.

"Stand up, Little Raven," he whispered, widening his legs to make room. I caught the shift in his eyes as they hooded and his tongue wet his lower lip.

As I stood up, Logan touched my bare legs and gradually slid his hands to my hips, reminding me that I didn't have any panties on.

"Not now, Logan," I said in a less-than-convincing voice. "You heard what the Relic said."

"Someday I'm going to devour every inch of your body with my eyes," Logan promised. "I want to admire you in sunlight, bathe you in moonlight, and drink you into my memory."

I twisted my hair around my fingers and dipped my nose into it. "I smell like you."

When his canines elongated, I fell into the chair, heart racing, sharp prickles awakening my nerves as I grabbed my neck.

Logan flew to his feet and clenched his fists. "I would *never* hurt you," he said, emphasizing each word.

"I know," I whispered. But his teeth reawakened a memory.

"No, you don't," he said harshly. "Stand up."

My eyes widened, scaling his tall physique.

"Please," he coaxed.

With a hard swallow, I scooted forward and stood up. Logan sat in my place and pulled me onto his lap so that I was straddling him. Both hands cupped my face and his forehead touched mine.

"I was made to protect you, female. I've claimed you, whether you accept it or not, and it's an honor that I take very seriously. If any male lays an unwanted finger on you, I will break it. If you hunger, I will feed you. If you're cold, then I will warm you with my body. If you're taken from me, then I'll track you. *Never* doubt my devotion to you." He gripped my head firmly. "I once gave a woman my heart, because that's all I had to give. But you, Silver, you're the pulse that keeps me alive. I was a soft man once, but no more. I don't know if you can accept the man that I've become, because all I have to offer you is my life. I want to shred Tarek apart for the fear he's made you feel when looking at me. He's made you afraid of something that is natural to my kind—an expression of my passion. My fangs are not just weapons." His voice strained and I knew.

I knew.

Denying a part of him was denying him completely. Maybe someday I could look at them without flinching, but it was too soon. They represented power and passion in his world. But in my world, they were death and pain.

I stroked his cheek and he leaned into me and closed his eyes.

"Give me time, Logan."

He slipped his hand behind the nape of my neck and brought his lips close to my ear—words melting into a soft whisper. "I'll wait for you."

CHAPTER 38

I PROMISED LOGAN THAT WE WOULD sleep in the same bed, but this wasn't the night. He fed me strawberries and kissed me fervidly before dragging himself away. I was unsettled—worried that his impulsive behavior might send him after Tarek. He said he had to take care of a few things at home but didn't elaborate.

Justus was gone and I grew listless and thirsty. I wandered into the kitchen, wearing my new slipper socks. The air had a different smell and I knew it was the odor-release crystals from the litter box in the adjoining closet. I snorted, thinking about Justus having to scoop the poop. Max twirled around my legs and darted into the living room to explore. It was going to be great having him around again.

Christian was perched on top of the counter, rolling a walnut between his fingers. "Your pussy has warmed up to me. Rubbed up on my leg and everything."

I shuffled to the fridge and reached for the handle. "Are you hungry?" I asked. "Disregard. I keep forgetting you only eat sugar." I tugged the handle and a sharp slice of light stung my eyes. I slammed the door so hard that something inside tipped over and rolled around.

"You'll live," he mumbled.

"Thanks for the warning."

Christian twirled the walnut on the counter. "I was testing to see if you were thinking about your actions. You should always consider the consequences of everything you do. I can't hold your hand, lass. You won't always have a guard. It's more than common sense. You need to develop your ability to assess every situation, read someone's facial tics and gestures, listen for hesitation and lies in their words. You're too trusting, too… casual. I blame it on being a human."

"You were a human once; don't be so quick to spit on them."

"Aye, to be human," he grumbled. "I once knew what hunger was. Not the kind when you go a day without a bag of chips, but real hunger that gnaws on you like an invisible animal. Life doesn't get any easier simply because you're an immortal. Weigh the consequences and make a sacrifice. You could have settled for food out of the cabinet or shut your eyes and blindly reached in."

"Ah, lectures on how to forage for food coming from a man who hasn't boiled potatoes since the turn of the century."

"Let me have a look at them." Christian hopped off the counter and examined my eyes closely, pulling the lids up.

"Hmm, they look smaller and I see a ring of green around the edges. How did you end up with an eye color like that?" he asked with a raised eyebrow. "Your mom's eyes are brown and I've never seen a color *that* vivid."

"They used to be brown."

"I don't believe I know your story."

"I'm sure the day you were made a Vampire was something you'll always remember—a ceremony, parade, maybe you even got a bouquet of flowers and a crown. But the day of my first spark haunts me."

"You need to eat something," he said, changing the topic.

"Logan fed me, so I'm good."

He folded his arms. "What did the Relic say about your… eye thing?"

"She has to do more tests," I said with a shrug. "I've never been normal, so I guess I've just learned to stop dwelling on it."

I glanced down at my hand and remembered the mood ring was still on the bedside table. I liked wearing it even though it never changed colors anymore and was always black. Maybe it was broken or I'd lost all my passion.

"How long did you guard Justus for?"

"Five years," he replied, pouring cold juice into a tall glass. "Don't think you're the only one who's all trouble. That man kept me on my toes."

"I bet." I chuckled as he set the glass beside me. "Why did he need a guard?"

"HALO. He was new and it was a dangerous time. The Mageri ordered a guard on every member after someone butchered the founders. You two have a lot in common," he said, slipping an enigmatic glance over his shoulder. "Stubborn. Me and him were in a good deal of knife fights and—"

"And what?"

He shook his head. "Nothing. Here, eat this."

I took a few bites of a banana. "And what?"

Something flashed in his eyes as he leaned against the counter on his elbow. "Don't tell him I spoke of this. There was a woman he was smitten with. She was different. In fact, he never spoke to her or got within thirty yards. He intentionally kept his distance."

"Why?"

Christian shrugged. "Many nights he went to her home and waited to catch a glimpse of her in the window. It was a strange thing to see, almost as if he was guarding her. There were nights she walked unattended and he kept in the shadows, following her until she was safely inside."

"Was she a Mage?"

"Yes. He knew her by association. She was the sister, so to speak, of one of the other HALO members, as far as them having the same Creator. Justus kept his affections a secret, especially from his HALO brother. I don't understand why he never spoke to her; he could have had her if he wanted to, with his charm."

"Because it would have been false," I murmured. "I would rather love someone who hates me than love someone whose feelings are a lie."

Christian considered that and brushed his hand through his disheveled brown hair. "Long story short, she was killed."

My jaw slackened. "By who?"

"Many didn't—and still don't—approve of the alliance between races. It's why the members never assemble in one place all at once. Anyhow," he said, pacing to the center of the room, "one of the HALO brothers was brutally slain alongside his sister—the woman that Justus had admired from afar. No one knows who the culprit was or what transpired in that room. It ruined Justus and it became a private hell since he couldn't mourn for her openly. I knew of his secret infatuation because I watched him day and night, shadowing closely as he continually put himself in harm's way to keep watch over this woman. It was *many* years ago."

I tossed the half-eaten banana in the sink. The womanizer I'd come to know had once loved—in his own way. I thought about the things I'd said to him regarding women. How can you know that an offhand comment could pierce another's heart if they don't open that heart to you and share their pain?

"Don't mention this to him, Silver. *Ever*." His mouth formed a grim line. "It is his own personal pain to suffer, and yes, he still suffers. I know him well enough that I see the vacant gaze in his eyes when he's near other women. The painting in the dining room out there—that's her," he said, jerking his thumb. "When he brought that thing over here, I knew he was still carrying the fecking torch."

"*What?*" All the blood drained from my face.

The painting mounted on the wall behind his chair—the one I'd stared at for a year while we ate our meals—was the woman he loved? The soft colors portrayed a beautiful woman in the water, reaching for a man. She touched the blue water with one hand and he held the sun with his other, but their hands never joined. The image of the man was from behind, but it could have very well been him.

"Justus painted that," he said solemnly.

I shook my head in disbelief.

Christian smirked and lifted his black eyes to mine. "You didn't know? Your Ghuardian used to be a painter; he was exceptionally good at it. He stopped after her death—destroyed everything he hadn't sold or given away, except that one. I'm certain when he went back to the house it was for that painting. The scoundrels assumed the cars meant more to him."

This revelation lay out before me like tapestry, weaving together the elements of his life that made him who he was. Hard. Cold. Distant.

"Not everyone's story has a happy beginning or ending," he said matter-of-factly.

"His story isn't over, Christian."

With his elbows on the cabinet, he rubbed his nose against his shoulder and stared at his black pants. "It's better not to fall in love. It never ends well and someone gets hurt. That's why it's called *falling*."

"Aren't you a ray of sunshine?" I slid off the counter and folded my arms. He sounded a lot like me and that was something I needed to change.

"And do you think you will fare any better?"

"Why don't you just stick to your job and leave out all the pearls of wisdom?"

"You *do* know that interbreeding is not highly looked upon," he pointed out. "Have you experienced the racism yet?"

I bit my lip. "Yes. We were on a date and someone approached our table."

"Sounds like a minor infraction. It gets worse. They spit on you, curse you behind your back, and call you a whore. They'll instigate fights with Logan, and some places will deny you entrance if they suspect you're a couple. That is a reality of our world and you should prepare yourself for it. Regardless of what DNA you may have, you are Mage first and foremost. I don't understand why you would take such risks with someone who is not a Mage; you only put yourself in further danger."

"Am I making you work for your money?"

Christian followed me into the hallway. I hadn't noticed before, but his position was calculated—in front of entrances or exits.

"My job isn't to judge you, Silver. But this puts you in a more perilous position—you'll make more enemies. I've never heard of a Mage and Chitah outside of a tumble in the bedroom and even then, not many. Most would never brag about sleeping with the enemy." His black eyes swallowed me up.

"I didn't plan on this, and I don't need to justify it to anyone. You don't date outside your Breed?"

Christian licked his lips and tucked his hands in his pockets. "No, I do not *date* outside my Breed. I won't turn away a good fuck from anyone, but it doesn't go beyond that. Vampire females are exquisite and incomparable. Not to mention hard to fucking come by," he mumbled.

"Why aren't you married?"

A burst of laughter escaped and he bent to his knees. His head suddenly snapped up with a menacing change in his expression. Without a word, Christian walked in hurried steps toward the front door.

"What's the matter?"

"Stay here and grab that." He pointed to the cell phone on the table. "Justus hasn't set up my security clearance, so I'll need you to get me back inside. We have a visitor."

"I'll go too," I said.

"No! You stay here."

Had Justus installed silent alarms? Christian left the house to go topside and I put on a pair of sweats as Max darted into one of the guest rooms. Several agonizing minutes ticked by and I sent a text to Justus to let him know something was wrong. What if Christian was hurt and needed my help? I walked through the secured doors until I reached the elevator that took me up to the garage.

It was late evening. A vibrant moon lit up the landscape, and a cold snap of air trickled into the garage, making me thankful for the socks.

I didn't sense the presence of a Mage as I stepped onto the driveway—although anyone could be concealing. A small animal scurried across the forest and I blew out a breath of air.

A cold hand slapped over my mouth. Christian's face burned with anger as he pushed me against the outer wall. "I told you to stay inside."

My pulse fluctuated and a hot wave of energy spiked in the tips of my fingers.

"We have company," he said to himself, looking over his shoulder.

Stretching my fingers, I moved his hand away from my mouth. "It's a Mage. I felt their light a second ago, so I don't think they're trying very hard to conceal."

"Go back inside," he hissed.

Under normal circumstances, I could have used my abilities to flash out of reach and fight, but my body was in no condition after what I'd been through over the past few days. What I needed was a stunner.

I had sidestepped toward the garage entrance when a burst of movement tore across the driveway.

Merc looked ready to inflict pain. His blond hair was stringy, thin, and the mist attacked it like a virus. More than moonlight danced in his eyes and I knew that he was charged with light.

"I thought you were in custody," I yelled out.

Merc flashed to the right and lunged forward. Christian knocked him away and Merc grinned like a demon, wiping the blood from his chin. He was faster and they both knew it. Christian pinned me against the wall with his back, locking his elbows on both sides and pressing against me like an immovable shield.

Twigs snapped beneath Merc's feet.

"Let me go," I said, pushing Christian's back. "He's going to stake you!"

Merc held a sturdy branch in his grip and studied the end.

"I'm serious, Christian. If he takes you out, what am I supposed to do?"

Merc spun the stick in his hand like a baton twirler marching in a parade.

Clearing my throat, I hoped to distract him. "Merc, what do you want from us?"

His expression tightened. Christian wasn't his target and he continued to roll the stick effortlessly between his brutal fingers. The air charged with Mage energy as if there were already a battle between us. Merc looked more like a man who'd done hard time than someone who belonged in politics.

"Learner, after I extract all that delicious power from your bones, I'm going to stomp on your skull until you're nothing but a corpse at my feet. Maybe I should cut off your head and mount it on one of his cars." He laughed maliciously. "I think Justus would like that, don't you?"

"Why did you come here?" I demanded to know.

Merc spit on the ground and scuffed up some dirt with his shoes as he stood on the edge of the driveway. "Someone like you doesn't deserve to live. You're nothing but a hybrid, a mutation that should've been killed at inception. You," he said, pointing the stick, "ruined my standing with the Council. I had plans. Doesn't matter." He shook his head slowly. "Things are set in motion. You'll never be a true Mage. You're an abomination that should be wiped from the face of the earth."

"And *you* are a traitor," I accused.

"Not everyone believes in the holy light of the Mageri. We are superior beings and it's time we quit hiding in the shadows of humanity. If we can't change them or kill them, then they'll be slaves to us and know how great our power is."

"You Mage and your little dreams of war," Christian spat. "I've been hearing it for centuries. Think you're going to be King of Connecticut?" he heckled. "Kill humans and you kill everything that has given you comfort. Packaged cakes, automobiles, movies—"

"Trite possessions. Did we always have them? No, and I could give a shit if civilization is altered and put on a new course. I want what's mine, and that's fucking dignity. Wouldn't mind knocking off Vampires and Chitahs while I'm at it. The hunger for war is a live grenade; you can't sit on it and expect it to disappear."

"Then fight your war instead of a woman."

Merc squinted and the pale moonlight cast shadows across his face. "I've worked for *years* keeping my political position and associations with other parties concealed. The one thing I will never tolerate is a snitch, and you can bet that as long as there is breath in my body, I'm going to make sure that a snitch is taken care of." He made a chilling motion with his hand, slicing across his neck. "Once I cut off her head, I'm going to shove this stick up your ass and set you to the fire."

"Threaten me, Mage, and I will yawn with boredom. Threaten Silver, and you will pay with your life." Christian's deep voice was so powerful that it vibrated against my chest.

Merc cocked his head to the side as I peered at him from behind Christian's right arm. "Are you her guard?" The bones in his jaw tightened and he nodded. "Now it makes sense. I thought you were only babysitting her at the park. If you're her guard then that means she's valuable to the Mageri or been given a position." He tapped the stick against his leg. "Novis, I presume. *That arrogant little prick*. His reputation as a peacekeeper makes me want to puke. Think you're someone important now, don't you?" Merc spit on the ground and dragged his murderous eyes up to mine. "You're a joke."

The hum of an Aston Martin rumbled in the distance. Merc was oblivious and I realized it was a residual effect of the Vampire blood allowing me to hear it. The adrenaline rush must have spiked what little abilities I had remaining. The engine shut off and doors clicked open. I felt no flaring, but if Justus parked that far out, then he was preparing himself for a fight.

Merc lowered himself like a football player on the offense. "You know, if I plug this thing deep enough in you, Vampire, I just might kill two birds with one stone."

"You're depraved!" I yelled at him.

Christian eased up just enough that when Merc flashed at him, I reached around and chopped my hand upward—snapping the stick before it was centered in his chest cavity. Merc yanked my wrist and flung me to the dirt. His heavy boot came down to stomp my head and I rolled over as Christian ran forward to swing.

Merc flashed out of his reach—laughing.

"Call the Council, Simon. We need Enforcers!" Justus panted urgently in the distance. He must have felt the energy swirling between Merc and me like a nuclear meltdown.

Justus emerged from the thick shadows and I could almost see the heat licking off him. This was a man built for battle, whose strong arms could wield swords, whose hands could expunge life from an enemy's throat. He was bigger than life as he strode forward, carrying an air of authority that made the trees quake. Those glittering cobalt eyes promised pain and punishment. Justus threw back his broad shoulders as if he were leading an army. The teeth of his boots bit into the earth as he neared the driveway.

Pride swelled looking upon my Ghuardian.

I'm not sure why the one thing that stood out was his shirt untucked on one side, but then it occurred to me— that was the side he carried his dagger. When I dragged my leg up, my right sock snagged on something and pulled off.

Justus stood with one arm behind his back. "Stand down, Merc. The Council has been notified and Enforcers are on their way," his glacial voice commanded.

"Always the tattletale, weren't you?" Merc chided.

"What was your intention? To murder an innocent Learner? I thought you a better man who respected our Breed."

"Flattery will get you nowhere," Merc grumbled. "You've never thought me a better man, so cut the bullshit. Your Learner is not entirely *our* Breed. She's nothing but a mutant gene that needs to be exterminated before it spreads like a virus."

"She is a woman; have you forgotten the code of chivalry?"

"Woman?" Merc laughed. "I care not that she's a woman; she would not be the first woman whose life I've taken, Justus, dear old *friend*." Merc unsheathed a dagger.

"We're not friends. You betrayed our trust."

Merc scraped his hair back and his bicep flexed. "HALO should be dismantled. You turned me in without any evidence; my reputation was *ruined*!" he roared. "My good name was soiled and I deserved retribution."

"Don't deny what we both know is true," Justus warned.

Merc glared down at me and sniffed. "I was incarcerated on charges never proven."

"Deservedly so. You took bribes in exchange for confidential information. You swore an oath to HALO to uphold the laws and respect your brothers."

He shrugged. "And? Nothing was ever proven by Nigel and that damn Chitah."

"Proof is irrelevant. You were guilty and if that fact only lies between us, then I'll be your judge and jury. Do you think that I've let this case go? I'm going to get the evidence I need one day, Merc."

"Fuck, did you just see that?" Merc asked, staring at his

ankles. "I think my legs just shook." He laughed. "The Mageri has a conscience, as I found out. Did you know that's how I got a position on the Council? To rectify what was taken—my reputation. Can't say everyone was in agreement about it, but they owed me."

Justus widened his stance a fraction and lowered his head. "Owed you for what? You *lied*. You deceived. You broke our trust for the sake of profit by selling information. You single-handedly placed doubt on our organization that took us years to reconcile!" he shouted in fury. The vein in his head stood out like a warning of the wrath to come. "And you still hold claim that you are owed for a punishment that was never fully rendered?"

"I broke nothing," Merc denied. "That was your own undoing by failing to produce evidence. The Chitah deserved a taste of his own medicine for the public humiliation that was served to me on a silver platter, and I'm glad that it ruined the alliance between our Breeds."

"He *knew* what you were up to and took an oath to expose the truth. Brother or not, the order and our principles come first. Do you think Nigel enjoyed knowing that he was going to turn in one of his own? He saw you as a brother."

Merc shook his head indifferently. "I care not. Had you anyone in your life that mattered to you… I would have also ended their life."

Justus shifted his stance and his jaw slackened. "What do you mean?"

Merc clicked his jaw from side to side and grinned. "You bastards really didn't figure out what happened to Nigel, did you? Thought it was related to one of the HALO cases or a personal vendetta. It *was* personal. Mage or not, Nigel was no brother to me. He was in too deep and when the Mageri didn't punish him, I got all the revenge I needed taking his life. His sister was *so sweet*." Merc's tongue caressed the words like a delicious memory.

When I looked at Justus, his face was ashen—frozen—lost in the horror of the answers that time had never given him.

Until now.

Merc scraped a heavy shoe along the concrete and I stood up, looking between the men. The tension was palpable and crackled against my fingertips.

"I invited myself over to talk man to man," Merc said. "He poured the alcohol and I put a stunner in his chest. I had propped him against the wall to sever his head when an unexpected guest tumbled into the room, screaming. What a gift that was. For what he did to me, his life alone was not enough retribution. I tasted the blood of Nigel's Breed sister and let him watch as she took her last breath. Every scream, every plea that fell from her rosy red lips—I made sure he was witness to. Even though all she said was *don't watch*," Merc said mockingly, mimicking her reaction. "Now that you have a Learner, I might get the same satisfaction. Paybacks are a bitch, aren't they?"

Without warning, Merc flashed at me from behind, ready to strike me down with his unmerciful intent. Christian spun me around and stood between us like a shield.

Color flooded into my Ghuardian's face like an erupting volcano. A vein protruded in a vertical line on his temple and his eyes blazed with light. Never had I witnessed such savagery and loss of control as in that moment. It was as if the lights went out and a warrior emerged—one without mercy, compassion, or recognition for all the laws he stood to protect. I sensed the heat funneling around him like a firestorm.

Merc tapped his blade thoughtfully against two fingers, watching the change that took over Justus. A knowing smile bled from his expression.

"*Of course.* Why did it never occur to me before? You *liked* Eleanor, didn't you?"

There it was—an open wound exposed for all to see. A secret buried, a truth revealed, and a vengeance awakened.

The pieces of what I knew began to fit together. Logan's father was part of HALO. He and Nigel had discovered Merc was accepting bribes in exchange for confidential information. The accusation had gone public without evidence. Logan's father walked away with a tarnished reputation; that was enough punishment among his own kind. The Mageri cleared all charges against Merc and he was free to walk, but not without a black mark on his name. Nigel received the same public scorn for slander, but in Merc's eyes, he hadn't suffered enough. So he exacted his own revenge against him and his sister.

Visceral pain spread across Justus's face and my heart constricted. Merc had crossed the line. Justus was more than my Ghuardian—he was *family*.

I approached Justus, but nothing existed in his eyes. Not the battered trees or the ancient moon smiling overhead. Only Merc. I cupped his face in my hands and it was rich with pain. His skin prickled the tips of my fingers as power surged through his body uncontrollably.

And the heat. My God, the heat.

"Look at me," I pleaded.

For the first time, he didn't pull away. Justus stared beyond me because in that moment in time, the only thing that existed was his nemesis. I tried to turn his head but it was granite.

"She didn't cry out for you when she died, Justus." Merc strutted around with mockery on his tongue. "Did you not consummate your love? I felt the heat between her legs and it was delicious. Had I known about your infatuation, I would have done the honors. Of course, with all the blood and crying, it would have been a stretch to tell if she was still a virgin."

"Shut up!" I screamed. "Justus, please don't listen to him. Please come back to me." I used his name, hoping that would bring him out of his blind rage. My heart was racing out of control and an impending sense of dread took hold.

Justus believed that emotions made you vulnerable and if you allowed them to consume you, then you would only know defeat. In this moment, he wasn't thinking rationally. He wasn't even thinking.

For once, Justus was *feeling*.

"Ghuardian, *don't* do this. Please don't do this." My hands traced over his sculpted jaw and I tried to pry his gaze away from Merc, but he was unresponsive.

Merc's dagger was eager to remove life from our bodies and a dark laugh rocked from his chest like a boulder tumbling down a mountain.

"I tasted her down to the last drop, Justus. Her light was *so* sweet when I plucked it out of her and made... her... mortal." He licked his thumb for emphasis. "You know what the real shame of it is? That gift of hers would have resisted your charm. She could block gifts; it was a tragedy when it leaked away from me. Had I known an Infuser, I would have sealed her light to my core. Blockers are so rare to come by." His grin faded as if he finally recognized a flavor on his tongue. "But you didn't know that, did you?"

Merc howled with laughter and darkness filled the contours of Justus's face.

It happened fast.

I spun around with an outstretched arm and used my gift to pull the dagger from Merc's hand. Christian stepped in the path and it sank into his abdomen. In the blink of an eye, Merc flashed forward and Justus shoved me to the ground, out of harm's way.

Their bodies collided like Titans and they fought in dark suspension—a blur of fists, muscle, and blood. Without a weapon, a Mage could only battle with another Mage using their hands and years of experience. I caught a glimpse of a blade planted in the dirt and realized that Justus had thrown down his weapon so that he could take down Merc with his bare hands.

The dagger was too far for me to pull.

"Christian, the knife!" I yelled.

He yanked the blade out of his side and slid it across the dirt. I used my gift to pull it the rest of the way. It left a cutting trail and I caught it.

Christian made no attempt to stop them, but kept his eyes focused on me.

I flashed into the chaos. Merc elbowed Justus in the eye, caught my wrist, and spun me around so that the biting edge of the blade I still held was cutting into my neck. He stood behind me with his hand firmly gripped over mine and the other arm wrapped around my waist.

"Stand back. One clean stroke and her head will be away."

"Release her!" Justus roared, blood trickling down his cheek.

Rage snarled on his curled lip as he assessed the situation the way he often did in the training room.

"No matter what happens," I ground through my teeth, "kill him."

Damn Merc for what he inflicted on that man.

Justus vanished; something I'd rarely seen him do. The speed of action was beyond comprehension. One minute he was standing ahead of us and the next, Justus appeared behind Merc. In a swift motion, he pulled Merc's wrist away from my neck and drove the dagger straight at my head. I winced, but the dagger had another target.

It plunged into Merc's eye, impaling him in the skull.

Gasping, heart racing, I staggered forward.

Justus had balled up his energy and, in one powerful burst, pushed himself in a position of control. Only a skilled Mage could harness their light in that manner. It was too advanced for me to understand, even after several attempts in the training room. Because it was a one-time shot and depleted an abundance of power, it's a last resort when there are no other options.

Merc collapsed to the ground in a heaping pile of worthless Mage manure. Justus kicked his legs to straighten them out and I winced at the gruesome image of the blade impaled in his eye socket. The wind shifted and a chill ran up my body as the leaves rustled in the trees.

Simon edged out from the road where he stood witness. "Come with me, Silver. This is a private revenge."

CHAPTER 39

Justus couldn't hear the empathy in the footsteps of his friends when he was left alone with Merc. He was only aware of the frost licking the back of his neck like an ice dragon. The pale moonlight gave a murky appearance to the blood that oozed from the mangled eye in Merc's head.

Unable to speak, he paced around the paralyzed body of a man who was born a Norseman.

Killing him quickly would be mercy that Nigel and Eleanor never had. Dirt and pebbles crunched beneath his boots and a narrow black shoelace dragged behind him as he stepped off the pavement. Years had elapsed and Justus would never know what might have been if Merc had only spared her life. Never had he imagined such a reawakening of suffering, proving that the laceration would never mend. Only now there was salt in the wounds with the revelation that she had been a Blocker.

Sweat trickled from his brow and he kicked Merc in the head. He continued to pace—arms thick with punishment, fists clenched with murderous intent, and a bitter taste of bile when the images of the confession swarmed in his head like angry bees.

Poison from Merc's lips. Acid from his tongue.

Justus kicked dirt up with every step, wearing a trail that circled Merc's soon-to-be incarcerated body. It wasn't enough. He wanted to know *everything*.

Being a Charmer was something of a disappointment to his Creator. Women were in abundance like the bounty from a vineyard, and Justus often selected the most beautiful and unattainable fruits until he was drunk with them. But after Eleanor's death, he'd felt more like an imposter with women. It became easier to pick the ones that were weak minded and easy. Every emotion they felt for him was a lie, and coming to terms with that fact was numbing. Sex was no longer a patient harvest but a quick bottle of cheap wine. Justus drank up the adoration, but in the end when the lights went out, it was only about the sex and the hangover was always the darkest part of the experience.

When Justus had first laid eyes on Eleanor, she was leaving a restaurant in a sage-green dress with a shawl wrapped around her shoulders. He'd stood on a busy corner and watched the lovely young woman with soft ribbons of long, silky blond hair looking expectantly up the street. Her smile was radiant when she waved at Nigel and kissed him on the cheek, with eyes that glittered like the Pacific Ocean. Such incomparable loveliness and grace. At first, he thought it was Nigel's woman, but later discovered that Nigel considered her a sister as they shared the same Creator.

Justus remembered the way her creamy complexion could make a man stutter, but most of all it was the innocence that played in her eyes.

Each day he followed her at the same times because she was a creature of habit. He watched her admire small trinkets and fabrics in the local shops. Her fingers were so delicate it made his own seem oafish and dangerous. From the opposite side of the windowpane, Justus's charm had no effect.

Eleanor had admired a sample of blue silk fabric once and walked away when she noticed the price. Justus must have ordered twenty yards of it and had it special delivered. He hadn't included a card and never knew what she thought of the anonymous gift. Nigel had money, so it didn't seem right that she denied herself beautiful things. Anticipation rose each day with the sun when she emerged from her door. He hoped to see her wearing the fabric, but a heavy sigh always followed when she stepped into the bright sunlight wearing a plain dress. There were many nights that he imagined her wearing it, and that would be the day that he would speak to her.

Eleanor often strolled along the streets alone with a pencil tucked behind her right ear. It bothered him that she didn't have an escort. She would spend hours on a park bench sketching inside her small notebook. What would it be like to touch her? Would her hair smell of fresh flowers as he had imagined? Her eyes looked upon the world with such adoration, sketching wild petals shaking in the breeze below her feet, or children lying in the grass and watching clouds drift overhead. It inspired him because he was also an artist, but Justus never looked at the little things the way she did. As much as he yearned for her affection—to hear her voice, to know her touch—it would be nothing but a lie.

Months passed and Justus was perfectly content with his routine. One Sunday morning, she never came out of the house.

Justus continued circling around Merc's body, each breath serving as a reminder of the one Eleanor no longer had. Light burned through his veins like hellfire, settling in the pit of his stomach as Merc's words festered.

Eleanor screaming. Eleanor screaming.

He squeezed his eyes shut because the stars burned too brightly. His right foot kicked up a chunk of dirt and it landed by Merc's arm. Justus sat on top of the former Council member's chest with his hand wrapped around the grip of the dagger buried deep in Merc's eye.

"We're talking," he said through clenched teeth. "Move an inch and I'll take your head."

Justus would wait until the Enforcers arrived because that's what law-abiding men did. In a swift motion, he pulled the dagger out and pressed it sharply against Merc's throat with his right hand gripping the handle and his left palm pressing the back of the blade. Justus wanted answers.

"Why kill Nigel? He would have faced punishment by the Mageri for not producing evidence."

Merc's lips peeled back as the blood pooled from his socket. "That's bullshit and you know it. The Mageri sat on it because they never had any intention of going against him. Nigel knew more and threatened he would talk." A rivulet of blood trailed down his neck.

"Knew what?"

"Where I was investing my money." He smiled. "How's your

gut these days?"

Justus paused and looked at him gravely. While he had little memory of the bombing at Novis's house, Merc had just indirectly admitted to being the responsible party behind the sword. It didn't matter. "You funded the experiments?"

"You see the world in black and white, Justus. This whole fucking mess we created ourselves—hiding from humans and letting their population explode. Working together in harmony? That's a joke. We built civilization. Deep down, everyone knows we don't belong in the shadows of mortals. Some just need a push in the right direction, but they'll follow. Peace is nothing but a bedtime story, and I think we're all big boys now and know that fairy tales don't exist."

"There is peace outside of the factions that threaten it. War never brings power, it only brings death." Justus leaned closer to Merc's face. "If you fight, it should be for a noble cause to protect, not to disembowel the laws that keep us civilized."

"Blah, blah, blah," he muttered. "My funding was a waste of money, so enjoy your monkey for as long as you can. When others find out what she is, they'll want her dead. Imagine the fear in knowing a mutation exists, one with powers they don't understand. Hell, maybe she's contagious," he said, huffing out a laugh.

The teeth of the blade bit into Merc's neck and he grimaced. He wasn't going anywhere, not with Justus using his knees to pin down his arms.

"That woman is a life to be valued, which is more than I can say for you."

Merc lifted his eyes to the sky. "You'll never win. You can lock me away, but my connections will bail me out. They have big plans and unlimited funds. The faith in the Mageri is fractured and it won't take much more to break that trust. The people will look for answers, and they won't look to you. Our time will come, Justus. Humans will know we exist. Ready yourself."

Justus sighed. "A fact we've long prepared for, and we will build relationships with them and—"

"Fucking kidding me?" he ground through his teeth. "Wake up

from your dream."

That struck a chord deep within Justus. Eleanor had been nothing but a dream, a floating petal on the wind who disappeared in the blink of an eye.

"Why Eleanor?" he nearly choked on the words. "Nigel, yes. Exact your revenge like the coward you are. But the woman—"

"No witnesses. I had the dagger in Nigel's chest and was ready to take his head. The woman should have fled before I saw her; she sealed her own fate."

More blood polished the dagger. Justus spoke each word slowly. "She was an innocent."

"Yes," he grunted. "Innocent and sweet. What a shame I had to ruin that silk dress."

The air seized.

"Blue?" Justus whispered hoarsely.

"What?"

Justus leaned in close so his lips were to Merc's jaw. "Was. It. Blue?"

Merc's eyes rolled up, plucking a memory. "Yes, it *was* blue. But it turned a deep shade of maroon by the time I was done with her."

After a thousand miles across time, the long journey for truth had ended. Sharp pain needled his lungs with each breath. Was it the first time she wore the fabric? Its silk was so lovely that it mirrored the Pacific waters, and he imagined how it paled in comparison to her sparkling eyes.

Visions of Eleanor splayed across the white marble floor of Nigel's house with blood pooling around her crept into his mind. The facts of their deaths were known, but never the details of the crime scene—not even to HALO. Nigel's Creator had spoken with the Mageri and any investigation that would have occurred was done privately.

His heart sank.

That stony heart he thought was long dead. One that beat on occasion when Silver was brought into his life, filling with pride and protectiveness, but one he kept guarded. One never meant to love.

"Blessing in disguise," Merc baited. "Gave me the pleasure of inflicting some real pain on Nigel for what he did to me. She sobbed like a baby and he was forced to watch her agony. In the end, he didn't even try to fight his own death. I removed the dagger, dragged him beside her and—"

With a violent roar, Justus rammed the knife so far into Merc's neck that his remaining eye widened with surprise. The gasping lasted seconds and then, just as sudden as the act itself, Merc's light flickered away.

A cool gust of wind carried fallen leaves and one landed on the dead Norseman's shoulder, tangling in his bloody hair.

Justus was fractured. He'd committed a crime by taking the life of a Mage. The situation had been contained and Merc never directly threatened his life. The implications were caked on the bottom of his boots.

He tossed the knife into the dirt and stood up. So much time had passed—could he even say that he'd loved this woman? Merc's revelation that she possessed an ability he never knew about broke him. Once the light was pulled from her body, she was rendered mortal and spared the atrocious death of a beheading. One detail made public was that Eleanor had been stabbed in the heart. It was a mystery never quite solved as it was not a common way for a Mage to die, but the assumption was that another Mage juiced her light and she was weakened enough to succumb to death.

He winced from the guilt of never having spoken to her. Not one word. She never even saw his face or heard his voice. Had he just once approached Eleanor, maybe she wouldn't have been in the wrong place at the wrong time.

In the wrong dress.

CHAPTER 40

THE ENFORCERS QUESTIONED US WHILE the cleaners removed Merc's body from the property. Due to the circumstances, members of the Council showed up and spoke to Justus privately. I was inside the house when he walked by with blood on his hands, leaving a trail of red mud in the hall. I cleaned the floor before the Council arrived. Merc's death was deemed justifiable. Unbeknownst to us, the Mageri had changed the status on his escape, labeling him an outlaw. This meant by law of the Mageri, anyone could hunt him—dead or alive. It was a fortunate turn of events, all things considered.

In the following days, Justus was despondent and locked himself away in his room. I never knew what transpired that night when we left him alone.

On the third day, he emerged from his bedroom as if nothing had happened. After six hours in the training room, a shower, and time in his study alone, he left the house to pick up some barbeque. The routine was the same, but Justus was not. *Was he upset with me? Was it the woman? Did he have remorse for killing a former Council member?* I wanted him to speak. I wanted him to yell, dammit.

I just wanted him back.

Justus mashed a few crumbs on his plate with his finger. The painting behind him would never look the same again. If it was true to her looks, then Eleanor was a beautiful young woman. I was awed by how romantic and evocative his painting was. Kindness colored her face as a man of fire dared to reach for her, a woman who was a reflection of innocence. Sadness encased it like a fragile frame. I wanted him to take it down, but it wasn't my place to make such a request. His torch had burned for that woman for so long that it was all he had left of an unrequited love.

The effects of the Vampire blood completely diminished and my eyes returned to their luminous green. The transfusion was a success, thanks to the Relic, although how I temporarily acquired Vampire traits was still a mystery. I liked Page and wondered if it would be out of line to have a girl's night out with her and Sunny.

Logan called with news that Leo had approached the Lord of their Pride for a personal meeting, but they would not bend in pursuing punishment against Tarek. His family ranked too high, and tainting their name with the affairs of a Mage would only ruin the reputation of the Cross family. Logan was infuriated, and I knew he would never let it go.

"Ghuardian, what do you think about everything Merc said about me being…" I averted my eyes. "…a mutant?"

He folded his fingers and stared at a candle on the table. "Mother Nature makes evolutionary leaps; one Breed is created and another dies out."

"But I wasn't a leap. I was a Petri-dish experiment."

His jaw tightened. "You are a Mage."

A quiet moment passed between us. "He deserved what he got," I said. "Merc would have never paid for his crime if we left it up to the Mageri."

His chest swelled with a thoughtful breath and Justus turned the rim of his plate.

I stared at my half-eaten cheesecake. "What's the plan?"

He scooped a large piece of the dessert into his mouth and wiped a smudge of icing on his plate. If Justus didn't have to use a fork, he usually didn't. It was the first meal he had eaten in two days, so I let it slide without a remark.

"Novis is right," he said. "We'll locate the labs and shut them down; the breeding must stop. HALO can no longer focus on Nero's case; we're expending too much energy hunting a lion when the forest around us is burning. He is in a league of men with a massive amount of money and connections; it would be a greater catastrophe to have them acquire this knowledge. It's more than the names on the list. There are doctors and scientists, papers and files—their progress may have expanded tremendously since you were born. It could compromise the safety of all humanity. Nero comes later."

"Are you afraid that we'll find a way to turn all humans into one of us?"

Justus lifted his eyes to mine. "We are not gods. My imagination is not large enough to fathom what the consequences of this could be. What if they found a way to extract gifts and plant them into anyone they wanted?"

I leaned back in my chair. That was a frightening idea.

He noticed my hands. "Where's your ring?"

My face must have turned the color of roses when I thought about Logan taking it off. "You know I don't wear it all the time," I said, concealing my smile.

He nodded and rested his chin thoughtfully on a fist. "No need to explain, I'm not a fool."

"I love the ring, you know that."

His large hands covered his face and rubbed away the hard edges. "Let's end this conversation before one of us leaves the table from embarrassment."

"If anyone finds out what I am, it could bring trouble. They'll see me as an abomination. I've had a good dose of criticism because of Logan and I expect there will be more to come. That list won't be made public, will it?"

"Over my dead body. Conceal who you are, Silver. Never let anyone see the truth."

The painting loomed over him like a black cloud and my gaze lowered. The carnage and devastation wrought on his face when Merc revealed the truth would live in my mind for a lifetime. The bloodstain in the dirt was enough for me to know that whatever was said between them would be buried with that blood. There was no struggle; Merc died in the exact spot that I last saw him. I couldn't imagine what was said between them that would have pushed Justus over the edge.

I knew the pain of living with a wound that no one could see, one that split you wide open beneath the surface. The woman he painted was the only woman who could have truly loved him, because she was the only one who could deny him.

Scooting my chair back, I abruptly got up and stood beside Justus as he tapped a fork absently against his plate. It didn't look like he'd been trimming his hair lately; it was growing out uneven.

I lifted his heavy arm from the table and sat on his lap. It startled him so severely that his fork tumbled from his hand to the floor. I needed to offer him the comfort he deserved to have that *no one* ever gave him. This man had a right to grieve.

My arms wrapped around his neck and I hugged him tightly. Justus predictably froze up like a statue.

There was something heartbreaking about how standoffish he was, now that I knew why. My cheek pressed against his so that he could hear the importance of my words. I doubted that anyone had ever given him these words before.

"I love you, Ghuardian. *I love you*." When he started to back away, my hands gripped his shoulders. "You're all the family I've got. You feed me, care for me, teach me, protect me, and put up with me. That's love—more than my own mother ever offered. You don't have to say it back." My voice cracked. "What can I do to take your pain away?"

My heart thundered in my chest when he dropped his head against my shoulder and his body sagged. "Don't speak of my charm. The jokes—they sting."

Tears welled in my eyes, knowing every sharp word I'd made about his gift was a dagger to his heart. It never occurred to me that behind the façade of a player was a man who had been played by fate. Justus could never feel a genuine word or touch from a woman without knowing it was a lie. I wept on the thick skin of his neck and his arms stroked my back softly. While he had initiated touch on his own in the past, Justus never wanted to receive it. Holding him this way was a privilege.

"Learner, don't cry."

"I had no idea."

I glanced up at the painting and tears blurred my vision. I'd always just seen a woman in the water, begging the man to help who didn't try. In reality, the man would never be able to reach her because she was just a memory.

Justus stroked my back, softening my quick breaths. His skin was splotchy and red, uncomfortable with the intimacy. For him, intimacy wasn't about sex; it was the act of receiving love.

My face contorted with frustration. I was supposed to be comforting *him*. "Stop doing that!" I wiped my nose and sat up to look at his face. "Dammit, just let me do this."

Amusement flared in his eyes as he stared at my tear-stained face and I caught a glimmer of wetness in the corners of his eyes. He never displayed emotions and I had struggled with that same behavior most of my life because it made me feel weak.

When I reached out and touched his tears, he flinched. His cheeks reddened and his lips formed a thin line.

I held his face in my hands, but the look in his tortured eyes devastated me.

"We're stubborn and we fight, but I care for you. I respect the man that you are and despite your horrendous table manners, you're an excellent Ghuardian. We're more alike than I think either of us will admit to," I said with a short laugh. "You have issues with personal space—I get it. Someone broke my trust a long time ago and that's what I have to deal with. It may not seem like it, but I trust you emphatically. This doesn't change anything between us, so let's keep talking to each other the way we always have. No one has to know."

My hands gave his shoulders a firm squeeze. "I want nothing more than to see you happy, even if I do make you *miserable*." My head fell on his shoulder, and I smiled thoughtfully.

"What am I to say to that?" he breathed.

"Nothing, Ghuardian. Say nothing. Just hug me and I'll leave you alone so you can enjoy the glory of ruining that dessert with your fingers."

His heavy arms slid around my hips, settling into the idea that I wasn't letting go until we had our moment.

"If Logan is unable to respect the unique woman that you are, I will teach him a lesson with my fists."

"Don't beat up my boyfriends," I said with a smile in my voice.

He sighed. "You choose who you want and I'll back you. They just better treat you right, even though you're the most cantankerous woman I have ever met."

"So that's why you tried to pick me up in the bar?"

He took a long breath through his nose and chuckled. "You were a puzzle."

"Well, have you figured me out yet?"

"No, Learner. All I can do is teach you what I know."

The loss he must have felt from severing the relationship with his Creator was difficult to imagine. Could I live without Justus in my life?

"You can have any woman you want, and that's not a curse," I said. "Choose someone who deserves you; just because they're charmed by you doesn't mean they can't see beyond that."

"I don't wish to discuss this, not now," he said in a sullen voice.

Eleanor may have never loved him the way he wanted because he never allowed himself to get close enough to find out.

I hugged him tighter. "Someday you'll have your happy ending."

"No ending is happy," he murmured.

So difficult.

"Then someday you'll have a happy beginning. No arguments."

While I could say that Justus gave me a short hug and we finished our cheesecake, the truth of the matter is that he held me like that for a very long time, allowing himself to finally grieve... and be comforted.

Printed in Great Britain
by Amazon.co.uk, Ltd.,
Marston Gate.